A Certain Slant
of Light

A Certain Slant of Light

MARGARET WANDER BONANNO

Seaview Books

NEW YORK

Manufactured in the United States of America.

FIRST EDITION

Trade distribution by Simon and Schuster
A Division of Gulf + Western Corporation
New York, New York 10020

Designed by Tere LoPrete

Library of Congress Cataloging in Publication Data

Bonanno, Margaret Wander.
    A certain slant of light.
      I. Title.
PZ4.B69745Cl   [PS3552.05925]   813'.5'4   78-31373
ISBN 0-87223-532-7

In memory of Marjorie F. Garhardt

There's a certain Slant of light,
Winter Afternoons –
That oppresses, like the Heft
of Cathedral Tunes –

Heavenly Hurt, it gives us –
We can find no scar,
But internal difference,
Where the Meanings, are –

None may teach it – Any –
'Tis the Seal Despair –
An imperial affliction
Sent us of the Air –

When it comes, the Landscape listens –
Shadows – hold their breath –
When it goes, 'tis like the Distance
On the look of Death –

EMILY DICKINSON,
"There's a Certain Slant of Light"

A Certain Slant
of Light

Prologue

"... No, I haven't read it," Sarah was saying to the girl on her right. "I don't get a chance to read too much contemporary stuff. Now, Gardner's last was an exception, a marvelous commentary on the age—do you know the one I mean? Can't think of the title...."

The girl on Sarah's right glanced significantly at her companion, who acknowledged with a slight smile that they were being tested. Sarah never forgot anything.

Naturally, both of them knew how important it was to stay on the good side of someone who, although not the chairman ("What the hell do I want to be a desk jockey for? Let me shuffle ideas, not paper!"), was the undisputed *grande dame* of the department. Besides, it was an honor to sit in the faculty lounge over lunch with Dr. Morrow. It happened, however, to be a little rough on the digestion—keeping a straight face being a virtual impossibility. Sarah Morrow had a reputation as a genuine pisser.

"... of course, I did enjoy *Grendel*, too," she was saying. "I assume you've both read Gardner's *Grendel*?"

Neither girl volunteered an overwhelming response.

"Well, you should have," Sarah said, narrowing her

eyes at each of them in turn. "It was on my supplementary reading list. Which is aside from its being a damned good book."

Not that I believe for even a fraction of a second that any of you actually read the supplementary material, Sarah thought with the half of her brain that wasn't monopolized by the headache. I suppose I should be grateful if *some* of you read *some* of the *required* stuff, but after I've broken my ass compiling this for over twenty-five years, and . . .

("... therefore, what we've inherited is this absurd notion that the medieval period was somehow under absolute control, that somehow people were inhibited by civil and ecclesiastical forces to the extent that free thought did not exist. We have the Victorians to thank for this galloping misconception. Nothing gratifies an uptight age more than trying to prove that previous generations were more restrictive than they. By the time they got through snipping out all the dirty stuff, what they had left seemed to them a bunch of pompous, papist piety—just try saying that after three drinks—and—ah . . ."

Sarah paused for the laugh. As usual, she was holding them in the palm of her hand.

"I know," she continued when they had subsided. *"I hear some of you mumbling—those of you who are still awake anyway—I hear you mumbling, 'What about the Inquisition?' What about it? It never crossed the Channel. The Inquisition was strictly a Mediterranean phenomenon. It flourished in Italy and Spain because it appealed to that bizarre morbid streak that is inherent in the Latin nature. It galloped through France because—well, because the French will try anything faddish. The French are odd, and that's that. The Germans flirted with it, but it was too fanciful for them; they'd rather solve a dispute by bashing someone on the head than by wasting time*

with racks and chains and such. The Flemish only suc-
cumbed to it because they were under Spanish domina-
tion. But the English—remember, please, that we are not
talking about the pallid variety of Englishman we know
today but thickheaded Anglo-Saxons who were only very
slowly being civilized by the Norman influence—the En-
glish would have laughed it from Calais clear back to
Rome. Picking on the Church was a national pastime in
England—perfected by Henry Plantagenet, who, as we
all know, hated bishops because they were robbing him
blind. And there was dissent on the Continent, too, despite
the cowls lurking around every corner. Dissent was con-
sidered a sign of health, a sign of growth, in the medieval
Church. Not so nowadays. Rome has become paranoid. A
sense of humor is no longer requisite for the papacy. John
was the only pope in this century who knew how to
laugh."

Some of them were still with her, but the others were
growing restive. The attention span of the average un-
dergraduate was really no greater than that of a four-
year-old, Sarah thought. It was time for a different tack.

"Of course there were things wrong with the Middle
Ages—which is a term, incidentally, that I dislike almost
as much as 'Dark Ages.' I trust you have sense enough
never to use that *phrase within my hearing. True, there*
was rampant illiteracy. But current statistics show that
kids these days—thirteen percent of high-school graduates
—can't write their own names. Education majors, please
note. There was also unequal distribution of wealth—
most people were either very rich or very poor. But would
anyone care to convince me that that's improved very
much recently? And of course, medieval women were
virtual slaves. Under German law, for instance, a man
was permitted to beat his wife in order to encourage
fidelity and compliance—on the condition that he did her
no permanent damage thereby. But when was the last

*time a wife beater was successfully prosecuted in this en-
lightened society of ours? True, we have made great
strides in science and medicine: We have, to our credit,
totally eliminated the Black Death; we've traded that for
fluorocarbons, genetic engineering, carcinogenic drinking
water, and abortion in the third trimester. All right, we
no longer piss in the moat, but I hardly think the flush
toilet is a fitting monument to the progress of the human
race!")*

They would be stunned for a fraction of a second, then
most of them would protest feebly but refuse to be drawn
into an argument. Some few would roar their indignation;
an even smaller group would agree with her. Their
bickering would resound in the hall long after the class
was over.

Sarah bounced back to the present with a jolt. That
had been yesterday's lecture. Or was it for this afternoon?
She always managed to squeeze it in before Christmas
recess, but whether she had done so already . . .

Encroaching senility, Sarah thought wryly. I'll have to
check my notes. I've never done that before. This frigging
headache . . .

Someone mentioned the time. Sarah's students had excused themselves somewhere in the middle of the blank
stare she'd had trained on them for nearly ten minutes.
People were gathering up books and notes and drifting
out of the room. Some lingered, finishing conversations.
Sarah made no effort to move. Her next class was just
down the hall, but the very thought of having to get up
and walk across the room . . .

At the other end of the table, Pietro was holding forth
with one of his moldy old Vatican Curia stories. Sarah
realized for the first time in nearly a quarter of a century
what an awful bore he was. If only this headache would
go away! It wasn't fair to assess a lifelong friendship on

the basis of one's own physical discomfort. Some people had apparently never heard the story he was telling. Was it possible? He'd been telling it for years, it seemed to her. They laughed deliriously when he finished.

The sound clattered unpleasantly against Sarah's ears. Wasn't one supposed to go deaf at her age? Instead, lately her hearing had become painfully acute. Her whole body was on edge—a single, taut, skittering nerve ending. This was absolutely the last year she'd do that tedious lecture tour. And maybe she'd abandon the monograph on Marie de France and tell her agent what he could do with the rest of the anthology. And next summer she would definitely, *definitely* return to England, to Stonehenge. . . .

Pietro caught the pained expression on her face as he was halfway out the door. Everyone else was gone. They were alone in the drab, narrow room.

"What's the matter, Sarah? You're looking distinctly peaked," he said, furrowing with concern. His words were garbled; she had trouble understanding him.

"Headache," Sarah said irritably, rubbing her left temple. Today was Friday. She's had it on and off since— Tuesday?

"Work, work, work!" Pietro shook his finger at her, looking foolish. "Christmas is just around the corner. Why are you pushing so hard?"

"I have c-commitments," Sarah said vaguely. As soon as the word was out of her mouth, she couldn't remember what it meant. "I—"

"Haven't been getting much sleep lately," Pietro finished for her. "It shows."

Sarah found his concern stifling. She wanted to bellow at him, to drive the great shaggy bear of him out of the room with the razor's edge of her voice. But she wasn't being fair, and she knew it.

Please don't! she wanted to say. Please, dear friend of my heart, don't make me tell you how awful I feel—you who are so attuned to me after all these years that every time I sneeze you get a cold. Don't make me tell you how much pain I'm in, because it will hurt you, too!

"Bug off, Pete," she said instead. "I'll cope. Eyestrain, that's all. Term papers and my own writing and all that. It's happened before."

"Are you sure?" He was looking at her with that kind of sad-eyed devotion she thought she'd beaten out of him long ago. "You'd tell me, wouldn't you, if something were really wrong?"

"Of course," Sarah lied brazenly, confident in the lie because she'd always been honest with him. "Not to worry. You're looking at Mother Earth right here. I have every intention of outliving you."

Pietro looked at her dubiously. It was hard to visualize this frail, white-haired academic as anything resembling Mother Earth. She was tougher than she looked, he knew that. God knew she'd had to be. But even so . . .

"Why don't you go home?" he suggested, bracing for the outrage he knew was coming. "The kids cut classes, why can't—"

"They don't cut *my* classes!" Sarah said, too loud, hearing it whanging off the inside of her head.

"Sorry!" Pietro said, hunching his shoulders and retreating like a chastened child.

Sarah plumped down on the squashed ancient couch against the wall with her hands clasping her corduroy-trousered knees—a thin, aging woman with a thundering, asymmetrical headache. She stared at the wall—painted, like most of the walls in the older buildings, that exquisitely neutral pastel-seafoam-lime-spring-left-over-stringbean-washed-out-institutional green. As she watched, the wall began to jiggle, to squirm with a million stabbing minuscule lights describing swhorls around each other, as if she were suddenly privy to the paths of the very atoms comprising the wall. Her neck felt stiff, and crackled when she flexed it.

"Absurd!" she said to the wall. "Migraines at my age."

The words sounded slushy and unfamiliar, a tape played too slowly, an alcoholic mutter.

It would not get the better of her. A couple of aspirin . . .

She stood suddenly to reach for her purse and—

The room swung like a pendulum and the heavy table in the center hurled itself against her pelvis and she—

Hit the floor as if it were a plate glass window shattering beneath her, gagging on something soft, saltwarm, clogging the back of her throat.

"Aaaaakkkk!" she heard—a death rattle that, no matter how bizarre, had to be her own voice as she hauled up as far as her knees and began pitching and yawing in the roaring fog until her right knee crumbled and she keeled over completely, mercifully, onto the dirty shag rug, unmoving.

Death.

Death, she thought. Dear dearth death knell knoll kneel know death done.

She could see nothing beyond the single chocolate-brown patch of shag rug lying directly in front of her. The rug smelled musty; she tried to hold onto that fact. Looking into a thicket and waiting for the rabbits. Don't black out! There are no rabbits. The rabbits are dead. There were noises, loud tinny noises, voices like carrion crows or scraps of metal dragging across each other in the desert wind. They were pulling at her, uprooting her from the soil she sought to meld with.

Cremate me, she tried to say, her lower jaw moving soundlessly. I don't want to stink, disintegrate in gobs. Dry, sterile ashes. Good fertilizer. Burn me.

"I knew something was wrong—she just looked so out of it," Pietro was babbling. The Roman collar hung loose

as he knelt over her, groping for her pulse, sweating pro-
fusely. "I came back to make sure she was—*where the
fuck is that ambulance?*"

When he heard the siren yowling erratically down the
block, he picked Sarah up like a broken doll and carried
her down the three flights to the street.

I

Here am I,
Little Jumping Joan.
When nobody's with me
I'm always alone.

ENGLISH NURSERY RHYME

The day after Brian left, Joan called the library to see if she could get her old job back.

She hadn't made any kind of decision when she saw him getting ready to go out that Saturday night. She knew where he was going, knew he would wait until the last minute to ask her to go with him so that she couldn't possibly get a baby-sitter and would have to say no.

She knew what he would say when he stood in the doorway with that hangdog expression on his face.

"Just a couple of beers and then I'll come home," he said, and Joan did not look up from her crossword puzzle. "I'll be back early."

Joan had nodded absently without looking at him at all, and he'd gone out. She knew he would spend the entire night and part of the early morning propped up on a barstool listening to his dead father's friends blathering on about what a fine lad he was, and trading stale jokes with his hang-on college buddies who were someday going to be actors, or going to be writers, or, like him, going to be lawyers. Most of them, as they approached thirty, were still driving cabs or working for the post office or, like him, working in brokerage houses and going to school nights for endless audited courses in photography or Kantian philosophy and writing melancholy songs for guitar at 4 A.M. (why always 4 A.M.?) in the kitchens of their three-rooms-with-wife-and-kid.

What Joan didn't know was that Brian would put his fist through the bathroom window in the hour before dawn because he'd left his keys on the dresser and, as he said by way of excuse later on the way to the emergency room, he didn't want to wake her.

He not only managed to wake her, he scared the shit out of her as well. He had torn the artery in his wrist and was bleeding all over his shirt by the time Joan got to the door. She drove him to the hospital shaking all over, though whether from fear or rage she didn't know. By then the something in her head that had been holding together all this time had finally snapped, even as she heard and comprehended the impact of the broken glass on the bathroom floor. There had been a rapid change in Brian's voice. He was still using the same monosyllable, his favorite, but his tone had changed from invective to terror in a millisecond.

"Fuck . . ." it had been. "Fuck . . . fuck . . . fuck . . ." sharply delineated by a tongue furry with alcohol and desperate to prove otherwise as he fumbled for the keys that weren't there. Then a pause while he thought of what to do next. Then the noisy, shattering impact and "Aw, shit!" And then "Fuckfuckfuckfuckfuck . . ." in rising crescendo as he tried to stem the gush and the pain, and finally "Joooan!" in primeval howl.

Yes, Joan thought, even as she threw off the blankets and staggered to the door. Of course. Identify yourself to the neighborhood, as if they don't already know who would be blundering and bellowing around at my door in the middle of the night. Embarrass me a little more!

She drove him to the hospital without even thinking about what to do with Eric, alone in the dark apartment with a three-year-old's nameless fears crouching at the foot of the bed should he dare to wake up, the January wind howling through what was left of the bathroom window. It never occurred to her that she should have sent Brian off in an ambulance instead of leaving her son, until she was already in the emergency room with her big baby, listening while he dry-retched for the fifth time as they stitched him up somewhere behind a curtain. She could call the landlady, Joan thought, but it was barely dawn, and there'd be an inevitable confrontation about the broken window, too. She sat in a battered plastic chair taking small consolation in the thought that, if Brian must puke, better here than all over the kitchen.

As soon as they got back, she rushed in to check on Eric. He hadn't stirred, had slept through the entire idiocy without nightmares, bed-wetting, or falling on the floor. Joan crawled back into bed, not because she had any delusions about sleeping but because it was the only way she could get away from Brian and postpone the argument that had been rising in her throat for an hour. She was not going to argue this time. This time she was simply going to tell him to get out, and this time he was not coming back. She would wait until the morning, when Eric was around, so that Brian wouldn't dare a confrontation.

Brian was coughing and shuffling around—Joan could hear him—first in the kitchen and then for a while in the bathroom, trying to decide what to do. He couldn't sleep on the couch like the chastened husband in the movies, because the bed *was* the couch. They'd never had a bed; they still slept on the secondhand convertible they'd

bought when they were living together. His options were
to sit up in the kitchen or to crawl into bed next to her and
hope she wouldn't say anything. Even his mother wouldn't
take him in at this hour, and the two yards of gauze
wrapped around his right wrist would require too much
explaining anyway. Neither he nor his mother cared to
acknowledge that he drank too much.

And so Joan waited, rigid and unmoving on her side
of the bed—as close to the edge as she could get without falling—and Brian eventually came out of the bathroom, closing the door to cut down on the draft from
the broken window. He struggled down to his underwear
with onehanded difficulty and got under the covers,
casually beginning to snore while Joan lay awake and
raging in the graying dark. *Damn him*, she thought.
Damn him!

She knew he was awake when she got up a few hours
later without having slept at all, but he faked sleep re-
markably well. His arm undoubtedly bothered him more
than his conscience.

"I want you out," she said, taking a deep breath. His
eyes flew open, but without meeting his startled glance
she went on. "I want you to pack and leave. I'm taking
Eric out for a while after breakfast and I don't want you
here when we get back."

She found a piece of cardboard to tape over the hole
that had once been a window, and pulled the curtain
across so Eric wouldn't see it. Now if she could only get
rid of the broken glass before he got up—

His small shadow fell across her from the doorway as
she crouched on the floor, gingerly picking up one splinter
at a time.

"What happen?" he asked anxiously, although Joan
was sure he had a fair idea.

"The window got broken," she explained with absolute
calm.

"Why?" Eric wanted to know, picking up a piece of glass and fingering it idly.

"Daddy broke it, by mistake," Joan said, her voice empty. "And please put that down before you cut yourself."

"Oh." The boy nodded. The two ideas were equally comprehensible. Glass could cut your finger, and daddy made a lot of mistakes. His pajamaed feet padded back into the bedroom, and Joan heard the television.

" 'Sesame Street,' " he crowed, waiting for the image to settle itself on the screen. "Super Grover!"

"It's too early, sweetie," Joan called from the bathroom, warmed a little by his presence. She dumped the broken glass into the garbage can and went to turn off the set. "Let's have breakfast first."

He followed her out to the kitchen without paying any notice to his father, who frequently slept late on Sundays.

"Whatcha want for breakfast, honey?" Joan asked the boy over her shoulder, fishing dishes out of the drainer and washing out the coffeepot. He tolerated such endearments only if they were offhand and no one else could hear.

"Pamcakes!" he bellowed, hurling himself at the refrigerator and trying to pry it open with both hands. "Mable siddup!"

"N-no, let's not," Joan said quickly, remembering that they had to get out of the apartment as soon as possible. She leaned on the refrigerator door to make him stop tugging. "No pancakes—we ran out of syrup anyway. Let's have cereal or something. Or I'll make you an egg."

She said it, knowing he hated eggs. Please have cereal, she thought. Risk being malnourished for a single morning so we can get out of here before I explode!

They ate, she stacked the dishes in the sink, stuffed Eric into his snowsuit before he could think about television, and they trudged down the block, the sled zigzagging behind them. The sun was out. It wasn't that cold. If they walked very slowly to the park, and stayed for about an hour, maybe Brian would be gone when they got home.

Eric's face was working, trying to put into words the questions he needed to ask. Joan had been keeping up a steady patter since breakfast to avoid these very questions. Now she had to stop; had to stop playing at Super Mom, had to wonder if the boy really had slept through it all last night. Had he been awake, listening in his silent, passive way, unable to interfere in the ugly games his grown-ups insisted on playing in the middle of the night? Joan's breath hung expectantly in front of her in the cold bright air as she waited for him to get it out, hoping he wouldn't stutter the way he did so often lately. Hoping she had the answers he needed. Deciding it didn't matter. She had gone numb sometime during the drive home from the hospital. She'd just do her best to answer any questions he asked.

"Daddy got sick again," Eric said finally, painstakingly, using Joan's euphemism, kicking at the dirty crusted snow.

"Yes." Joan sighed, wondering how far it would go this time.

"Why him gets sick?"

"I don't know why, Eric," Joan said. "He just does."

How to explain? How to tell him what she didn't know herself? Why did Brian drink? Was it something simple, like the fact that his father had died when he was twelve, and his mother had made him the man of the house while treating him like a baby at the same time? Was it because he had a little talent in several areas and no great intelligence for any one? Did he resent being coerced into fatherhood before he was fully grown up himself? Why *did* he drink? More importantly, why had she married him when she knew he drank?

("It sucks," Brian said for about the fiftieth time, holding himself up against the sink in the too-small kitchen.

Joan was sitting at the table that straddled the archway between the kitchen and the living room/bedroom to create a kind of artificial dining area. She didn't want to listen to him—she knew the speech by heart—but she knew if she didn't stay in the same room with him he'd only raise his voice to reach her in the next room. He would get louder and louder until he succeeded in waking Eric, and she would have to spend the next hour trying to get him back to sleep. Besides, she had reached the point where she didn't have to hear anything Brian said while he was under the influence. She sat there with her crossword puzzle, blocking him out.

"It sucks," Brian said again. "The whole system sucks. It's very simple—jush nobody's bothered to figure it out. There's too fucking many of us, that's all it is. You remember that article I showed you in the—wherever it was—and I told you to read it, but of course—"

"I remember the article, Brian," Joan said quietly, deliberating over a synonym for "apothegm."

"—said it's all the fault of the baby boom." Brian drained the beer he'd been using for a chaser. The pint of Seagram's was almost gone. He hadn't had enough money for a fifth this time. "There's too fucking many people born in our generation. Always hafta struggle for everything. Fight to get into high school. Fight to get into college. No jobs when we get out. Graduate school? Forget it!"

"I know, Brian," Joan said without looking up. She erased something that didn't fit, cursing herself for using a pen instead of a pencil, shifted to a different part of the puzzle.

Brian took the last beer out of the refrigerator.)

There was a rock between Joan's shoulders. It had been crushing her into the ground for so long now that she couldn't remember when it hadn't been there. All she had to do was figure out how to shake free of it.

She'd thrown Brian out before, but always with the understanding that he could come back when he straightened out. He'd always come back; she had always known he would. But she hadn't left him the option this time. She didn't want to live like this, ever, anymore.

She knew that it would take forever to find a job, knew she might even need welfare or something to tide her over. She'd certainly have trouble with the utility companies for a few months because Brian's jacket pockets were full of unpaid bills—bills that went unpaid for months because there was a bar between home and the bank where he went to pay them. As for the emotional cost—she had no way of even estimating it. She only knew she could not go through another weekend like this, and that was worth whatever else happened. It was even worth trying to raise a three-year-old without a father. She could not explain that to Eric right now; she wasn't even going to try.

"Daddy goes away again?" Eric broke into her thoughts. He knew the answer without having to ask. He'd seen the ritual repeated since he was old enough to pull himself to a standing position by the screen door to watch the car swerve erratically away from the curb with his father at the wheel.

"Yes," Joan said, clamping her teeth down on the rest of the sentence that rose in her throat like vomit. *For good this time. For good!*

There was nobody else in the park that early on a Sunday morning. Most of the snow had melted off during the week, though the tracks of other sledders were still visible on the side of the slope ending in a frozen mudhole near the sidewalk. Joan belly-flopped on the sled with

Eric clinging to her back like a monkey, and they pushed off, jolted down the hill, and dragged themselves up again perhaps a dozen times. But it was useless. Bone-shaken and with frozen toes, they would have to go home. Joan cursed herself for not thinking of something else.

"Let's go to Baskin-Robbins for hot chocolate," she proposed, capitalizing on one of Eric's weaknesses.

"Nope," he said, and she should have known. "I cold. Hafta go pee-pee."

Okay. Joan dragged the sled with him on it down their block as slowly as she reasonably could, the runners making insane screeching noises on the concrete with its inadequate covering of snow. Brian would still be there anyway; Joan would be amazed if he was even out of bed.

The car was still in front of the house, angled weirdly ass-out from the curb the way she'd parked it earlier that morning. Exhausted at the prospect of what lay ahead, she turned the key in the lock, wondering as she did whether her whole life might not be different if Brian had only been able to do as much last night, and kicked the door open, hauling the sled in behind her.

Brian was sitting on the rumpled bed, rubbing the back of his neck and blinking stupidly. He'd made no apparent headway against the tangle of dusty lawbooks, records, dirty sweat shirts, and guitar that comprised his contribution to the history of civilization. Was it only the injured arm that impeded him, or was it his chronic inability to ever make a decisive move?

It was Joan who began throwing everything into shopping bags, an old suitcase, and a lone corrugated box—flinging books in with business suits in with sneakers in with half-empty bottles of aftershave that clashed angrily against each other in the bottoms of the bags as she hoped with a kind of viciousness that they would smash and soak everything with their sickly-sweet stink and drown out the smell of alcohol that had permeated all their lives.

(Brian took the last beer out of the refrigerator.

"Even if I did finish law school," he said, wiping his mouth on his sleeve. He was beginning to slobber. "Even if I had, I wouldna been able to practice. Firs' of all, the bar exam'd hafta be real tough—they were last year, y' know, and the year before—f'the same reason the College Boards were such ass-busters when we were going to school—you remember?"

"I remember, Brian," Joan said, hoping he'd run out before the crossword puzzle did. Who would win this round—he, she, or the crossword puzzle?

"And even if I did by some miracle pass the bar, I don' have the connections. My father wasn't a lawyer. He was practically a bum. I don' know the right people. In this business it isn't what you know—"

"But who you know," Joan finished, hurrying him.

"You're not listening to me," Brian accused her, trying to look menacing. The result was more pitiful.

"Yes, I am," she said quietly, staring straight into his eyes until he had to back down because he could no longer focus. It was the moment she'd been waiting for.

You're drunk, her stare said, though she said nothing. You're smashed out of your skull, and you stink. She knew he knew it.

He took his beer into the living room and turned the television on gingerly, sobered enough to remember to turn the volume down.

"Anyhow, when you quit working, we didn't have the bread for law school," he grumbled softly at the television.

A sad smile crossed Joan's face for a moment. She'd never tried to rub his nose in his failures. Brian managed to do that all by himself. Whenever he'd been drinking, he got this overpowering urge to explain himself. It was her task to cut a potential three-hour monologue down to an hour or less. She had done that tonight. Now if she could just get the better of this crossword puzzle . . .

She couldn't. It was Wednesday. She'd been working on it in spurts since Sunday. She never used a dictionary. Only once in ten times was she able to finish it. Tonight was not one of those times.

When she came out of the shower later, she handed Brian the earphones for the television set. He plugged in without protest. Joan got into bed and turned her back to the set, and to Brian, knowing he would lie there staring at the screen until nothing was left but the test patterns.)

When she'd finished packing Brian's things, Joan flung the whole mess into the back seat of the car—her car, since she'd made most of the payments, but she was willing to give it to him if only he would go. Brian stood watching passively, his only defense being to grip the guitar protectively to keep her from smashing that in on top of everything else. When she had finished, Joan handed him the car keys, showing him that she was taking them off the ring that held her house keys. He was not to come back this time.

Brian got the message. He paused only long enough to put his hand on Eric's hair until the boy shrugged him off, then he shouldered the guitar and slammed the storm door behind him. Joan could see him cursing and fumbling the key into the ignition with his damaged hand. The car started, stalled out in the cold, started again, and jerked away from the curb.

She watched until he had turned the corner, wondering if he'd have the presence of mind to clean the bloodstains off the front seat. Wondering where he would go. Deciding she didn't care. She wondered, too, if he'd taken all the money with him. He'd gotten paid Friday, and if he hadn't left her enough to get through the week . . . She checked the top bureau drawer and saw that he'd left

most of it with her. She could survive the next two weeks.
After that . . .

She was settling in for a good cry after she got Eric into
bed that night, figuring she deserved it. But Eric didn't
stay in bed. He came padding in to stand by her side of the
still-unmade convertible, owlish and concerned.

Joan held out her arms to him. "Come here, baby," she
said, and he didn't object to the endearment. Fuck the
child psychologists, Joan thought, tucking him in beside
her.

"Was a monster," Eric said, jostling into her rib cage
to get as close as he could.

"Was there?" Joan murmured into his hair. "Just a
dream. Just a bad dream. It wasn't really real. You know
that, don't you? That monsters aren't real?"

"Yup," the boy breathed. "Was scary."

"What did it look like?" Joan asked absently, anxious
to soothe him away from it before he fell asleep. "Big and
green with fourteen eyes and lots of teeth?"

"Nope," Eric sighed, drowsiness taking over his voice.
"Like daddy. Daddy when him—when him gets sick."

"Shh. It's just a dream, baby," Joan whispered, as if
Brian might overhear. She blinked back the tears. "Go
to sleep."

She felt him relaxing, growing heavier against her,
his head pressing into her shoulder while her tears trickled
silently down her chin and lost themselves in his tousled,
fresh-air-smelling hair. Only when she was sobbing so
hard she thought the shaking would wake him did she
let him go, easing him onto the pillow where Brian had
feigned sleep last night. She turned on her other side and
continued to cry, clamping her teeth down on the pillow
to keep the sound back in her throat.

II

Maid Margaret would ariding go;
Her horse was but a nag.
She wore of two her better gown—
The other was a rag.

She met her lover in the wood
And neath the pines they lay.
When from the wood again she rode
Maid Margaret was no maid.

A jewel she did her lover give;
A flower 'twas he took . . .

"How bad is it?" the man in the Burberry topcoat asked the attending physician.

"I can't tell you that now, Mr. Gartenhaus," the doctor said. "Your sister's been semiconscious for the past several hours. We're giving her anticoagulants, and we think we've got her stabilized. But it's been my policy over the past few years not to venture an opinion on this kind of thing for at least twenty-four hours."

"All I want to know is what the hell happened to her?" the man said angrily in a tone that indicated he expected some damn good answers. "I keep hearing the term 'cerebral accident.' Does that mean a stroke, or what? I'd like something specific, not a lot of medical bullshit."

The doctor sighed. This was the the aspect of medicine he liked least.

"All right," he said. "What I can give you so far is this. Based on the X rays and the EEG—that's an electro-encephalogram—"

"I know what that means," Gartenhaus said gruffly.

"I beg your pardon," the doctor said, holding himself back. "As I say, based on these and a couple of other tests, I think we can safely assume that what caused your sister's problem was a blood clot. There was no evidence of an aneurysm, and there was no massive hemorrhaging inside the brain. It seems to have been a localized clot, and not a piece of something else that could give us a thrombosis elsewhere—a heart attack, for instance."

"In plain English, a stroke," Gartenhaus persisted.

"That's right," the doctor said.

> ... And many centuries anon
> 'Twas written in a book:
>
> How poverty did not prevent
> Two of such passion strong
> From dallying beneath the trees
> And spending time in song.

"What I'm really driving at," Gartenhaus continued, "is how much damage was done? Will she recover from this thing? Assuming—God forbid—that she doesn't die, is it going to cripple her or affect her brain in any way? Do you understand what I'm getting at?"

The doctor had a fair idea, but he was too polite to say so.

"I thought I made myself clear when I said it was too soon to tell, Mr. Gartenhaus." The doctor was getting annoyed. "Your sister has no previous history of high blood pressure. There's no telling how this thing flared up all at once. We have to take her age into account—a woman in her sixties will not recover as quickly as someone twenty years younger. We'll monitor her over the next few days, and we'll let you know whenever we get something definite. Right now there appears to be some paralysis of the right side, but we can help that with therapy. We also suspect aphasia, but, considering the mildness of the stroke, it's probably only temporary."

"Aphasia? What in hell is that?"

The doctor smiled slightly. Might as well throw a scare into the old tightwad.

"Loss of speech," he explained. "It means the patient can understand part or all of what is being said, but is unable to respond. As I said, in your sister's case it's probably only temporary."

Gartenhaus was looking uncomfortable. He shifted uneasily inside the heavy topcoat. Figures were clicking inside his head.

"But now, what about after she gets out of the hospital? She won't need a nursing home or anything, will she? Or need a visiting nurse? What I'm trying to get at—she never saved much money. Always lending it to people who never pay back. I don't know what shape her finances are in, but if it comes down to it, I'm not doing so hot myself. All right, I own my own little ad agency, but I got kids still in school, and with the recession—"

"I'd suggest your accountant could give you better advice than I could," the doctor said nastily. What did the bastard want from him anyway? "Does your sister have any other family?"

"She's a widow," Gartenhaus said. "Her husband wasn't what you'd call steadily employed, and he's been dead now for—and she's got no kids. I'm next of kin."

"That's too bad," the doctor said sincerely. "Does she work?"

"She taught—I mean, she teaches. I mean, she will, if

she can get back on her feet." Gartenhaus seemed to have
lost himself. "English lit at one of those Catholic colleges.
They don't pay much, and like I said . . ."

> Maid Margaret was not got with child
> That first time in the wood;
> It took a marriage and one year
> To prove the seed was good.
>
> Three pretty girls she later bore
> And also three stout boys.
> Her husband was a woodcutter
> Who made them wooden toys.

The doctor shrugged. It was none of his business.

"I can't give you any simple answers," he said. "I've had
patients make a complete recovery from two or three
strokes. You remember that actress—what was her name
—Patricia Neal? But then she was in her thirties. I've had
other patients who never made it back from one stroke.
I'm not sure where your sister falls between those two
categories. We have to wait and see."

Gartenhaus looked at his watch. He hadn't gotten his
damn good answers.

"You want to look in on her again before you go?" the
doctor asked him, nodding toward the intensive-care unit
down the hall.

"I don't think that'll be necessary," Gartenhaus said
abruptly, looking uneasily down the hall as if he expected
to see a white-haired wraith floating toward him, finger
pointed accusingly. "My sister and I—I'm not exactly one
of her favorite people."

The doctor could see why, but he didn't say anything.
They shook hands perfunctorily, and he watched the
elevator doors close between himself and Gartenhaus with
a feeling of relief. He checked the time. He wanted one last
look at his patient before he signed out for the night.

For fifty years one bed they shared,
Until his axe fell still.
No hewing heard in wood nor bed
Once he had lived his fill.

Old Margaret yet lived on awhile,
Her children at her side.
"Enough!" she cried at ninety-three,
And that is how she died.*

The doctor pushed aside the curtain that separated her bed from the adjacent one and looked first at the monitor, then at the patient.

"Mrs. Morrow?" he said softly, addressing her formally only in deference to her age. "Sarah? Come on, Sarah, wake up. Talk to me. Tell me how to get your brother off my back."

Sarah's eyelids flickered, then parted. Two luminous gray pools stared up at the doctor, looked through him, retreated. She sighed, and slipped away from him again.

The doctor sighed too, and took advantage of her loss of consciousness to study her closely.

It was a habit of his, an idiosyncrasy, studying the faces of patients he had never seen before, and might never see alive and whole and well. He tried to imagine what they had been like before, who they were, what they sounded like when they talked—particularly the aphasic ones who might never speak again. It was morbid, he supposed. Maybe he should have been a coroner. Maybe he never should have gone into medicine in the first place.

It was a strong face, he thought, studying Sarah. Not pretty—"handsome" was probably the old-fashioned word for it—boyish and unlined despite her age. It was not a face that could lie, not a face for delicacy or pretension.

* Sarah Morrow.

This was a woman who would guffaw rather than giggle. The doctor thought of what she'd looked like in Emergency this afternoon—skin blue-white and clammy, face twisted grotesquely, thin chest heaving brokenly in an effort to keep up with the oxygen. She looked better now, calmer, cleaner, though the face was still pulled slightly to the right. But her mouth was closed over a fine set of teeth— he'd noticed this afternoon that one of her upper incisors overlapped the other slightly—and her breathing was normal. Well, almost normal, just as she looked almost normal, despite the monitor and the IV and— And her hair annoyed the hell out of him.

She had very long hair, naturally white, not blue or whatever color older women were using these days—coarse and strong, with traces of the neat braid she must have woven for herself that morning before she went to work. He could see her, annoyed and squinting into the mirror against the sudden blurring of vision. What was left now was a mass of tangled, matted rats' nests, torn free from the pragmatic fat rubber band by the events of the day. He wished one of the nurses had had the presence of mind to find a hairbrush and do something about it.

He would mention it to the night nurse, who would, he knew, pass it on to the day nurse, who would . . . They were superstitious in the ICU. There was an unwritten law that said you did nothing extraordinary for a new patient for the first twenty-four hours. There was no point in wasting the effort on someone who was going to kick off without being able to appreciate it. When they'd passed the crisis point, when they were conscious and could take fluids, that was different. There was even a rumor that someone was running a numbers game based on patient survival rates.

The doctor passed a hand across his eyes. He'd been on call for thirty-six hours—not counting the forty-five minutes he'd spent trying to get rid of Gartenhaus—and he supposed that accounted for his irritability. Still, if they didn't do something about her hair . . .

He checked his watch again, checked Sarah's intravenous, wrote something on her chart. Then he sighed again, and pulled the curtain back into place.

He was almost past the nurses' station when he spotted the tousled bear of a man who'd been sitting in the hall for hours. He'd come in the ambulance with Sarah Morrow this afternoon, and had apparently not moved since then. It was a little past midnight; he'd been there for nearly nine hours, smoking, drinking coffee, reading magazines, patient. He got up from the couch when he saw the doctor coming. There was something oddly styleless about him, whether it was his clothes or— Of course. The doctor caught a glimpse of the Roman collar half-hidden by the heavy black beard. No doubt a fellow teacher. Perhaps Sarah's parish priest?

"Father?" the doctor inquired, extending his hand.

"How is she?" He was much taller than the doctor, though stooped somewhat by fatigue. "Dr. Morrow, I mean. What's the prognosis? I wanted to speak with you before I left."

The doctor gave the priest the same story he'd given her brother. Then he stopped.

"You said *Dr.* Morrow?"

"Ph.D.," the priest explained. "Medieval literature. Rather well known in scholarly circles, actually. Her husband was Sam Morrow—the sculptor? I guess you're too young to have—"

"And you?" the doctor interrupted, wondering whence this flood of information. There was something about this priest he couldn't pinpoint.

"I'm sorry," the priest grinned sheepishly. "Pete Giangrande. I'm on the faculty with Sarah. I was with her when she keeled over this afternoon. They let me ride in the ambulance. I thought she was going to die."

That's all it was, the doctor told himself. Just a good priest looking out for a member of his flock. Yet he wondered what it was about some people that made their friends more loyal than their families. At any rate, it was none of his business.

"Well, I don't think she's going to die, Father," he said. "But that's all I can tell you tonight."

Nothing could be kept secret on such a small, self-contained campus, at least nothing that roared up to the front entrance in an ambulance and screamed away bearing two prominent members of the faculty with it.

They clustered in the hallways and the lounges, blocked traffic, held elevator doors open to the consternation of those inside. Talking about it, spreading the news more quickly than would seem possible. Each of them wanted to get all of the facts absolutely straight.

"*Was* it old lady Morrow? Jesus, what the hell was it— a heart attack or what?"

"A stroke? That's what somebody told me, too. I don't know. I didn't see anything—just the two weirdos running around with the stretcher. I fucking near got trampled. We're on our way up to the chem lab, you know? Walking real slow, so the experiment's started before we get there, so we can just hang out and watch. When all of a sudden these two guys come tear-assing past us with this stretcher and an oxygen tank and I don't know what all else—"

"Yeah, well, that was because Giangrande was carrying her down the stairs on the other side of the building. I mean, carrying her like a baby or something, and his face turning purple like *he's* having a stroke—"

"How'd she look though? Shit, I missed the whole thing. I was in the john and I heard all this yelling—"

"You think they made it to the hospital yet? Jeez, maybe she's *dead!*"

"Yeah. Yeah, maybe. I wonder what they'll do about finals. And that term paper she gave us for after Christmas. I was almost finished with it. Shit, the first time in my life I get a paper done on time and this has to happen. All that work for nothing. . . ."

The professors knew within moments, even before the students did, though they were scattered around the campus; the news seemed to reach them by telepathy. Most of them quietly went on teaching, with the exception of one of the French teachers, who was forced to quell a near riot in Father Giangrande's freshman theology class. Their uproar when he did not appear had been threatening the conjugation of irregular verbs in her classroom, and she had to do *something*. And there was the librarian who crept upstairs nearly an hour later to the phonograph room to dismiss the six English majors who met with Sarah twice a week for a noncredit study of medieval polyphonic music. They seemed to be the only ones on the entire campus who hadn't heard. Two of them went home crying.

And so the gap was closed. The event had transpired. It had been witnessed, reported, impressed upon everyone's memory for as much as an hour, and as the afternoon progressed it was discussed anew from time to time. But the ponderous weight of schedule took over, and almost everyone went back to whatever they had been doing before they heard the news. Almost everyone.

"Well, I don't suppose there's any point in calling the hospital quite yet. I would imagine she's still in the emergency room."

It was a poor choice of words. Sister Francis Anne was not given to imagining much of anything. Imagining, after all, was not her job. Her job was to hold back the tide of evil that threatened her young Catholic ladies and gentlemen, to forestall their entrance into the twentieth century for as long as possible, while still providing them with that near-extinct commodity, a liberal arts education.

This was to be accomplished in the face of economic quandaries, the sociological dilemma of operating an essentially white middle-class institution in a neighborhood that had once been inhabited by the likes of the Clintons and the Vanderbilts but which now, alas . . . Well, no one had ever assumed that the job of a university president was easy.

"That's true. I doubt if they'd be able to tell us anything yet."

After thirteen years of being in second place, the other nun had developed a Pavlovian affirmative response to whatever her superior said. In this case, however, as in all matters pertaining to Sarah Morrow, she was in genuine agreement with Sister Francis.

"One wonders if she will be all right," the president mused half-aloud. "If it *was* a stroke . . ."

"I stopped by the chapel for a minute before I came here," Sister Aquinas, the other nun, said. "To say a prayer for her."

As soon as it was out of her mouth, she realized she shouldn't have said it. In confirmation, she caught the cold blue glint in Sister Francis's eye. You are not authorized to pray for a member of the faculty before I do, the look said.

Aquinas did not react, but inside she seethed. It shouldn't get to her after all this time, but it did. She was the older of the two—Francis was not quite fifty—and certainly equally qualified to be president. But Francis had a doctorate in classical languages; she had only a master's in speech. It was obvious which had more weight. This was not to mention the fact that Aquinas was short and dumpy and didn't photograph well, whereas Francis, with her patrician profile, always made such a hit in the yearbook and in the order's newsletter.

"On the practical side," Francis said after a pause, "it was thoughtful of her to fall ill so close to Christmas.

We'll have ample time to find a substitute to take over her classes."

Her expression told Aquinas that this area might possibly be open to discussion, even opposition. Aquinas took the plunge.

"That would depend," she said. "One could get a graduate student to fill in for the end of the semester. But if she's not well enough to come back for the spring semester—"

"If it *was* a stroke," Francis interrupted quietly, "she might not be well enough to come back at all."

Aquinas did not reply. She was not required to. She was but the sounding board—the idea had to be given voice, and someone had to hear it for the first time. She waited. After a few moments, Francis took off her reading glasses and rubbed her eyes.

"Naturally I intend to pray for her recovery," she told Aquinas weightily. "But practically speaking . . ."

Aquinas nodded. That was all that was required before she could excuse herself and leave.

"Is there anything else?" she asked from the doorway.

"No, dear." Francis shook her head, putting her glasses on again. She always called people "dear" to put them in their place. "Except, if you see Mario in the hall, please tell him I'd like to speak to him about the rug."

"Yup, she did," Mario nodded. "Threw up all over the rug. Then she passed out. I seen most of the whole thing. Horrible!"

He had stopped by the cafeteria for his afternoon coffee a little earlier than usual, figuring "the girls," as he called them, were entitled to hear his gossip firsthand. He had been mopping the hall just outside the faculty lounge when it happened, had heard Giangrande bellowing like a bull, and rushed in to see what was wrong. And he had the honor of cleaning the rug after all the excitement had died down.

"My sister-in-law had a stroke three years ago," Mae said, her substantial back toward him while she scraped the hamburger grease off the grill. "Paralyzed she was— lost the use of her legs, sure. They give her therapy and all and she can walk a bit now, but she's still confined to a wheelchair, God help her!"

Bertie pushed the cart full of dirty dishes past and began stacking them in the dishwasher, but she did not turn it on. It was deafening as a rule, and she wanted to hear the rest of the conversation. She wanted to listen, though not to participate. If anyone cared to hear about illnesses, she could tell them plenty, but she was not like that. Mae could talk enough for the two of them anyway.

Mae wiped her hands and settled herself heavily behind the cash register.

"D'you find out what hospital she's at?" she asked Mario.

He shrugged, spilling coffee on his pants.

"Who was I supposed to ask? I didn't see no ambulance."

He was trying to dab the spots off his fly without attracting too much attention. He was notorious for spilling things.

"Long Island College Hospital," Bertie said in spite of herself. The other two stared at her. "I see the ambulance in the street when I brought Sister Francis her afternoon coffee."

Mae nodded sagely. "We oughta send her a card or something. Or flowers. Though, sure, flowers always makes me think of wakes." This reminded her of something. She turned to Mario, who was still wiping his pants. "How did she look? You said you seen the Father carrying her down the stairs?"

Mario shook his balding head. He didn't want to be reminded of the scene. "Horrible thing!" he said. "She looked all white—blue almost. Her eyes all rolled up in her head. *Madonna mi'*, she looked dead!"

"Just passed out," Bertie said, trying to convince herself as well as the others. She'd already said more in five minutes than could usually be dragged out of her in an hour, but she couldn't seem to stop herself. "Don't nobody die from a stroke. Not the first time."

Mario gave up on the coffee stains and put down the empty cup. He laughed a little at Bertie's way of putting things.

"If you say so, Miss Alberta," he teased, a kind of joke he had going with her because she was always so serious. "I guess that's the gospel on it."

"I just wish we could find out is all," Mae said, her fat lips pursed. "Hate to see something like that happen to anybody, but especially someone who's such a doll. She never looked through you because she had all that education, know what I mean? She was always so polite. Always called me 'Mrs. Connaught.' 'Mrs. Connaught this' and 'Mrs. Connaught that,' until one day I says, 'No offense, Dr. Morrow,' I says, 'but my name's Mae.' And she says, 'And my name's Sarah.' Just as nice as that! I'm telling you!"

"She was a real lady," Bertie said somberly, not realizing she was speaking in the past tense. With a sigh, she turned on the dishwasher.

Sarah's eyes flicked open again, as they had been doing for some time without any direction from her. Sometimes faces swam in front of her—mouths opening like fish, the sound slow-motion garbled as if they were speaking underwater. They were gone now. The place where she was —rune? ruin? *room*—was green, lit eerily in-can-des-cent. She might very well be underwater. A new kind of therapy.

Runes, she thought again. *Runes!* she wanted to shout. Rune Ruin Ruinous. Ruin us. Us. Chaos.

"*Ssssshit*," she mouthed softly. "Ex cre ment."

She was trying to get a fix on—on what? On the blank patches in her brain. There were things she could not remember, but she had forgotten what they were. What was I saying? she asked herself, knowing she hadn't because she couldn't get her mouth to—what *was* it?

Clink clink clink—pieces of her memory like the bits of colored glass in one of those—calliope?scopes that you turned and—your ears hummmmedbuzzed and one eye couldn't focus—flashing lights procuring the field of vision.

Runes.

My mother, Sarah thought. My mother imagines—what *was* it?

Why was her write side so numb? Dumb. Novo-something. They've invected me with—supernova, that was it—like at the—at the tooth-fixist. Novus, novarum. Le Pont Neuf/Neunzehn hundert sieben und—

My mother imagines I'm—

Nees. Knees. My knees are two white earless elephants. I am looking at them from the back of the elephants' necks which are my thin-girl hairy thighs under the sheets my calves form the trunks tucked up so that my heels almost touch my buttocks. My hands are two equine animals also earless with three legs on one side and the thumb as the fourth leg on the other my index finger forming the head and neck. The left hand is decidedly feminine the right masculine, a curiosity in that I am both female and right-handed. These two creatures inhabit the island of my flat fishwhite stomach with the largish freckle just to the left of the navel as I float in the ocean of my bathtub, the tide coming in to cover the mass of tangled reddish seaweed where my belly ends. My Mother iMagines I'M Mastur-bating. SoMetiMes I aMmmmm. . . .

III

. . . I love you so
You bind my freedom from its rightful path;
In mercy lift your drooping wings and go.

          AMY LOWELL, *A Fixed Idea*

When she had finished crying, Joan sat up slowly and flicked on the light, shading Eric's eyes so it wouldn't wake him. She blew her nose silently and considered carrying the boy back to his own bed. What the hell, she decided. He'd only be back and forth with nightmares all night. And he looked so peaceful, the flushed daytime color gone from his face so that he looked like marble, his damp black curls tangled over his forehead in what her father would call a "sissy" haircut, his mouth half-open as he breathed. She couldn't move him now. An Oedipus complex couldn't blossom overnight.

She went to the bathroom to wash her face. After an hour of crying, it looked like someone had been beating her. Tomorrow her voice would be hoarse; she would sound like she had a terrible cold. Fine fettle for job hunting.

Tomorrow. God, tomorrow. Where to begin? Should one find a job first, or arrange for a legal separation first?

How did one go about convincing a three-year-old to like nursery school full-time when he didn't care much for it three mornings a week? There would have to be backup baby-sitters, and endless arrangements to be made. What were the priorities in a situation like this? When one had never been divorced before, it was difficult to jump in feet-first.

And then there was telling people. How did one go about announcing this sort of thing? Whom to tell first?

She ought to call her parents. It was a masochistic idea; if she expected any kind of understanding or moral support, she would be looking in the wrong place. They'd disliked Brian from the beginning. And Joan supposed they were right, but for all the wrong reasons.

Still, she really ought to tell them first. It would serve them right. She'd always called them with the good news —to tell them she and Brian had decided to get married after they'd lived together a year, to tell them when she got pregnant, when Eric cut his first tooth, said his first word, and all the other things long-distance grandparents missed out on. Why not tell them the bad news, too? Joan could just hear her mother.

"How could a marriage just fall apart like that?" would come the voice from Houston, shrill even at that distance. "Your father and I have been married *thirty years*, and while it hasn't always been a picnic—and I told you when you first started dating that boy, and I told you again when you two began—well—cohabiting—and I said to your father he might just as well pass up the transfer to Houston because I couldn't see us moving all those miles away and leaving you alone up there to make a fool of yourself, and I felt all along that Brian wasn't *right* for you, but still I fail to understand and I wish you would explain to me how a marriage could just *fall apart* like that. . . ."

If I can get a word in edgewise, Joan would always think, without having the nerve to say it.

It wasn't just that Brian drank. Joan knew he was a drinker from the moment she saw him, although she might not at that innocent point in her life have been conversant with the details of what it was like to live with an alcoholic. No, it wasn't the drinking, but she couldn't put into words just what it was. Maybe she'd just gotten tired of being leaned on.

The first time she'd met Brian he'd had a can of beer in his hand, and she'd been the one who had leaned on him, to extricate herself from an awkward situation that threatened to become unbearable. It amazed her now what adolescence found unbearable. . . .

It was the fall of her senior year of college, a time of year that usually found her climbing the walls out of sheer disgust with herself and her total lack of accomplishment. What she meant really, when she took the trouble to examine it, was that she'd never had a sexual encounter, and had never been close enough to a man to honestly say she could have if she'd wanted to. She knew she was slow by contemporary standards—half the girls she'd gone to high school with had already scored before graduation, if you took their word for it—but at that time in her life she'd been preoccupied with other things. Until almost a year ago she'd thought she might someday be a great dancer; but after several years of struggling to keep up with everyone else in her classes, that dream had crashed resoundingly around her ears. She was bored with college, and less than enthusiastic about her future career.

And on her last birthday she had vowed she wouldn't be a virgin at twenty-one.

All of this had something to do with her having dragged

herself to one of those idiotic mixers that were so intrinsic a part of the mating ritual at Catholic colleges. She was there that particular night—a cup of foamless beer in her hand; her callused, disciplined feet refusing the insistent pounding of the rock band bouncing off the walls—not because she anticipated getting laid that very night but because she was creating the framework around which to arrange to get laid at some future, unspecified date. She was looking, and looking intensely.

Somewhere in this room, she thought, surveying it through a haze of cigarette and grass smoke and the equally dense fog of her own inebriation, somewhere in this room, in the midst of this ugly glob of dull and commonplace people, is the man-boy-faceless-person who will deflower me. I do not know who he is, or what he looks like, or what there will be about him that will turn me on, but he is even now bringing his circle of existence into contingency with mine, and I will not leave until I find him.

But one ought to know what to look for, and how to go about it. Joan might be desperate, but she was still discriminating. She avoided the grabbers and gropers, although one of them might have made it that much easier. Instead, she panicked, swinging toward the opposite extreme. A science major would be nice, she had thought. An astrophysicist or a marine biologist who's too wrapped up in his work to be anything but clinical in his approach to sex. Nice and neat and clean, and over and out with no recriminations.

She ended up with a horn-rimmed ornithologist, whose interest in mating rituals was significantly different from hers.

". . . so there I was blowing the entire summer slogging around in the woods upstate with my tape recorder, trying to tape the white-throated swallow, which happens incidentally to be one of my particular favorites, and . . ."

"Really?" Joan murmured at intervals, sloshing the beer around in the paper cup and resisting the urge to drop it on Bird Boy's shoes.

". . . to give you an example, there's a guy from the University of Toronto who's been tracking the redwing blackbird for the past *twenty years*. This is without portable taping equipment—he used to have to string his speakers out over a hundred yards or more just to . . ."

Trapped again, Joan thought. He would finish his monologue and ask her if she wanted another beer, and then they'd dance a little—he would still be doing the Freddie or something sad like that. At the end of the evening he'd ask for her phone number and she'd be too gutless to say no—and that old gimmick of giving him the wrong number never worked. He'd drive her home in his father's LeSabre and they'd kiss antiseptically on her front stoop, and he'd call her the day after tomorrow and they'd go to the campus film festival the following weekend to see *No Exit* or *Ulysses* complete with free coffee and a discussion period afterward, or—

She couldn't stand it. She'd replayed this scene so often she knew it by heart. She'd been raised in a culture that said that young girls did not go prowling alone at night, that they had to have an "escort" in order to be let out of the house. This escort paid for the movie tickets and the dinners, spent his own money on gas for his father's car, and got little in return except a little harmless kissing and handholding. The trick was to find a guy who was as disinterested in you as you were in him; if he got to like you too well, things could get sticky. And if you really liked him, why the hell would you put him through all of that expense and inconvenience without at least offering him a little bit of good, dirty fun? The way Joan saw it, the whole scene stank.

She would have to lose Bird Boy, and quickly, before she went berserk and started shouting things. Maybe she could tell him she had to go to the john, and then sort of keep walking toward the coatroom. But anyone who could spot a white-throated swallow at twenty yards—

". . . and when you finally tape that particular boundary call and get it on an audiograph and slow it down about two hundred times . . ."

Joan gulped down the rest of the beer, wishing she could get fuzzy enough to tell him to fuck himself. She'd never used that word in front of a man; seldom used it at all, really. Maybe it would scare him off. Or maybe it would make her seem more exotic, more of a turn-on. Joan sighed, and noticed for the first time that someone was staring at her. She discovered the fact that he'd been hovering in her peripheral vision for a long time, but she hadn't really seen him until this precise moment. She rotated her head imperceptibly *à droit* and stared back at him.

She was immediately attracted to him—at least he seemed appealing from the far side of the room, where flaws were hard to notice. He was very tall; she liked tall men. He looked Irish—dark wavy hair and almost milk-white skin, with probably blue eyes. Her mother would approve. But he was thin, hungry-looking, and he smoked as if his life depended on it and drank his beer straight from the can. From this distance he didn't seem to be drunk. Why was he staring at her?

Six years of dance training, while totally useless from the point of view of a career, had made Joan acutely aware of her physical presence, of ways to enhance her good points and make herself look most attractive. She began subtly to rearrange her body, to give her admirer—if that was what one could call him—the come-hither without a word spoken.

Her pulse skipped slightly as he detached himself from the pillar he'd been holding up and began zigzagging across the boozy, noisy crowd. He did not take his eyes off

her, as if she were the star he steered by. Joan turned
away from him when he came within ten feet of her. She
smiled frostily at Bird Boy, who was still talking, unaware
of what was taking place beyond the range of his myopia.

It's up to you, Joan thought in the direction of the
stranger as she turned away from him.

"Well, well! Hiya, Henry!" the stranger said too cheerfully, clapping Bird Boy on the shoulder and nearly
knocking the horn-rims right off his beak. "I didn't know
you and my best girl knew each other."

Stupidly, Joan almost put her foot in it. She thought
he was mistaking her for someone else. It took her several
seconds to realize what he was doing. Idiot! she berated
herself. Are you *that* drunk?

"I didn't know that you—that she—that—" Bird Boy
was stuttering, looking up at the stranger, his erudition
knocked clear back into his esophagus.

"Hey, don't get uptight, Henry," the stranger soothed
him. "You know me. Brian Tierney always picks the best.
Right, baby?"

Your cue, stupid, Joan told herself frantically. Even if
he does sound like he just picked you off a tree, say something!

"That's right, Brian," she said sweetly, trying not to
spread it too thickly.

Brian yawned suddenly. "This place sucks," he announced. "You ready to split?"

"Y-yeah, sure," Joan nodded. Oh, God, now what? Was
she in deeper than ever this time?

Brian took her hand as they were leaving, but held it
loosely, indifferently. Joan was relieved. What the hell—
just because he'd done her a little favor didn't mean he
owned her.

The sudden silence out on the street made their ears
ring. It was cool and clear; the darkness actually glittered.
There was no one around; it was the perfect setting for

a rape-murder. Even if he gave her time to scream, who would hear her?

What now? Joan thought. She had no idea who he was, or what he was. She didn't know what he wanted from her, although she had a fair idea. But what now? Had she chosen him, or he her? Would she decide by the end of the evening that it was all right to sleep with him?

Joan sat on the edge of the bed and looked at Eric. He was curled on his side now, fetal, and a slight adenoidal snore came from his open mouth. She loved him so. How could that be possible, though, when she hated his father, hated the terrible wasting of the years that had brought him into being?

She'd tried one feeble time to get rid of Brian that night, but it hadn't worked. She hadn't really wanted it to.

"Listen, thanks a lot, Brian, you know? It *is* Brian, isn't it?" she heard herself saying, her voice giddy and rasping. "I mean, like, you probably saved me from a slow death by boredom in there. Thanks a whole lot, you know?"

"What's your name?" His voice was utterly flat, completely different from what it had been inside. He cut across the crap she was trying to give him. Joan cringed.

"J-Joan," she stuttered, wondering why she didn't at least try to lie to him. "Joan Dalton. Listen, I—"

"Yeah. I dig it. You're eternally grateful."

He said it without the sneer she expected, deserved. His voice was still flat, toneless. A wall he was hiding behind.

"Listen," he said, "would it be too much trouble for you to just sit and rap with me for a while? That's all. Just talk?"

"Sure. Okay," Joan nodded, pseudo-effusive. She felt completely at ease with him, but her hands had suddenly gone ice-cold, and she felt excited, as if something momentous were happening.

There was a church halfway down the block. She slid her hand out of his and sat down at the top of four steps, patting the place next to her on the worn marble to indicate where he was to sit. She smiled at him. I like you, the smile said. That's all I feel about you, and don't ask me why, but I like you. Don't expect anything else.

He still had the beer can in his hand. It seemed to be a permanent extension of his right arm.

What were they going to talk about?

"In case you were wondering, I was gawking at you for a reason," he began, finishing off the beer but holding onto the can.

"You were?" Joan asked brightly. She didn't want to talk. She wanted to sit here and squint up at the stars through the September trees and just enjoy sitting next to a man, without having to say anything to him. She felt herself being sucked into another meaningless conversation.

"Yeah," Brian said.

He had a habit of weighting his monosyllables to make them bigger, more significant than they really were.

"Never seen you at one of these gigs before," he continued.

"I don't go to them. Not my thing," Joan said airily, clasping her hands together and flexing her fingers backward until her knuckles cracked. It was a despicable habit, but a little more genteel than picking her nose. She was telegraphing her total disinterest in this conversation.

"I mean, these things are usually populated by cheerleaders," he said, looking sideways at her, making the word sound like an obscenity. "Or dogs."

"Are they really?" Joan asked naïvely, though she knew damn well. She would not look at him; she was staring at a gas lamp in front of the house across the street. She turned toward him suddenly. "If that's what you think, what were you doing there?"

Brian snorted. "Because I sneak in the fire exit. Friend of mine leaves it open. I can get free beer," he explained. "To someone of my means, that's important."

"Oh," Joan said, hitting a dead end. Was she supposed to ask him why he was so poor? Or was she supposed to sound sympathetic and then change the subject?

"You want to know something?" Brian interrupted before she could opt for either. He had slid from the step she was sitting on to the one below it, so that his long legs stuck out onto the sidewalk. The wind had shifted suddenly, and the pounding of the rock band filtered erratically out of the auditorium and toward where they were sitting.

"I don't want you to get insulted or anything," he began. "I mean, I don't know how to put this without you getting mad. . . ."

"What is it?" Joan asked warmly, almost tenderly. There was something desperately appealing in his concern. He was so gentle, she thought. So diffident, so considerate, so damned sexy—

"I just wanted to say that you have the most gorgeous legs I have ever seen. Do you know that? I mean, you've got absolutely the most—"

"I used to take dance," Joan cut him off, embarrassed by what he thought was a compliment, illusion shattered. He really was just another horny male.

"No kidding?" It apparently freaked him out, but not enough to make him take his eyes off her knees. "Ballet, you mean?"

Joan nodded, sighed. Here we go again, she thought. What do you do? I'm into such-and-such; how about you? Would she ever have time, with anybody, to talk about the stars, about Plato, about experimental theater, about her own gut feelings about life and the nature of things?

"Far fucking out!" Brian exclaimed, with no intention of apologizing. "You're a dancer? *Really?*"

"Well, not exactly," Joan said, almost sorry to dampen his enthusiasm. "I mean, I studied dance for six years, but then I found out I wasn't—that it wasn't—what I wanted. Right now I'm going for a degree in library science, of all things. What do you do?"

"Me? Just bum around mostly." He put the beer can to his lips, forgetting it was empty, making a face when he came up dry. "I've changed schools and majors so many times I've lost count. I'll be twenty-four next month, believe it or not, and I still don't know what the fuck I want to do with my life. I keep dropping out, falling back in again. The big hassle was trying to get a C.O. status. They kept calling me back down to the draft board and hassling me. Finally they gave me a four-F and told me to to stuff it. Shrink I know convinced them I was 'psychologically unfit' for military service. He forgot to mention that I couldn't do anything else either."

Joan's maternal instinct had long since gone into overdrive. She'd never met a male under thirty who didn't consider himself God's gift to humanity, specifically to women. But he was so humble, so unassuming, so—

"Hey, you're shivering," he said, breaking into her thoughts.

"No, I'm all right," Joan said. She wasn't cold; she was shaking all over from sheer exhilaration. She was happy. It was an emotion she wasn't terribly familiar with; the last time she remembered experiencing it had been sometime back when she was studying with Maestro. Yes, she was happy, and trembling from the effort of restraining herself from turning cartwheels in the street, short skirt and all.

"Shit!" he was mumbling. "I don't even have a jacket to give you. Here, take my shirt."

He was already unbuttoning it. Joan could see how frayed it was, how the buttons slid so easily out of the threadbare buttonholes.

"No, really. I'm not cold," she said, daring to put her hand on his arm. Her fingertips tingled when she touched him; there were goose bumps on her arms. He felt so warm, so real.

"Shit, I can't even take you someplace for coffee or something," he said with an air of great tragedy. "I got two bucks and change on me, and I don't get paid until Monday. Listen, I'm gonna ask you something—and I'm not propositioning you, I swear to God—but if you could get on the subway with me, I've got a room on President Street, and I'd really like to just rap with you awhile. I mean, if you don't mind. And I'll take you home."

"I have to be home by one," Joan said, gritting her teeth on the indignity. "My parents sit up all night and have shit fits. And I live all the way out in Bay Ridge."

"I'll get you home," he promised, lacing his fingers through hers and pulling her to her feet.

They got off the train at Grand Army Plaza, emerging into the midnight-still socialist-larger-than-life nightmare, an animated newspaper whirling aimlessly in the wind the only visible form of life. Joan shuddered at the great openness of it, and they scrambled across the wheel-rim streets where murder-intent cars roared at them, blinding and deafening, until they reached the safety of one of the tree-dense streets that spun away in all directions. The heels of Joan's shoes staccatoed sharply against the broken sidewalks, except at every fifth step or so when her bad ankle turned and broke the rhythm. She breathed in the aura of the brownstones—wooden-shuttered, crowded with plants, golden glow of light from high-ceilinged rooms with fireplaces and spiral staircases. She loved it.

The night around them was eerie in its silence, abnormally crisp and clear—or so it seemed to Joan's heightened awareness. This night was momentous, she told herself, though she didn't know how she could be so sure. She tried to walk more softly, reverently, to attract less attention from the eyes she felt certain were watching from behind the closed shutters. The result was that her bad ankle turned more often. Dancers were inordinately clumsy, she'd heard somebody say. They could only look graceful when every step was choreographed. It was true. She herself couldn't walk across a room without tripping over the rug, barking her shins on the coffee table. But on stage she had been—well, but that was over. Now she kept bumping into Brian as they walked, though he was gripping her hand tightly and she was sure she was walking in a straight line. She resented the possessive way he clung to her, but supposed she ought to get used to it. She would, after all, have to learn his rhythm, learn how to walk with him.

They had been walking for several blocks, and the houses were beginning to deteriorate. There were fewer one-family houses, more broken up into apartments and furnished rooms. Windows were dirtier, there was garbage in front yards, and here and there whole buildings had been burned out. Brian led her up the steps of a building next to one of these hollow shells, and Joan suppressed a shudder as she followed him down the too-narrow-for-two-people-to-walk dirty green hallway and up two more flights of stairs. The array of drop-bolt locks on the battered door to Brian's room was impressive; they were probably worth more than the valuables they were meant to protect.

The room was fairly large, but so passionately cluttered one could hardly turn around. There was a bed; a crippled swivel chair; a small electric stove; bathroom down the hall; and boxes upon cartons upon crates of books. Empty beer cans, several unmatched scummy coffee mugs, cans of sardines and Dinty Moore Beef Stew, and a half-loaf of Sprouted Wheat Health Bread lined the top level of books. Every available inch of wall space was covered with a PLAYBOY centerfold.

Joan laughed wildly, a little panicked. The sound echoed down the stairwell as she hovered in the doorway.

" 'Smatter?" Brian turned toward her, startled by the sound.

"I love your wallpaper," Joan said, pushing herself through the door and plopping down awkwardly in the swivel chair, which tilted brokenly and threatened to dump her on the floor.

"Bed's more comfortable," Brian said, without innuendo. Joan looked alarmed anyway. "Hands off. Promise."

"Okay," Joan nodded, giggling nervously, relocating at one end of the bed. When he sat next to her, she clasped her hands between her knees and didn't move.

"You're very uptight," Brian observed.

"I'm not," she lied, wondering what she could possibly do if he tried anything.

"Then why're you all scrunched up like that?"

"Am I?" Joan hedged vaguely, belying her surprise by releasing her hands from their prison.

"I won't rape you," Brian said quietly, studying the part in her hair because she refused to look up at him.

"I know that," Joan barely whispered, staring at the incredible amount of litter on the floor. If she could get her hands on a vacuum cleaner. . . . Her shoulder was touching his arm, and she didn't move away.

"Why'd you come up here with me if you're so scared?"

"I'm not scared!" Joan protested, shaking the hair out of her eyes and looking up at him. But she couldn't look him in the face for long. "And I don't know why I came with you."

"I wouldn't try to talk you into anything you don't want," Brian said.

"I know that, too!" Joan blurted impatiently. "Jesus,

will you stop being so damned nice to me? I'm sorry, but I just—I don't know how to make this sound like sense, but I've been very depressed for a long time, and I don't know if that has anything to do with tonight or not, but the minute I saw you I felt like I could talk to you. Like I could trust you. Maybe I'm crazy, but that's what I want to do—like you said—just talk to you, without all of the usual boy-meets-girl kind of shit. Does that make any sense?"

"Yeah, yeah, it does," Brian nodded, as close as he could come to enthusiasm. "That's perfectly cool. I mean, to tell you the truth, I haven't had a really good rap with somebody in a long time—just the usual bullshitting with the guys. And talking up the war with people. Tell me the truth, little lady, whatcha think about Vee-yet-nam?"

"Oh, God, do we have to?" Joan breathed, putting her hands over her ears as if she could block it out.

"No," Brian shrugged. "We don't have to if you don't want to. That applies to talking as well as to—anything else."

He put his arm around her shoulder, good-buddy-style, and Joan did not shrug him off. And they talked.

Talked about the stars, about Plato, about experimental theater, about their own personal gut feelings about life and the nature of things, and they wound up curled against each other under a blanket with just their shoes off and their arms around each other until Joan realized it was after three and she was going to get killed. She had to take a cab home with her own money and sneak into the house, hoping against hope that for once her mother would be asleep.

And as she got into the cab, she kissed him once— tenderly, innocuously, and it was as if from that moment on they both knew that the thing was sealed, that they were entangled in each other's life and couldn't get free without a great wrenching.

Easily done, impossibly undone, Joan thought, studying Eric's face once more before she shut off the light and tucked herself in next to him. And tried to sleep.

And as soon as the bus picked him up for nursery school the next morning, she called the college law library where she'd worked until two weeks before he was born.

IV

. . . Allas! syn I am free,
Sholde I now love, and put in jupartie
My sikernesse, and thrallen libertee?
Allas! how durst I thenken that folie?

CHAUCER, *Troilus and Criseyde*

The sky faded down, down, until it caved in and wrapped itself around her. Sarah blinked, trying to focus, her twisted face honed to a fine point of concentration. The fluttering lights from the corner of her right eye were beginning to dim a little, to be less painfully bright, though by now they had almost completely blanketed the vision in her right eye and were overlapping into the left. Sarah sighed. Until yesterday it had been double vision. This, she supposed, was an improvement.

She tried to speak.

"Air," she croaked.

The speech therapist looked up from her notebook and flash cards with something resembling hope, anticipating a breakthrough. Her mouth was open, and she seemed to have stopped breathing.

Air, Sarah thought desperately. It had been running around in her head for days; it was important to get it right. She wanted Pietro to bring it from home so she could be sure—be sure of something. What was it? Praetorius—she had it now, could almost reach out and grab it—Praetorius's Air for Tenor Recorder and Krummhorn. Were there several? What key was the one she wanted? It was extremely important—Air for—

"Air," she repeated doggedly. "Crumbles."

It was daring, she thought. Distinct and bell-clear, defiant against the incessant humming in her ears.

The therapist let the pencil droop in her hand, defeated. More gibberish. Some patients simply could not be impressed with the importance of what she was trying to do, and sometimes the more educated they were the more difficult—

"All right, Mrs. Morrow," she said, looking at her watch. "That's enough for today."

She buzzed the nurses' station, and the sound of the aide's shoes slip-slapping down the hall relieved Sarah immeasurably. Fuck the therapy, she thought. And fuck the therapist—might do her some good. Take that perpetual sour look off her face, the one that's hidden behind the plastic smile. Fuck the therapy. If she could just listen to some real people talking, she could get it back.

She closed her eyes as the aide took the wheelchair down the hall. Her voice, the mellow West Indian accent, was punctuated by the sound of the rubber-soled shoes.

"They really giving it to you today, aren't they? Poor old thing! Speech therapy an' physical therapy an' this an' that an' the other. Seem like they'd leave a nice old lady like you alone once in a while, let you get yourself together. Lord, honey, if they push me around like they been pushing you, I'd've wheel myself outta here day before yesterday."

Sarah nodded, half-smiling, able to understand without being able to be understood.

"By the way," the aide said, smiling secretly, "that big

handsome fella with the beard be waiting in your room for past an hour. I told him over and over you got therapy afternoons, but he hang around anyway. Stubborn, but he don't get in anybody's way. He some good friend to be hanging around all afternoon, hmm?"

Sarah nodded again, delighted at the description of Pietro.

"Real good friend, hmm?" The aide nudged Sarah gently. "A good-looking man like that an' an old lady like you? Don't be insulted, but, my, I hope I got that much energy when I get that old. You sure got taste, I'll give you that."

She was still laughing when they got to Sarah's room. Pietro got up from the edge of the bed and tried to take the wheelchair from her.

"Thank you," he rumbled.

"That's okay," the aide smiled, positioning the wheelchair at a comfortable distance from the bed. "Always glad to help a friend of a friend." Her laughter echoed down the hall.

Pietro frowned. He never wore his collar to the hospital, but even so . . .

"What's the joke?" he asked Sarah. "What's going on between you two that I don't know about?"

Sarah's good eyebrow told him what her voice could not.

Pietro shook his head, trying not to smile..

"Sometimes I think you create new gossip when the old stuff runs out," he said. "I think you enjoy it."

He'd been talking to her normally, as if nothing had happened, for weeks, but Sarah was only fully aware of it now for the first time. There was a new depth to her perception that had been absent as recently as yesterday. Not only could she understand ninety percent of what Pietro, or anybody, said to her, but in many cases she knew what they were going to say before they said it. She had known Pietro for years—that could be part of it—but she'd found herself doing it with strangers as well. Was she suddenly psychic? She'd never been before. Or was it simply a new part of her brain taking over for the damaged areas? Whatever it was, she had to get away from the opaque minds in this hospital and try out her new talent. She really *had* to get out of here.

"A lot of people have been asking about you," Pietro said, as he must have said every day for weeks, feeling foolish perhaps at talking to this inanimate wrinkled mannequin who moved nothing but her eyes. "A lot of them have been asking if they can come and see you once you're out—the nuns, a few of the students—and the cafeteria people had a mass said for you in the chapel last week."

He was testing her; if anything would get her mad, that sort of news could do it. He'd been testing her almost daily, waiting for that precise moment when the light would dawn.

"They want to come and visit you when you get out of the hospital," he said weightily.

Sarah kept her eyes closed when she shook her head; the room broke loose otherwise and rattled around her, making her dizzy. She shook her head violently. No! Absolutely not. No one but you must see me this way. No one.

"I know," Pietro said, taking her icy hand between his own, sparing himself one nervous glance at the open door, though who would notice them here . . . "I know you have your pride, and you don't want people to see what's happened to you. Naturally it hurts you to think that they'd all be sitting around laughing and talking and your usual brilliant repartee would be missing."

Sarah's eyes flashed at him. She did not answer.

"Come on," Pietro urged her, seeing the recognition in

her eyes that had not been there yesterday. "I'm right. Admit it."

Sarah opened her mouth, listening intently. It had to be the right word.

"Yes," she sighed.

Pietro waited, trying to control himself. There would be more if he could just hold off and not frighten her.

"Pietro," Sarah said bluntly, making no attempt to disguise how immensely pleased she was with herself.

"Thank God!" Pietro breathed, throwing his arms around her and sweeping her out of the chair.

They sat in silence and marveled at it for what seemed a very long time.

"Well!" Pietro exhaled finally, slapping his knee, too hearty. "It's about time! What shall we talk about now? Now that you've got it all together, as the kids say."

"Talk," Sarah said, not parroting him, but giving the word a shading of her own. "Talk—people we—people— teachers. Friends. Names. I—forget. How they *are* . . ."

Pietro could hear the concepts rattling into place in her broken brain. How much reconnecting was necessary? Would she be normal again? The process demanded his respect. Yes, he would talk, and she would listen, and somehow his endless gregariousness would be of help to her.

He'd been here almost every day for the past eight weeks, watching her day and night during the coma, waiting for the involuntary wakings to become voluntary, waiting for the suddenly deathlike face to regain its precious animation. He'd prayed over her, knowing she'd curse him if she knew, wondering what transpired behind the sometimes blank, sometimes bewildered eyes. He'd run down a dozen different doctors, nurses, technicians, asking for explanations, making sure he understood the reasons for her various medications, making sure she got

the right dosage at the right time. He called her brother—
who was too busy to visit regularly and who, when he
did come, sat looking at his watch the entire time—with
daily progress reports. He read to her for hours though
he knew it was probably useless, lifted her effortlessly into
the wheelchair for marathons up to the solarium and back,
and he never once stopped talking and explaining, searching for the spark of recognition. He had helped them
wash her waist-length white hair—

"Ought to have it cut," one of the nurses kept insisting.
"It's unsanitary that way. She don't care what it looks
like at this point."

"She's always worn it this way," he would say stubbornly, trying to rebraid it with his thick masculine hands
until the nurse got exasperated and did it for him.

And he would leave her for the night with a single,
passionless kiss on her sleeping forehead. A balm for
the curing of damaged minds.

He went to her house every few days when he got the
chance, letting himself in with the key he'd taken from
the handbag she'd left in the faculty room the day she had
the stroke. He would straighten up a little, look for
papers the hospital or her brother or the college needed,
forget to water the plants. He would bring her fresh
nightgowns, taking the rumpled ones back to the house
and washing them in the bathroom sink. And he watched
as she gradually unfolded again from the protection of
her interior.

"Did I tell you about the kid they've got subbing for
you?" he asked her, though he knew he had told her
every day since the time, just after Christmas, when she
first opened her eyes deliberately, shaking off the coma
like a too-heavy blanket. "Nice guy. Right out of grad
school, I understand. The kids like him. Spent a year in
England doing brass rubbings—all the authentic stuff—
and he knows his material. Of course he had a helluva

time getting started because he couldn't read a word of your notes. . . ."

He had no idea how much she was absorbing, but he babbled on. The barrier had been broken. She was not aphasic. She would speak. She would return to a normal life. She would go back to teaching. And she would return to the lifelong friendship of a certain priest in his fiftieth year.

What was his category? Where did he fit into the schemata of the countless philosophies he had studied in his lifetime? He taught—or tried to teach—Teilhardian philosophy to jocks and prospective kindergarten teachers and frostbitten nuns. Occasionally a student would challenge him, question his abject belief in what he taught. He would respond with complex metaphysical reasoning; he couldn't possibly tell them the truth. How could he explain that his own philosophy was based in essence on his love for a woman? Because he could not bear the thought of being separated from Sarah by something so idiotic as death, he simply postulated that it would not happen.

But what was his category? What sort of eternal *ménage à trois* would he make with Sam Morrow?

He loved Sarah. He loved her as much, he dared say— though he had never met the man—as Samuel Morrow the Famous Sculptor could have, and he'd spent a considerable amount of time wondering what might have happened if he'd met Sarah before he'd yoked himself with the Roman collar. But he had no delusions that she would have accepted him even then. There had always been the nagging question about her reasons for rejecting him. Was it really because of the collar, or because she could not respond to him as a man? Was it something about him personally, or only the fact that no one could follow Sam?

It amounted to a hill of bullshit anyway, Pietro thought

wryly. Even after all these years he couldn't think of five things they agreed upon, in any area. Would a sexual relationship have altered that in any way? He doubted it.

What was his category?

He would go home soon, back to his tranquil blue room in the rectory, back to his predictable dinner and the little frog of a housekeeper and his obligatory chess game with Father Lipinsky. He would grade some test papers before he went to bed, his feet up on the ottoman and the stereo on, Sibelius rumbling. Sarah hated Sibelius. That was another thing. He must remember to play her Bach and Purcell and Albinoni and Mozart and all of that anonymous Renaissance stuff she loved, when she got out of the hospital.

He would take care of her when she got home. He had talked it over with her brother, who had no objection, who was grateful for having saved the price of a private nurse. Sarah didn't need a nurse anyway, only a companion. Who better than he, who had been her constant companion for twenty-five years?

He would drive over every afternoon after classes, cook supper for the two of them, and read to her and talk and play the stereo, and buy the groceries, and pay the bills, and do the laundry, and add all of the other domestic touches save one. And he would lock up carefully when he left.

Left to come back to his cool blue room with its private bath, where he would shower with his mind a deliberate blank, and put on his pajamas—his lifelong habit of sleeping in the nude had recently been abandoned on esthetic grounds—and fall asleep in his narrow bed with its too-soft-to-be-good-for-his-back mattress. He would fall asleep within minutes, his voluntary thoughts fading into the tranquillity of sleep without so much as a bump, and he would sleep as one at peace with himself and his philosophy. The fires were banked. He hadn't masturbated in years. Whether he'd at last been able to force the drive underground, or sublimated it in his work the way they said you were supposed to, or simply outgrown it— it was gone, that was all.

"Nothing," Sarah said suddenly, bringing Pietro back to the present with a start. "Remember—nothing."

Of course, Pietro thought. They'd been talking—or rather he'd been talking—about the day she had the stroke. He'd been describing the situation as it had happened, leaving out a few of the uglier details like the convulsions, and the subsequent chaos left by her absence. All of this while his mind had been functioning in a completely different groove. It was lucky she'd interrupted before he got his wires crossed.

"It's just as well you remember nothing," he said comfortingly. "It was a very traumatic experience, and your mind is wise in blocking it out."

A traumatic experience indeed, Pietro thought. So traumatic that I've been getting the shakes on and off for weeks. So traumatic that I've been on the verge of the kind of emotional display I thought I could avoid with you. Thank God you're talking again so I can shut up before I say anything I—

"There were a few things I—decisions I had to make for you," he said. "While you were—out of commission. I mean, everything was in an uproar. Someone had to decide on certain things, and I thought I knew what you would want in a given situation. I told them that, regardless of the outcome, they should count you out at least until September."

Sarah just looked at him. Dates meant nothing to her, but there was something in his tone, in what he was *not* saying, that made her wary. Where intellect failed, instinct was intensified.

"September?" she asked.

"Next fall," he said, then clarified: "About eight months

from now. Time enough to get you back to your old self. Yesterday you couldn't speak. Today you can. Within six months we'll have all those multisyllables rolling out of you like always. And we'll have you walking again, too. The doctor says—"

He had to stop himself. He would have to draw the line at an outright lie. What had the doctor said? Certainly none of what Pietro had just told Sarah. The doctor had said she could make a total recovery, or a partial recovery, or none at all. The doctor had said in effect that he had no idea what would happen; that certain physiological damage had been done, and could not be repaired, but that psychological conditioning would determine the degree of recovery. In other words, if Sarah thought she could get better, she probably would.

That was why Pietro permitted himself these outrageous conjectures. He no more saw Sarah back in the classroom in eight months than he did in eight days. In terms of what was going on on campus at the moment, it might be better for her if she *could* return in eight days. But how could he tell her that now? How could he tell her that the wheels were already in motion; that there were rumors the administration was going to force her into an early retirement? He couldn't destroy her motivation, but he had to somehow warn her of what to expect should she want to go back to teaching.

Sarah watched him, listened to what he was saying, and what he was not saying.

I do not understand your words, she thought, but I understand their meaning. Caution! they shout. Danger! You are being threatened by the very things you do not understand!

She watched him as he talked and talked. She only half-heard his words as she searched for the meaning behind them. What did it mean, this new sixth sense of hers? It frightened her just a little. But having come back from where she had been, what right did she have to be frightened by anything now?

She would not discover for some weeks yet what she had lost, had exchanged unwillingly for the power to read minds. She did not know that she had lost the power to read the written page. At this moment she was too taken up with the sudden rediscovery of speech to even notice.

I know you, Sarah thought, looking warmly at Pietro, sifting through all the languages her mind had once mastered. Ichot yow. Ichot ne just yir mien and manner, aber auch seine herte und seele. And of a sudden ich understanden how twas that ich colde love thee sans the must of sexualité. It war ne al the excusen I gave yow sae long agone, now wot ich wel, though swich I helde athen. Nae, but tis this: I dorst ne think ye wast nat a thinge of perfectioun, und had ich so with yow yslept and found yow lacking swich grandeur as I yhoped, ich wolde so sorwed be an disappoint—or worse, had I so yow yfailed as I colde nat yow satisfie, ich wolde againe' so sorwed be ich colde nat meet yow in thi yë. Suffice it thus: Wir hae lived this mony yere in preciouse harmonie and trew friendshippe, and yow hae folwed thi destinie and I myn, withouten an syngle partyng of our lyves or seriese quarrl, and we colde say—as few ywedded couple can—that our twae myndes are sae complementarie blent as we can speke the daylong withouten any worde yspoke. Ichot yow wel, and am plesed with my knowlege. Had I betorn yow fro yir priestlinesse, what manner man wolde yow be anon? I dorst nat think that it wolde be to yir goode, and certes nat to myn, to have swich thyng on myn consciousnesse. Ist nat better thus? Consider this: Wir haben both our freedom and our choise. . . .

V

You don't believe—I won't attempt to make ye:
You are asleep—I won't attempt to wake ye.
Sleep on! Sleep on! while in your pleasant dreams
Of Reason you may drink of Life's clear streams.
WILLIAM BLAKE, "You don't believe"

On Tuesday of the second week of her new life-style, Joan met Vicki for lunch.

She hadn't really seen Vicki for months; it was hard to think of something to say when people asked you what was new and the only thing you wanted to say was "I've decided to get rid of my husband." And that sort of thing didn't go down well with Vicki at all.

They sat in a small Italian restaurant around the corner from the main building of the college. Joan agonized over the menu. She really shouldn't be here; right now she couldn't afford to order a tuna sandwich in Woolworth's, much less . . .

Joan agonized, and she and Vicki made small talk, avoiding the things that were really on their minds. It was ridiculous and phony, but there it was. The whole thing was an exercise in masochism. Why had she agreed to do this? The last person in the world she felt like explaining herself to now was Vicki.

She and Vicki had both majored in library science. They had taken most of their classes together, and had both gotten work in the college law library after graduation. They went on to graduate school together, although Joan had dropped out and Vicki had gone on to finish her master's. This handful of facts were the only things Joan and Vicki had in common.

One did not have to be any sort of genius to be a librarian. All one required was an innate sense of order, a mania for accuracy, an appreciation of the silences inherent in high-ceilinged rooms full of inanimate objects, an immunity to the allergic propensities of the particular type of dust found between the pages of seldom-used volumes, a fairly prodigious memory for trivia, and an illimitable supply of patience. The similarity to housework and child-rearing had not escaped Joan in the past three years.

It was a secure job. It paid well, considering. And as long as there were lawyers and judges to write more laws to be put into more books to be kept in more libraries, there would be a need for librarians. And it was legend that lawyers reproduced by spontaneous generation, or perhaps by secret couplings with the laws themselves, which always burgeoned in Malthusian proportions.

The problem was that the academic institutions that housed the libraries were easily shaken by little things like recession, and when Joan left her job to give birth to Eric—with no particular plans for returning earlier than several years from that event—she had not been replaced, for economic reasons. The library now managed with two librarians instead of three.

Joan knew her job no longer existed; she'd acknowledged as she thumbed through the Sunday *Times* that the chances of her getting a library position anywhere this side of Canada, Europe, or possibly New Zealand were at best slim. She did not have time to send out

résumés and sit back for weeks and wait, either. She had
to get a job now, before the end of the week, if possible.
If she'd had any sense she'd have thought about this before she threw Brian out, and it was perverse at this point
to even bother calling the library. But she'd reached for
the phone anyway.

I have to call Vicki sooner or later, she reasoned. If she
finds out what happened between Brian and me by hear-
say, she'll never speak to me again. Besides, if I can tell
Vicki, telling my parents will be a breeze.

But what am I going to say to her? Joan had agonized
in the interminable moment between dialing the last
number and the onset of the first ring. God, how she
hated telephones!

Vicki was probably the only person from college that
Joan still kept in touch with. Most of the people she'd
known had drifted away to various parts of the world,
desperate to get out of the city for some reason, and it
was hard to keep in contact. As for the people she'd
studied dance with—well, dancers were bitchy and mer-
curial, and it was next to impossible without a scorecard
to tell who was snubbing whom in a given week. And as
for Brian's friends, what was the point of staying in touch
with them?

Vicki was impossible to figure out, really, and Joan had
given up on her for months at a time. It was hard to say
what was wrong with Vicki exactly, except that she had
been born about a century too late.

Vicki was the product of, the oldest daughter in, a
large Irish family, and she had become convinced from
birth that the shortest route to heaven was the ability to
quote chapter and verse in support of every action from
brushing one's teeth in the morning to not sleeping with
one's boy friend at night. Joan never knew whether to
laugh at her or feel sorry for her. Never had anyone of
such wit, intelligence, energy, and education been so

completely taken in by the monolithic piety of countless generations of sainted grandmothers and undereducated grammar-school nuns. Vicki had faith and, as far as Joan could see—though she kept coming back for another look —not much else.

So there she was calling Vicki to tell her about Brian, to try out on her what she would have to say to her parents, her landlady, any potential employer, the credit-card companies, her son's nursery-school teacher, the paper boy . . .

She got past the switchboard and listened to the ringing, wondering how the hell she was going to accomplish this.

"Hello, Vicki," she began, hearing the familiar voice.

"Hello?" the voice echoed, puzzled. Joan could see the pinched white space between Vicki's eyebrows as she frowned.

"It's Joanie," she said flatly, disgusted that she couldn't even do that much right.

"Oh, for heaven's sake!" Vicki near-shouted, enthusiastic as always. "Well now, isn't that funny! I've been thinking about you all weekend. As a matter of fact, I was going to call you tonight—it must be weeks since we talked. How's everything?"

"I guess it depends on your point of view," Joan said, trying to sound breezy and cheerful, when all she wanted to say was "Fine. How's everything with you?" and lie like a bastard for the entire conversation. But her words were already beginning to fray at the ends, and she knew she wasn't very convincing.

"Joanie? What's wrong?" Again the white space would appear between Vicki's eyebrows. "How's Brian? You haven't been—"

"Yes, we have," Joan snipped out quickly. "Or that is, we were, and to make a long story short he has split for good this time after pulling a scene that you wouldn't

believe and—I can't go into details over the phone, but—
but this is it. I've had it. I can't take it anymore. I'm going
to get a divorce."

"Oh, no! Oh, Joanie, please don't say that! I know
you can't possibly mean that. You're upset at the moment—I can understand that—but when you've calmed
down . . ." Vicki loved missionary work. Joan could hear
her warming to her subject. "I know how angry you must
feel in the wake of the argument, or whatever it was, but
when you've had a chance to think it out, you will realize
that nothing good can come from divorce—"

"Vicki—" Joan attempted to interrupt, though she
didn't know what she would say if she could get
through.

"You have to think of Eric," Vicki went on, not notic-
ing the interruption. "No matter what has come between
Brian and you, you have to take into consideration the fact
that a little boy needs a father, and—"

"Hey, look, Vicki, I didn't call you to get into this—
this kind of—" Joan felt as if she were choking. "I can't
explain what this is all about. I'm not going to try. Look,
if I gave Brian visiting rights on weekends, it would be
the most he's seen of his kid since Eric was born. You
have no idea what it's like—that a home without Brian is
less of a broken home than one with him blundering
around drunk and talkative all night long. You've never
had to live with an alcoholic. I hope you never do. And
I'll thank you to mind your own business."

"Did you call me to tell me that?" Vicki's voice was
brittle. "Or was there something else?"

Joan was out of breath. "Something else, yes," she
gasped. "Something completely idiotic. I need a job. I
know what you're going to say. I know there's nothing
on campus. I just thought maybe you might have heard
of something—an office job, legal secretary, like that. I
have to have something, and fast."

"Have you tried the *Times*?" Vicki asked coldly, in the tone of one who had no intention of aiding and abetting a sinner.

Joan's temper was going. She took a deep breath, letting it out in short pants like transitional labor.

"Oh, sure," she said airily. "But I don't think I can finance a move to Canada. Or did you mean Australia? That's where they used to send hardened criminals, isn't it?"

"Oh, really!" Vicki was dismayed. "I wish you wouldn't be melodramatic. I am trying to help, even if I don't approve of the situation. It's only fair to warn you that I'm going to pray for you and Brian every night."

Save your breath! Joan wanted to shout. She restrained herself.

"Can you type?" Vicki asked suddenly, getting a flash of inspiration.

"Sixty words a minute!" Joan said proudly. It was a major accomplishment for someone with a purely academic background. "I used to type papers for Brian when he—"

She stopped. How many evenings and weekends wasted on Brian's papers, papers for courses that led nowhere but to more courses?

"Well, you're in luck then, aren't you?" Vicki asked primly. "In that case I'd suggest your best bet would be something along the line of a paralegal, or a legal secretary."

"Right," Joan said dispiritedly. "I'll keep you posted."

"Yes, do that." Vicki brightened, relieved of a great moral burden. "In fact, call me as soon as you get something and we'll make a date for lunch. Unless you change your mind about—about the whole thing. Call me right away in that case."

"Sure, Vicki," Joan had said, reaching for the *Times* with her other hand.

After she had checked all the listings under "Secy-Lgl," Joan called her parents in Houston.

Her father's company had transferred him right after she and Brian had started living together, which, as it turned out, was convenient for everybody. Joan didn't have to listen to her mother's nagging, and her parents could escape the shame of having a daughter living in sin. They had seen each other less than half a dozen times in as many years. She couldn't really talk to either of her parents. If she couldn't get a word in edgewise with her mother, she fared little better with her father, who spoke hardly at all. With him there were long silences, punctuated by the fact that he could never forgive her for moving in with Brian.

Joan had a little speech prepared; she'd been running it through her head all morning. It went something like:

"Hi, mom, I just called to say that we're all fine, but I have something important to tell you which I hate to say over the phone, but here goes: Brian and I are separated, and the way things look now we'll probably be getting a divorce, but don't worry because Eric's taking it very well, and . . ."

But for some asinine reason she dialed the operator and placed a person-to-person call, even though her father would be at the office and her mother didn't let the housekeeper answer the phone. Maybe she'd just needed the operator's voice as a buffer before she hit smack up against her mother's grating monotone, but the delay threw her timing off and she ended up blowing the whole thing.

"Hi, mom—" she began, faltering for a fatal half-second.

"Hello, sweetheart, you sound like you have a terrible cold it must be freezing up there you know we hit eighty last week why the hell did you make it person-to-person that's so expensive what's wrong?"

Shit! Joan had thought. Shit, shit, shit! This wasn't it at all.

"By the way, stop looking at the prices and relax," Vicki ordered. "My treat. You can have anything except the lobster."

"Yes, ma'am," Joan said meekly. She couldn't protest, but she knew the price of the lunch entitled Vicki to lecture.

"You've got an interview in Manhattan?" Vicki was concerned. "Will you have time to get there?"

"Oh, sure," Joan assured her. "It's downtown, and it's not until three. Last chore before they close up for the weekend."

"What kind of job is it?" Vicki wanted to know.

Joan shrugged. "Legal secretary," she said. "Sounds like a small firm—family, kind of a mixed bag of cases. Maybe I can get a break on my divorce."

What the hell, might as well get on with it, she thought. Maybe we can beat it to death quickly and I can enjoy the rest of my lunch. God, I haven't had a meal in a restaurant since—

"Speaking of divorce," Vicki began, swallowing it hook, line, and sinker.

"I thought you might want to," Joan said, waiting.

"You're still serious about going through with it?" Vicki's eyebrows pinched together, and she answered the question herself. "Even after two weeks of looking for work and seeing what you're up against out there? If you could just wait awhile and think it over. When Eric's a little older and you can look at it objectively—"

"Vicki," Joan said with deadly calm, "you don't know what you're talking about."

The calm was a new phase. She could talk about her

situation quite rationally now, at least in public. It was only at home, alone, that she spent any time crying. And that time was getting shorter almost daily.

"I'm sorry if I've offended you," Vicki said. "But I have to say what's on my mind."

"Feel free," Joan said airily. "But then let me have a word when you're through."

She had to stop while the waiter brought their order, and by the time he was safely out of earshot she'd scrapped the neat little speech she'd prepared.

"Look, Vicki," she began, closing her eyes and exhaling slowly—a habit she'd acquired when Eric was going through the Terrible Twos and she'd had a choice between making him listen to reason or slamming him into a wall—"we really don't have anything to talk about. You can look at it objectively all you want, but I'm sitting plunk in the middle of something that has been snowballing for years and which finally got too big for me to push against anymore. All I did was stop pushing and let it roll over me. I have no desire to drag it up the hill and start all over again. I couldn't love Brian again no matter how hard I tried. I'll be grateful if I can just learn to *like* him again once all this is over. My advice to you is to try to see it from my mother's point of view, which is that I never should have married him in the first place. But I did, and I can admit now—objectively—that I made a mistake. That's my confession, and now all I have to do is get absolution, in the form of a divorce and whatever penalties it entails. I think I'm being very orthodox about the whole thing."

"You're twisting it to your own advantage," Vicki said primly.

Joan was watching her with fascination. She had meticulously cut her veal cutlet into bite-size squares, and was arranging them on the plate to be eaten clockwise. Joan thought she'd seen all of Vicki's fussy habits in action;

this one was new to her. She almost expected Vicki to say grace.

"What God hath joined together—" Vicki began instead, intoning the punch line of her original text.

"If God joined Brian and me together, it was one of the bigger blunders of his recent career," Joan snorted, losing patience. "I'd prefer to think we fucked it up all by ourselves."

She watched with a kind of sadistic pleasure as Vicki's cheeks went bright scarlet. Vicki always blushed when hit in the face with a dirty word.

"You've made your point," Vicki said finally, recovering badly from her shock. Blasphemy and obscenity in the same breath. "Now that we've apparently exhausted that subject, what shall we talk about?"

"I don't know," Joan said airily, finding that she enjoyed winning arguments by default. "I mean, that's what's been monopolizing my life lately. Nothing else is new. What's new with you? How's your love life?"

"Well, I shouldn't think *that* was so important." Vicki attempted to laugh; it was a sore point with her. "If you asked me about my intellec al life, or my career—"

"Nobody on the horizon since you broke up with whatsisname—the actuary? I could have told you he was a dead end." Joan was being nastier than usual; she couldn't believe what she was hearing.

"You *hardly* seemed like the person to ask for advice," Vicki snapped, getting her Irish up.

"Point for your side," Joan acknowledged. "I'm crazy. You just seem very uptight about the subject."

"Well, I've been busy lately," Vicki said, almost a plea for understanding. "They've asked us to put in a lot of overtime at the library, and my grandmother hasn't been feeling well, so I've been spending the evenings with her, and I'm getting to an age where my family is beginning to nag a little."

"But other than that, you don't feel the need for it."
Joan shook her head. "Don't you ever get lonely?"

"We all have our crosses to bear," Vicki said in all
seriousness.

"Oh, Jesus, Vicki!" was all Joan could say. Vicki pre-
tended not to hear. Joan groped for something they could
talk about without arguing. "Look, we're both very touchy
today. Is there anything we can talk about? What's new
at the college? Any juicy gossip? Please, can't we just
talk without killing each other?"

"What's new at the college . . ." Vicki mused, taking
her literally. "Nothing juicy that I can think of—a lot of
policy meetings, a few new faces on the faculty—I guess
it's not interesting if you're not involved. I really don't
think—"

"Well, what about the people who've been there since
we were there?" Joan asked, suddenly enthusiastic. Nostalgia, escape from the gritty realities of the present to
the good old days of college, even if they weren't so good.
"You know, the old-timers. Is Turner still there? Is she
still as dotty as ever?"

"Miss Turner is still with us—a little more *absent-
minded*, you might say." Vickie tried to be specific. "Not
changed much, I wouldn't think."

"And what about—oh, whatsisname—the music teacher,
the one with the rose in his teeth—come on, you know
who I mean—"

"Of course. Father Arpino, our resident hypochon-
driac," Vicki said severely. "In view of what happened
to Dr. Morrow, nobody's been paying much attention to
his palpitations recently."

"What happened to Dr. Morrow?" Joan felt a chill
that had nothing to do with the environment. She had
been about to ask—

"You didn't know?" Vicki was puzzled.

"Know what?" Joan gasped. She's dead, Joan thought.

Don't tell me that. I can't bear to hear things like that about people. "How could I have?"

"Oh, I'm sorry." Vicki laughed nervously. She only believed in personal revelation where gossip was concerned. "How stupid of me! I thought surely you must have— well, Dr. Morrow had a stroke. A rather severe stroke, as we have been led to believe. Just before Christmas."

There was a finality in Vicki's voice that made Joan dread the answer to her next question. People didn't always die of strokes, did they?

"H-how is she now?"

Vicki shook her head to indicate that she was chewing and could not be interrupted. She swallowed the final mouthful, carefully crossing her knife and fork at right angles to each other on the plate before she spoke.

"No one really knows," she said at last. "We were informed that she was to have no visitors, and the hospital keeps saying her condition is 'guarded.' It's been about six or seven weeks now. She may be home already, but no one's been able to get in touch with her. Her phone's unlisted, and there's a possibility she might be staying with relatives for a while, or—"

"You were informed?" Joan asked, puzzled by the wording. "By whom? The hospital?"

"No," Vicki said slowly, weightily. "By Father Giangrande. He's the only one who's been in touch with her. He took her to the hospital, you know—carried her into the ambulance like a knight in shining armor and drove off with them, leaving his classes in an uproar and half the campus buzzing with rumors."

"It's a good thing he was there," Joan said, puzzled by a note of self-righteous nastiness in Vicki's tone. What now? "They were always close."

"*That* they were," Vicki said, and Joan saw the color coming up in her cheeks again.

"Now what's that supposed to mean?" she demanded.

"I think it's perfectly obvious," Vicki said primly, fighting back the blush.

"Oh, for God's sake, Vicki!" Joan looked at her in disbelief, tempted to quote her one of her own lines about judging not. "Those rumors have been thundering around on campus so long they've got hair. You don't really believe they could carry on an affair for—what—twenty-five *years* without some kind of slip-up? Particularly Giangrande—he's so goddamned orthodox he couldn't carry on an affair for twenty-five minutes without trotting off to confession. And don't you think somebody in administration might have been grilling them if they thought anything was going on? And how come she never talked him into marrying her? She's pretty good at persuasion. Come on, Vicki, really! I'm surprised at you. Under that cold exterior beats the heart of a true romantic."

"Oh, horsefeathers!" Vicki said heatedly, as close as she could come to obscenity. "I'm only thinking of how it looks. He's the only one who's been allowed to see her at the hospital. He drives off right after class every day, apparently to be with her, wherever she's staying now. And you should see them together, even before the stroke —interrupting each other's stories and everything. Like an old married couple."

"And they always were. What's wrong with that? The trouble with you is you've got a dirty mind." Joan shook her head, not sure if she was teasing Vicki or if she really wanted to pound on her for making it all sound so rancid. She pushed her chair back from the table in disgust. "Damn!"

"What's the matter?" Vicki's eyebrows puckered.

Old age, Joan thought. People you knew, people you respected, starting to age on you. A heart condition was one thing. Gradual senility was embarrassing for others, but relatively painless for the victim. But a stroke—a brilliant mind broken in half—

"Oh, poor Sarah, that's all," Joan said. "You have no idea how bad it was? How is she now?"

"Nobody knows," Vicki said solemnly. "Nobody except that priest."

Joan chose not to respond to the remark.

"Did you ever take one of her courses?" she asked. "The Chaucer or anything?"

"I don't remember," Vicki said. She was lying; Vicki never forgot anything.

"You'd remember if you had," Joan said, smiling a little at the memory. "I had her for freshman lit—you know, that deathly-dull survey course? Other people's classes used to bitch about it like crazy, and I could never understand why. I used to laugh so much I'd wet my pants. God, she was good! I almost switched my major on her account. Once she assigned me a paper on—oh, what was it?—something dirty, anyway—and I got thrown out of the library twice for laughing so loud in the middle of all this heavy research. Incredible! She had to be the best teacher I ever had."

"How nice for you," Vicki said, totally unable to relate to the experience.

The waiter brought the check finally, and Joan looked the other way while Vicki studied it and reached into her purse.

I shouldn't have been so bitchy, Joan thought. If I weren't so desperately poor . . .

"What hospital?" she asked, unable to get Sarah Morrow off her mind.

"Hmm? Oh, Dr. Morrow." Vicki nodded, already having dismissed the entire subject. "Long Island College. Nearest to the college, except for Brooklyn Hospital, where one simply *wouldn't*—"

"Naturally." Joan understood the instinctive terror of municipal hospitals. "I wonder if she's still there."

"I doubt it," Vicki said. "Once you're off critical they

usually want to get rid of you on something like a stroke."

"I guess so. Maybe I can get her address and send her a card or something," Joan said, not half believing it herself. "Listen, I'm sorry for being so nasty."

"I'll live," Vicki assured her, but with a trace of mortality in her voice. "I'll just chalk it up to your present unsettled state of mind. It's time I was getting back to the library. Why don't you stop up for a few minutes and say hello?"

"I—I don't think so," Joan said, suddenly panicked. Enough memories had been dredged up by their conversation. "I'll call you if I get the job."

"Do that," Vicki said.

They bundled up against the cold, standing on the corner for a moment to kiss each other with antiseptic propriety before they went their separate ways. Vicki cut across the campus to the library, and Joan trudged toward the subway and a dubious future.

"Missed you at lunch. Did you go out today?"

Vicki had been hanging her coat in the back room when the other librarian came in. The two of them always took overlapping lunch hours in the cafeteria in the basement of the library, leaving an undergraduate to supervise the main desk while they were gone.

"As a matter of fact, I did." Vicki flashed her slightly too saccharine smile. "I met a friend for lunch."

"How nice," the other librarian said. "Where'd you go?"

"Joe's Place," Vicki said. "I don't happen to care for barbecued ribs. It's the only civilized place in the neighborhood."

Bigotry was apparently permissible in Vicki's moral code, as long as it was honest bigotry.

"Joe's Place," the other librarian mused. "Gee, I haven't been there in years. Is it still as romantic and cozy?"

Vicki had to think for a moment. "I guess it is, yes," she acknowledged. Such descriptives rarely occurred to her.

"Someone from the college?" the older woman asked. "Male or female?"

She was considerably older than Vicki, silver-haired and plump, the kind of person who wore fur-trimmed boots and tweed skirts all winter. She hadn't married until she was thirty, so she could appreciate the loneliness she imagined Vicki was experiencing. She couldn't resist matchmaking.

"Mm?" Vicki had her mouth full of hairclips, a brush in one hand. "Who?"

"The friend you had lunch with," the woman prompted.

Vicki put her hairbrush back in her purse and shut it with a bang. "Oh, Mildred, for heaven's sake!" she said. "I wish you wouldn't be so obvious. Female."

"Oh." Mildred was crestfallen. "Well, you missed some interesting gossip. So there!"

"Really?"

Gossip was Vicki's only vice. She never succumbed to the common addictions of cigarettes or liquor or sex that enslaved most people. Her weakness was gossip. She wallowed in it.

Conscientious, she ought to have ended her lunch hour precisely at the hour of two. She would ordinarily be out at the desk by now, or pushing the book cart ahead of her, reshelving. Succumbing, she leaned one hip against the cataloguing desk, folded her arms over her well-Maiden-formed breasts.

"What did I miss?" She was trying not to drool.

"Well—" Mildred hesitated, peeking through the open doorway to make sure that the sophomore at the circulation desk couldn't overhear. "Let's just say that a certain party was called into Sister Francis's office this morning, and questioned closely as to the health of a certain member of the English department who—"

Vicki shook her head, exasperated. "Honestly, Mildred, you should have been a lawyer," she said. "You can mention names. The room isn't bugged."

"That's not funny!" Mildren protested. She gave Vicki a furtive look. "Years ago, when the library was in the old building, with the intercom . . ."

Neither wanted the other to see that she was looking for the device they both *knew* had not been installed in the new building.

"What you're saying," Vicki said a little too confidently, masking her paranoia, "is that Sister Francis called Father Giangrande into her office this morning. How do you know what they talked about?"

"Vera Neil told me," Mildred said simply.

That made it gospel. Vera Neil was the president's secretary, a little prune of a woman with extremely acute hearing. Her desk was directly against the wall of Sister Francis's inner office; and despite the excellent construction of the old building, a curious acoustical freak made most conversations held above a whisper easy to overhear. And Father Giangrande was not notoriously soft-spoken.

". . . I'm not an authority on her condition, Sister," he had said when asked. "I'd recommend you speak to her doctor."

"Since I cannot speak to her directly," Sister Francis said coolly. "That *is* what you are telling me—however obliquely—is it not?"

Francis had nothing against Pietro, really. In fact, their paths seldom crossed beyond an occasional faculty meeting. The theology department was a relatively autonomous unit within the university. Most of its members were diocesan priests, with a handful of Jesuits like Pietro and one very old Franciscan. The diocesan priests answered directly to the bishop, the others to the superiors of their respective orders. Any measure of control by the ad-

ministration of the college—that is to say, by the nuns—
was pure formality. Besides, Sister Francis and the other
nuns went to confession to these very same priests. It was
hard to say who controlled whom.

So Francis neither liked nor disliked Pietro. She had
no power over him, hence no reason to be polite to him. He
was here to provide her with information, and she saw no
reason to be deferential in extracting it.

"Sarah can speak!" Pietro said, a little too forcefully, in
answer to Francis's accusation. "True, she tends to hesitate, to think out what she's going to say. It isn't easy to
pick up after something like this. Her vocabulary's a little
on the fuzzy side. But she understands anything you say
to her. She'll get the rest back in time."

"And whose prognosis is that—yours or the doctor's?"
Francis watched with the beginnings of a smile as he gave
himself away.

"The doctor's," he said. "Mine as well. I know her. She's
not a quitter. She's willing to fight her way back."

Francis's smile broadened a little, turning up the corners
of her mouth by a few millimeters. Condescending.

"And how much time do you suppose—" she began, but
interrupted herself before he could. "You see, I have to
make my decision well before the end of the term. There
is the matter of finding a permanent replacement for her
during the summer. And I must inform Mr. Spensieri
that he must look for another position. All of this has to
be done sensibly, and not in haste."

Spensieri was the graduate student who was filling in
for Sarah. Pietro felt obligated to rise to his defense.

"Suppose Sarah can't—doesn't come back next year?"
he asked. "Maybe Mr. Spensieri would like to keep his
job."

"I doubt it." Francis looked at him blandly. "He accepted
it on the basis of its temporality. You see, his wife is—

expecting—and she's going to leave her job shortly. They couldn't possibly afford to raise a family on what I'm paying him."

The absolute indifference of her statement stunned Pietro. Of course he knew there was a huge difference between the salaries paid in this place and those of the big universities, but to hear it put so casually . . .

"I assumed you were paying him something comparable with what Sarah earned," he said naïvely.

"Why on earth should I?" Francis was incredulous; it was the first true emotion she'd expressed all morning. "He's not a full professor. He has no previous experience. You know the rules regarding the pay scale."

Pietro was about to protest, but realized he had been successfully sidetracked. He was here to defend Sarah, not some kid who could pick up a new job anywhere in the country on the basis of his youth and the shiny newness of his degree. He started to speak.

"You understand my problem, then," Francis stopped him, knowing he did nothing of the sort. "You see, less than a decade ago, when the majority of our faculty belonged to religious orders and received a minimum monthly stipend from the diocese, salaries were not a difficulty. However, with the recent changes in the Church, and the departure of so many of our nuns and priests, it has been necessary for us to hire many lay people, and the total output for salaries—well, I won't bore you with details. The point is this: Dr. Morrow was a full professor with tenure. She was at the highest salary level. Now, unfortunately, she has suffered an illness which, as I see things, renders her unable to teach at full capacity. There is also her age, which, if I am not mistaken, is sixty-two—"

"What you're trying to say"—Pietro rose from his chair, a little angry and rather loud—"is that you'd rather hire the kid at half the price and put the old gal out to pasture."

Francis tilted her head imperceptibly to look up at him. She did not really feel intimidated by his height, but even so . . .

"I would prefer to put it less bluntly than that," she said. "However, in essence, I cannot see retaining Dr. Morrow on the basis of sentimentality rather than competence."

"Sarah is competent!" Pietro all but roared, remembering the little secretary just in time.

"Is she?" Francis's voice was steely.

"Not—not right this minute," Pietro stumbled. "But she will be. Six months' rest, and therapy—"

"—is six months too long," Francis said simply.

Pietro stared at her grimly.

"I am not an ogre," she said, as if his expression warranted a plea for understanding. "I have enough compassion to realize that such things cannot be broached to Dr. Morrow at this time. That was why I wished to speak to you, to elicit your help in making clear to her—"

"Enough compassion?" Pietro repeated wryly. "I think only just enough."

He strode out, resisting the urge to make obscene gestures at the peaky-faced little secretary, whose typewriter—silent throughout the interview—was suddenly hyperactive.

"Imagine!" Vicki was wide-eyed. "Imagine his speaking to her like that!"

"It's a touchy situation," Mildred agreed. "You can see Sister's point, of course, but it seems a shame."

"Oh, I'm not so sure," Vicki said, weighing it. "I think, for the amount of tuition the students have to pay, they'd prefer to have an inexperienced but competent professor to one who—well, of course we really don't know how bad the stroke was. It's my suspicion that it was worse than we were told."

"But it makes you wonder," Mildred pointed out, stacking the books that needed reshelving onto the cart. "What if you or I were in the same position? Sarah's under the mandatory retirement age. She has tenure. They can't just bounce her out. There's going to be a big stink before this is over, you mark my words. What if it happened to you?"

"Well, I'm hardly likely to find myself in a similar situation for another thirty years or so," Vicki said airily. "And if I were—well, I'd consider it perfectly fair for them to let me go."

"I wonder." Mildred looked at her skeptically. "Besides, they could stretch a point about health and competence pretty far. I'm a diabetic. Maybe they could prove that made me a less effective librarian. And what if you got pregnant?"

"Mildred, really!" Vicki blushed furiously. "You do have a way of making a big issue out of an individual case!"

She pushed the book cart out toward the elevator. Mildred watched her go, unwilling to return to her own work.

"I'm not so sure" was all she said.

"Level with me. You need this job badly?"

"Yes, sir, I do," Joan said quietly, breaking all the rules of successful employment-seeking. One was to remember that the employer needed an able employee as much as the prospective employee needed the job. One was not supposed to be humble and gauche and practically mendicant, but when one had been rejected in twelve interviews in less than two weeks . . .

"Without prying, might I ask why so badly?"

He was the middle partner in the firm of Goldmark, Werner, and Goldmark. His brother-in-law and his nephew, the two Goldmarks, were identically tanned, identically die-cut at a thirty-year interval from the same Ivy League, Brooks Brothers mold. Uncle Sid, by contrast, was bookworm-pale, educated at City College, and still retained his Flatbush-Yiddisher accent. He was the nice guy in the firm, the one who got the odd jobs like interviewing the new secretary. Joan liked him already.

"Well—" she began, looking for a subtle way to outline her difficulties. Oh, what the hell! she thought. They'll find out sooner or later. "I'm separated from my husband, and I have a three-year-old son."

"Two excellent reasons," Mr. Werner nodded. "You're separated how long?"

"T-two weeks," Joan blurted, realizing how asinine it sounded. "Actually less."

"And you're so desperate for money?" Mr. Werner raised his eyebrows. The hurt look on Joan's face softened his approach. "Forgive me, I'm being indelicate. But I have to ask. Someone with already a B.A. and half a master's is obviously not wanting to type for the rest of her life."

"That's true." Joan looked down, her voice barely audible. It was time to start putting her coat on again.

"This was why I was assuming you needed the job in a hurry," Mr. Werner continued. "If you had time to browse, you'd want something much fancier than this dump. Someplace to meet interesting young people. The problem being, if you're taking the job in a hurry, you're also leaving someday in a hurry."

Joan said nothing. Monday morning would find her at the Department of Social Services. Maybe they could give her enough to hold her over until—

"You know something, though?" Mr. Werner studied Joan intently. "I'm going to hire you, and I'll tell you why. I've interviewed already five other girls for this job, and most of them figured out pretty quickly this wasn't what you'd call a glamour position, and most of them would last two weeks, if that. But every one of them swore to me how important this job would be to them. You gave me no such assurances. I am hiring you on the basis of your sincerity."

Joan wanted to kiss him. She wanted to gush about how eternally grateful she was, but he raised his index finger to stop her.

"And also," he said, "because my grandson will be three tomorrow."

He had taken out his billfold and was counting out five twenty-dollar bills. "Take," he said, putting the money down on the corner of the desk nearest Joan. "A little advance on your salary. Please not to argue. I insist."

If anyone on the subway wondered why Joan's nose was running and her eyes were red, no one asked. Allergy, she would have lied.

Tomorrow morning she would ride the same train in the opposite direction, safely sealed inside the special airtight plastic personality one wore as armor on public transport. She would enter the cluttered little office with its floor-to-ceiling bookcases in the cramped three-room suite, dirty venetian blinds hiding windows that looked across a sunless courtyard into other windows, broken-down couch stacked with unsorted briefs and ragged little piles of rubber bands and paper clips, rolls of postage stamps. She would make a home for herself at the oversize, scratched and battered desk, typing until the small of her back ached and all her fingernails were broken. She would bring her lunch from home, never tempted by the three enticing sandwich shops and the pizzeria between the subway and the office. She would eat at her desk next to the clanking old-fashioned radiator, and have her very own key to the communal bathroom down the hall. She would hoard every dime she earned, and open a checking account in her maiden name and a trust account for Eric, and—

That was tomorrow. Today she was going to get home before Eric did and soak in a hot tub for half an hour, and after supper she would set out her clothes and go to bed early and . . .

VI

Ink-a-bink
A bottle of ink
The cork fell out
And you stink.
Not because you're dirty
Not because you're clean
But because you kissed a boy
Behind a magazine.

CHILDREN'S COUNTING RHYME

She had done most of her traveling over the past three years within a few blocks of the apartment, wearing dirty jeans, accompanied by her son. The only men who honked at her were the transcontinental truckers and, being chronically horny, they offered no true measure of society at large. She had forgotten what it meant to be a sex object.

For years she had gone almost daily to the small park near their apartment, pushing the carriage or stroller, later lugging tricycle, sled, skates, Frisbee, football. There were always figures in the background—junkies, resident wino, pill-trading kids swearing at each other over endless games of stickball. And there were the lovers, usually the ones who were married to someone else. The most consistent had been the guy in the Con Ed truck who for two years parked at the end of Joan's block on his lunch hour while his girl friend, a fortyish kind of dog, turned her two dirty-mouthed kids loose to tear up the park while they grunted and thumped in the back of the truck. Joan wondered where they went in the winter.

There were the three blocks from the subway to the office—all the three-piece-suit varieties and the Wall Street clerks eating yogurt or pizza and making remarks. Three blocks to be walked twice daily, subway to work, work to subway, and even the cold and the long winter coat had no effect on the comments. And there was the park to be passed mornings and evenings, and weekends with groceries and laundry.

And for years she'd had the kid with her and she hadn't traveled on a regular basis, and Joan had forgotten what intestinal fortitude it took for a female person to take a three-block walk.

"Hey, baby, whatcha doing tonight?"

"Dig that one. She's got a nice ass. Good legs, too."

"Yeah, but she's got no boobs. A chick's gotta have boobs."

"Hey, girly, your skirt's too long! They're wearing them short again, right? Aren't they?"

"Forget it. That one's a real dog."

"Hey, listen, guy I know says the flat ones get hot faster than the ones with big boobs. That right, sweetheart?"

"Aw, look, maybe she's married. How's your husband like it, baby?"

"Hey, you do blow jobs?"

"Nah, that one's a real dog."

"Nice ass, though."

Joan couldn't remember it happening with quite this frequency as long as she was married. Maybe it had, but she hadn't noticed it. Or maybe there was something about her that told them she had no man around to protect her now. Maybe it was because until recently she hadn't had to deal with the irrational fear that one of these pricks might follow her home. Instead of becoming immune to it, she was getting more and more paranoid. She was beginning to read sinister motivations into every male she encountered: the store clerk who let his fingertips brush her palm as he handed her the change; the bus driver whose eyes met hers a fraction of a second too long when she asked him for a transfer; the neighbor across the street who mentioned, only once, that he and his wife weren't getting along. Joan added them onto the list with the others: the ones who moaned and made kissing noises behind her back, the flasher on the subway platform, the one with garlic on his breath who squeezed her ass from Court Street through the tunnel to Whitehall during the morning rush hour when she couldn't move away from him—and if she hadn't had an umbrella to push between herself and his hand, there was no telling what else he might have tried.

It's no worse than it's always been, she told herself. You've just forgotten how bad it can be. One must not be terrified of half of the human race just because some of its members are vile.

I must have been awfully dumb when I was twenty, Joan thought, trusting Brian the way I did. Trusting anybody, for that matter. It's a good thing twenty-year-olds are naïve, or the species would be extinct by now. There is a certain kind of fatalism inherent in adolescence—it has something to do with rock music, I think, or courses in existential philosophy—which forces one to spend a great deal of time thinking, This is all I've got, and I could be hit by a bus tomorrow and never know what I've missed.

And it took me longer than most to fall prey to this, possibly because I was so taken up in my dance classes. But once that came crashing down around my ears— once I took the trouble to think that maybe all I had was what I saw around me—I started getting high a lot at parties, and wanting to get it on with every guy and half the girls I met

Except that I've always been cursed with the talent for watching myself while I'm in the middle of things so there wasn't the slightest real possibility that I was going to start screwing around but I did have an elaborate secret fantasy life in which I imagined every possible way there was of Doing It and just what It would be like

And I'm sure to this day that I picked Brian up at the beer blast and not the other way around but at the time I wanted to think he had chosen me and that I would quite naturally have the nerve to Do It—for what else could he ultimately have on his mind?—the minute he suggested that we should He would have to suggest it first of course but I would be more than compliant And the only thing that sobered me was the thought that I might get pregnant and however irresponsible I might have been it always struck me that that was a singularly irreversible thing to do

So we dated a few times in the standard way mostly just taking walks in the park or trips to the zoo or to the Metropolitan back when you could get in for free when I had to do a paper because he never had any money and he was too proud to let me treat so we spent a lot of time holding hands and talking instead of necking in the movies which is all I'd ever done with the three or four other guys I'd dated and I discovered that not only could I welcome the idea of going to bed with him because I liked his body except for the slight hint of a beer belly evident in his round-shouldered way of walking but I could also talk to him and listen to him although he never said much and it wasn't until much later when we'd been married for a while for God's sake that I realized I talked just like my mother too much and sometimes we could have fun without even thinking about sex so that when we finally Did It it seemed so natural

I was very careful and slunk into a drugstore in a strange neighborhood the week before to buy the aerosol foam they sold over the counter if you looked overage and it was supposed to be ninety-nine-percent effective but I made him buy some new condoms though he swore he had some old ones lying around somewhere and I tried not to be hurt by his crassness The alternative would have been getting in on the vast campus black market in Sanger Clinic pills garnered wholesale to avoid embarrassment to the individual but I didn't want to take a chance on screwing up my hormones or forgetting to take them

And I'd already convinced myself that Doing It wasn't going to have any harmful effect on me either psychologically or physically nothing lost but an insignificant little all-but-invisible membrane that some girls didn't even have or had such a thin one that they never felt a thing when they

But I practically heard it pop when he lowered himself into me and it pinched and burned like hell and I must've stopped breathing because he stopped heaving in and out and asked if I was all right and I gasped Yes! which he must have interpreted as ecstasy because he kept on going when except for the burning I felt nothing nothing at all except so tired I could hardly keep from yawning and couldn't wait until he finished and heaved himself off me and covered me with his old ratty blanket and I guess I fell asleep

Because the next thing I knew he was asking me Was it good Did you like it and I lied Yes it was good and I love you while all I kept thinking was that if this was all there was to it I couldn't see what all the fuss was about

And it wasn't until we'd lived together for nearly a year and we got married much to the relief of Vicki and my parents in the college chapel with Vicki as maid of honor although she must have done a lot of rationalizing and consulting with her confessor before she took on the assignment and maybe that's why she's so anxious to have Brian and me reconciled to justify her assumption that we knew what we were doing when we got married And within about six weeks of the wedding I got pregnant even though I'd wanted to wait a year and I'd been faithfully using a diaphragm the whole time we were living together but one night I forgot and Brian used it as an excuse to drop out of law school for which he didn't need much of an excuse because he'd decided almost as soon as he started that it wasn't what he wanted although how he could tell when he'd never found anything he did want was beyond me.

And it wasn't until I was four months pregnant which is the best time of it because your insides have settled after the first three months of being perpetually seasick and you're not all bloated and morbid and sleepy like the last three months It was that far along when I really discovered one crazy night for no reason that I could hit the top and go over the edge into a real live orgasm howling until I was hoarse and for once in my life forgetting to rationalize

And I guess that was when if you really want to calculate it down to a specific date I guess it was from that night on that my relationship with Brian began to deteriorate or maybe the holes just began to show through the pretty gauzy fantasy I'd thrown over the concrete fact of his drinking which was getting worse because he couldn't cope with the idea of being a husband and a father all within a few months of each other

And it was also because it bothered me intensely to think that any man who could do *that* to me would not even know that I'd been faking it before Any man who could do *that* to me and then roll over and go to sleep—

I'd been getting used to the ritual of it without having to climax and I gradually learned to enjoy being petted and stroked and lightly mauled just long enough for him to peak and slip inside right away before he went off like a geyser without there being any danger that what was usually only a mildly annoying pleasure might spill over into anything approaching uncontrol and I didn't want to lose control was afraid somehow of losing myself and never being able to come back Of being swallowed up in that great big hole where the babies come from until like a snake swallowing its tail I would disappear into nothingness

But whatever it was this particular night maybe it was that he was too drunk to get it up as fast as usual and so he was playing with me and playing me until I sang better than his shitty guitar and playing me to buy time for his ego until I went higher than I'd ever gone before and wanted to stop it to shout No but I shouted Yes and let go trying to watch from the outside but losing control even of that and

letting go until

letting go until I was engulfed thrashing gasping until I was over the top and hurtling down into obliteration of the distinct-human-female-being-person I thought I was

becoming only skin singing nipples pulsating cunt roaring my secret tongue big as a mountain and blocking out the sun—

and just as it was ebbing away into something like what I was accustomed to Brian finally got stiff enough to get where he was going and went off with a single convulsive grunt before he fell asleep or passed out I didn't care and I had to roll out from under him and try to find the pieces of myself and remember my name and whether these hands belonged to me and contemplate without recognizing at first the strange shock of dark hair against the pale skin all sticky and still pulsating vaguely tingling despite the cold realization that the bastard didn't even know what he had done

The path of divorce, once chosen, meant gradually forgetting the smell of liquor on someone else's breath. It meant losing touch with the special mannerisms he had, forgetting that his hair smelled musky like a dog's fur, that he had freckles on his knees and a tiny black speck in the iris of one blue eye. It meant forgetting how he ate, and the expressions he used, and what he looked like when he was sleeping, until on the few occasions when you saw him these things seemed foreign to you.

It meant you felt shy with him for a long time, because he knew what you looked like naked, because he had heard you talk in your sleep, because you had confided so many of your secret thoughts to him.

It meant running over in your mind like old movies endless scenes of the two of you together and happy, even if they were glamorized and sometimes outright lies. It meant you'd never be able to ride a merry-go-round or go ice skating or look at Van Gogh's *Starry Night* again without thinking of him.

Divorce also created a war of nerves between you and your son, who increased his quota of sudden loud noises that drove you up a wall, lied about things, nagged you to give back the pacifier you'd thrown away six months ago, peed the bed oftener than necessary, and, in a final act of defiance, flushed a washcloth down the toilet and waited to see what you would do about it.

"You little bastard!" Joan shrieked at him, forgetting what his being a bastard made her. She jiggled the handle on the toilet frantically, watching the water back up, up, spill over ever so slightly onto the tiles, and then stop churning with a gasp at the very rim of the bowl. "What the hell did you do that for?"

She tried to control her language in front of him, primarily because the other mothers in the neighborhood did not approve, and she didn't want him to become a social pariah, but this . . .

"Well?" she demanded when he didn't answer, only stood in the bathroom doorway with his lower lip stuck out far enough to park a car on. "Answer me! Why did you do that?"

"Just because," Eric said sullenly, folding his arms and daring her to do something about it.

He knew without being able to tell time or read a calendar that it was Friday evening and almost seven o'clock, that his father would be here any moment to rescue him from this witch, his mother. He knew with the uncanny prescience of a three-year-old that she wouldn't hit him now and have him crying when Brian arrived, knew also that she would have forgotten all about it by the time he came home Sunday evening.

"You're a rotten little kid, you know that?" Joan hissed at him, narrowing her eyes to scare him. It used to work when he was two, but no longer. "Now I have to call the plumber. We can't use this toilet until it gets fixed. You've made a terrible mess!"

"Don't care," he said imperturbably. He had figured out that he wouldn't be here to be inconvenienced, but she would.

Brian came to pick him up, and there was nothing else Joan could do.

She really couldn't blame the kid. There was so little time—she was always hustling him off to school or nagging him to finish his supper before he fell off his chair from exhaustion, and by the time she got him in bed he was nodding off before she had a chance to talk or read to him. She couldn't even count on Brian to skip a weekend, or to be so drunk she could refuse to let him take the boy. He seemed to have given up drinking altogether, just to spite her.

Brian took Eric to the park on Saturdays, let him stay up

late, let him watch television all day Sunday. She had always limited him to "Sesame Street" and other educational programs. Brian and Eric went to McDonald's; they went horseback riding and got circus tickets and rode the Staten Island ferry. Joan got to clean up Eric's room when he wasn't there, pack and unpack his clothes every weekend, calm the nightmares he got from the scary programs Brian let him watch. She made him take his vitamins and supervised his toothbrushing and dragged him to the doctor's for shots. And she got to call the plumber when he avenged himself on her for being his mother and not his best friend.

When the two buddies had left, Joan poured a whole bottle of Clorox into the toilet and tried flushing it again. It overflowed with a vengeance this time, bleaching out her only decent bath mat and stinking up the entire apartment with the smell of bleach. Joan mopped up the mess for the second time and looked in the Yellow Pages for a plumber who was on call twenty-four hours. Even though it was a weekend and she'd have to pay time-and-a-half . . .

She got the answering service. Sorry, there was no one on call right now, but someone would try to get there tomorrow. She understood it meant paying overtime for a Saturday? Fine. Sometime tomorrow, then, Mrs. Tierney. Thank you for calling.

Why was she still using Brian's name for things like that?

The plumber came when she was still in bed. Ordinarily she slept until noon on Saturday, luxuriating, but she'd deliberately set the clock for eight. Plumbers, exterminators, and special-delivery packages always came first thing in the morning or while you were in the middle of supper.

At five minutes to eight the doorbell rang.

The hair on Joan's arms stood upright. Shit! What to do now? She scrambled out of bed and grabbed her robe, wishing it were cleaner, less frayed, groping under the bureau for the slippers she never wore, wishing there weren't so much unshaved leg showing between the hem of the robe and her feet. He would know that all she had on under the robe was one of Brian's old undershirts. He would see that her face was scummy from sleep, her hair stringy and uncombed.

The bell rang again, and then there was a knock—insistent, aggressive. Would *he* put his fist through the bathroom window if she didn't answer?

Joan didn't wait to find out. She unlatched the door and swung it toward herself, forgetting she kept the chain on all the time now in case Brian, some night in a drunken frenzy, or someone knowing she lived alone, unprotected . . . She heaved the door shut again, fumbled the chain off, and swung it wide.

"Sorry," she said with a weak smile. "Forgot about the chain."

He seemed awfully big, not as tall as Brian, but broader, heavier, for some reason more ominous. She'd never been afraid of Brian; maybe she should have been, but she knew him, knew he wouldn't have the ambition to hit her. Now she found herself sizing up every man she met. How tall was he? What did he weigh? Did he have a quick temper, or was he easygoing? Could she outsprint him in a short race? If he hit her, how much damage could he do?

Her plumber was extraordinarily clean, and smelled of aftershave. His nails were particularly neat, almost manicured. Joan made note of the red hair, the requisite freckles on his thick arms, and the tattoo—badge of membership of the blue-collar class—a small blue dagger half-hidden in the red forest on the back of his left hand. No wedding ring.

He asked her something. She responded. Joan was never certain what she said to people in everyday exchanges. She somehow knew she had given him the necessary answers and that he had understood her.

She flattened against the wall to let him pass, then

followed at a safe distance. No one had ever instructed her in the etiquette of home-repair situations. Was she supposed to hover over him, keep up a conversation while she watched to make sure he did it right? Should she go off someplace and putter with the coffeepot or read a magazine and leave him in peace?

Joan said nothing, but hung around in the bathroom doorway while he squatted in front of the toilet and contemplated it.

"So what's the problem?" he asked, looking up at her.

"My son threw a washcloth down it," Joan explained. "I tried putting Clorox in it. I know you're not supposed to use drain cleaner or it might explode, but the bleach didn't do anything. So that's when I . . ."

He was nodding slowly, letting her talk herself out.

"Got the picture," he said. "I'm gonna have to get down inside her. I left the snake in the van. Sit tight!"

The minute he closed the door behind him, Joan grabbed the first clothing she could find, scurried to the door to see if he was coming back, ran to the bathroom to agonize over whether she had time to wash her face *and* take a leak, or if not then which to do first since he could be here for hours and she . . .

Ever since last night, she'd been relieving herself into an empty orange juice bottle and pouring the contents down the sink, forcing herself not to eat any fruit or anything that might create other urges that could not be met under the circumstances. She could always use the landlady's bathroom, but she was not the sort of person who could . . .

She ended up pouring the still-warm contents of the orange juice bottle into the bathtub, splashing a little Lysol in after. She barely had time to zip her jeans when she heard him coming back.

She was positive he gave her a strange look, but he said nothing, so she squeezed past him out of the bathroom to

resume her hovering in the hall. She still had no idea what
to do with herself. She ought at least to make the bed.

She did. Then she floated past the bathroom into Eric's
room. In its occupant's absence, the room was unnervingly
neat. Everything was exactly where she'd put it the night
before, the Grow-with-Me books smugly perpendicular on
their shelf, the mobiles immobile. Defeated, Joan went to
the living room for the proverbial magazine.

And all that time, which wasn't really all that time,
Joan's plumber was engrossed in his work. The toilet made
strange sloshing, gurgling noises as he worked. Joan
half-listened, unnerved by the inconvenience. At least,
thank God, he wasn't the conversational type. The thought
of carrying on a shouted dialogue between the two rooms
and over the sound of the toilet . . .

She sat with the magazine in her lap, too far from her
line of vision to be readable if she'd wanted to read it,
wanting to cross the room and watch him from the hallway, to see what he was doing, perhaps to catch another
glimpse of the little blue dagger which for some reason—

*(Fascinates me. I don't know why, but it does. I've al-
ways thought tattoos were gross, immature, phony-macho.
But this one is so small, unobtrusive, almost attractive,
an afterthought half-hidden in the copper-red hair.*

*Red hair. What am I thinking of? So what if he has red
hair? All those bullshit superstitions about red-haired people—quick-tempered, untrustworthy. Redheads ought to
form a union, become a recognized minority group, and
then—*

*When all I'm really thinking about is the things other
than little blue daggers that can be hidden in a forest
of red hair.*

*And it's not just that. God, just because I haven't had
sex in over three months, and what I was getting then was
not exactly—I'm not really horny, but he's so goddamn*

healthy-looking. Like he spends a lot of time outdoors, and maybe he plays football or jogs or—

Brian was thin, but he always had a paunch, possibly a latent distended liver. Lately he'd begun to stoop a little. He was always pale, even in the summer, as if he liked to live on the underside of things. I always tried to drag him outdoors—for a walk, down to the beach. He always found some excuse, stayed sulking indoors, rebreathing his own stale air.

I need some excitement, dammit! I've spent four years of wife-and-mother push the stroller to the park and sit with the others talking La Leche versus Enfamil, Pampers versus diaper service versus let-them-go-bare-ass like the one three blocks over whose kids used to irrigate her front lawn until the neighbors got a court order, Spock versus Salk versus Skinner versus Basic Common Sense

I've exchanged nearly four years of five-dollar jeans and overdue utility bills and secondhand furniture and sneakers instead of shoes because my kid had congenital interior tibial torsion otherwise known as pigeon toes and wears orthopedic shoes at twenty-five bucks a six-week pair when he uses his feet to brake his tricycle from here to the bottom of the block The orthopedist says it's hereditary and undoubtedly comes from Brian's side of the family since my legs are perfectly parallel and I try to tell him that's from dancing because when I was a kid I turned my feet out so much duckfooted that I used to bang my ankles with the heels of my penny loafers until they bled But the orthopedist never listens since he is worth I figure at thirty dollars a five-minute visit approximately three hundred sixty dollars an hour which is even more than plumbers

Exchanged all of this for what?

For a half-dozen cheap dresses and cheaper pantyhose that snag on the corner of my desk and run like mad and an approximately eighty-hour work week when you count the commuting and the cleaning up and the laundry and in all this time I haven't been out of the house to see a movie or even go to the library and all I'm asking for is a tiny bit of something new to happen to me

When Brian and I were living together we found a stray cat roaming the hallway of the apartment we had then and we adopted it or it adopted us and it must have been altered because it never sprayed on the furniture or tried to get out and fight And the damn thing only had one freaky habit which was that it was crazy about a certain kind of hand lotion I used something with menthol in it that gave the cat a kind of high and every time he smelled it on my hands he'd go nuts and start licking and licking with that crazy raspy tongue until he damn near licked the skin off and I'd have to knock him on the floor to make him stop And I always sort of wondered what would happen if on one of those nights when Brian was out late I took the bottle of hand lotion and rubbed some of it on my breasts and up my thighs and even—although that stuff is probably hell on mucous membranes— And anyway the stupid cat got himself splattered by a car the year Eric was born because he was jealous and decided to end it all by sitting in the middle of the street waiting

And if I only had a cat now

Or even a bottle of that hand lotion.)

"All fixed, ma'am."

"What?" Joan looked at him blankly. She came back to earth with a thud. "Oh, right. How much?"

Ma'am, she thought. Christ, he must be younger than I am. He's a mere child, and here I am an old hag of twenty-seven. He called me "ma'am."

She paid him, and saw as she walked past the bathroom that he'd cleaned up the floor when he was finished. She could still smell the aftershave, even over the odor of Clorox.

And when she saw his truck pull away from the front

of the house she wanted to cry, wanted to run after him and ask him his name and how old he was and . . .

Brian brought Eric back earlier than usual on Sunday. Eric immediately threw a tantrum.

"Wanna stay with daddy," he growled when Joan came near him.

"Get out of the doorway so I can close the door," she said patiently, nudging his backside with her foot. "And take off your jacket."

"No!" he grumped, settling in more firmly. "Wanna stay with daddy."

Joan gave Brian an exasperated look. "Will you do something?" she demanded, hand on hip. "What's the matter with him?"

Brian shrugged. "He's been bitchy all weekend. Put him to bed early, that's all."

Eric began to roar. "Wanna stay with daddy!" he bellowed, sudden tears streaming down his distorted red face, dripping into his open mouth. "Wanna stay with daddy!"

Joan glared at Brian, who refused to participate. He lowered himself onto the couch and lit a cigarette. Gritting her teeth, Joan dragged Eric bodily into the bedroom. He struggled, kicking her more than once with his heavy orthopedic oxfords. She slammed him down on the bed and forced his arms out of the jacket. She left him to howl, shutting the door, caging him and cutting down some of the noise.

Brian had not moved, except to flick ashes into her perfectly clean ashtrays.

"I can't take him next weekend," he said, exhaling it with his smoke. "I gotta do something else."

"Something else what?" Joan demanded. "Did you tell him that?"

"I guess I did, yeah," Brian said noncommittally.

Joan stood over him, fists clenched to keep from throwing something at him. This dumb passive act was one of his favorite weapons.

"And it never occurred to you that *that's* why he's having fits?" she half-shrieked at him. "He thinks you're abandoning him. That you're never coming back for him."

"Bullshit." Brian put his cigarette out. "That's hysterical."

"Not to a three-year-old!"

Brian looked up at her, unruffled. "So what did you want me to do—leave it to you to tell him? Jesus, I can't do anything right by you!"

Joan tugged at her hair, disgusted. "Oh, get the fuck out of here, will you?" she steamed at him. "You always have to make my life as difficult as possible."

By the time she had locked the door behind him, some of the noise from the next room had subsided. Joan waited a few extra minutes and then went in.

Eric was a crumple of corduroy and damp tangled hair. His face was wet, mottled, snotty. Joan grimaced and went to the bathroom for a washcloth.

"Cold," Eric whined as she scrubbed his flushed face.

"Too bad," she replied, rubbing vigorously. "It's good for you. Calm you down. What's the matter with you anyway?"

"Wanna stay with daddy," Eric said raggedly, threatening to start all over again.

"Well, you can't," Joan said flatly, smoothing his hair and looking into his eyes, trying not to remember that they looked just like Brian's. He was such a beautiful little kid, if only . . . "Sometimes you stay with daddy, and sometimes you stay with me. You have school tomorrow."

"Hate school," Eric decreed.

"But you don't really," Joan reasoned. "Most of the time you have fun at school. You told me that."

"No," the boy said, irrefutable. "Hate school. And hate you! You made daddy go away!"

He cringed, expecting her to hit him. She ought to hit him, Joan thought, except that it was such a glorious surprise to hear him expressing an active emotion. At least she ought to yell him into submission and then try to explain all over again.

"It's time for bed," she said instead, leading him toward the bathroom.

She kept him the following weekend. He'd forgotten the uproar by then; three-year-olds confused the days of the week at the best of times. The battle Joan expected didn't materialize. Everything was fine, until Sunday afternoon.

It was a beautiful day, sunny and mild enough for him to be outside most of the time. If he kept within certain prescribed boundaries, Joan could see him from the window. He was old enough not to run into the street. And unstructured play was a novelty for a kid who spent forty-five hours a week in nursery school.

She zipped up his jacket and held the door open for him. All she had to do was look out the window every five minutes. She could clean up the apartment, start dinner, possibly even sit down with the paper for a while before he got bored and came thundering inside.

At first he was content just tooling up and down the block on his tricycle. Then he had to go through the obligatory ritual of tipping the bike upside down and revving the pedals around and around. Then a small gathering of other kids materialized, and an impromptu game of tag had them shrieking and tumbling up and down sidewalk and lawns. Joan watched Eric. He seemed to end up being It more often than anyone else. It wasn't that he was slow, only that he was so damned trusting.

The other kids would entice him, trap him, and he would be tagged twice for every one time another kid got chosen. They teased him mercilessly, but he didn't seem to react. Joan had to force herself not to rush out to his defense. What the hell was wrong with him?

The next time she looked out the window, he had disappeared.

All right, don't panic, she thought. He probably went off with the others. All you have to do is stand in the doorway and look up and down the street until . . .

She stuck her keys in the back pocket of her jeans and grabbed a sweater. Goddammit, hadn't she told him . . .

She searched all his usual hiding places, finally finding him in the last place she could think to look before she called the police. He and two other boys—one his age, one a year older—huddled in a neighbor's driveway, engaged no doubt in some surreptitious activity. They scattered guiltily at Joan's approach.

They're just playing doctor, Joan thought. Perfectly normal activity for his age. Don't overreact.

"Whatcha doing?" she asked them, trying to sound casual.

"Nothin'," they replied in unison.

"I told you to stay where I could see you." She turned toward Eric, frowning slightly. "Come home."

He said nothing, submitted without so much as a tremor. That damned passivity, Joan thought, leading him by the hand. Come on, throw a fit like other people's kids. Throw yourself on the sidewalk and kick and scream and tell me you hate me like you did last week. Be normal, for God's sake.

She led him into the house and closed the door, still without encountering any resistance.

"What were you guys doing out there?" she asked again, following him to his room and sitting on his bed.

"What?" Her son was an expert in evasionary tactics.

"You and Scott and Anthony—what were you doing in Mrs. Wisniewski's driveway?" Joan repeated with dogged patience.

"Just playin'."

"Playing *what?*" Joan persisted.

"Hostibal," Eric blurted, staring at the floor.

Joan wanted to laugh. Her face must have brightened. The boy interpreted her expression as one of approval and became suddenly talkative.

"Yeah," he grinned, warming to his subject. "Scott-nanthony was the doctors and I was got the shots!"

"Shots?" Joan frowned at this new twist. "What shots? With what?"

"With a stick," Eric said, not catching her mood quickly enough. "Right in the ass!"

Joan got the picture. Lousy little perverts, she thought —of the other two, of course. She didn't even think to correct Eric's terminology. She was furious. Dirty-minded little bastards!

And her son, as always, was their unprotesting victim.

She turned her anger on him. "You stupid little idiot!" she spluttered, unnaturally loud. "Did they hurt you?"

"Noo," the boy whimpered, his face crumpling.

Thank God for corduroy pants, Joan thought, and thank God I got there before they talked him into taking them off. It made her angrier.

"I don't want you to do that ever again!" she shrieked, seeing their snot-nosed snickering faces. "You stay away from those kids! They're disgusting!"

Eric had worked himself into a good cry by now. A buzzer was going off in Joan's head. She knew she'd lost control, but couldn't stop herself.

"Stop crying!" she shouted. "You dumb little bastard— you're as bad as your father!"

It was a cheap shot, but it brought Joan to her senses.

The incident had exhausted her. She and the boy hardly spoke during supper, and she went to bed early.

Just for half an hour, she told herself. I'll just catch a little nap because I still have to do the dishes and set out Eric's school clothes and . . .

(They still lived in the same apartment, though most of the furniture was different. Not new, but different. It belonged to her lover, and when he moved in with Joan he had brought it with him, so she'd had to get rid of her own. It didn't bother her; the old stuff reminded her of Brian, and Brian was long gone. She and her lover spent most of their free hours in bed, a real king-size bed that took up most of what had once been Eric's room. Eric slept on the convertible in the living room now, when he slept at all.

Joan's lover didn't like Eric. "He don't look like you,"
he would say. "So he must look like his old man. I don't need that."

Joan had murmured something vague, hoping to divert his attention and take the coldness out of his eyes.

He started with verbal abuse—picking on the boy for the slightest fault, aping the way he stuttered, forbidding him to cry. And then—

"If he pisses the bed once more, I'm gonna beat the shit out of him."

At first he only used the flat of his hand, though some-times hard enough to knock the boy down. Then he used his fists. Joan tried to intervene. He told her to shut up or she'd get some, too. Once she came home from the laundromat to find him holding a screaming Eric down with one broad hand—the blue dagger taut against the red-furred skin—and holding a lighted cigarette against the boy's—)

Eric's scream melded with the white-hot shriek Joan

had let loose into the darkness. It was minutes before she could distinguish what she had dreamed from what really . . .

Eric was having a nightmare, that was all. That was why he had screamed. All the rest . . .

Joan stumbled out of bed, tripped over the sofa cushions, and ran toward the bedroom. She scooped her son out of bed and cradled him like an infant.

He had wet the bed. She would have to change his pajamas, and the sheets, and—

It didn't matter. Nothing mattered right now.

"Baby, baby," she crooned to him. "Mama's here, puppy. Nothing bad's gonna happen. Mama's here."

He couldn't remember what he had been dreaming about. Joan changed his pajamas and he fell asleep on the floor while she changed the sheets.

It was only after she'd lugged him back to bed and closed the door that she realized she was trembling all over.

I am going to pieces, Joan thought. My mind has become a squirrel cage. I can't function much longer like this. I can't afford a shrink, my family is hundreds of miles away, and the only friend I have doesn't have the vaguest idea—

If I don't talk to somebody soon, I'm going to go right over the edge.

Joan clung desperately to the phone, hating it, searching the old woman's voice for signs of decay or senility.

"Of course. I—remember you. Worked in the—library —until—the baby. Little boy—wasn't it?"

The words were halting, painstaking, but the memory seemed fine, excellent in fact, considering how little an impression Joan usually made on people. Maybe the stroke hadn't been as bad as Vicki said. Vicki tended to exaggerate. Maybe Vicki had wanted it to be bad, to prove out one of her moral theories.

Why was she calling Sarah Morrow? How was a crippled old woman supposed to help a screwed-up young one? Why bother now—as if she didn't have enough troubles—to get in touch with an old woman who at one time, when life was simpler, had been her teacher, and who was now ill and probably unrecognizable and didn't remember her at all? And couldn't help her at all?

Joan didn't know, but she was doing it anyway.

". . . and I meant to send you a card, but I never got around to it, and since no one's heard from you in such . . ."

On and on she babbled, wondering how much of it was getting through to the old woman. God, how she hated sickness, and old people, and the whole scenario she was setting herself up for with this crazy phone call! Why was anyone as squeamish as she was going out of her way to contact someone she had once admired who was now probably old and grotesque and drooling and incoherent?

It will take my mind off my own troubles, Joan thought wryly and with an air of Christian martyrdom, to see someone who's in worse shape than I am.

She blundered her way into an invitation for the following weekend, and said goodbye.

Sarah scowled at the phone after she had replaced the receiver with her good hand. She looked quizzically at the figure across the room.

"Let me know when it's Friday, will you?" she asked. "I keep—losing the days. . . ."

VII

The choice of servants is of no little importance to a prince . . . the first opinion which one forms of a prince, and of his understanding, is by observing the men around him.

MACHIAVELLI, *The Prince*

"To my way of thinking"—Miss Turner put her tea-spoon on the saucer, leaving the maelstrom of milky tea to spin itself out in her cup—"to my way of thinking, one ought to stay out of it altogether. Taking either side is apt to be dangerous."

Miss Turner taught Victorian literature, and lived with her invalid mother. She wore harlequin glasses, flowered polyester dresses, and lavender eau de cologne. She prided herself on not having read any twentieth-century fiction because, as she put it, "it has not yet been proved by time." As she remembered it, the last major campus disturbance had occurred in 1968, when female students fought for and won the right to wear jeans to class. Vietnam was someplace they talked about on television, and Miss Turner did not watch television. Her mother, on the other hand, liked to watch the soaps.

"To my way of thinking," Miss Turner went on, "it

ought to remain a matter between the administration and
Dr. Morrow. I cannot see the purpose of the rest of us
getting involved. The faculty ought to present a united
front."

"Crap!" Sister Brigid said, slashing a red line through
a test paper she was marking. "Pardon my French, Agnes,
but you don't know what you're talking about."

There were four of them, sitting at the long table in the
room where Sarah Morrow had had her stroke some three
months before. Sarah had often sat with them during this
hour; conversations had been lagging in her absence. Even
so, they sat there, out of habit—two nuns, a priest, and a
slightly cracked spinster—each in the same seat, at the
same distance from the others, every Wednesday afternoon. There was Miss Turner, drinking tea and whining;
she never had anything else to do with her free periods—
she saved all her class preparations and test marking for
home. There were fewer distractions at home, and there
wasn't much else for her to do there.

There was Sister Brigid, a truck driver in a nun's habit,
marking blue books as she talked. She had no time to do
her schoolwork at the convent; she spent her nights writing
the definitive book of theater criticism, under an assumed
name. There was Sister Rosalie, teacher of dead languages,
soft-spoken, other-worldly. And there was Father Arpino,
professor of music, who sat fingering his nitro capsules,
lamenting the demise of the Latin mass, and convincing
himself it was simply another indication of the imminence
of the Second Coming.

"But what will the girls thinks?" Miss Turner almost
wailed, still concerned about the turn the gossip about
Sarah Morrow and the administration had taken of late.
"Dissension among the professors! What sort of example
are we giving them?"

Miss Turner always referred to the students as "the
girls," oblivious to the fact that the college had gone coed

five years ago. Not many of "the boys" were interested in Victorian literature.

"Crap," Sister Brigid repeated, though less vehemently. "They'll think we're capable of making up our own minds, that's what they'll think. If we don't speak out, we come across as a bunch of saps. And if the people upstairs can knock off one tenured professor before the legal retirement age with this incompetence angle, wait'll they start looking all of you over. Who knows, Agnes? You might be next."

Miss Turner blanched until her usually pale complexion began to resemble the mauve dress she was wearing, the same dress she wore every Wednesday. Sister Brigid was not one to mince words at the best of times, but really . . .

"W-what do you mean?" Miss Turner was bewildered. "I'm only fifty-thr—I mean, I'm nowhere near the age—"

"It's not age, Agnes. It's an intangible called incompetence, and it's so intangible they can interpret it any way they like. Take my word for it, heads will roll," Brigid said, pointing her red pen at Turner as if to mark her for the guillotine's next round. "If they can throw Sarah out, none of you are safe."

Brigid wanted to say more, but the question of competence was not one to be examined too closely where persons like Miss Turner were concerned. Excluding the half-dozen nuns who were past eighty and sometimes couldn't find the staircases—but they would be kept on until they dropped in harness; they cost less than the lay people. It was the lay professors who were walking a tightrope right now; if they didn't recognize it, someone ought to point it out to them.

Someone like Brigid. She considered herself safe. She was the only nun in the entire order with a doctorate in theater. She constituted the entire theater department at the college, and had been gradually expanding a two-course curriculum into an entire department over a period of years. That and the ridiculously small stipend she earned were her insurance against being transferred to some grammar school in Canarsie for opening her big mouth once too often.

Sister Rosalie spoke up for the first time, her voice as always barely a whisper. "One wonders if it is necessary to be quite so vociferous on the matter."

"Why? Because I live under the same roof with the people upstairs?" Brigid cocked one eyebrow. It made her look whimsical. "Is that supposed to make me lose sleep? They can tell me to shut up, but other than that there's nothing they can do to me. I'll have my opinions."

"One might refrain from marching about the halls roaring about academic freedom and neofascism," Rosalie said, repressing a smile.

"Was I doing that?" Brigid was amazed at herself. "I guess I got carried away. The entire situation pisses me off, though."

"Delightful!" Father Arpino bellowed from his seeming slumber at the far end of the table. "Such gentility, such precise turn of phrase from the mentors of our youth! Really, Brigid! Your language is enervating!"

"Can it, will you, Joe?" Brigid said without bothering to look at him. "You haven't had any nerves to speak of since I've known you."

"Don't fight, dears," Rosalie advised, and they subsided like chastened children. She had that effect on people; no one knew why. Her mild blue eyes were leveled at Brigid. "Agnes is right. In some respects we must maintain a united front."

Brigid opened her mouth, but said nothing. She contented herself with writing a particularly vicious comment in the margin of one test paper.

"God knows what some of these people are doing in college," she sighed. "It's beyond me."

"It's just possible they're here to get an education,"

Father Arpino rumbled. "Not like that noisy rabble we had here eight, ten years ago."

It may have been the mention of neofascism, but something had triggered a memory, hidden in his brain behind the complete choral works of Bach, the piano transcription of *Pictures at an Exhibition*, and the death dreams that would not let him alone since his first coronary coming home from Europe on the *Leonardo da Vinci* some years ago—a memory of the feeble, sad, misplaced antiwar movement that had tried to hold its own on this backward little campus in those years. The thought of something similar happening again, even over a domestic matter like the firing of a professor, filled him with horror. Besides, Sarah Morrow had always given him palpitations.

"Those kids had guts," Brigid told him. "They had ideas, they had creative energy. The current batch are as boring as hell."

Rosalie could see the turn events were taking. They would be at each other's throat in a moment if she didn't stop them. They often ended up not speaking to each other for weeks, and in a place as small as this it was important to get along with others.

"In the event that Sister Francis *does* ask Sarah to retire—" she began softly, hoping to end things quickly so she could sit and chuckle over her Juvenal in peace, "and might I remind everyone present that this has not yet transpired? We are operating solely on rumors—but in the event that this does happen, are we prepared to offer some sort of stand? Will anyone bother to ask us for an opinion, do you suppose? And will our opinion have any weight? There is of course the faculty committee to handle matters of this sort, but, other than that, what actual power do we have? And are we prepared to use it?"

"They've already heard from me," Brigid said belligerently. "Aquinas made some sort of remark at the last department meeting, and I let her have it. They know my opinion."

"As if they needed to be told!" Arpino said. "You've taken the left side of every position that's come down the pike. If they sent you to do missionary work at the Kremlin, you'd outleft the Reds. Your opinions are worthless."

"He has a point." Rosalie put her hand on Brigid's arm to silence her. "Although it ought to have been put more kindly, Joseph, really. But one *would* know your position on such a matter. If nothing else, you are consistent."

"All right, then," Brigid said, trying to ignore Rosalie's remark. "At this table we have one for Sarah"—she counted on her fingers—"one against." She glared at Arpino.

"Damn right!" he nearly shouted, feeling his blood pressure change gears and trying to remain calm. "This institution has no place for prima donnas! When I am sixty-five, should I live that long, I intend to leave quietly. I am going to enjoy my retirement years in peace, if not in good health. You'll hear no protests from me."

"If they weren't paying you so little they'd have thrown you out when you had the first heart attack," Brigid said without mercy. "Instead they allowed you to fart around in the rectory for an entire year, racking up doctor bills and moaning about the Last Rites."

"What's that got to do with anything?" he sulked. "Are you saying a bad heart affects my teaching? I'm not teaching pole vaulting, only music. My heart condition does not affect my brain."

Brigid looked as if she were going to say something vile, but Rosalie interrupted.

"Shall we get on with your poll?" she suggested. "One for, one against. Agnes, we come to you. What is your opinion?"

"I—I thought I made myself quite clear," Miss Turner faltered, as though she were being asked that question in the presence of Sister Francis, with her own future on the line. "I choose to take no stand at all. While I respect Dr. Morrow as a member of my department, I do not see that it is pertinent for me to offer an opinion."

"Chicken!" Brigid muttered, before she turned to Rosalie. "And what about you? Can you allow yourself to descend to our mundane level for that long?"

Rosalie smiled her mystic's smile. She was not hurt by Brigid's bluntness, nor by any of the often less-than-good-natured teasing she took because of her other-worldliness. She simply was what she was. If people saw fit to ridicule her because of it, so be it. It did not disturb her.

"I shall tell Sister Francis—if and when I am asked—that I feel she is being subjective in her decision to remove Dr. Morrow, and that perhaps she ought to examine her motivation—I hesitate to say her conscience—before taking such a step."

"And you'll get away with it," Brigid said with a kind of wonder. "You're the only one in the place who can!"

Bertie's feet made no sound on the carpet in Sister Francis's inner office. Bertie herself made no sound coming into the office with the coffeepot. Ordinarily she had to get past Vera Neil's careful guardianship, and some sort of conversation with her was necessary. But Vera was home with one of her biannual head colds this morning, and the door to the inner office was half-open. Without knocking, Bertie crept inside, intending to place the coffeepot and the clean English china cup and saucer on the credenza just inside the office, and creep out unobserved. But some sixth sense, or perhaps only the odor of freshly brewed coffee, brought her presence to the attention of the formidable woman behind the big desk.

"Good morning, Mrs. Byrd," Sister Francis said mildly, her pen poised in midsentence.

" 'Morning, Sister," Bertie said solemnly, about to leave.

Nobody who knew her first name ought to call her Mrs. Byrd, she thought. Ever since she'd married, at the age of thirteen, her older sisters had teased her to death, calling her "Bertie-Bird, Bertie-Bird!" and imitating her slightly off-center walk—she'd been born with one leg shorter than the other—and her downcast, introspective manner. Alberta Byrd, she would think to herself. Alberta Byrd. It sings, she would think, not knowing what a pun was and unable to recognize that she'd made one. Call me Bertie, and don't put on airs.

"Thank you for the coffee," Sister Francis said, as always.

Bertie had begun bringing the two-cup pot and the clean china upstairs from the cafeteria years ago when the entire college had been crammed into this one building. Now that the cafeteria had been moved to the basement of the new library building, Bertie still brought the coffee up fresh every morning and every afternoon, walking half a block and crossing the street sometimes in two feet of snow or ankle-deep rain. She didn't have to do it, but she did. It gave her an excuse to get out of the nearly windowless basement of the library, gave her a chance to roam on rubber-soled feet through the echoing corridors of the old building that she liked so much better despite its being overheated and roach-ridden.

And Sister Francis always thanked her, when she brought the coffee in the morning and when she retrieved the empty pot in the afternoon, but it was always as an afterthought; she never looked up from her paper work. That was what made today so strange. The even stare of the austere blue eyes fairly gave Bertie the jumps.

"You welcome, Sister," she managed to say, wanting to sidle out the door.

"Are you very hurried?" Sister Francis asked, a little too

suddenly, so that Bertie nearly jumped out of her skin. "I thought you might have a moment to sit."

The suggestion, more in the nature of a command, threw Bertie completely off-guard. In her fifteen years at the college she'd never once sat down anyplace but in the cafeteria, excluding the day she was hired, when she sat in an old wooden chair next to the bursar's desk to fill out the job application. Sit where? There were two green leather armchairs facing the president's desk. Surely she couldn't mean—

"Would you like to sit down?" Sister Francis rephrased it, as if she weren't quite certain she had been understood the first time. She was pointing with her pen at the closer of the green leather chairs.

Bertie sidled up to the chair, a little frightened as it squooshed beneath her, as if it, or she, were releasing a great deal of pent-up gas. She looked at Sister Francis in alarm, but the nun seemed not to notice. Apparently green leather chairs were supposed to sound like this.

"How are you this morning?" Sister Francis asked, actually putting her pen down and folding her alabaster hands on top of her paper work.

"Just fine, thank you," Bertie murmured, and let it stop there. When she was a child, her mother would prod her to say "And how are you, ma'am?", especially to white ladies who inquired after her health. She never asked that now. Somewhere in the forty-odd years since her childhood, she had discovered that people in a position of authority asked how you were because they wanted something from you.

"And your husband? I hope he is well?"

"Mr. Byrd be fine, Sister," Bertie said, trying to be easy and conversational. She'd had no idea Sister Francis even knew she had a husband. "Only his artheritis sometimes—"

"Oh, I know!" Sister Francis nodded solemnly. "It's

this terrible dampness. Some mornings I can hardly move my hands."

"Yes, ma'am," Bertie said, hitting a dead end. She was trying to imagine a resemblance between the sculptured ivory of those fingers and the great knobby protrusions that had begun to form on Henry's shoulders when he was barely forty. A lifetime and a half of lugging other people's burdens, he would say.

"And the children?" Sister Francis wanted to know.

Bertie was startled. Nobody ever asked her about her kids, not even Mae, with whom she worked shoulder to shoulder every day, and who was always banging her ear with stories about her own children and grandchildren. Nobody ever asked Bertie about her kids.

She had no way of knowing that Sister Francis kept a private file full of information about every one of her employees, and that only five minutes earlier she had pulled Bertie's card out and studied it. It was still tucked into the corner of the blotter on her desk for ready reference. If pressed, she could recite the names and approximate ages of Bertie's five children. There was Henry Junior, she would say, age thirty-two; and Amalia, thirty; Jackson, twenty-five; Azalee, twenty; and Gloria, seventeen.

But Bertie didn't know about the card, and couldn't read it upside down anyway. Flattered at what she thought was personal interest, she smiled for the first time.

"They all fine, last I heard," she said. "I only got the girls with me now—the two youngest—and Azalee be graduating nursing school in June so I'll lose her. But they calls me now and then, except Jackson. Last I heard he was out in California, but he don't like to write, and with the phone rates . . ."

She went on and on, a tide unleashed, not realizing that Sister Francis's smile of eager expectation had frozen into condescension and that she was nodding more often than was necessary. When at last Bertie realized how much she was talking and frightened herself into silence, Francis said nothing for a longer time than she should have.

"I'm so glad everything's fine with all of you," she said finally, drawing a deep breath as if to terminate any further variations on the theme. "Now, if you have a moment more, I'd like to ask your advice on something."

Bertie was almost completely bewildered. Almost, because she had discovered once again that the concern for her health and that of her family had an ulterior motive. But why could the president of the college possibly want advice from her?

"How old are you, Bertie?" Sister Francis asked without further preamble. She had the information on her card, but thought it would be better to do it this way.

"Fifty-two, Sister," Bertie murmured, wondering.

"Are you really?" Sister Francis seemed genuinely surprised. "Isn't that amazing! You certainly don't look it!"

"Thank you, Sister," Bertie said warily.

"And you've been with us—let me see—fifteen years, I believe. Do you like it here?"

"Oh, yes, Sister," Bertie said, thinking of some of the other jobs she'd had in her lifetime. "It's the best job I ever had."

"But you'd be glad to retire when you turned sixty-five, wouldn't you?" Sister Francis prompted her.

"Well, yes, ma'am. That's when my pension starts." Bertie was surprised. "And I got no intention of dropping dead in the traces."

She didn't know where she'd gotten that expression; it might have something to do with her mother's upbringing in rural North Carolina. But it made Sister Francis laugh, a rare occurrence, and one that Bertie had never witnessed.

"But now suppose"—Sister Francis suddenly grew fearfully solemn—"suppose, God forbid, that you became ill or incapacitated—unable to work—before that time. Suppose you were, let us say, in your early sixties, and you suddenly . . ."

Like Dr. Morrow, Bertie thought, getting the whole picture. You want me to say that if I was in her shoes I'd sit still and let you retire me, but I'm not going to say any such thing. You want to sound me out so's you'll know what the rest of the hired help thinks, so's you don't have some kind of protest on your hands. But you ain't getting any assurance from me.

"If it was me," Bertie said carefully when Sister Francis had finished her hypothesis, "I'd just as soon retire early. As it is, I get days when my feet don't want to get out of that bed. But I ain't about to speak for anybody else."

She left the office moments later, enthralled at her own eloquence. She'd never done anything so momentous in her life. She could hardly wait to go home and sit with Henry in the kitchen and tell him about how she'd stood up to the president of the college herself.

"And she had the gall to ask you that?" Mae stage-whispered past her clasped hands as she and Bertie knelt side by side in the back pew of the chapel. "The brass of that woman!"

Bertie had to laugh. Mae always said things like that about Sister Francis, except on the rare occasions when the president deigned to visit the cafeteria on one of her announced tours. At such times, Mae bowed and scraped enough to make you want to vomit.

When Father Giangrande turned around to give them the final blessing, they pulled themselves up from the kneeler like two middle-aged women who spent most of their lives on their feet, Mae crossing herself and kissing the crucifix of the glittering noisy rosary before shoving it unceremoniously back into her purse.

"That was fast!" she gusted. "Sure, he don't waste any time about a mass, does he?"

Mae always went to mass on the weekdays of Lent. Bertie seldom entered the dark, odorous little chapel. She was a Baptist, and realized the dangers of working in this Romish institution, but some of the staff had asked Father Giangrande to say a special mass for Sarah Morrow every week, and Bertie saw no harm in attending, as long as she said her own prayers and blocked the strange ones from her mind.

"Come with me," Mae said as she was about to leave, taking Bertie's arm and half-dragging her toward the sacristy. "I want to talk to the Father."

Bertie hesitated. She'd heard that women were not supposed to go past the altar rail, that dire things would happen if they passed into the little room in the back where the priests donned their ecclesiastical robes. She'd heard . . .

But Mae was a Catholic; she ought to know if it was all right or not. Reluctantly, Bertie tagged along.

When they found the priest, he was wearing his street clothes and sharing a cigarette with Mario, who leaned on his broom and dropped ashes on the floor as he talked. Mario didn't go to mass, but he was concerned about Sarah anyway.

". . . well, we figured the best way to find out was to go to the source, know what I meant?" Mario was saying. "Right, girls? Isn't that what we said?"

Father Giangrande noticed the two women for the first time. "It was very good of you to come," he said, as if at a wake, taking each of them by the hand. Bertie thought he looked tired.

Mae immediately launched into the tale of her sister-in-law's stroke, and the priest listened patiently, though he'd heard it all before several months ago when Sarah was still in the hospital. Mario and Bertie exchanged knowing looks behind Mae's broad back. When she was finally through, the priest spoke thoughtfully.

"It's not that we're trying to be mysterious," he said, seeming to look around him as if he might be overheard. "But it's understood that sometimes rumors get started—"

"Sure, don't they ever?" Mae shook her head in dismay. "But you don't have to worry about us, Father. We're not about to go spreading any rumors."

Mario seemed to be having trouble with his cigarette. Bertie didn't trust herself to say anything.

"Sarah is feeling much better," Giangrande said. "And she's grateful for your concern and for your prayers. She may not be able to come back to the college for a while yet, but she's on the road to recovery."

"And you tell her not to worry, Father." Mae patted his hand solicitously. "If they give her a hard time—about coming back, I mean—you tell her we're all of us on her side."

Giangrande was taken aback. Did everyone know *everything* around here?

"I'm sure you are, Mae," he murmured uneasily. "I'm sure you are."

He ground out his cigarette on the sole of his shoe, looking at Mario before he let the butt fall onto the parquet floor. Mario swept the ashes and butts ahead of him down the hall as they went their separate ways.

Being the youngest department chairman had its disadvantages. So did having the reputation for being extremely gifted and intelligent, when you also happened to be a nun. The other nuns in your class tended to be a little vicious toward someone who'd been sent to Bryn Mawr to do graduate work, and who spent her summers in Europe while the rest of them sweated out education courses at the motherhouse and squabbled over whose turn it was to do the dishes. And when you'd earned your doctorate before you were twenty-five, only to find yourself doing advanced clerical work at the age of thirty-four, you were bound to feel depressed.

At least, a lot of people thought Sister Maryann ought to feel depressed, and told her as much. The others thought she ought to feel honored at having earned such an important position so young. Maryann's actual emotions were somewhere between the two.

Of course she thought it was nice to be department chairman, and to get to go to all sorts of important policy-making meetings, and to have control over curriculum, and to help solve people's intradepartmental problems, as well as sometimes their personal ones (were only English teachers this neurotic? she wondered). But it would also be nice if she could teach more than one course, if she could spend her free time doing what she wanted to do instead of catching up on her paper work.

And it would be extremely nice if she hadn't been put in the position she'd found herself in this morning. She was still fuming about it.

"So what are you going to do?" Herb asked her later.

Maryann blinked at him through her thick glasses. "I'm not going to do anything," she said in an injured tone. "I'm certainly not going to do their dirty work for them."

"Them" referred to Sister Francis and Sister Aquinas, who had spent a good part of the morning trying to persuade her to talk to Sarah Morrow about resigning. They had not put it quite so bluntly, of course, but the intention was obvious. Maryann had a sunny disposition; she rarely got angry. Now she was so angry she couldn't see straight.

"But you're not going to try to obstruct them," Herb

said, which didn't help matters. He'd meant it as an observation, but Maryann took it as a criticism and jumped on him with both feet.

"Do you think I have the freedom to do that?" she demanded.

"Of course not," Herb said, backing off. "I was just going to suggest—"

"Forget it," Maryann snapped, and stormed out of the room to get something to eat.

The others in the small faculty dining room exchanged glances, but said nothing. They were the so-called younger generation, the lay people, most of them in their thirties or early forties, most of them from the arts and philosophy, who seemed always to be on the wrong side of the fence on matters domestic or political. They were the ones who, however quietly, had come out on the liberal-to-radical side of things like Vietnam and Watergate, the ones who had petitioned for black-studies courses back when minority students comprised less than five percent of the campus population, the ones who treated the students like equals. Some of them even encouraged the students to call them by their first names. Some of them weren't even Catholic, and some of the ones who were supposed to be Catholic were shockingly overt in their agnosticism. And they talked about things like contraception, and homosexuality, and—

And Maryann was the only nun in the group, although some of the nuns from sociology drifted in and out from time to time. She aligned herself with this batch of outcasts for several reasons: because she was of their generation; because she shared many of their views; and because once in a while she liked to forget she was chairman of the English Department, and wanted to talk about something besides Gerard Manley Hopkins and the altar flowers for Palm Sunday and everyone else's diseases.

If the truth were told, she was deathly sick of being the

youngest department chairman, and of being a credit to the order, and of all the other meaningless honors the older nuns were always patting her on the head about. She resented the total lack of freedom that being in a position of power sometimes brought with it.

She had been annoyed that she could not attend the impromptu little meeting Herb had organized to draw up a petition in support of Dr. Morrow. Her presence would have drawn too much attention to what was going on, would have tipped off the administration and put the whole project out of operation. She couldn't even sign the petition without bringing half the staff down on her neck—the same people who tolerated Herb and the others because they were only assistant professors or worse and couldn't do much damage. All she could do was dig in and refuse to help the opposition.

She jostled among the students on the cafeteria line, almost blending in because she didn't look her age and didn't wear any sort of habit and because the students weren't impressed with her title but with the fact that she was a decent human being. She wondered if any of those owlish individuals she'd just left at the table could have held their ground the way she had in the president's office this morning.

"Hey, Sister! Where's your skateboard?" one of the kids yelled, coming up beside her.

It was a joke. Some of her students had presented her with a skateboard for Christmas, saying it was the only way she could possibly get around faster than she already did. Maryann loved it. She lugged it to class almost daily, and would sometimes glide around the deserted halls when she thought no one could see her. She had never seen any reason to stop doing certain things because of her age, her important job, or the fact that she happened to belong to a religious order. She wore flame-red dresses, could get through a transatlantic flight without groping for her rosary, adopted stray cats, and advised the kids on their sex lives, and somehow this morning's meeting seemed to threaten all that.

She was still kicking herself for not having gone to see Sarah much earlier. Pete Giangrande had said Sarah preferred to be undisturbed; Maryann had listened to him. She should have known this was going to happen and tried to warn Sarah.

What galled her was that Sister Francis actually thought she would cooperate with them in their nasty little scheme. Didn't she know that Maryann owed her chairmanship to Sarah, that Sarah had always been her mentor and friend? Was she supposed to forget that solely because a higher authority tried to intimidate her?

The intimidation had been thorough. Sister Aquinas did most of the actual talking; it was one of Sister Francis's favorite techniques for dealing with inferiors. Maryann had survived it before, but she could feel her kidneys going into overdrive.

"What I'd like to know is why no one's talked directly to Dr. Morrow," she'd said matter-of-factly. "No one even knows how she *is*, how she's feeling. Whether she even *wants* to come back. Why hasn't someone spoken to her?"

"We feel at this time, dear," Aquinas began while Francis nodded, "that it would not be judicious."

"Lest you warn her ahead of time," Maryann ventured.

Aquinas opened her mouth like a fish and glanced toward Francis, whose smile had quite vanished.

"I think that's rather harsh." Aquinas looked wounded and misunderstood. "We have no intention of forcing Dr. Morrow to do anything that she doesn't want to do—"

"Then what do you need me for?" Maryann demanded, her glasses misting over with the effort to control her temper. "Am I mistaken, or do you want me to talk to her and suggest—not insist, of course, but suggest—that she take the easy way out and retire?"

She was looking directly at Francis, ignoring Aquinas as if she were an extension of the furniture. Francis still did not speak; she met Maryann's myopic stare with a steady gaze of the utmost serenity.

"We simply feel that you, as her immediate superior, could point out to her the difficulties she would face in coming back here with handicaps—mental as well as physical," Aquinas explained. "We feel it would be less cold and impersonal than if it came from someone higher up."

"As far as I'm concerned," Maryann said, wanting more than anything to leave in midsentence and head for the john, "it should be up to Sarah to decide what she wants to do. And I don't think it's fair to start making plans around her without speaking to her first. I'm sorry, but I'm not going to do what you want."

Francis leaned forward for the first time. "Suppose we were to leave the decision to her? Suppose she is incompetent but refuses to acknowledge that fact?" she asked evenly. "Suppose she is unable to speak, or can speak only in monosyllables? Suppose she is confused, unable to find her way about? Suppose she doesn't recognize people, can't keep track of her notes? As chairman of the department, the burden will then rest on you. Wouldn't it be cruel to let her come back and embarrass herself, and then tell her she must leave? Are you prepared to do that?"

"If necessary," Maryann barely whispered between clenched teeth. "But we will not know what is necessary until we talk to Sarah first."

There had been more in the same vein, and neither side had budged. At last Maryann excused herself because she had a class in the other building, and they parted company on a sour note. Once past Vera Neil's desk, Maryann had bolted for the hall, and barely made it to the john in time.

Now she paid for her coffee and cheeseburger, substituting an apple for the piece of pound cake she really shouldn't have, and went back to join the others in a less hostile frame of mind. None of them had condemned her outright for what she had done, or not done, this morning. She was just being paranoid.

She was met by Herb and his infernal petition. Maryann gritted her teeth. He'd been circulating the thing among the faculty for over a week. He'd even mentioned wanting to distribute copies among the students, who had not even thought of it themselves.

Herb knew how Maryann felt about the petition. When he saw her coming, he slipped it back into his briefcase.

"It's premature, Herb," she scowled at him, setting her tray down a little too forcefully. "You can't take any action until they make an overt move to force her out."

"It's only tentative," he said. "And as far as I'm concerned, their calling you into the office this morning is tantamount to a declaration of war. This thing is beginning to heat up."

"But you have no idea what went on in there this morning, do you?" Maryann asked primly, adding onions to her cheeseburger to keep him as far away as possible. "At least not from me you don't. I thought Kierkegaardians didn't jump to conclusions."

"I can surmise an awful lot from the way you've been stomping around here all day," Herb said. "And if they're mobilized, it's about time we got there ourselves."

Maryann concentrated on the cheeseburger to keep from snarling at him. Sometimes she felt sorry for Herb. His vocabulary and his tactics were beginning to date him. He hadn't been content to try getting himself fired over Vietnam; he was starting again. He seemed to disregard the fact that he had five kids to feed now instead of two, and that he was one of the few salaried members of the philosophy department and they'd be only too happy to replace him with a priest or a nun who didn't cost as much. Maryann wondered why he had to jump on the wagon and make noises every time a cause happened by, as if he doubted the strength of his own liberalism and had to keep proving it to everyone else. She sighed. He was such a nice guy, really. Too nice for his own good.

"All right," she said, swallowing. "Let me get this straight. You are asking people for signatures as a declaration of solidarity with Sarah. But, as I said to the boss this morning, and I may as well say to you, nobody has taken the trouble to talk to Sarah. Maybe she doesn't want our solidarity. And you still can't do anything until the administration actually comes out and says they're letting her go."

"This is just ammunition," Herb said, tapping the briefcase that housed the petition. "If nothing happens, I'll throw it away and there's nothing lost. But I want to be ready to jump in the minute trouble starts."

"And I suppose yours is the first signature?" Maryann asked, knowing the answer.

"How else can I ask others to sign?" Herb asked mildly, leaning back in his chair and lighting a cigarette.

Maryann sighed and shook her head. "You missed your calling," she said sadly. "You should have been an early Christian martyr."

Herb made a face at her, exhaling smoke. "That shits, and you know it." It was the closest he would venture to a personal attack. "As far as I'm concerned, what happens to one member of the faculty could happen to any one of us. So aside from the fact that I think Sarah is a marvelous, warm, brilliant person who is being short-shrifted, I'm also covering my own ass."

Maryann blinked at him skeptically. "How many people have signed so far?" she asked, as curious about the petition as she was wary of it.

Herb slid it out of his briefcase and handed it across the table to her. She scanned it briefly, recognizing Herb's barricade rhetoric, seeing that the liberal contingent had once again lined up and declared itself. She laughed a little when she saw Sister Brigid's signature, then handed the petition back.

"How'd you get Brigid to sign?"

"Oh, Sister Brigid approached me in the very beginning to see if anything was being done. She said she'd do whatever she could to help. I think that's damn courageous of her. Why are you laughing?"

"Because it's just like her," Maryann chuckled. "She lets you stick your neck out and all she does is tag her name onto it. She's going on sabbatical next year to finish her theater book, and Francis can't touch her."

The Kid came in just then. Everyone called him The Kid—because he was all of twenty-eight, because as Sarah's replacement he was the newest member of the faculty, and because there was something almost too fresh and eager about his approach to his job and the people he worked with. Certainly he must have some inkling of what was going on, but no one was crass enough to talk about it when he was in the room. Guiltily, Herb stuck the petition back into his briefcase and everyone changed the subject.

"How's everything, John?" Herb asked, too loud, too cheerful.

"Fine," The Kid nodded. "Just fine. How's by you?"

"Can't complain," Herb said, stubbing out his cigarette and stretching idly. Maryann wanted to choke him. "How's your wife feeling?"

The Kid brightened. "Six months and counting," he said. "Doctor says she can keep working for another month if she takes it easy. It looks like we'll be able to keep this one."

He'd known them all only a few months, and already everyone knew his wife was miscarriage-prone, that this was their third try for a healthy baby. Herb sighed, thinking about his own menagerie. Only the first two had been planned; the other three had just happened. And the third was hyperactive, and the fourth had allergies, and the fifth needed corrective shoes, and only since his wife had gone back to work last year and he had taken up selling stocks as a sideline to teaching philosophy had they been able to afford more than groceries. Small wonder, he thought, that there were no great female philosophers, or that philosophy and child psychology were incompatible. And here was this kid earning, he figured, somewhere in the neighborhood of eight thousand a year, and hoping against hope that his wife could have this baby.

"Say, what time is it?" Maryann asked suddenly, all of this good-fellowship getting on her nerves. "I dropped my watch in the sink yesterday and I've got this meeting at two—"

"You're late then," Herb said pleasantly. "It's two now."

"Damn!" she said, surprising everybody, shoving her tray aside and knocking half her books off the table.

When she'd finally made her noisy exit, Herb stretched one last time, picked up his briefcase, and clapped John Spensieri on the shoulder.

"I hope she makes it, John," he said sincerely, realizing how inconsistent his feelings were with what he'd been doing ten minutes before. "You tell your wife we're all pulling for her."

The Kid smiled and opened his brown-bag lunch. When Herb left, he had the faculty room virtually to himself. He took out the notebook filled with Sarah's neat, minuscule writing, and studied it as he ate.

He knew what was going on. From the very first day, he'd been anxious to know about the woman he'd replaced, and there had been more than enough volunteers to tell him. He absorbed all of the stories, even the apocryphal ones, and pored over the rich illuminated manuscript of her class notes—observations written in such a witty and amusing vein that they could not have been intended for her eyes alone. Possibly she was planning a complete text-book someday, or another volume of essays. Spensieri had read some of her monographs during his graduate studies and he was a little overawed at being the replacement for this brilliant and talented woman. Whatever effect it had upon his own future, he hoped she could get back to teaching.

Still, he could hardly come out and ask his colleagues what course of action they were planning. He'd heard rumors that Sarah was to be asked to retire early, and felt somehow instrumental in her potential downfall. He didn't know about the petition, but suspected something was in the works. While they were all as warm and helpful and gracious as they could possibly be, he hadn't missed the almost consistent lull in the conversation whenever he entered the room. And so he spent many of his free periods alone, reading over Sarah's notes, thinking about his wife and the baby, and wondering what he would be doing this time next year.

In the president's outer office on the morning that Sister Maryann had had her grilling, Vera Neil had sat disconsolately blowing her nose, the traces of her head cold making it impossible for her to hear what was transpiring inside. She was disconsolate also because she would have to make a decision, and it was not an easy one. So far no one had asked her to commit herself on *l'affaire* Sarah Morrow, but eventually someone would. And what could she do? She liked Dr. Morrow, who, unlike some of the grander members of the faculty, or the great insensitive mass of students, never treated her like an extension of her typewriter. And the injustice of the situation was quite apparent to her. She had been the unseen auditor of all administrative machinations for over a decade, and this one struck her as the most unwarranted. But what

could she do? Give lip service to her employer for the sake
of her dull but comfortable job? Or say nothing either
way and risk antagonizing Mae and the others who were
willing to shake things from the bottom?

She was caught in the middle. Like the rest of the clerical staff, she felt a little too good to mix comfortably with
people who made sandwiches or swept floors, yet she was
kept in her place by an academic and administrative
hierarchy that reminded her daily of her inferiority to
those with initials after their names. The other secretaries
could seek the cozy anonymity of the typing pool in the
registrar's office, or the security of being paired off with
someone else in one of the departmental offices. Only Vera
Neil had an office, and a decision, all to herself. Neither
fish nor fowl, she agonized in silence behind her typewriter.

VIII

Ki Deus a dune escience
E de parler bon eloquence
Ne s'en deit taisir ne celer
Ainz, se deit volunters mustrer.

(He to whom God has given knowledge
And the eloquence to speak well
Ought not to remain silent nor conceal what he knows,
But should willingly make it known to others.)

MARIE DE FRANCE, *Prologue: Lais*

Halfway up the subway steps, Joan realized she should have brought some kind of gift with her. Some people, she thought, had absolutely no reverence for the social amenities. To walk up the front steps of a strange house with nothing to hide behind but a foolish grin . . . When one visited sick people one brought flowers, or something.

But Sarah wasn't sick, she reminded herself. She had sounded fine on the phone, lucid as anything. And if they'd let her out of the hospital, then she must be fine.

At least Joan hoped so, because she couldn't bear the thought of spending an evening in the same room with an invalid. She shuddered just thinking about it. She was beginning to wonder why she had started this whole crazy project in the first place. Being noble could screw up an entire weekend.

It was Friday night. People traveled in couples, never alone, on Friday nights. Joan saw them gliding past her on the street—the middle-aged twosomes off to stuff themselves with heartburn and cholesterol at their favorite restaurants; the younger ones of whatever sexual persuasion with their arms around each other, engrossed in heavy dialogue; the panting kids in platform shoes groping and slobbering on stoops and in half-lit doorways. Where were the lone waddling figures who walked their dogs on the other nights of the week? Why were only matched pairs allowed out on Fridays?

Why was she doing this? She hated sick people, loathed the overheated air breathed by those recently out of hospitals, exuding odors of cheap dusting powder and disinfectant, skin papery and dry to the touch. It wasn't the sickness itself; she loved the sight of a child shaking off the cobwebs of a high fever. But old people, as they sickened, became more like the sickness than themselves. There was nothing so horrible, Joan thought, remotely remembering a time when she was about six and her grandfather . . . nothing so horrible as watching someone waiting for death, letting it take over cell by cell until it was irreversible, and the eyes—always the last external feature to surrender—glazed over even though the lungs still struggled to keep themselves afloat, and the heart . . .

Reluctantly, Joan started walking away from the subway, dragging her heels and squinting at the addresses on the houses to make sure she was going in the right direction, if slowly. The rows of closed white window shades, wooden shutters, bamboo blinds, endless windowsills of coleus, hanging planters of asparagus Boston fern spider plant wandering Jew, an occasional opaque-eyed Siamese cat scowled at her as she passed. Do-gooder! they hissed at her. Nobody said you had to do this. You got into it all by yourself. Stop bitching!

If only she'd brought something with her. There were a lot of stores in the neighborhood, but most of them would be closing by now. There might be a florist or two, but was that where she ought to go? Flowers, candy, a plant? Poor excuses for not knowing what Sarah would really like. Better to arrive empty-handed.

Sarah's house would be on the next block. She would have to make up her mind now. As she crossed the street, Joan got an inspiration. A book! There *had* to be a bookstore somewhere. Maybe she would be lucky and find it still open, keeping late hours to attract last-minute browsers. How simple could it be?

Well, not quite that simple, perhaps. In the first place, she would only be able to afford a couple of paperbacks; hardcover books were something she couldn't afford to buy for herself, so why be ostentatious? Then there was the problem of what kind of book to get. Sarah's library had to be extensive. One would have to get something light, undepressing, but whether to venture into mystery, sci-fi, or—God forbid—Harlequin romances . . . Maybe that last was the answer, the way to avoid the possibility of colliding with topics like old age, sickness, death—regions too recently visited to make travelogues desirable.

And, true to form, she had only five dollars in her wallet, and if it got too late and she had to take a cab . . .

Joan recrossed the street the way she'd come and scanned the storefronts on both sides. As usual, the decision was taken out of her hands; there wasn't a bookstore in sight, not even a drugstore that might have paperbacks. The only thing that looked remotely hopeful was a candy store wedged into the middle of the block. She crossed the street for the third time, feeling paranoid.

The store was little, dark, smelly. A front for a dope

den, no doubt about it. Its literary accouterments were limited to a small collection of scabby cheap novels of the genre of the blindfolded, scantily clad blonde tied spread-eagle on an airplane propeller. Joan decided to do without.

She picked up a pack of gum—sugarless—avoiding the storekeeper's hostile glare, then saved herself at the last minute by grabbing a handful of magazines. She picked up *Saturday Review*, *Time*, *Atlantic Monthly*, and, just for laughs, *The Ladies' Home Journal*. What the hell, she thought, each of them ought to be worth an hour or two. Coming out of the store, she felt positively smug.

She would have known the house without looking at the address. She had covered three blocks of near-identical brownstones, trying desperately not to think of that first night with Brian when she'd . . . Each house had a little concrete apron in front, beside the steep flight of stairs—the celebrated Brooklyn stoop—that led to the front door. This tiny patch of concrete, never more than six by eight feet, framed by a wrought-iron fence, bespoke the kind of neighborhood it was—artsy-bourgeois, but not terribly imaginative. They were all the same—the small circle of ivy or nondescript shrub struggling to get enough light and water, the obligatory identical gas lamps.

And then there was Sarah's house, similar to the others if one did not look too closely. There were the same shutters and houseplants, the same wrought-iron fence. But the concrete was gone—broken up, gotten rid of—and in its place was a miniature rock garden, painstakingly nurtured, a small gem that probably couldn't be seen from the parlor windows and hence served only one purpose—to delight the passerby.

Joan would have been delighted, but the rock garden was choked with dead leaves. Nothing grew there except a rampage of weeds and a patch of quarrelsome irises, strangling each other for lack of attention. The garden was emblematic of Sarah's illness.

Suppressing a final shudder, Joan took the steps two at a time and jabbed the doorbell while her nerve still held out. Then she began to wonder how Sarah would get to the door. Even if she could get around, would a woman her age, living alone, be terribly eager to answer the door at this hour even if she was expecting someone? Suppose she was upstairs—could she get to the door without falling? Would it be wiser to ring the bell a second time to let her know her visitor was still waiting? Unsure as always, Joan stood there, doing nothing.

The door opened with such force that it nearly knocked her right off the step. A large male figure dominated the doorframe; Joan cringed involuntarily.

"Yeah?" he demanded.

He was not consciously unfriendly, Joan assured herself, trying to size him up. Type: Joe College. Classification: endangered species. All-American, square. Football sweaters, straight-leg jeans, Hush Puppies, defiant absence of facial hair, never smokes pot, wouldn't be caught dead in a disco. A can of Budweiser in his hand, the sound of a baseball game in progress somewhere in the interior of the house behind him. Did she have the right address after all?

"I-I-I've come to see Dr. Morrow," Joan burbled, ready to bolt if necessary.

"Oh, right! She told me about you." He did not explain his relationship to "she," but swung the door wide to indicate that Joan was to be permitted to enter. Joan squeezed past him and stood just inside the foyer.

She gave her surroundings a quick, encompassing glance while her reluctant host relocked the door. She was entranced with the place almost immediately. There were wall-to-wall books, Oriental rugs, furniture that was more comfortable than stylish; any spare wall space was covered with an original painting or sketch. Sarah's husband had been an artist, hadn't he? Or a sculptor? Something like that. Joan didn't see any sculptures around, and wondered why. The paintings fascinated her—apparently Sarah knew a number of people who could make a living at the business end of a brush. Then Joan looked at the plants, and a chill went through her. There had been a jungle of them, but now they were horrible—unwatered for months and petrified in their pots at the precise moment when thirst had become unbearable. Joan began to notice the grime on the windows, the cobwebs on the ceilings, and the migrant bits of dust and lint on the rug. The place was not a total shambles, but it looked as if sporadic efforts at orderliness had been made by someone who simply lacked the strength to follow through. A small portable television teetered incongruously on the coffee table. This was the origin of the ball game.

The boy with the Budweiser went to the bottom of the long, steep staircase and looked up into the twilight thoughtfully.

Boy? Joan thought. He was probably no more than five years younger than she was. Why did he seem like such a kid? And since he'd looked right through *her*, what kind of old bag must she seem like to him?

He remained motionless for a number of minutes, seeming to listen, though Joan could hear nothing beyond the sound of the television. Finally he nodded his head in her direction. "First door, top of the stairs," he said. He went back to the armchair and put his feet up on the coffee table, adjacent to the set, indifferent to whether Joan went up the stairs or stayed where she was or melted back into the night whence she'd come. Accepting her dismissal, Joan began the ascent.

As she got further from the television, she could hear music coming from upstairs. Gregorian chant, she thought, wondering if it had been chosen for her benefit. Sarah loved to create the proper setting; Joan remembered that from school. This particular music was symbolic. See how much I've recovered? it demanded. Come see how nice and healthy I am!

The door to the back bedroom was only slightly open, letting out the music and a warm slit of light. Sarah's universe, Joan thought, mildly apprehensive. Why the hell must the door be closed? What was waiting for her on the other side? She knocked lightly.

When there was no response, she waited. And waited. Finally, uncertainly, she pushed the door slowly away from her. She inhaled sharply when she saw the figure framed exactly in the center of the doorway.

Whistler's Mother in Sensurround, Joan thought, letting the breath out.

Sarah didn't look that much different from when Joan had had her in class. God! Could it have been six or seven years ago? There was the white hair, of course, but other than that . . . Sarah's hair had still held traces of auburn when Joan saw her last, but the white was striking and didn't make her look any older. She was thinner, if that was possible, but that was to be expected after a long illness. But there she was, regal and ramrod-straight in the overstuffed chair, wearing a flowing purplish caftan of some shimmering material, her long narrow feet slippered and propped up on an ottoman. There were the same laugh lines around the eyes; the large masculine hands—no tremors, no liver spots; the fine white teeth with the peculiar lap-over upper incisor; and the eyes—God, those eyes!

"Welcome—to—the Twilight—Zone," Sarah said slowly, but with no less irony, and the eyes fairly crackled.

Every Catholic schoolgirl is raised on a number of superstitions, one of which being that the eyes are the "windows of the soul." If you couldn't look your fourth-grade nun in the eye, so it went, it wasn't out of shyness but out of a basic evilness of character. And light-colored eyes were the easiest to see through.

Joan's eyes were brown and, she liked to think, impenetrable. But any attempt to read the thoughts in Sarah's gray eyes was deflected as if by mirrors.

What is she hiding? Joan wondered, feeling distinctly uncomfortable.

"H-hello," she managed to say, still hesitating in the doorway.

"Come in," Sarah urged cheerfully. "I promise—it's not —contagious."

Her tempo was slow, painfully deliberate, as if every word had· to be bolted into place before it fell out of her memory, but there was none of the stereotypical slurring Joan had expected, none of the tendency to leave sentences and ideas trailing. The completion of a thought, the choice of the multisyllabic, were good signs. Maybe the visit wouldn't be as grueling as expected.

Joan sidled awkwardly into the room, sizing it up the way she always did a new place. Her glance devoured the brilliant blue walls, the bare parquet floor, the brick fireplace with the huge Boston fern growing out of it. This one plant, at least, had survived its owner's absence. The large brass bed was unwrinkled, defying anyone to think that its occupant was too feeble to stay out of it during the daytime. In spite of the freakishly cold evening, the windows were open slightly, shades thrown up to reveal the darkening sky, curtains swaying energetically. There was a small cluttered desk, two mismatched chairs and the ottoman, the stereo, and more books. The walls here were bare except for a reproduction of the Bayeux tapestry, which snaked its way around the room several times. Certainly an atypical sickroom.

Sarah's positioning herself in the center of the room, profile toward the door, had been deliberate, Joan discovered, seating herself on the edge of the other chair, wishing she could sit on the floor. The old woman could not disguise the fact that she was ghostly thin. She could not deny the existence of the cane leaning against the desk at arm's length. She could try, however, to disguise the inertia of the right side of her body by turning her left side toward the door and her visitor, and her right toward the wall. The illusion was destroyed, unfortunately, when she reached past herself to turn off the stereo with her left hand. The knob lay only inches away from her right, which did not have the power to grasp and control it.

Joan realized she was staring. She cleared her throat against the silence.

"H-how *are* you?" she asked brilliantly.

"Well. Quite well." Sarah smiled, and Joan saw that her face was pulled to one side by the smile. Only the left side moved; the right side of her face was frozen, a mask that reduced the warmth of Sarah's emotions by half. Joan felt herself getting the shakes again.

There was another silence. Joan realized it was her turn to speak, understood that the older woman could not waste a single newfound precious word on small talk. How *would* they get through the next hour?

"I—I hope I'm not keeping you up too late," Joan bumbled along. "You know, it occurred to me after I spoke to you on the phone the other night that maybe the evenings would be a bad time for you—"

"It's all—right," Sarah said. Her eyes, fixed quite firmly on Joan when the younger woman spoke, would veer away and focus on the wall as she herself searched for the right words. It was as if she half-expected to find the words she needed floating around the room at random; it was only necessary to seize them as they drifted by.

"I sleep—very little," she said carefully. "I—seldom—go to bed—before one or—two."

"It's just that the rest of my time is so bogged down," Joan said lamely.

Sarah nodded. "Of course—when you have—a child," she said dreamily.

"Oh, that's not the problem," Joan blurted. "Brian has visiting rights on weekends, so I—"

"Visiting rights?" Sarah frowned. The phrase was meaningless to her. Contextless.

Joan misunderstood the problem. "I thought I told you on the phone," she heard herself saying, wanting to bite her tongue as she said it. "Brian and I are separated. We're going to get a divorce."

"Divorce," Sarah said, digesting it. It must have jarred a memory somewhere, because she looked up at Joan with startled pleasure. "And so you are—free to—come and go—on weekends. Now I see. You must be—patient— sometimes I lose—words—ideas—whole sentences, even now. . . ."

Joan felt stupid. Now she would have to explain the whole tumultuous scene of the past few months, when if she'd only kept her mouth shut . . .

"You are getting a—divorce," Sarah said slowly. She'd gotten a fix on it now, and wouldn't let it alone. "Do you want to—do that?"

Joan sighed "It's what has to be," she said wearily.

"Tell me," Sarah said gently, but with the weight of a command.

And so Joan recited her tragic tale as fairly as she reasonably could. As she spoke, she wondered if it sounded as flimsy and made-up to an outsider as it was beginning to sound to her. Did she really know what she was doing? She babbled on, unable to stop, watching Sarah soak it up hungrily. Was she really concerned about Joan's problems, or was she just trying to reassimilate as many words as she could? At least the time was passing quickly, and there were no more awkward silences.

Joan peeked at her watch and saw that it was past nine. She could leave soon, as soon as she stopped talking about herself and let Sarah speak for a while. She finished her sad story and waited for the comment, or the lecture, but neither was forthcoming.

"You've been through—a lot," Sarah said finally. "Hard on you."

Not nearly as hard as the past few months have been on you, Joan thought, feeling selfish. She didn't say it.

"I'll live," she shrugged. "I'm talking too much."

"I enjoy—listening," Sarah smiled. "Talk as much as you—like."

Joan smiled, dried up. Mustn't talk about sickness, have exhausted the topic of self. What now?

"How's your anthology coming along?" she tried, not sure if that was quite the way to put it. "Vicki told me—"

Something about Sarah's face stopped her. Bewilderment, momentary confusion she might expect, but this was pure sadness—an overwhelming sadness.

"Anthology," Sarah repeated. "What anthology?"

It was not a question of a word misunderstood, but simply a fact forgotten. Sarah had no idea what Joan was talking about.

"Vicki said you were—a collection of essays—international scholars contributed—that you were editing it before you . . ." Joan was hopelessly enmeshed, frightened of what she'd gotten herself into.

"If—Vicki said—"—Sarah's face had lost the tragic look—"then it must be so. The fact is—I don't—remember."

"Oh," Joan said, kicking herself. How would she get out of this one gracefully? "I guess it must be difficult putting back the pieces after such an—experience. In fact I'm amazed at how well you've recovered. You must get a lot of help from—" She gestured in the direction of the stairs.

"Oh—you mean Charlie." Sarah laughed slightly, a bell

tinkling. "My nephew. No. He's not here often. Only when he—has to be."

She did not elucidate. In a way, Joan was relieved. The image of the ball game superimposed over the Gregorian chant nightly, the refrigerator stocked with Bud alongside Sarah's vegetarian delights, did not sit well with her. But how did the old woman manage?

"I see," Joan said, although she didn't. "Then you're here alone most of the time?"

She wasn't prying, only being concerned, she told herself. But it was only half true.

"Most of the time," Sarah repeated, without elaborating.

Joan had run out of steam. She didn't want to be nosy, but she couldn't help wondering how the old woman had gotten this far. Who had taken care of her when she first got out of the hospital? Who helped her daily to dress herself and get breakfast and cope with all the other taken-for-granted things that people with two good arms and two good legs and a whole memory could do for themselves? Did her family look after her, or did they come—like her nephew—only when they had to? Did her neighbors bring her hot casseroles and do her laundry and take out the garbage? Did her friends stay in touch, come over to read and tell her the latest gossip? Did one friend in particular come around on a regular basis?

And what business is it of mine? Joan wondered, distrusting her usual lead-footed subtlety and not daring to ask any further questions. Maybe what Vicki said was true, and maybe it wasn't.

They chatted aimlessly for a while longer, Joan carrying the conversation for the most part single-handedly, with weighty comments about the weather and other safe topics. The evening had turned out to be a bomb, she thought, forgetting how much saner it was than spending the entire weekend in her own company. She hadn't exactly expected scintillating dialogue, and at least Sarah had proven to be not quite the near-vegetable she'd feared, but she'd ended up listening to herself repeat her own stale monologue and filling in with a lot of meaningless chatter with what was really a very boring old woman, and that was almost as bad as the other possibilities. More than once she had to choke on a yawn.

I know! Sarah thought, almost uttering it aloud. I know your mind! I know what you are thinking as if it were written on your forehead! I know what you are thinking, though it is all I know!

"You'll have to—be leaving soon," she suggested, offering Joan the escape she sought. "I can ask Charlie to—make some tea."

"Oh, no thanks, really," Joan assured her, all but jumping out of her chair. "I *do* have to get going. The subways at this hour—"

"The subways," Sarah ruminated. "You have no car?"

"I *had* a car," Joan said ruefully, "but I was so glad to get rid of Brian, I just let him take it. I got the apartment and the furniture and everything else, so I guess I got the better of the deal. It was a nice little car, though, and I feel kind of stranded."

"I have a car," Sarah said, as if discovering it for the first time. "I won't need it. Perhaps . . ."

"You'll want it when you go back to teaching," Joan protested, not sure if the old woman meant she should borrow it or actually keep it.

"I shall not—go back," Sarah said with finality.

Joan became suddenly, unreasonably angry. It was none of her business, but, goddammit, it wasn't right. All right, a stroke was no minor thing, but it didn't mean you had to lie down and die. She'd thought Sarah was a fighter.

Look at Patricia Neal, she wanted to shout. How can you give up so easily?

But it wasn't any of her business.

"That's a shame," Joan said distantly, realizing how singularly asinine that sounded. She sighed. "Well, I really do have to go. I can come back another time. Maybe in a few weeks," she lied.

She was halfway to the door when she realized she still had the magazines in her hand. "I almost forgot—these are for you," she said, holding them out to Sarah. "They're not much, but I thought they might pass a few hours. I didn't know what else you might want."

Sarah's crooked smile faltered for a moment as she took the magazines. She held them lightly in her lap without looking at them. "Thank you," she said softly, looking up at Joan. "That was very kind of you."

Her reaction irritated Joan. What now? Why didn't she at least look at them? Was she offended for some reason? The natural thing to do when someone handed you a stack of new magazines was at least to flip through them and look at the titles. Why was she sitting there holding them like a pile of folded laundry?

"Is something wrong?" Joan heard the shrillness in her own voice.

Sarah looked startled. "No," she said almost humbly. "It's just that I—can't read them."

Of course, Joan thought. How stupid of me! People in their sixties were farsighted as a rule. They wore reading glasses. She would have to supply what the old woman lacked the capacity to explain.

"I'll find your glasses," she said, scanning the room.

The desk would be the logical place. Joan rummaged through the clutter and found a red leather case. The glasses were inside, all right, but the outside of the case was filmy with dust. Joan frowned.

"It's not the glasses," Sarah said in a strange, faraway voice. "I don't—remember how to read."

Joan was staring again. What was she talking about?

"The therapist—at the hospital—says it's called—let me get it right—alexia," Sarah said, her lecture-hall voice all but restored. "Pretty name—deadly affliction. I got over the—usual thing—aphasia, that's called—ability to understand but not—*be* understood—gibberish. Sometimes I still get—scrambled—but not so much— But this other thing—they wouldn't say—but I think it's—permanent."

A kind of feverish light was gathering behind her eyes. She grew almost eloquent.

"I understand almost anything I hear—anything spoken or—read to me. But the words on a page—print—scribbles —numbers, symbols, all the alphabets—runes—I'm an illiterate child again—without the child's flexibility for— learning. I have to start—from the beginning."

Joan felt as if she were suffocating. "You!" she gasped. "You of all people!"

"Why do you say that?" Sarah asked innocently.

Joan shook her head. How could she explain?

"I didn't know," she said, terribly embarrassed. "I had no idea—nobody told me."

"Nobody knows," Sarah explained. "Except—close friends. It's not something one cares to—advertise."

"But why did you tell me?" Joan wanted to know, panicked a little by the sudden confidence.

Because Pietro has been reading to me all these months, Sarah thought, and because he's being sent back to Rome for the summer after they've treated him like a pariah for twenty years because of his radical opinions but now somebody at the Vatican needs the benefit of his scholarship in the blinding heat of a Roman summer when even the Great White Spinster himself is cooling it at his summer castle The time he was going to use here with me in the garden they want him to waste instead rooting around in some papal library using his unsigned efforts for the greater glory of Ignatius's order of soldier-priests Because Pietro was going to spend the summer reading to me and instead must spend it writing tripe that will supposedly teach the laity to think Because I can't bear the thought of spending the summer—most debilitating of seasons— alone, and because you have all but dropped from a cloud at my doorstep—

"Because I need somebody to read to me," Sarah said simply, offering it as an option, almost a gift. "Not often. Not even—regularly. Just whenever it's—convenient for you. Now and then."

Joan was trapped. No! she wanted to shout. Not me! I'm too fucking busy as it is, thank you. Too bogged down in my own life to get mixed up in yours. I can't stand the sight of you in this condition; can't stand to wait while you struggle for every phrase when I can remember how the words used to roll out of you like distant thunder; can't stand how old you've gotten, and how pitiful. I haven't got the time. Haven't got the patience to sit still and read to you as if you were a baby. Not to you, the great scholar, the brilliant teacher, the scintillating intellect—all of that now broken in two like a fragile heirloom, shattered. No! Joan thought, her eyes misting over at the incredible waste of it all.

She flipped through one of the magazines, sitting down again in the chair across from Sarah, and, clearing her tightening throat, began (just this once, and then you can get your nephew or one of your famous artistic friends, or a former student or that crackpot priest) to read.

IX

I and Pangur Ban, my cat,
'Tis a like task we are at:
Hunting mice is his delight,
Hunting words I sit all night.

OLD IRISH POEM

"There. It's done," Sister Francis said, replacing the receiver with ladylike gentility. "She will be coming in the day before exams, and we shall get the entire matter settled."

"How did she sound?" Sister Aquinas wanted to know. "Did she sound like the old Dr. Morrow?"

"I'm sorry?" Francis asked, preoccupied with her thoughts. "I'm afraid I didn't hear you, dear."

"I asked you how she sounded," Aquinas repeated, knowing perfectly well that she'd been heard the first time. "Did she sound well? Normal? Recovered from her illness?"

"Oh." Francis considered for a moment. "I couldn't say. I'm hardly the person to judge that."

"All right, those ought to do it," Vicki's mother said, handing three phonics workbooks over her shoulder to

Joan. "Oh, and take this one, too. It's kindergarten level, but it might be all right."

She closed the cabinet where she kept all her teaching materials and turned to Joan, dusting her hands. "Come into the kitchen and talk to me while I do the dishes," she said.

Joan followed her, picking up a dish towel and grabbing the dinner plates as they came soapy and steaming from Mrs. O'Dell's efficient hands. She tried to imagine what it must be like to wash dishes for upwards of seven people every night.

"I don't usually get stuck with this," Helen O'Dell said, reading Joan's mind. "But since Kathleen got married, the chores have been a little jumbled. I'll have to bribe someone else now, I suppose."

There were five children in the O'Dell house—or had been until the second daughter, Kathleen, had been the first to leave the nest at twenty-five. Vicki was the eldest, of course, and after Kathleen came the twins, Maureen and Mary Frances, and after a gap of fifteen years there was little Frankie, whose real name was Francis Xavier. In between, the house had been inhabited by a platoon of foster children, a few cousins whose house had burned down, two dogs, seven cats, and innumerable hamsters, gerbils, and goldfish.

Mrs. O'Dell was also part owner of a summer day camp. She was never happy unless surrounded by at least a dozen children. She taught Confraternity of Christian Doctrine classes at the local parish, tutored neighborhood kids in remedial reading on Saturday mornings. Somehow her own kids survived, and the housework got done, and nobody was particularly traumatized. Four of her offspring had apparently turned out neurosis-free, despite ironclad laws about attending mass on Sundays and not leaving the house until one married. As for Vicki, "I'm afraid I botched it with Vicki," Mrs. O'Dell confided to Joan once, trying to patch up an adolescent quarrel between the two girls. "Remember, I was only nineteen when I had her. Maybe I tried too hard. Then again, she was always a model child—never got dirty, always did what was expected of her, got the highest grades in her class. She was born a little old lady. Thank God the others are normal!"

Joan had thought of getting in touch with Mrs. O'Dell right after that first evening at Sarah's house. If she said she was trying to teach Eric to read before he started kindergarten, she could borrow enough workbooks to help Sarah. She could also get some advice on how to go about teaching someone to read, without bothering to mention who the individual happened to be. She hadn't bothered to consult Sarah about all of this.

"By the way," Mrs. O'Dell said, handing the last dish to Joan and pushing the damp hair up off her forehead, "how old is Eric now?"

"Three and a half," Joan said. "He'll be four in September."

"Don't you think it's kind of early to start him?" Mrs. O'Dell asked, turning off the teakettle that had been whistling erratically for some minutes. She dumped some teabags into the boiling water and sloshed them around absently. "I know the current trend is to have them reading before they start school, but it's not wise to push. Boys especially—"

"Oh, I'm not going to *force* him," Joan explained. "But he's hooked on 'Sesame Street,' and he already knows the alphabet, so I thought the next logical step—"

"But you have so little time together now," Mrs. O'Dell objected. "Don't you think it would be better if you just enjoyed being with each other? If he gets his back up about learning now, you'll have awful trouble with him later."

Joan was not good at lying. She'd thought her story would be a convincing one, but the very thought of trying to do anything at all with Eric, under the present circumstances and with the way they felt about each other now, was pretty ridiculous. It must show on her face; it must be apparent that she wanted the books and the advice for something else. How much could she tell without violating some kind of confidence?

She groped for a way out of her story while Mrs. O'Dell rummaged through cabinets and the refrigerator to come up with a box of Mallomars and a half-eaten coffee cake. When she finally sat down at the table, she was looking at Joan pointedly. Joan said nothing.

"That's not the real reason you wanted those books," Mrs. O'Dell said at last.

Joan bit her lip, deciding.

"No," she sighed finally. "I didn't tell you the truth because—well, because I'm doing something that maybe I'm not qualified to do and I wasn't sure— There's this old lady I know, a friend of my mother's—before my parents moved to Houston, I mean—someone from the neighborhood . . ." Even this lie wasn't going to work, she thought ruefully. Why was she doing this? Sarah hadn't sworn her to secrecy or anything; but then, Sarah had no idea what she was up to either. "Well, this old lady had a stroke, and she needs someone to read to her—she can't read anymore, because of the stroke, and—"

"Is this the truth now?" Mrs. O'Dell asked, carefully stirring her tea.

"It is, yes," Joan said, not at all convincing. She couldn't help it; she would have to tell the whole story. She took a long breath, and identified the "old lady."

There was a long silence when she finished her story. Joan sat crumbling the edge of her piece of coffee cake; Mrs. O'Dell just sat.

"What a terrible thing," she said at last. "And here you are trying to protect her, to keep her identity a secret."

"I didn't think it was necessary to—I wasn't sure if you even knew her," Joan babbled. "Vicki said she never had her for a course."

"Oh, I know Dr. Morrow," Vicki's mother nodded. "I can tell you a story— But how awful! For a person to lose the most important thing she has—it's as if God had made me sterile. How awful!"

"Yes," Joan said soberly.

"And it's a great thing you're trying to do for her," Mrs. O'Dell said sincerely. "I guess it's what Vicki would call storing up grace for eternity."

"Yeah," Joan laughed dryly. "Vicki's Sermon on the Mount. I've heard it."

"You've abandoned your religion," Mrs. O'Dell said, sipping her tea, making no judgments.

"Yes," Joan said quietly, vaguely ashamed. "I kind of outgrew it, I guess."

"Have you given any thought to what kind of religious training you'll give Eric?" Mrs. O'Dell asked, but without the urgency of Vicki's moral inquiries.

"I imagine Brian must take him to mass. Brian always gets religion in times of crisis," Joan said airily, trying to make it seem insignificant. "I—I'm really not equipped to handle that kind of thing right now."

"I see," Mrs. O'Dell nodded. "More tea?"

"No thanks." Joan was struggling to maintain her composure. Any mention of religion unnerved her.

"What will you do with Eric for the summer?" Vicki's mother asked suddenly, as if the previous subject were really not that important after all. "Nursery lets out in a couple of weeks, doesn't it?"

It was a problem that had been haunting Joan's waking hours for weeks. He was too young to go to a day camp, surrounded by strangers, bounced around on school buses to faraway, unfamiliar wastelands, sitting in the hot sun all day. She wasn't poor enough to be eligible for free day-care. Should she hire a baby-sitter who would let him watch television all day and stay mushroom-pale indoors all summer? She might almost consider shipping him down to her mother in Houston for the summer, though what kind of monster he would turn out to be as a result of that she could just imagine. There hadn't seemed to be an answer to the problem, until now.

"Because I could slip him into our summer program," Mrs. O'Dell was saying. "We usually don't take them younger than five, but he's bright for his age, I'm sure, with you for his mother."

"Well, thanks," Joan said, embarrassed. "But—"

"I started Frankie at three and a half just so I could get back to work," Mrs. O'Dell continued, not to be stopped now. "Believe me, I know what you're up against, and I'd like to help you out. We could make Eric our mascot. I'm sure he'll love it. And if you ever get caught up at work and you can't get home right away, I'll bring him home with me and he can have supper with us. We've always got room for a couple of extras."

"That would be fantastic," Joan said, wanting to believe it could be this easy. "But what are the fees like? I mean, I'd pay them eventually, but I'd probably have to budget it out a little every month—"

"I'm talking about a freebie," Mrs. O'Dell interrupted, proud of herself for being able to use the idiom correctly. "And before you start gushing, let me tell you I've got an ulterior motive."

Joan frowned. She disliked mysteries.

"To explain, I'll need to go over a little ancient history," Vicki's mother said, pouring herself a second cup of tea that would be cold long before she finished her narrative.

"As you've probably figured out just on basic chronology," Helen O'Dell began, "I got married less than a year after high school and, like a good little Catholic girl, got pregnant on my wedding night. That was Vicki. Two years later I had Kathleen, and three years after that the twins came along. Needless to say, there was a period of over ten years when all I did was change diapers and collapse in bed at nine every night from sheer exhaustion. It wasn't until Mary Fran and Maureen were in first grade and I was past thirty that I had time to consider anything as self-centered as going to college.

"But that's what I did. I packed everybody off to school, got myself a Knights of Columbus scholarship, and off I went to college. I knew I wasn't much of a brain, so I went into early-childhood education, figuring I'd certainly done enough fieldwork already. Anyway, half the courses were boring and the other half were too deep for me, but I made up my mind I was going to get through this. So I started taking all sorts of crazy electives in my senior year to keep myself interested—anthropology, earth science, and, of all things, medieval literature. That was where I first met Dr. Morrow. And what an experience!

"You see what Vicki's like now? What she's been like all her life? I don't have to tell you, everything is either black or white with her—she never questions anything. Her life is very simple, but, good Lord, how dull! I was like that then—I'd been brought up in a strict Irish family and I guess I just carried on the tradition with my own kids when I got married. I never questioned the values I'd been raised on until I was in my thirties and sitting in Dr. Morrow's class listening to what she was saying. I remember a quote of hers; she was talking about the psychological makeup of medieval man—if you can even imagine figuring out how people who've been dead six hundred years must have thought about their world—and she said, 'Remember that these people believed that God had a sense of humor.' That sentence knocked me right on the floor the first time I heard it! God having a sense of humor? God being able to laugh? The God I met in Saint Mary's Church every Sunday morning never laughed! All the philosophy courses I'd taken had gone right over my head, but this was something I could understand. And I don't think my life's been the same since.

"Well, to make a long story short, I got my degree and went right on for my master's without a whole lot of breast-beating. For once in my life I was going to do what *I* wanted to do—no qualms about neglecting the kids or the housework. And everybody survived it, as you can see. I even—God forbid—started using birth control, although Frankie snuck up on me anyway. All those years of playing Russian roulette with rhythm, and the little monster snuck up on me anyway. But I love him. Maybe he's an example of God laughing at me; I don't know. But my whole outlook had changed. I wasn't as tensed up around the kids, and they relaxed too. Of course, Vicki didn't change. I wish I'd gone through my transformation early enough to help her so it had some effect on her, but . . . Well, maybe something will change her life before it's too late. . . ."

She had talked herself out, and sat fingering her tea-cup, thinking.

"That's an amazing coincidence," Joan managed to say.

"What is?"

"You and Vicki and I all ending up at the same college, with the same professor."

"Oh, no!" Helen O'Dell shook her head vehemently. "No coincidence. When Vicki was in eleventh grade and trying to decide where to go to college, I desperately wanted her to choose my alma mater. I kept telling her about all the things I knew would appeal to her—that it was an all-girls school, that they held chapel services at lunchtime—things like that. I didn't exactly *insist* that she go there—"

"You just steered her in the right direction." Joan smiled.

Helen shook her head, and they both sighed over Vicki's impossibility.

"What you're doing for Dr. Morrow is a very good thing," Helen said again, as if she had not emphasized it strongly enough before.

"She sort of talked me into it," Joan said, excusing herself.

"Even so," Helen said. "It's like restoring a great painting or a rare work of art to what it originally was. Even if she never teaches again, you are helping her to have a whole mind."

"Don't say all that," Joan laughed nervously. "You're embarrassing me."

"If you need any help—advice on special teaching techniques or whatever—let me know," Helen urged. "And the secret is safe with me."

"What's all *that?*" Sarah demanded the following weekend, pointing an agitated finger at the phonics books Joan had as unobtrusively as possible taken out of her tote bag, along with a few magazines and that day's newspaper.

"Educational materials," Joan said, trying to sound glib, but feeling flustered. She wasn't prepared for an immediate confrontation. "I thought we'd see if we can bring back what you've lost. Then we can progress through some crossword puzzles, which are my favorite, and word games and—"

"Kid stuff, you mean," Sarah snapped, narrowing her eyes at Joan. "See Dick run. See Jane play with her dolly. See Dick grow up to be a—whatsis—nuclear engineer— while Jane stays home and does the laundry. All of that shit. Oh, no you don't!"

If nothing else, her temper had elongated her vocabulary. After a half-hour of badgering, Joan surrendered.

"I asked you to read to me," Sarah said for perhaps the fifth time, "not to teach me how to read. To read to me. Is it too much trouble? You said your weekends— most of them—were free. Nothing to do. The—implication—I got was that you were lonely. Until you—catch a new boy friend or whatever, can't you spend a little time with me?"

She wasn't pleading; she was showing Joan the error of her ways. Joan was embarrassed.

"I want you to read to me," Sarah repeated with something approaching obsession. "You can come here whenever you—have the time. If you're too busy, if your weekends suddenly—fill up with—other things, well, then, so be it. But my house is air-conditioned. Is your apartment? Do you enjoy the heat? I don't. It's cool here. I'm inviting you—as my guest. You can read, we can talk, I will cook supper. Perhaps I will interest you in vegetarian cooking. You can stay the night if it's late —or take my car. Keep it."

"Are you serious?" Joan asked abruptly. They'd had this conversation before, and the repetition, the whole idea of what she was getting herself into, was beginning to drive her a little mad. And the car—it was a late-model Volvo, undoubtedly expensive. She couldn't possibly—

"What do I need with a car?" Sarah was exasperated. "Even if I could—fake my way through the road signs, the leg isn't strong enough for the brake, and anyway I have nowhere to go. Take the car, please."

"But I can't just *take* it," Joan objected. The car was becoming the metaphor for the whole situation. "Maybe I could borrow it once in a while if I stay very late, but I'd bring it back the next morning."

"You're right. Of course," Sarah nodded, thinking she understood. "If I gave it to you outright, there'd be in-

surance and all—I didn't think about that. All right.
Keep it in my name. But take it. Pay for the gas if it—
soothes your conscience."

"That's not what I meant—" Joan started to say.

"*Fuck* the car then!" Sarah half-shouted. Joan had
never heard her use that particular word before. It effec-
tively shut her up. "Just answer—*will* you read to me?
Will you come here—*damn*, I keep losing the days—
Saturdays—when you are free, and read to me? No more
funny business with the kindergarten books—just read?
And talk, and stay for supper? I'll contract you for the
summer. After that . . ."

She wasn't pleading, but Joan knew she was powerless
to refuse.

"All right," she said quietly. "If that's all you want."

"*All?*" Sarah repeated. "My God, child! If only you
knew how *much* that was!"

It developed into something Joan looked forward to—
an exactly scheduled oasis from a too-predictable week.
A kind of tranquillity settled over her as she let herself
into Sarah's house with her own key at precisely two
o'clock every Saturday afternoon.

She never told anyone where she spent her weekends.
She supposed the neighbors thought she had a new boy
friend. Her landlady rather pointedly admired the Volvo,
which Joan reluctantly took to driving home occasionally
"just to keep it in shape." Joan told her she was minding
it for a friend who was in Europe for the summer, and
left it at that. Let her decide whether the friend was male
or female. Joan even thought she detected a quizzical look
in Brian's eyes now and then when he brought Eric back
on Sundays, but since she didn't inquire into *his* private
life . . .

At the beginning it occurred to her that this was a
peculiar situation. She ought to be out doing the singles
thing, like all the other young divorcées she kept reading

about in those women's magazines. She ought to be gar-
nering herself a rich lover and a Bloomingdale's charge
card instead of wasting her weekends reading to some
old lady, like something in one of those missionary magazines her mother doted on.

But I want to do this, Joan thought. What's wrong
with that?

She started reading cautiously, using easy things like
the daily paper, unsure of Sarah's capacity to understand,
even less sure of her own ability to read to someone without inducing sleep. She'd never analyzed the quality of
her voice; the only person she'd ever read to was Eric,
and at least part of her motivation had been to put him to
sleep. But apparently her voice neither bored nor unnerved Sarah, and this made her more secure. She began
choosing books from Sarah's library, which was vast—a
Dickens, some Shakespeare—though only the poetry because Sarah couldn't keep a straight face if she tried to
do the plays—a little Dostoevski (which put Sarah to
sleep), a Faulkner, some Tolkien. She avoided anything
medieval, partly because she didn't dare the language,
partly because it seemed like rubbing Sarah's nose in her
weaknesses.

And over the ensuing weeks, Joan would read from
world histories and the Britannica until Sarah began to
yawn. She would read Thurber short stories and *Me-
chanix Illustrated*. She would read from the *I Ching*
and the Old Testament. She would read Yeats and Eliot
and Donne and parts of the *Iliad*. She would read Egyp-
tian art history and biographies of famous composers.
She would read articles on ecology and strategic arms
limitation. She finally had the nerve one day to pick up
one of Sarah's own monographs—she'd found it wedged
in the back of a bookcase behind the Chaucer—and from
then on she read all of them, on Chaucer and Abelard
and Erigena and Spenser. Sarah was not offended, but

rather surprised, and they spent some time analyzing the style as if they'd just come across something written by a total stranger.

And they talked.

They began with casual discussions of current events, ending up in philosophy and autobiography. Joan remembered that there had been a time not too far past when she'd been considered intelligent. It was nice to feel that way again. She would be satisfied with this, for now; the rich lover could come later. She'd always hated the clothes in Bloomie's anyway.

Vera Neil was frantic. Here she was only a few feet away from what could be *the* confrontation of all her years as the president's secretary, and she wasn't allowed to listen to it. It was all the fault of that unbearable priest.

He had come in with Sarah Morrow a full ten minutes before their scheduled appointment with Sister Francis, although they both knew perfectly well that Sister Francis never saw *anyone*, not the bishop himself, until the moment the clock struck the hour. Then the two of them had sat in the outer office to wait in uninterrupted silence, as if they'd rehearsed everything beforehand and had nothing to say now. It drove Vera mad. She'd finally ventured to buzz Sister Francis on the intercom at three minutes before the hour, and Sarah had risen from her chair with great deliberation and gone inside alone, leaving the priest to stub out his cigarettes in the immaculate onyx ashtray and continue to say nothing.

Vera had thought of striking up a conversation about the weather, or exams, or summer vacation, but she was certain he would respond in monosyllables, if at all. He made her terribly nervous. All men made her nervous, but he and his silence made her nervous to the point where it was all she could do to keep from screaming.

The only thing that kept her in control was her suspicion that he was as curious as she about what was going on beyond that wall.

She'd thought of accidentally leaving the intercom open, but that would mean she would have to trust him to stay absolutely silent so they wouldn't be discovered. If either of them should so much as cough . . . Besides, how would he interpret her actions—as concern, or as snoopiness? No, she could not take the chance.

So she fidgeted. She filed and refiled every piece of paper on her desk, simply because the file cabinets were nearer to the door to the inner office. She watered all of her plants, some of them twice. She wished she had the nerve to bring the watering can into Sister Francis's office to do her plants, as she often did when more mundane visitors were there—in fact she had been encouraged to do so by Sister Francis on more than one occasion; it served to hurry the more boring visitors on their way. But such activities in this case could only earn her a reprimand, and the conversation would probably grind to a halt the minute she opened the door.

So there was nothing she could do. She could hear the three voices—Sister Francis, Sister Aquinas, and Dr. Morrow—humming along in seemingly equal segments, but she could not make out a single word.

Exasperated, she looked at the priest one last time. He smiled affably and blew smoke rings toward the ceiling, as if what transpired in the next room had absolutely no effect upon him or anyone he knew. Defeated, Vera Neil switched on her typewriter and rattled away with a vengeance.

"Prove it," Sarah said softly.

Francis raised an eyebrow. "I should think the burden of proof in this instance would rest with you," she said.

Aquinas's face was immobile. She had been instructed carefully this time: She was to play a supporting role, and only speak when Francis indicated that it was her turn.

"Put me back in a classroom," Sarah said. "Right now. No preparation. No notes. No textbook. I can teach."

Francis looked at Aquinas. Aquinas leaned forward in her chair, oozing solicitude.

"We're quite certain you could stand before a class and recite your material by rote," she said. "But if someone were to ask you a question—"

"As to the textbooks," Francis interrupted, "they'd hardly do you any good, would they?"

Aquinas actually gasped. Francis tended to be incisive, but that sort of remark bordered on downright cruelty.

"Point for your side," Sarah said without a flutter. "But that is temporary. And I *can* teach."

"But how long are we supposed to wait?" Francis asked reasonably. "Suppose we were to consider this term as part of a sabbatical, and the fall term as well? It is highly irregular. The inconvenience for the gentleman who is substituting for you— And what assurances can we have regarding your recovery by next January? Suppose there is no progress?"

"I have tenure," Sarah said, cutting to the heart of the matter.

"Indeed." Francis nodded tersely, drawing back in her chair. "And you may fight us if you wish. But I'd advise against it."

"Would you?" Sarah's voice was acid.

It was Aquinas's turn.

"It could be extremely embarrassing," she said with what could pass for genuine concern. "If it came to a departmental hearing—well, suppose you couldn't— If you were to lose—"

Francis cleared her throat, reducing Aquinas to silence. She was in grave danger of fumbling it.

"To clarify the situation," Francis said, her mouth pinched at the corners, "would you rather make a voluntary and graceful decision or be coerced into a public admission of—"

"Of incompetence?" Sarah's half-smile fairly glittered. "I repeat—prove it."

"We'd prefer not to be forced into that kind of position," Aquinas explained. "This is not a vendetta. We mean you no personal ill will."

"I shall not leave—in this—manner," Sarah said, beginning to falter. The ordeal was exhausting her, but she had to hold on. "It is my—desire—to return next—January. I shall request a departmental hearing—to prove that I am—competent to teach."

Francis exhaled slowly, folding her hands on the for-once-empty blotter on her desk. The battle was met.

"As you wish," she said curtly.

There was a silence.

"When?" Sarah spoke up suddenly.

"I beg your pardon?" asked Francis.

"How soon can I have my hearing?"

Francis looked at Aquinas, who looked back at Francis. A bell rang somewhere in the building, and the sound of feet and voices reached them from the halls.

"Examinations begin tomorrow," Francis said, using the noise to help her get through what she intended to say. "The semester is over. Everyone will be scattered during the summer. I do not see how it would be possible to hold a departmental hearing before September."

"How—convenient for you," Sarah said dryly.

"And for you, I should think." Francis raised her eyebrows in surprise. "It might give you an advantage in regaining your—health."

Sarah made no reply. Aquinas looked uneasy, uncertain whose turn it was to speak. Sarah fumbled for her cane, rising from the chair with some difficulty.

"If you manage to—force me out," she said with unusual vindictiveness, "I may—take others with me."

It was a reckless, insane thing to say, and Sarah never said reckless, insane things. But there was no other way to express the hurt, the anger, the outrage. It would have to be her parting statement; she was too incensed to give voice to anything else. Leaning on the cane, she made for the door.

Pietro sat in the outer office, pleased with the fact that he was driving Vera Neil up the wall. He didn't know why he felt so calm, so certain Sarah could cope. They'd argued only the night before about whether or not he should go into the office with her.

"Now what in hell is that going to look like?" Sarah had managed to get out in one breath. "Should I sit on your lap while you—make my mouth move?"

Pietro had not deigned to reply.

"You may—assist me up the steps and—over the doorsills," Sarah said, "but I go inside alone."

He'd seen the reasonableness of her viewpoint, had only wanted to make sure she was recovered enough to make the decision herself.

Perhaps that was what made him so confident. He was as desperate as Vera Neil to find out what was going on beyond the wall, yet he could sit here calmly blowing smoke rings and smiling like a Cheshire cat.

He could not have anticipated what was going to happen. He had been half-listening to the unintelligible sound of the voices, lulled into near-indifference by the evenness of their tone. That was why he was thrown off guard by the sudden rise in pitch of Sarah's voice, and nearly knocked out of his chair by the impact of her wrenching open the door.

"You! You miserable bastard!" she hissed at him, looking as if she would belt him with the cane if she could risk her balance without it. "You could have told me!"

Pietro was stunned. He shot a nervous glance at Vera, seeing that she was as horrified as he. Did Sarah even realize her scene had a witness? Did she realize that the two nuns in the office behind her could probably hear every word as well?

"What's wrong?" he managed, finding his voice. "Calm down, can't you?"

"You never told me!" Sarah hissed. "You bastard! You made it sound like they were—like they cared—concerned about me—welcome me back with open arms instead of—throw me out on my ass to—to save a little money. You didn't tell me!"

Pietro grabbed her by the arm, trying to shake some sense into her. "What did you want me to do, scare the shit out of you?" he whispered violently, leading her bodily out of Vera Neil's office into the hall. "I tried to give you a vague idea. If I'd told you the whole thing, you'd have gone suicidal on me. Stop creating a scene. What can they do to you anyway?"

"The question is, what can I do to them?" Sarah half-shouted, listening with satisfaction as her voice echoed down the hall.

It took a few moments for her to gain control of herself, and then she was more than a little frightened at the scene she had caused. On the one hand, it might have shown them she wasn't one to be intimidated. On the other hand, it might have made her look like a senile old crackpot who shouldn't be running around loose.

"Drive me home!" she growled at Pietro. "God forbid I should bump into anyone I know. I'm not in the mood for—hearts and flowers."

He had relaxed his grip on her arm, but did not let her go completely, supporting her while the cane made hollow thumping noises on the deserted staircase.

"Son of a bitch!" Mario said when Mae told him what she'd heard Vera Neil say to the librarian over lunch. "Son of a bitch!"

"Sure, it's a shame though—her making such a scene," Mae said grimly. "It can't but hurt her."

"At least she proved she can still fight 'em," Mario pointed out. "She ain't gonna sit still and take no crap from 'em."

"Hst! Will you keep your voice down?" Mae frowned.

It was a little after one; the cafeteria was crowded. Students filed past the cash register in droves, and Mae was having difficulty talking and making change at the same time. Mario was on his self-imposed lunch hour. He'd heard some of the shouting in the hall, had abandoned his mop to see what was going on, but had missed the actual confrontation. He knew better than to ask Vera Neil; he was not in her social class. But he knew Mae would get the story somehow, so he'd hurried over to the cafeteria as soon as he reasonably could. He'd pestered the story out of Mae as she rang up frankfurters and chicken salad sandwiches and ice cream sodas, but only on the understanding that he was not to breathe a word of it to a soul. That made him laugh. Once Mae had the story, whom could he possibly tell?

"Excuse me for living," he said, lowering his voice. "But you mean to tell me they don't know what's going on?" He jerked his head at the students, for whom he had particular contempt. It wasn't just that they had the luxury he'd never enjoyed of postponing their wage-earning life for an extra four years, it was the absolute disdain with which most of them treated him. Obviously only a person of inferior intellect would opt to spend his productive years pushing a broom, they reasoned. That was why they threw still-burning butts in his path, walked on the patch of floor he'd just mopped, and *almost* hit the wastebaskets with their garbage, this generation of intellectuals. Mario returned their contempt in kind.

"Sure, they're always the last to catch on," Mae said with something approaching a sneer. "All they care about is cramming for their exams. Six months of lollygagging and now they start to sweat."

"Screw 'em" was Mario's opinion. He stretched, looking for a cigarette. "Whatcha doing for the summer, Mae?"

Mae shrugged, as if she were weighing several options. "My daughter and her husband have a locker down at Breezy," she said. "If I baby-sit the kids, they'll have me all summer."

"Breezy Point?" Mario repeated. "That damn shantytown beach you micks stole from the Jews? You gone integrated yet, or is it still all Bay Ridge beer bellies?"

Mae swatted at him and missed. "You're nervy," she scowled. "Anybody's allowed in, long as they're Catholic. We got Porto Rickans and colored. We even got Eyetalians. First I ever met that take baths regular."

Mario grinned at her. "You know what I love about you, Mae?" he asked sweetly. "You're such a doll, that's what. I mean that. And I'll betcha I take more baths than you do any day."

"I hope you're satisfied," Pietro growled, jumping a red light with his fist on the horn. "You pretty well blew it."

"Maybe," Sarah sighed, closing her eyes against the glare of the sunlight off the chrome and a recently acquired headache. The interview had left her completely wrung out, and, since she couldn't take aspirin with her anticoagulants, she could look forward to having the headache for the rest of the day. Had she been out of her mind to let them goad her into a fight so easily? If she couldn't stand up to an hour's debate in Francis's inner sanctum, how the hell could she teach again? How the hell could she even consider fighting for her job when a five-minute temper tantrum left her so drained? Was she out of her mind?

"You're leaving tomorrow," she said to Pietro, wanting to drop the subject.

"Yup," he said. "Bags packed, passport updated, airline tickets ready. They're even forwarding my exams to Rome so I can mark them and send the grades back before commencement."

"What time is the flight?"

"Eleven in the morning," he said, keeping his eyes on the driving and his voice disinterested, hiding the fact that he hated to be away from her for three entire months, especially after this morning's little fiasco.

"It's been a long time," Sarah said carefully. "Perhaps it has changed."

"Rome?" Pietro snorted. "In a mere twenty-odd years? Not likely. There'll be more traffic, more smog, more Communists, more pigeon shit. Superficial stuff. But in her heart of hearts the old whore won't have changed a bit."

"Do you—want to go back?" Sarah asked searchingly.

Pietro shook his head. "It's anticlimactic," he said. "They had no reason to keep me away so long. And to bring me back now—it's almost insulting. I've paid my dues. What the hell can I offer them now? Or vice versa? No, if they're trying to make it up to me, it's twenty years too late."

They drove in silence for a while. When they were

almost at Sarah's house, Pietro looked at her solemnly. "Will you be all right?" he asked.

Sarah smiled her half-smile. "I can manage the motor things now," she said. "And I have Joan to read to me."

Even as she said it, she wondered if she might not have been rash in rejecting Joan's efforts to teach her to read again.

"You were going to be a dancer," Sarah said out of the clear blue that Saturday.

Joan had dutifully brought the morning paper, and had been halfway through the editorials when Sarah interrupted her.

"Yes," she said carefully. "Years ago."

"That's what I mean!" Sarah said. In the month or so since Joan had first appeared on her doorstep, the gaps in Sarah's speech had all but disappeared except under stress. "I've been thinking back—all the years I was teaching, certain students I remember—and all I could come up with for you was this obsession about dancing. You were always on your way to a ballet class, or just coming from one, dragging those damn toe shoes with you everywhere, wearing your hair pulled back—very unattractive, by the way. And it was all you talked about. Dance, dance, dance. Then all of a sudden you stopped. Started dressing and talking like everyone else, trying to blend in. What happened?"

Joan was embarrassed. It was not something she cared to talk about, even now, so many years later.

"I just—it didn't work out," she said vaguely. "One of those things that happens. You lose interest, go on to something else."

"But so suddenly?" Sarah was incredulous. Her sixth sense was working. She knew Joan didn't want to talk, but she herself had things on her mind that were destroying any pleasure she might have in listening to Joan read. Now, if Joan could talk . . . "Tell me about it?"

It was a request, not an order, spoken softly, but Joan decided to comply. For some reason she decided the time had come to talk about that time in her life, and that she could do it now without getting emotional about it.

For as long as she could remember, she had wanted to be a dancer. . . . No, that wasn't accurate either. It had begun when she was fourteen, the victim of a single performance of *Giselle*, the birthday present of a well-meaning great-aunt, now long deceased. What she saw that night haunted her waking and sleeping hours until her parents signed her up for lessons in a desperate attempt to prevent her from mooning away her entire life. Before that one event, there had been nothing, nothing she had ever especially wanted to do or to be. She remembered nothing about her childhood, her school life, her friends—anything. It was as if she had sprung from the womb at the age of fourteen, hobbled by three-day cramps every month and disadvantaged by a figure that could fill out a blouse without benefit of a padded bra but which was not considered—well—balletic.

She took lessons three times a week, the money supplied partly by her parents and partly by whatever she could grub up from baby-sitting and mowing lawns. She swore off Christmas presents, begging family and friends to give her cash instead. Not exactly gracious behavior, she admitted, but a necessity. There were, she would try to explain, the endless pairs of toe shoes. She had no time for movies, dating, the masochistic mating rituals that were *de rigueur* for girls of her generation. Her life meant nothing without The Dance. She got tickets for every classical company that performed in the city, scrunched up in the last row where the two-dollar seats were, her feet performing restless imitations of the steps as she watched. Her hair was always *au chignon*, and she wore leotards with *everything*, even in the summer. She would stay up all night to watch *The Red Shoes* on television, crying through the entire thing. Her parents were relieved; at least it wasn't drugs or sex.

She did have *some* potential, her teachers said as she worked her way up toward the advanced class, but of course in order to be a true *artiste* one ought to have started no later than the age of eight. The bone structure, after all—

"Bull-sheet!" was Maestro's response when Joan offered this as an excuse for some minor infraction the first day in his class. "If there is in one the dancer, I shall find it!"

Maestro taught only advanced students. His graduates were scattered throughout the *corps de ballet* of nearly every international company. There was even a certain *première danseuse* in a Brazilian company who had been his student—perhaps, as some said, his lover as well. Maestro himself had danced, briefly, with the Bolshoi.

"I make not so big the splash as Nureyev when I defect," he would shrug, bemused. "Small potatoes."

He was small, not quite at eye level with Joan, but beautiful, elongated, disciplined. He had a few minor affectations, like tearing his hair out in exasperation, but the principal one was the immaculate white towel draped around his neck. It was purely decorative. Maestro never perspired.

He prodded, he barked, he bullied. No one left his studio a bad dancer. One was either a good dancer, or one was convinced that one had never been a dancer at all.

"You are no *prima ballerina*," he told Joan almost immediately. "Never in a million years! But with great effort one can do something with you."

It was enough. She was seventeen; her whole life was

ahead of her. She practiced endlessly, staying on, bruised and aching, to watch the others after class, the proficient ones, working out their idiosyncrasies at the *barre*. It was obvious what one had to do, and that was to blend in, to become indistinguishable from everyone else.

Joan's feet bled, grew callused, bled again. At the end of the day she stank, regardless of how often she showered. The sleeves of her leotards rotted away from the perspiration. She ached all over. What was worse was that everyone else stank, too. The dressing room reeked. Stage makeup did grotesque things to her skin. The most gorgeous costumes, close up, were lurid and tacky—hooks-and-eyes hanging by dirty threads, armpits stained and stale-smelling, the entire thing dingy and frayed. The floor of Maestro's studio was filthy, gritty. It seemed a mark of professionalism that it was never cleaned, seldom even swept. Joan's mouth was always full of dust. Her eyes burned and her nose ran continuously. She developed a chronic cough. She did not get along with the other dancers. They grubbed cigarettes from each other and sneered at her for not smoking, left gobs of hair in the sink, picked their noses with dirty fingers, waited gleefully for the scourge of Maestro's wrath to fall on someone else. The male dancers were worse. They bitched, fucked up her cues in progressions, pinched her ass as she slunk past them from the dressing room.

But stage lights cover everything.

Joan was permitted, along with several other students from Maestro's class, to dance in the *corps* of a professional production during her second year. She was allowed to sit in the same rehearsal circle with well-known dancers, making an idiot of herself by staring and thus missing cues. Her days became an infinite whirl of rehearsals crammed in before, during, and after school hours. Her nights hummed with the metronomic monotone of Maestro's voice, invading her restless sleep.

". . . and-from-the-third-*now*-one-and-two-and-three-and-four-and-*plié*-so-the-left-arm-forward-five-and-six-and-seven-eight-and-*arabesque*-the-arm-brought-back-and-one-and-two-and-three-and-four-and-slowly-slowly-again-and-again-and-again-*finis*. *Enfin*. Five minutes, *mes enfants*, then back to work."

There would be a spontaneous scuffling of feet, subdued hum of voices. The mirrors threw their figures back at them, straggling sweaty shapes in dirty tights and elbowless leotards, Ace bandages, hair pulled up and steaming slightly, damp tendrils clinging to foreheads and stalklike necks. They patterned endlessly, narcissistic—posing, stretching, tapping out the ghosts of *enchaînments* with tentative feet. Joan had to search for her own figure in the mirror, so uniformly did it now seem to blend with the others. That's me! she thought with a kind of awe. I am a dancer!

She remembered little of the performances, except that they were not at all what she had anticipated. She'd steeled herself against the dirt and the stench. She'd expected overextensions, with the resulting agony the day after. But even ignoring these, she was unable to find the euphoria, the mystic sense of control, the glory. She never mastered the seeming floating effortlessness of the others. She was ruled by the sound of the metronome in her head, reeling off series after series of steps as if the entire choreography had been blueprinted on the inside of her skull. Her teeth ached with the strain of maintaining the essential relaxed smile. In her heart she knew her dancing was boring, mechanical. She was a failure.

It had to show, though Maestro said nothing. He seemed to be avoiding her, giving her fewer criticisms as he gave the others more. Joan began overextending herself, wallowing in self-doubt, pestering him after class, half-deliberately making mistakes, to attract his attention. Finally he exploded.

"You have made this same mistake every day for the week! You ask me the same questions over and over until I am sick of the sight of you. Do *you* doubt *me?* I tell you such-and-so is the way it is done—do you dare to question me? All right! I will tell you what you seem to must hear: You are not the dancer! You will never be the dancer! You are a robot—a doll one pulls the strings to make the movement. There is no heart. No feeling. I no longer be nice to you. Go away! Leave! I can teach you nothing! Do not waste my time!"

He went looking for her later, in the dressing room. She was huddled in a heap on the floor, still in her leotard, her face bloated and splotchy from crying. Maestro loved histrionics. He frequently roared at someone in front of the entire class. But everything he had said to Joan was absolutely true. Now he felt sorry for her. He patted his pocketless person in search of a nonexistent handkerchief to offer her. In an attempt at humor, he offered her the towel around his neck. Joan looked at him miserably. Maestro shrugged.

"Jon," he said softly, never able to twist his Slavic tongue around her name. He crouched beside her, staring at his own splayed-out hands while she hiccupped and mopped at her eyes with a ragged soppy tissue. "Jon, you must stop the cry and listen to what I am saying to you.

"It is this way," he began when she was quieter. "There are the three things which work against you. One is the structure of the body. It is not—how does one say? —balletic. The dancer's body is small, compact—long neck and limbs, small head, no breasts, no hips. Your body is too full—too much torso, no legs. You do not elongate. For the *ballet classique* this must be, unless one has the talent *extraordinaire*, and you—you, alas, do not. Perhaps if you tried instead the modern dance—"

Joan made a face.

Maestro nodded. "I understand. Like myself, you are the snob. But it would perhaps be better than nothing, no?

"Now we come to the second thing, which is the lack of early training. Your talent is limited—I think even you must see this. If you had begun at eight, even ten, one might be able to save you, but fourteen . . . But there is no purpose. This is all nothing to the last problem."

Joan's crying had dried up by now. She waited for what she knew he was going to say.

"What is here insurmountable," Maestro said carefully, "is that you do not *feel* what you do." He held up his hand to keep her from interrupting. "I know what you would say. Of *course* you feel for being the dancer; you will work to the death for a little glamour, for the little magic world of the stage lights. But you have not the feeling for the dance itself. For the true dancer, the difference between the stage and the rehearsal is as nothing: Both are dance, and both are the same. But you will not give all that you have unless there is the audience, and then you try so hard you become the mechanical doll. All of your effort is visible to the audience, they feel how hard you work, and there is no beauty, there is no poetry. And this will always be so."

Joan began to cry again. She could not deny what he was saying.

"How old are you, child?" Maestro asked gently, patting her hand.

"Nineteen," Joan gulped. "A-almost twenty."

"Almost twenty," Maestro mused. "At such an age some girls have—well, but you have been sheltered. Would it be indelicate to ask—you have never had the *affaire*?"

Joan blushed violently. "N-no," she stuttered. "But it's not as if I—"

"So." Maestro nodded, smiling a little. "Perhaps this explains. *Enfin*, a last word for advice. Go out and live, little girl. Throw yourself into the life as you have tried to do with the dance. Do not think so much."

He left her alone. Joan pulled herself up from the floor, threw her toe shoes into her satchel, slipped her jeans on over her tights, eased her battered feet into her sandals. She wound down the echoing metal staircase, treads worn paintless by the friction of a thousand feet, and pushed the heavy fire door open to the blinding sunshine.

When Joan looked at Sarah again, she could see that the old woman was nodding. Bored to sleep. But her eyes opened as soon as Joan stopped talking.

"Beautiful," Sarah said without sarcasm, as if she had heard every word. "You tell it with such passion. Who would think you had all that lurking beneath that cool exterior. You never went back?"

"Nope," Joan said wistfully. "Maestro offered to get me into someone else's class, but I couldn't face it after that day. I still exercise to keep in shape, but that's it."

"And what have you found to replace it?" Sarah asked, her eyes hooded, watching. "On the artistic level, I mean."

"Nothing." Joan shrugged. "There's nothing else I know how to do."

"Oh, come on!" Sarah was incredulous. "Nothing at all? There must be something—painting, writing poetry —something. Even needlepoint. But not nothing."

Joan couldn't think of a thing.

"Beware of letting your creative juices back up on you," Sarah warned, shaking her head. "Someday they're liable to explode."

"I don't have any creative juices," Joan said flatly.

"Wanna bet?" Sarah demanded. Joan was looking for the newspaper, to change the subject. Sarah motioned her to forget it.

"What's the matter?" Joan frowned.

"Nothing," Sarah lied, not looking her in the eye. "I just don't want to be read to at the moment. I'm enjoying the silence."

"I talk too much, you mean."

"No, no. Nothing like that," Sarah began. "It so happens—"

"Something's bugging you today," Joan interrupted. The old woman's inattentiveness had not escaped her entirely. "Are you going to tell me about it or not?"

"I don't know what you're talking about," Sarah said.

"Wait a minute," Joan said, remembering something. "This was the week you were supposed to talk to Sister Francis! What happened?"

"Did I mention that to you?" Sarah was genuinely surprised; she couldn't recall saying anything to Joan. She must have been subconsciously building new bridges even as she set fire to the old ones.

Joan narrowed her eyes, using one of Sarah's techniques. "You did," she said. "What happened?"

Sarah shrugged, trying to pass it off. "Perhaps I should not have—dissuaded you from teaching me how to read" was all she said.

Joan sat back in her chair, taking a deep breath, trying to comprehend what was not being said. "Let me get this straight," she said. "Did you go in there and *tell* them you can't read?"

"It doesn't matter," Sarah said, trying to play it down.

"It doesn't matter because they want to let you go anyway," Joan enunciated slowly. "Holy shit!"

"Indeed," Sarah said, not looking at her.

"Well, Christ, are you going to just sit there?" Joan pounded on the arm of the chair for emphasis. "What the hell are you going to do about it?"

"Get off your soapbox, please," Sarah said mildly. "And stop shouting. What I'm going to do is wait until the fall, and then I'll appeal. They can't bounce me. I have tenure."

Joan could not believe what she was hearing. Had the stroke done something to Sarah's memory? Had she forgotten the iron-fisted control the administration had wielded during the Vietnam years, squelching any attempt at protest before it could start? Had she forgotten how easily half the psychology department had once been let go for holding late-night coed bull sessions—Sister Francis had termed them "orgies"—and refusing to get haircuts?

She said nothing else to Sarah on the subject; but that night when she got home, Joan made several phone calls.

"Hi, Vicki?" she began. Only Vicki would be home on a Saturday night. "It's Joanie. . . . Yeah, hi. Listen, I'll talk to you in a few minutes. Is your mother around?"

X

Twirling your blue skirts, traveling the sward
Under the towers of your seminary,
Go listen to your teachers, old and contrary,
Without believing a word.

JOHN CROWE RANSOM, *Blue Girls*

"The first thing we ought to do," Helen O'Dell said, pushing her hair back and looking at the other two, "is contact the bigwigs. Get in touch with the influential alumnae—the rich ones who always give big contributions to the college—and see if we can talk them over to our side. And the board of trustees as well. We'll go right over Sister Francis's head."

"No way," Celia said firmly. "I mean, why don't we just march into her office and let her know what we're up to? Don't you think some of those fat-cat conservatives on the board would just love to rat on us? No, this thing's got to be sewn up before anybody upstairs knows what's going down."

"What do you suggest then?" Joan asked wearily, fiddling with the air conditioner and sweating all the same.

It had been her idea to contact Celia. There had been less than two dozen genuine student radicals on campus in the Sixties, and Celia had been their unofficial leader. They were a scruffy, disorganized minority, largely ignored by nearly everyone else, in spite of their underground newsletter, antiwar poetry events, and consciousness-raising moratoria. They'd boycotted classes on the first day of every month to protest the war, but the smallness of their numbers defeated their purpose. They'd worn funny clothes and stuck flowers in their hair, and their fingers were always purple with mimeograph ink. Most of them grew up to be social workers or public-school teachers. Having tried and failed to shake the system from the outside, they had surrendered to some degree in order to infiltrate from the bottom.

Celia would have graduated with Joan if she hadn't dropped out in her junior year. Their circles of friends had overlapped, though they themselves had never been close. Joan had heard that Celia was involved in theater work now, that she worked in some sort of technical capacity in a small off-off-Broadway theater. She had contacted her anyway, hoping to find that the student activist had not changed too much in the near-decade since their paths had diverged. Her hopes had been justified, but she had not counted on the endless bickering about tactics that would go on nearly all summer between Celia and Helen O'Dell. The role of mediator was getting her down. And Sarah was averse to the entire project.

"Cart before the horse!" she would bellow. "Who needs the lot of you? If they refuse me a hearing in the fall, *then* you can make an uproar. Right now you're all falling over each other to give me help I don't need. I can do this myself."

The present debate had been going on all morning. Disgusted, Sarah had hobbled up the stairs to take a nap. The three went on arguing.

"What do you suggest then?" Joan asked Celia wearily, wishing she'd never started the whole thing.

"You have got to get your grass-roots support together first," Celia said doggedly, repeating a variation on the theme she'd been harping on all day. "If you get a couple hundred signatures from students and *recent* graduates—to hell with the old farts—people who know Sarah and will stand behind her—*then* you take that list to the big contributors and say, 'Dig it. This is what's going on. What are you going to do about it?' And you don't go near the trustees. Letting those fascists in on what you're doing is like going to Frannie's office and telling her directly."

"I don't agree," Helen said, entrenched.

Joan resisted the urge to scream.

"I'm glad you weren't with us during the Stop the War days," Celia said without malice.

Helen O'Dell blinked at her "No danger of that," she said. "I was *for* the war. And I still think we need a full accounting of all the MIAs—"

"Oh, wow!" Celia said, collapsing against the back of the couch and covering her eyes with one hand. "Shit, man, I don't believe I'm hearing this!"

"I said I *was*," Helen specified. "Looking back on it, I can see where we probably shouldn't have—"

"Hey!" Joan yelled, surprising herself as well as the others, but she simply couldn't let this thing spin off into pacifism or they'd be here all night. "Look, ladies, can we get down to cases before she wakes up, or are we going to waste the entire day?"

She listened to herself talking. She was being forceful, decisive. She couldn't believe it. She ought to capitalize on it before she lost it.

"You're right," Celia nodded, agreeing with someone for the first time since she'd walked in the door. "Besides, I have to split soon. We have a tech run-through at five and, unlike you rich chicks, I have to rely on public transport to get me there."

She avoided Joan's sympathetic look. Celia's husband

had been out of work for over a year, but it seemed to bother other people far more than it did her.

"Okay," Joan said, taking a deep breath. "Compromise. Contact recent grads first, rich alumnae a few weeks later. Leave the trustees out until the last minute."

"No way!" Celia interrupted. "Leave 'em out altogether."

"I don't think so," Joan said, considering it. "If we let them know last, it'll throw a scare into the powers that be. At any rate, we'll put that off until we see how the rest of it is going. We'll start sending the letters out this week, so we get a jump on the fall semester. I'll draft the letter and you two can make corrections on it when we get together next weekend. I can run off copies at work, and we'll chip in on stamps and envelopes. Any complaints?"

"What about the students?" Helen asked.

"Waste of time," Celia remarked.

"Why?" Helen asked, trying to be patient. She wanted very much to understand this grown-up flower child, but she hadn't been getting much encouragement.

"Because they don't give a shit," Celia said, looking her directly in the eye. She, like Joan, knew how Vicki always winced at dirty words, and wanted to see if her mother did also. She didn't. Celia was a little disappointed, but she respected Helen a little more, too. "See, the current genera-tion—and they really are a whole different generation from those of us who grew up under the onus of Johnson and Nixon and all that jive—are even more apathetic and self-interested than the people we went to school with. They're so paranoid about their grades and getting good recommendations for jobs and grad school that they wouldn't stand up against the administration if they were holding public executions. There's no point in wasting the stamps on them."

"She's right," Joan nodded sadly.

"Really?" Helen was dubious, suspicious of generalizations. She looked at Joan, then Celia, and then she thought of Vicki. Here were three contemporaries among whom very little could be said to be held in common.

"All right," she said. "We can't get in touch with the kids until September as it is. We'll do it the way Joan suggested."

"Groovy. I'm glad it's settled," Celia said, gathering up her belongings. "I have to go."

She embraced Joan, and shook hands tentatively with Helen. "I'm sorry if I hassled you," she said sincerely.

"That's okay." Helen smiled. "We're all entitled to our preconceived notions, I guess."

"She doesn't mean to be so abrasive," Joan said later, relieved that Celia was gone. "She's always come across that way on political things, or human-rights issues. That's probably how she sees this—the rights of the underdog or whatever. On anything else she'd fall over backward to be nice to you."

"It doesn't bother me," Helen said, listening to sudden sounds of activity from the back bedroom. She went to the stairs and called, "Do you need any help up there?"

She began the ascent without waiting for a reply, but Sarah was already at the top of the stairs. "Down!" she ordered gruffly, waving the cane at Helen, who retreated dutifully. "Well! Has Anarchists International adjourned for the day?"

"We're not that bad," Joan said lamely, watching the old woman settle herself in her favorite chair and haul her weak leg up onto the rattan footstool like a stick of firewood.

"You're not that good, either," Sarah said ironically, propping her cane against the side of the mantel. "My question is, have you finished? I'd like to do something useful with the rest of the day."

". . . and we can contact the ACLU if all else fails," Joan was saying, clearing away the supper dishes.

"Are you out of your mind?" was all Sarah said.

Helen had left before supper, so it was just the two of them.

"I'm serious," Joan said, rearranging the refrigerator so that the leftovers would fit. "There was a case a few years ago—some high-school teacher from New Jersey, I think, went blind from diabetes and called in the ACLU. Won the case, too. He proved that he could keep up with the material with Braille transcriptions and cassettes, and proved he could still stand up to a classroom full of screaming kids. They had to reinstate him."

"And you think this applies in my case?" Sarah was trying to act distinterested, but there was a gleam in her eye.

"Sure," Joan nodded, turning on the hot water. "It's almost a complete parallel. If anything, you've got a stronger case. You're teaching college kids; they're more civilized than high school. No discipline problems. And you've got an outstanding record."

"Leave those," Sarah frowned, meaning the dishes.

Joan went on running the water. "I don't mind," she said.

"I said leave them!" Sarah shouted. "You never get the glasses clean. I'll only have to do them over."

Joan wrenched the faucet off and threw herself into a chair. "You're not even listening to me!" she hissed. "Why do I waste my time on you?"

"I've heard every word," Sarah said placidly, tracing an invisible pattern on the tablecloth. "There are just a few things you've neglected to consider."

"Such as?"

"Such as the fact that they have promised me a departmental hearing," Sarah pointed out. "That hardly indicates that they intend to throw me out."

"Suppose they back down?" Joan demanded. "Or suppose they give you the hearing and still refuse to reinstate you?"

"No chance of my blowing the hearing?" Sarah was bemused. "Maybe I am incompetent after all."

"Bullshit," Joan said.

"You're so persuasive," Sarah sighed in mock-amazement. "You should have been a lawyer!"

Joan glared at her. It was a sore point between them. It was something that had occurred to her more than once since she'd started working and come to the conclusion that she could do what her three employers did without any great mental strain. However, there was the question of how on earth she was supposed to finance law school and still eat.

"Don't change the subject," she told Sarah. "What's going to happen if they don't let you go back?"

Sarah shrugged. "I'll get to that when I get to it," she said.

"Afraid to rock the boat, is that it?" Joan challenged her. She had an ace up her sleeve, something she'd heard about a long time ago and was dying to know the truth about. "Did they teach you that in the convent?"

It stopped Sarah in her tracks. "How did you know about that?" She narrowed her eyes at Joan.

Joan didn't flinch. "Rumors," she fenced. "Weren't you?"

"Yes," Sarah acknowledged. "Several centuries ago."

"How long?"

"Too long," Sarah sighed. "Much too long."

"But why?" Joan was incredulous. "I mean, you're so unorthodox now. It's hard to imagine you were ever any different. Why did you do it?"

"Why did I become a nun?" Sarah repeated. "I was very

young, although that's hardly an excuse. To this day I'm
not completely sure. My mother was convinced it was to
avoid having to work for a living—that's how she put it.
It was nineteen thirty, you understand, and even if there
hadn't been a depression, people of our social class never
wasted money putting a *girl* through college. After all,
sensible girls got married and had babies, and their husbands took care of them. What on earth did they need all
that education for? If my parents had had any idea how
I'd turn out—not that I did either the day I first put my
suitcase down on the front steps at Brentwood . . .

"But to get back to the reason for it—or the reason I
can give now, looking back on it—it was for the same
romantic, obsessive, semihysterical reasons that made you
want to be a dancer. Sounds ridiculous, doesn't it? But it
is the curse of adolescence that one becomes interested in
only a very few things—everything else is so *boring*—and
those few interests become obsessions. For the general run
of kids, it's just sex in one form or another, or drugs, or
alcohol, or fast cars, or whatever, but for the oddities like
you and me it's something else."

Joan said nothing, savoring the preciousness of the
narrative, wishing she could tell Sarah how flattered she
was to be included in the same category as she. Sarah
continued.

"So, I entered the convent because it seemed the logical
extension of my religious upbringing, and because I was
madly in love with the idea of sailing around in a long
black habit, and because I desperately wanted to be
different. Other girls got married and had babies and were
absorbed into their husbands' last names, or, God forbid,
became secretaries and shriveled up in dry little offices and
made novenas every evening so they wouldn't have to go
home to their widowed mothers' houses and lie awake and
alone in their cold narrow beds masturbating in the dark.
No, sir, not me. I was going to sun myself in the aura of

witty, educated women, and never have to change a diaper or put up with the—ugh—degradation of sex. The convent, you know, was probably the first forum for the liberation of women in Western society. When you consider the alternatives for a woman in, say, the fourteenth century, who, if she wasn't dead of childbed fever before she was twenty-five . . ."

Sarah heard herself babbling, missing the point. She had thought about none of these things when she was seventeen, could not have had the background necessary to put such thoughts into words. All she knew at seventeen was that the world was an evil place—or so her mother said—and one ought to stay as far away from it as possible.

Sarah's mother had married a German, a not unheard-of thing for a working-class Irish girl to do, except that he wasn't Catholic. She had converted him before she would marry him, and, after that single concession on his part, had proceeded to lose herself in his identity, to sit at home and cook and try to make babies for him. She labored part-way through seven pregnancies, completing only two. She was sick most of the time after that. Hers was a morbid household, filled with dark corners and faded rose-twined wallpaper and the smell of camphor, the endless winter dampness of laundry drying in the kitchen by the wood-stove. Even so long removed from it, Sarah could remember every texture of it with the agonizing clarity of childhood. The smell of mothballs tied her stomach in knots.

In comparison, life as a nun seemed wholesome, almost frivolous. Sarah fell into the convent headfirst. Within six months she knew it wasn't what she wanted, but it took seven years more for her to pull free.

Brentwood, in the autumn of 1930, was a small farm town about twenty-five miles from the county line of Queens, New York, about a third of the way inland from the south shore of the tapering fish body of Long Island.

The late-night train of the Long Island Railroad sent shrieking echoes over the flattened-out hills that surrounded the motherhouse of the Community of Sisters of Saint Joseph. The train echoed the unvoiced cry in the heart of Sarah Elisabeth Gartenhaus, who lay unsleeping in her long white nightgown in the postulants' wing of the dormitory. Despite getting up at dawn and putting in a working-study-prayer routine that would exhaust any adolescent to the point of tears, she still woke at the exact moment nightly that the train shrieked past, raising goose bumps on her arms under the long white sleeves, lifting her cropped hair on end, answering her loneliness.

She had cried about the hair. It was, after all, the only beautiful thing about her, this breastless praying mantis with horn-rimmed glasses and chronic sinusitis. Her hair was the color of a copper penny, thick and straight and swinging to her waist, brushed nightly until it gleamed. She had plaited it into two strong braids under the little cloche hat she wore on the train. Her cardboard suitcase, full of long cotton underwear and heavy black stockings, lay tucked under the wicker seat as she rattled along, alone in the seat (her parents had refused to go with her; could not understand her need to do this thing), clutching a mangled handkerchief and staring at the endless parade of countryside clattering past the window. She had dreamed of how she would look in the voluminous habit, its pleated weight lending importance to her thin figure, the big wooden crucifix clanking against her ribs, the fathomless pockets and jangling key rings, the starched linen bib and wimple, the almost floor-length veil somehow transforming her into someone else, someone more perfect, more real, than the pale adolescent she saw in the tarnished mirror in her parents' room the night before she left.

She'd paid the cabdriver with her own money by the gate and was let inside the main building, where she and the other new arrivals sat in the parlor smiling nervously at each other. Then she had been led down a series of hallways and ushered into a small white room and sat in a chair with a sheet wrapped around her while a fat, smiling nun with rolled-up sleeves who called her "lovey" took a pair of sewing shears and began to chop and chop until nothing was left but the masses of coppery strands tumbled around her on the floor and the cropped bony head she couldn't even see because mirrors were considered worldly vanities and hence forbidden.

She did not know exactly when, or why, the glamour of it began to slip away from her, leaving her with the knowledge that she was making a big mistake. All she knew was that there was a moment, a definite instant, when she looked up from the textbook she was craning her neck over, and decided that what she was doing was not normal. She would have been hard pressed, with her background, to say what "normal" was; but after nearly twenty affectionless years, it suddenly occurred to her that something was missing. She had never been overtly friendly; she was too shy, too awkward to simply warm up to a stranger. But she had seen—and been warned about—the kind of heads-together whispering and surreptitious handholding that went on in the halls of the novitiate. What she didn't understand was why that sort of thing was forbidden. Wouldn't it be wise to be friendly with the people with whom one would have to spend a lifetime, inside the limited orb of a few dozen convent houses?

Sarah wished she had just one close friend. There had been constant warnings about the necessity to "renounce all ties with the outside world." It had been easy for her; she had always been a loner, given to bumping into things and talking too loudly to cover her shyness. Her range of interests, her multisyllabic vocabulary, the long sickly childhood that had given her more than the usual opportunity to stay home from school and read endlessly on her own, all made her freakish to girls her own age. The ones she'd known in high school were mostly interested in snaring husbands. Those she met in the convent were forever absorbed in that elusive pastime known as "offering oneself to the service of God." The way Sarah saw it, both amounted to approximately the same thing—sacrificing one's own personality to the will of another. All she wanted for herself was one strong friendship, and that, it seemed, was forbidden.

"It is our purpose, and our commitment, to make ourselves receptive to the grace of God, and to serve the needs of His people," Mother Superior would say. "Personal attachments distract us from the voice of God speaking within each of us, and through Holy Mother Church, and are therefore to be discouraged."

They were disquieting words from this particular woman, who, though she seemed at first impression to be quite austere, was in fact a warm, gracious person when approached in private. She was not a storybook nun with posture so upright that her back never touched the chair. She smiled often, suffered from asthma, and had an extremely hairy mole on her chin. The mole haunted Sarah, who had more than once been given an audience with Mother for the purpose of reviewing her eating habits.

"You're so thin!" Mother would say with genuine anguish. "Are you certain you're eating enough?"

"I never gain weight," Sarah shrugged, embarrassed by the attention. "I eat like a horse—really," she finished inelegantly.

"Your health concerns me," Mother went on. "Do the sinus headaches still trouble you?"

"They're not as bad," Sarah murmured, wrestling with what she had to say. It might be the last time she could speak to Mother privately for some time. "Mother, I . . ."

"Child, what is it?" The warm smile hovered beneath the wimple, anticipatory.

"Mother—I—what you said in your talk this morning . . ." Oh, hell, Sarah thought, get it out. "Well, dammit, why can't we have close friendships? We have to live under the same roof and share the chores and eat the same food and study together and sleep in the same room and—well, why not? Why make life more difficult than it already is?"

Mother was panting slightly, whether from her asthma or from the effort to ignore the abrupt profanity, Sarah couldn't tell. She stared hard at the mole on Mother's chin, wondering in a perversely objective way if it wouldn't be less noticeable if Mother tweezed it, or at least trimmed the hair back occasionally. Of course, without a mirror it would be difficult, and Sarah excused Mother on that account. She hadn't yet become aware of the subtle vanity of women devoid of the usual outlets for beauty like hairstyles and makeup, who had to resort to extraordinary means to make themselves visible despite the uniformity of clothing. Even something as ugly as Mother's mole might be interpreted as beautiful in that it made her face, cut out of the huge obliterating wimple like everyone else's, different. But Sarah was new to this life, and hadn't discovered these secret affectations. As it was, she was concentrating on the mole so much she barely heard what Mother was saying.

"The reasons," Mother wheezed, her eyes closed, two bright pink spots appearing on her cheeks, "the reasons you have mentioned are precisely why one must not become too close to one's sisters in Christ. Discord occurs where a too-strong friendship must endure separation— as when one of you is transferred to a different convent,

for example—and friendships which are too exclusive
detract from the amount of ourselves we are able to give
to others in charity. Then, too, a friendship between two
women in such circumstances may lead to—occasions of
sin—temptations to commit—actions which are—found
to be sinful under the sixth commandment. . . ."

Lesbianism was a concept difficult for a girl of Sarah's
background to grasp, but somehow what Mother was
hinting at began to filter through. Sarah became fear-
ridden—fearful of the outside forces watching, spying,
talking behind their hands; fearful of herself, of a body
stifling under too many layers of clothing and too many
layers of restriction, fearful of a mind made small and
peevish by too much moralistic minutiae. One was never
alone, but always lonely.

Sarah received her bachelor of arts degree and took
her final vows within a single week. The ceremony for
taking the vows always came first; the awarding of degrees
seeming to be an afterthought. Sarah wondered why.
Was it to keep possible opportunists from skipping out
with a free degree? Banishing such evil thoughts from
her mind, she left the following day to teach in a run-
down grammar school in Brooklyn, not far from where
she'd grown up.

As the weeks and months went by, her dreams became garish and disturbing, and she was having day-
dreams as well. They soon monopolized every waking
moment when she was not in the classroom, directly involved with her students. She did not like the life she
was leading, and so formed another, fantasy life around
it. She began having chronic crying spells.

The order sent her on retreat. This sort of thing happened frequently after one took one's final vows, she was
told. It would pass. When it did not, she wrote a letter
to Mother Superior asking to be allowed to leave. She
was advised that this was a serious matter, and not to

be taken cavalierly, and why didn't she wait a year, and pray, and reconsider? Sarah began to lose herself in books as she had when she was a child. She read voraciously—comparative religion, philosophy. She was advised to concentrate more on the reading of her divine office, and given extra duties in the kitchen—a place where she was singularly inept—lest idleness become an occasion of sin. She became desperately involved in the lives of her students, writing endless letters of concern to their parents for trivial reasons, exasperating the principal of her school.

At the end of the school year, she repeated her desire to leave. She was transferred to a newly constructed high school and given permission to study for a master's degree. As a placating gesture, the order allowed her to study medieval literature instead of taking the usual education courses, thinking the newfound interest would make her forget her ephemeral miseries. She had a brilliant mind, and they didn't want to lose her.

Sarah began to cry less, but to withdraw more. She began writing horrible manic poetry during the long sleepless nights. The few tentative friendships she'd tried to establish with the other nuns began to disintegrate. They didn't really understand what was wrong with her. On her twenty-fourth birthday, exhausted after a week of marking exams and cramming for her graduate courses and staying up all night to finish an epic poem (burned in a wastepaper basket with kitchen matches upon completion) on the nature of guilt, Sarah developed severe bronchitis, had no resources to combat it, and ended up in the hospital with double pneumonia.

Her convalescence was slow. She had lost nearly twenty pounds; she had a cough that shook her until her ribs ached. It was nearly May before she could walk the length of a block without wheezing. She'd been exempted from teaching for the rest of the term. As soon as she was strong enough to write without her hands shaking, she once again submitted her case to Mother Superior.

"I want to leave. I am not made for this life, nor it for me. I want to be free," she repeated to anyone who came near her, until they were tempted to send her to a psychiatrist, so madly did her eyes glow when she said it. By June, when she was on her feet again, her request was reviewed, and they let her go.

She came back to her parents' house by car this time, her younger brother, wearing his newly acquired army uniform, carrying the cardboard suitcase she was too weak to pick up. They gave her back her old room in the camphor-smelling house. The room had been unoccupied all the time she was away, filled with unused furniture, stripped of her adolescent possessions. It resembled nothing more strongly than the countless bare, white-painted rooms she'd inhabited for the past seven years.

At least, she thought, now everyone will leave me alone.

She spent the summer sitting in the sun in the yard, sending résumés to the local high schools, enduring the clucking of the neighbors. Some of them felt sorry for her. The others thought it was a disgrace: Bad enough to become a nun and deprive your parents of grandchildren, but to come out of the convent again . . . ! Sarah was beginning to feel like a fallen woman.

By September, a few of her résumés had brought replies. Sarah chose a Catholic girls' school run by a different order of nuns, and began teaching English in the fall. She was doing almost the same things she had been doing as a nun, but it was the freedom to come and go that made all the difference. Her mother tended to ignore her; she was overage and could not be told what to do, so it was easier to let her alone. She could go to bed whenever she wanted to, go out for a walk without asking someone's permission or taking another nun along, and absolutely no one called her "child." They were simple things, but Sarah treasured them.

She did not get on well with the handful of other lay teachers in the school—dumpy, resigned, small-minded spinsters—mostly because she dreaded becoming like them. As soon as she had put enough money aside, she got her own apartment. She was going to live the adolescence she had cheated herself of.

The apartment was a cold-water flat with only one window, and a woodburning stove even her mother would have despised. Sarah let her hair grow long, and kept it straight instead of bobbing or perming it the way everyone else did. She wore trousers whenever she wasn't in school. She abhorred makeup, especially the bright red lipstick and nail lacquer that were considered *de rigueur*. She practiced the art of swearing, went to the movies every single weekend and cried like a schoolgirl. She did not get up for mass one Sunday, found she was not struck by lightning, and decided she had outgrown the religion of her birth. She developed her own version of the Judaic tradition of speaking to God directly, without the necessity for an interpreter. It suited her.

She was completely alone now. Her parents, laboring under the disgrace of having a daughter who had reached her advanced age without showing the slightest interest in marriage, began to grow more and more distant. Sarah didn't mind. She still had no friends. Most of her high-school chums were married. One or two of them tried inviting her over, ostensibly for dinner, but also with the intention of matching her up with the Wall Street type at the other end of the dinner table. Sarah always arranged to bump into the coffee table and swear at it, or quote Kierkegaard at dinner, or begin a tirade against fascism or the papacy over dessert. She was not invited again.

It all worked splendidly until Christmastime. It was

her first Christmas out of the habit, and school vacation lasted an interminable two weeks. She assigned her students long compositions that were due just before vacation so she'd have something to do to pass the time. Christmas Day would be a dreary time at her parents', out of duty, but the rest of the time looked to be a dismal void.

On the last day of school, she packed up her books with infinite slowness, listening to the laughter of the girls freed from their prison into the cold crisp air. Sarah wondered if she'd ever been that happy, even in high school. She was the last to leave the building. The Christmas decorations in the hallways struck her as tacky and meaningless as she said goodbye to the custodian, envying her the seven children she scrubbed for on her hands and knees, and went home.

She went to the beach that weekend. It was a mad sort of pastime she'd begun early in the fall, going to the beach when no one else was there—to walk at first, and later, when her scarred lungs felt a little stronger, to run a little, and then a little more, until by December, with its burning-cold air, she felt almost as strong as before she'd gotten sick. She was not affected by the cold, and she loved the remote beauty of this landscape in the winter.

And that was why she was there the weekend before Christmas, jogging along the shoreline in her baggy clothes, hair flapping, her speed the only thing that kept her from freezing right into the sand. The cold was bitter, alarming. She would have to leave soon.

"Olympics are over," a voice rumbled at her, cutting across the wind and knocking the breath out of her.

He'd been nearly hidden by a little hummock of sand he'd been crouching beside. As he stood up, Sarah prepared to bolt. Rape! she thought, assessing quickly whether she could outdistance him in a sprint. It must have been written on her face.

"Relax," he almost barked, laughing a little. "Didn't mean to scare you."

He was a gnome. Stravinsky, was Sarah's first impression, only younger—not yet forty—swathed in an oversize muffler and an ancient overcoat, his huge scarred hands bare against the cold. Such large hands for such a small man. And scarred from what? The fatalist in Sarah made her stay where she was. What could he do to her?

"What the hell you doing out here?" He spoke as if words were an effort, as if the shortest phrasing were necessary with or without the biting wind. "Know it's twenty-five degrees?"

"Yeah," Sarah shot back, adopting his tone. "Cold doesn't bother me."

"Hell," he spat. "Whatcha doing out here, though?"

A number of sarcastic answers occurred to Sarah; she did not use any of them.

"Getting some fresh air," she snapped, tossing her hair back over her shoulders. "What the hell're *you* doing here?"

He laughed, pleased with the answer and the question. Sarah liked his laugh.

"Sculptor," he said, tapping himself on the chest as if he were an immigrant struggling with the language, though Sarah could detect no accent other than that of the streets. "Looking for inspiration. Freezing my ass off instead. Shit!"

Sarah laughed with him this time. He was a discovery, an adventure. Her fear was gone.

I am a survivor, she thought. If something's going to happen, it will happen. *Carpe diem*, and consequences be damned.

She watched him trying to light a cigarette against the

wind. After the third attempt, he let out a string of obscenities that shocked even her. He turned toward her
and went to grasp her arm.

"Coffee?" he asked, his aboriginal simplicity sounding
almost chivalrous. "Diner just up from the beach."

Sarah had seen it on her way here, so she knew he
wasn't up to anything. Yet. Why not? she thought,
though she shied away from his touch.

"Okay," she nodded, falling into step beside him.

The windows of the diner were steamy with warmth.
It was crowded, mostly with truckers, the kind of people
who would come to the aid of a lady in distress. As her
newfound friend held the door open and the hot air hit
her in the face, Sarah realized she hadn't eaten in a restaurant since her sixteenth birthday. There was still so
much catching up to do!

"Two coffees, Mabel," the gnome shouted to the wait-
ress as he led Sarah to a booth in the back.

Safe, Sarah thought. If they know him here, he won't
risk a scene.

"May I—" she began, feeling ridiculous.

He turned to her like a hawk, looking surprised. "Something wrong?"

"I can't drink coffee," Sarah said weakly. "Gives me the
runs."

"Hot chocolate then," he offered, not startled by her
frankness. "Or tea?"

"Tea," Sarah nodded, greatly relieved.

Within minutes they sat staring at each other across
the steam from their too-hot drinks.

"Most girls holler for a cop when you jump out from a
rock at them," he observed, positively eloquent. "Whatsa
matter? Your mother never tell you not to talk to
strangers?"

"I'm old enough not to have to—listen to my mother,"
Sarah said grandly. She had almost said "obey," magic

word of Catholic upbringing. How long would it take to outgrow the formulas?

He was laughing, a kind of wheezing in the back of his throat. It made his eyes crinkle, relieving what was otherwise a melancholy face. There were sharp creases at the sides of his too-full mouth that made him look unnecessarily serious. His only beauty was the luminous brown of his eyes, and the big rough hands with their chipped dirty fingernails, hanging absurdly from the almost woman-thin wrists that stuck out of his frayed shirt cuffs. He wore the same kind of clothing as the truckers—faded flannel shirt, work pants shiny with age, both spotted with what looked like dried clay. He apparently was what he'd said he was—a sculptor.

"You're a sculptor," Sarah said, repeating the obvious, deciding to let him talk so she would have time to study him. Men liked to talk about themselves, she'd been told, and it sure beat hell out of discussing the weather.

"Yeah," he grunted, waving it away like the smoke from the cigarette he finally managed to light. He clutched his forehead suddenly. "Oh, hey! No manners. Sam—Sam Morrow," he said, holding out one dirty hand to her across the table. "What's yours?"

"Sarah," she replied, shaking his hand in what she hoped was an assertive manner. His hand was warm, dry, strong. "Sarah Elisabeth-with-an-S Gartenhaus."

"Gartenhaus?" he repeated, making sure he got it right. "Gardenhouse, no? Krauts aren't too popular these days, are they?"

It was a safe topic, and they talked about the Nazis and the probability of war until they'd pretty well exhausted it. He had not let go of Sarah's hand, but held it down on the table with his own, not forcibly, but firmly enough to keep Sarah's attention fixed on it. She did not pull away. She had never held hands with a man before; she saw no harm in it.

"Thank God I'm too old for the go-round with the draft board this time," Sam was saying. "Not that they wouldn't try. They snagged me for the Great War, but I had rheumatic fever when I was a kid. Left me with a heart murmur. So they had to let me off the hook. Never even gave me a chance to give my spiel about pacifism."

"Are you a socialist?" Sarah asked with more than a little awe. The idea was a deliciously dangerous one.

"Nah, not me." He shook his head. "I'm not political in the least. It's all a lot of crap—any of these earth-shaking movements. I stay out of it. Too wrapped up in my work."

"Tell me about your work," Sarah said abruptly, then thought better of it. Was this the way to handle a real live artist? "I mean—I don't want to be nosy, but—that is, if you want to."

"I'll do you one better," he said, gulping down his coffee and releasing her hand. "I'll show you."

Sarah looked at him blankly.

"Studio's a few blocks from here," he explained. "I've got a truck. Drive you home after."

After what? Sarah's brain flickered momentarily. Did she look so naïve? Or so easy? Why was she ready to go with him anyway?

His truck was a battered, rusty pickup, the back filled with bags of concrete and rusty garden tools. Did he do lawns and sidewalks in his spare time? Sarah didn't ask. She jounced along beside him on the springless seat, her hands clenched deep in her pockets. It was an adventure, nothing more, she told herself. Nothing was going to happen.

It was exactly the way she'd imagined a sculptor's studio would look—the top floor of a warehouse, with twenty-foot ceilings and skylights. But the sculptures were nothing like what she'd expected. They were not hulking ultrarealist forms looming out of their equitably socialistic corners, but something almost impossible to classify, at least with her limited knowledge. Certain pieces were airy and elongated, seeming to float. Others squirmed, agonized, battled invisible enemies that came from within, struggling in vain for calm, for serenity. They were in all media—primarily stone and clay, but also in bronze and even wood. They were the most frighteningly beautiful things Sarah had ever seen.

She remembered something then, something that had been teasing the back of her brain since he'd half-introduced himself back in the diner. She remembered coming across an article in *Time* magazine, during the early years in Brentwood when she'd thirsted so desperately for news from the real world outside. She remembered brooding over the postage-stamp-size picture of the artist and one of his works, wondering what it must be like to be talented, to have a gift that brought you to the attention of the world. The face in that picture was as vivid as if she had the magazine still in her hand. The article had described this young artist as promising, if difficult to classify. The young artist's name had been . . .

"You're Samuel Morrow," Sarah said with a kind of awe.

"Thought I told you that back in the diner," he growled, but his face was not angry.

"But I had no idea you were *the* Samuel Morrow," Sarah gasped. "When I saw all of this . . ." She waved her arms to encompass the entire room. If she looked hard enough, she could probably find the sculpture that had been in the photograph. Judging from the crowd of them jostling each other in the shadows, he was either extremely prolific or he never sold anything. "That write-up they gave you in *Time*—"

"Shit," he cut her off, unimpressed with her admiration. "All that's terrific, but it don't sell sculpture. I got the name but not the game."

"But they're magnificent!" Sarah objected. "Why can't you sell them?"

"I do, sometimes," he shrugged, "but not enough to eat on. I make my living teaching other people how to fuck around with the stuff—excuse my French. But my own stuff is too 'individual,' see, which is another way of saying it's too weird to sit in the parlor or crouch under a birdbath; and since it don't belong to any 'school' of contemporary sculpture, most galleries won't touch it. So for the most part I'm stuck with it."

He said it lightly, but there was pain in his voice. He lit a cigarette and dismissed the subject. "Hey," he said softly, nodding at Sarah to get her attention. "Listen, something I wanted to ask you. I didn't bring you up here for the scenery."

Here it comes, Sarah thought, assessing the distance between where she stood and the nearest exit.

"Look," he was saying, "I'm not good at fancy words, so I'll get right to it. I need a model."

"Do you?" Sarah asked archly, her eyes widening with incredulity rather than fear.

He laughed his smoker's laugh. "Yeah, I do," he grinned. "What'd you think I was looking for—a quick lay? I don't do that in the studio. This is business, not pleasure. Yeah, I need a model. And I want you."

"I'm not for sale!" Sarah nearly shouted, suppressing the fact that the idea excited her.

"Look, don't get hot about it," he said. "I can pay you."

"I *have* a job, thank you," she snapped, trying to make him understand. "That's hardly the problem. The problem is—well, among other things, my age. I'm twenty-five."

"So?"

"And hardly of classical proportions," Sarah said, feeling her face grow hot. "Perhaps a younger girl, with

something of a figure. You'd have to be desperate to settle
for me."

"Hey," he said quietly, exasperated. "What do I want
—a Willendorf Venus? Not a de Milo either, for Chrissake. That's been done already, and too much. I work
with angles. And you got angles. When I saw you galloping along that beach, you looked like some crazy frigging
antelope. You got cheekbones, collarbones, elbows. No
blubber. I want you."

"I'm not for sale," Sarah repeated, but quieter than before. She was curious about how he could see all of that
through two sweaters and a pea coat.

"Listen," he said, taking her gently but firmly by the
shoulders. "Weekends. Broad daylight. Clothes on. No
monkey business. Bring a girl friend along even, so long
as she keeps her mouth shut."

"I don't have any girl friends," Sarah said weakly,
knowing she'd already made up her mind.

The Saturday after Christmas, she climbed the stairs to
his studio, firmly convinced that she was out of her mind.
She'd spent Christmas with the family, bearing up as
well as she could under the constant lamentation. She was
flirting with evil out there in the cold, cruel world, they
told her. Living alone, dressing like some sort of Bohe-
mian, stubbornly remaining an old maid when she ought
to be giving them grandchildren by now. Yes, sir, as God
was their witness—and He usually was—she was flirting
with evil.

If they only knew, Sarah thought now. I'm not only
flirting with it, I'm jumping right into the back seat with
it and waiting to see what it will do next.

She acknowledged the fact that her mind had finally
snapped. There had been a madness in his eyes that after-

noon. A monomaniac, no doubt about it. They might very well find her body in the river by New Year's.

So what? Sarah thought, pushing the door of the studio open with the toe of her galosh. I will have died in the cause of Art. It's better than living for nothing.

He was waiting for her, wearing what looked to be the same flannel shirt and work pants he'd worn that other afternoon. She smiled at him without speaking, trying to be nonchalant as she shed her coat and scarf.

"Hey," he said warmly by way of greeting. He was wiping some clay off his hands from the huge lump that sat plunk in the middle of his worktable. Sarah realized it was as cold here as it was in her heatless flat.

He saw her shivering and immediately opened the valves on the huge radiators suspended on the walls some three feet above the floor. They started clanking and hissing pleasantly.

"I like to keep it cold while I putter," he explained. "But I don't want my models with goose bumps. Spoils the effect."

Models? Sarah wondered. How many, and under what circumstances? And what business is it of mine? And why am I doing this when I've already refused the money —and I notice you said no more about it after the first time—and what am I going to do if you want something more of me as well?

When the room was thoroughly heated, he rummaged in a corner filled with what at a distance seemed to be only debris, producing from it a brown paper bag. He threw it toward Sarah, who fumbled and dropped it. It fell with a soundless plop, as if it held something soft and shapeless. When she opened it, Sarah found a kind of tunic, knee-length and sewn clumsily out of a thin brownish material. Perhaps he had made it himself. She could see him hunched over it the way men did with detailed work, stabbing his fingers and scorching the fabric with obscenities. The picture made her smile.

"You want me to wear this?" Sarah asked.

"Unless you'd rather do without it," he suggested, watching her ears go red. "But I can't exactly shape a timeless work of art out of a girl in pants. It's a compromise."

"Is there somewhere I can change?" Sarah asked carefully, weighing each word.

"There's the can," he said, jerking his thumb toward a door in the opposite wall.

Sarah opened the door, found a light bulb with a string, pulled the string. The room was scarcely big enough to turn around in, windowless, housing a sink and toilet, both surprisingly clean. There was a small hook on the door. Sarah stuck it into its ring with an audible click.

"And take off your brassiere if you're wearing one," she heard him shout through the door. "Don't need them phony pointy things staring at me. Why the hell a girl with your shape needs one of them things . . ."

Sarah was blushing again. It was a good thing he'd waited until there was a door between them to come out with cracks like that. All right, she would show him. She slid out of her underpants as well, slipped the odd-looking garment over her head, and was about to open the door when she found she had to urinate suddenly. She availed herself of the toilet as quietly as possible, saw too late that there was no paper, and began to swear. She didn't even have a tissue with her; she'd left her purse outside. Still cursing, she rolled up her underpants and used them, stuffed them under the rest of the clothes she'd piled on the sink, flushed the john, and came out.

She stood motionless while he appraised her, the worn wooden floor undulating beneath her bare feet. She never walked around like this even in her own apartment, mostly because of the cold. Wearing this flimsy thing with nothing under it, she might just as well be naked.

To make matters worse, he kept staring at her, walking around her several times and looking her up and down, nodding and grunting, apparently with approval. She could feel his breath on her, though he did not touch her. It was a kind of subtle seduction, and not unpleasant. If he didn't try anything now, she was safe. She was hardly breathing, and yet she became aware of an odd, relaxed feeling somewhere in the pit of her stomach. Her skin began to crawl, and she knew that her nipples were alert against the thin fabric. And she wished she'd kept her drawers on.

"Okay," he said finally, in a voice so sudden and loud in the big shadowed room that Sarah jumped violently. "Better than I thought. C'mere."

While she'd been in the john, he'd dragged out a sort of platform about six feet square and a foot high. It was covered with a threadbare old piece of carpet and didn't look too uncomfortable.

He began to instruct her in how he wanted her to sit, directing her with his voice from a few feet away. When at last she had achieved something of what he desired, he touched her for the first time, tucking one foot under the other leg and moving her elbows forward a fraction of an inch. He was gentle, detached. Sarah relaxed completely.

He worked and she sat, both in total silence. He had arranged her so that she could not see the lump of clay he was working on; it was just beyond the range of her peripheral vision, and she dared not move even her eyes. She didn't have her glasses on anyway, so the whole effort would have been wasted. After what seemed like hours, he told her to take a break; by the time she moved her head, he'd thrown a cloth over the thing. Sarah's curiosity was overwhelming.

"Can't I see it?" she pleaded.

"Not until it's finished," he growled. "You hungry?"

"Starved," she grinned. "You must have heard my stomach rumbling all the way over here."

"Good," he grunted. "Go home then. See you next week. Same time."

Sarah wanted to hit him, but he would have expected that. Instead she strode grandly into the lavatory, changed her clothes, and thrust the tunic at him on her way out.

"Take it home and iron it," he said evenly. "Wash it, too, if you think it needs it."

Sarah stuffed the thing into her purse and stormed out. What made him so damn sure she would come back?

When she showed up the following Saturday, after spending New Year's Day huddled by the stove grading test papers, she found him in a rage.

"Where the hell've you been?" he demanded with such violence that she nearly bolted down the stairs. She was here; she was on time. What the hell was he bitching about? "I've destroyed the other one. Completely wrong. Soon's you left I smashed it into the wall. Shoulda been going in a completely different direction. All wrong. Must have been frigging out of my mind. Been eating at me all week. Have to start from the beginning."

Sarah saw the huge greasy splat on the wall by the doorway. The thing must have weighed over fifty pounds. Maybe he'd been aiming it at her.

"I don't read minds," she said icily. "You could have called me."

His anger left him. "I'm sorry. You're right." He grinned—the sun coming out from behind a cloud. "Guess I thought I was shouting so loud you could hear me in the Heights. Relax awhile and we'll get started."

It was always "we," as if Sarah were somehow an

active part of his creative process instead of something as inanimate as the clay itself. The strangeness of their relationship impressed itself upon Sarah as she stood this time on the threadbare carpet, shifting her weight from time to time to keep the pins and needles out of her feet. All he knew about her was her name, her age—only because she'd volunteered it—and whatever he could see of her through the homemade tunic. All she knew about him was what she saw about her in this room, and she never tired of studying them whenever he let her rest. She knew him from his sculptures, and from the pendulum swings of his moods. Yet within a span of less than two weeks she'd begun to feel as if she had known him for a very long time, as if they had grown up together in adjacent spheres of influence, and that if only the right conditions existed to break down the barriers that separated them . . .

Staring at the same blank patch of discolored wall made one's mind wander. Sarah was about to ask him if she could rest—her right leg had gone completely numb —when she heard him begin to curse.

"Shit!" he shouted, and Sarah swung her head involuntarily in time to see him mash an hour's work into oblivion. "All you need is the bow and the greyhound!"

"I beg your pardon?" she inquired, although she knew perfectly well what he meant. She broke her stance and sat down in a heap.

"Diana of the Virgin Snow," he sneered, slamming his tools around on the table. "Look, I know I promised you, but that—that frigging nightgown is distracting as hell. It's like I'm trying to work in a fog. Couldn't you—I don't know—make believe I'm a doctor or something?"

"I can't," Sarah almost pleaded.

"Hey," he was saying, avoiding her eyes, "I've kept my nose out of your business, but if you expect me to believe that in twenty-five years no man has ever seen you bare-ass—"

"Hardly," Sarah said grandly, sadly. "Six months ago I was a nun."

He was laughing, wheezing until she thought he would choke.

"Holy shit!" he gasped finally. "Holy shit, I sure can pick 'em!"

"I'm sorry," she said miserably.

He stopped laughing. "No. My fault," he said seriously. "The way you looked on that beach—loping around like a wild thing, so fucking free—I thought—"

"It's a front," Sarah sighed. "I'm really hopelessly inhibited."

He looked profoundly depressed, she thought, quite out of proportion to the disquietude one would expect of an artist deprived of a passable model.

"Hopelessly, huh?" he repeated.

She nodded.

"That's tough. That's a frigging shame. Sorry I wasted your time. You can go if you want."

Sarah did not move. She could not go; could not stay under the circumstances. Why did she refuse to do what he asked? She'd long ago decided that sex had been invented by God, not the devil. She would not be struck by lightning for posing in the nude any more than she had been for passing up Sunday mass. What was the matter with her?

"Are you afraid of me?" He was trying to figure her out. "If I was going to pull any fancy stuff, I would have done it long ago—on the beach, in the truck, last week with you running around pantsless. You think that little rag you're wearing would protect you if I made a grab for you right now? I could, you know. Nobody'd hear you."

"It's not that," Sarah said softly, knowing it, completely enervated.

"I swear to God I wouldn't touch you," he said sincerely. "It's not like I'm taking photographs. Nobody's gonna recognize you. Shit, time I'm through with it half the critics won't even know it's a female."

Sarah didn't answer, locked in her indecision.

"Hey, if it'll make you feel better, I already know what you look like." She must have looked terrified, because he quickly explained. "I'm an expert anatomist. You think that little rag can hide anything from me? All right, maybe a mole or a scar, or maybe you got more or less hair than I figured, but the rest's been right there in front of me since I saw you on the beach. Winter clothes and all."

"Then why—" Sarah began, but he interrupted her.

"So why do I still want you to take your clothes off?" he asked, cocking his head to one side and looking at her almost tenderly. "Because I'm not a scientist. I'm not just looking to see if you got the right number of ribs, and if your tits are in the right place and all that. I have to see the planes, the shadows, the goddamn beauty of you, for Chrissake. Whatta you want from me? I ain't a poet. I'm a sculptor. I can't explain any better than that."

She was beginning to yield. He was using the same arguments she'd been using herself.

"Look," he rumbled, his voice taking on a strangely emotional tone that caught Sarah off-guard, "all I'm asking for is the outside of you. You know what's all around you? All them funny-looking chunks of rock? Do they look like anything special? Those are my guts, little Miss Gartenhaus. These are the monsters I dream about. I was naked the minute I let you walk through that door."

Sarah knew it. It was what had brought her back here when everything reasonable pointed in the other direction. With a sigh she got to her feet, struggled with the fastening at the neck of the tunic, and awkwardly, self-consciously, slipped it over her head.

He looked away the minute he realized what she was

doing, retreating behind his worktable, posing her with
his voice while his eyes stayed averted, focused on his
tools. He waited until she was in the desired pose, her face
turned so that she could not see him seeing her, and then
he looked at her for a long, serious minute, and began to
work.

Sarah's whole body began to pulsate. The pins and
needles she felt this time were not in her feet.

The following Monday she was back in the classroom.
Anyone who studied her closely might have noticed a
more brilliant tone to her voice, more pride in her walk, a
secret glimmer in her eyes.

She went to Sam's studio every Saturday. She found
after a week or two that they didn't always start to work
right away, but would sometimes sit and talk for as much
as an hour. Their kinship deepened.

He told her about his childhood, about leaving home at
sixteen and never going back, about working on the piers
and going to school nights, about the woman of forty
who'd "adopted" him when he was broke, feeding him and
giving him a quiet place to work in exchange for an anti-
dote to loneliness. About the Art Students League, and
the various people he'd studied with. About the girl he'd
almost married who died of tuberculosis. About the fifteen
years of partial success and limited notoriety; about
battles with critics and fistfights with stevedores in the
waterfront bars he still frequented; about the endless
struggle to carve his own name in the art world without
being squeezed into some little category or "school."

Sarah listened—absorbed—understood. She told him
about herself, and began to find in her strange and mysti-
cal young adulthood not wasted time but an ordeal survived.

January melted into February. Sarah's birthday passed uncelebrated in her cold-water flat. Europe rumbled oppression, holocaust, and war. Sam abandoned his other projects and concentrated on Sarah. She began showing up on Sundays, on weeknights, and he drove her home in the battered pickup. Occasionally their hands would touch briefly on the cold seat just before she got out of the truck. In the studio, naked, she no longer felt awkward but walked around casually, without putting anything on, and without apology.

Sometime in March she stepped off the carpeted platform to take a breather, tripped lightly over to where he was soberly covering the clay model with its cloth, and kissed him, flutteringly, on the mouth.

He was startled for a moment, and then returned the kiss, his hands upheld like a bandit's to show that he wouldn't touch her without permission. His tongue began to work its way lazily into her mouth.

When she was in high school, they'd told her French kissing gave you mononucleosis, and babies. Sarah giggled wildly, slipped around the table that separated them, and threw her arms around him.

He pried her loose, gently, from his neck. "Whoa!" he grinned. "Hold your water a minute."

He shed the flannel shirt and the worn pants like a snakeskin, fumbled with underwear yellowed and ancient. Sarah watched him, drank him in—pale, concave-chested, almost hairless except for his legs and the heavy black thicket that— She inhaled sharply as he pressed himself against her, and they tumbled slow-motion to the floor.

She took him when the time came, without a sound, with no pain or bleeding, felt him pulsating inside her as he sucked her nipples at the same time the way a short man can do. She was still coming when he retreated, still throbbing and sighing on the worn wooden floor—

"God," Joan broke in rudely, unable to bear the preciousness of the mood Sarah had created. "And to think I bled like a pig!"

"Not me," Sarah murmured, lost in a memory almost forty years old. "We were a perfect fit."

XI

Every Saturday that Joan spent at Sarah's now began in exactly the same way. Joan would take out of her bag a set of flash cards with the alphabet on them. Patiently, doggedly, she would sit and recite them for Sarah, flipping each card toward the back of the deck as she said each letter. Good-humoredly, patronizingly, Sarah would recite along with her, trying not to betray by her tone of voice that she thought the entire thing was laughable. Joan was still convinced that the day—the moment— would come when the code within Sarah's brain would be broken, the light would penetrate, and the simple basic building blocks would become familiar again. Once that was accomplished . . .

". . . W, X, Y, Z," Sarah finished too quickly as Joan lingered on the V. "Shall I recite them backward? Inside out?"

"Will you have a little patience?" Joan demanded crossly. "You're not even looking at the cards!"

"It doesn't make any difference!" Sarah tried to explain for the thousandth time. "You could shuffle those cards right now—throw them on the floor and scramble them any way you like—put them back in a stack and start reciting 'A, B, C' all over again, and I would recite with you in total faith that the letter you said was the same one printed on the card, *because no matter how many times I see them I do not recognize them!*"

"But you *will,*" Joan insisted. "It's just a question of persistence. According to all the books I've been reading —I can read you one right now if you'd—"

"Never mind," Sarah interrupted.

"But they all say the same thing," Joan went on, not to be distracted. "It's impossible to replace brain cells that have been destroyed, but other cells can be trained to function to some degree like the old ones. . . ."

"A, B, C, D . . ." Sarah began to recite, blocking Joan out. "E, F, G, 'Twas brillig and the slithy toves did gyre and gimble in the wabe. All mimsy were the morogroves—' "

"All right!" Joan yelled, flinging the flash cards across the room. They scattered against the fireplace. "Shit, you've made your point! I just wish you'd explain to me how you intend to get your job back if you can't read!"

" 'Whan that Aprill with his shoures soote the droghte of March hath perced to the roote, and bathed every veyne in swich licour of which vertu engendred is the flour . . .' " Sarah said without batting an eye. "That's how. By referring to the brain cells that remain intact, to that fantastic storehouse known as the human memory. Do you think I have to look in the books to remember the

things I need to teach? Ask me a question—ask me anything about anything that was written in Europe from
the sixth century to fourteen ninety-nine, and I'll quote
you chapter and verse. Go on!"

"I wouldn't know what to ask you," Joan muttered
crossly. "And I wouldn't know if the answer you gave was
the right one. It's not my field."

"Neither is remedial reading," Sarah snapped.

Joan muttered something inaudible while she crawled
around picking up the flash cards.

"I beg your pardon?" Sarah tilted her head to one side.
"Forgive me, but I think the old ruin's getting hard of
hearing as well."

"I said 'screw you'!" Joan said heatedly, aiming the
flash cards at the wastebasket. Several missed and had to
be picked up a second time.

"That's the spirit!" Sarah said, pretending to be impressed. "Although I thought your generation preferred
'fuck.' "

Joan did not answer, but glared at the old woman.

"I appreciate what you're trying to do," Sarah said in a
quieter, more sincere tone. "Really, I do. I only wish I
could convince you that it will not work. Of course I'd do
anything to be able to read again, but it is not going to
happen. The important thing is that I can get around it.
Why do I ask you to read to me? Is it solely to keep me
amused? Rather, it's to keep my mind sharp, to keep the
rust off, to discover for me things I didn't know, to remind
me of things I may have forgotten. I hope it does the same
for you."

"I've been out of school a long time," Joan said sullenly.
"I can think of much better things to do with my time."

"Such as?" Sarah asked archly, but altered her tone
when she saw the resentment on Joan's face. "You're right,
of course. I'm not doing you any favors. I'm monopolizing

your time. But I'll remind you that I'm not pointing a gun at your head."

"There are other methods of coercion," Joan sulked.

"Oh, shit, leave then!" Sarah shot back. "Go—go hang around in singles bars, or whatever it is you'd do if you didn't come here. What else *would* you do on a Saturday afternoon, except spend it at the laundromat? Go. Maybe you'll meet the man of your dreams on the rinse cycle. I don't believe you!"

Joan said nothing. What difference did it make what she said, when Sarah already had all the answers? Yes, she had been tense lately. Yes, she did have trouble getting to sleep. Yes, she had been having strange erotic dreams when she finally did get to sleep. But how did Sarah surmise all of that from an argument about flash cards?

"I know what it is," Sarah said, narrowing her eyes at Joan. "I know. You get used to sex, however mediocre it may be, and then when you haven't got it at all anymore— I've been that route. On the one hand you feel very horny; on the other you start weeping about how old you are and how nothing good is ever going to happen to you again. Well, buck up, old girl. It's never as bad as it seems. How old are you now?"

"Twenty-eight."

"An absolute antique." Sarah shook her head. "My, my. Over the hill. I want you to know I was over forty the last time I was propositioned."

"Did you accept?" Joan couldn't resist it.

"Another time!" Sarah evaded. "Find something to read."

"I don't feel like reading now," Joan said. "Could we just talk for a while?"

"You mean could *I* just talk for a while." Sarah frowned, retreating into herself. "You've managed to get quite a lot out of me lately, haven't you?"

"Does it bother you?" Joan inquired archly, turning one of Sarah's techniques back on her.

"Yes and no," the older woman said cautiously. "At my age one spends a considerable time reliving the past. But it's not until one tries to tell it to someone else that the details become acutely—I might say painfully—clear again."

"You don't have to say any more," Joan said warmly, suddenly aware of how much she was asking.

She felt she and Sarah had become close friends in the past few months. But a true friend ought to know when not to ask. Was she being too nosy? There were so many things she wanted to know—why Sarah never had any children, why she never remarried after Sam's death— but did she have the right to ask?

"And leave you in midair? Leave you to conjecture all sorts of romantic crap?" Sarah demanded, mischief glittering in her eyes. "My dear, the position I'm in regarding what I've told you of my past is like being a little bit pregnant. If I don't tell you the whole story, the one you'll surmise will be far more lurid than the truth. Besides, maybe someday you can write my memoirs."

Joan opened her mouth to object, but Sarah shushed her. "Have a sense of humor!" she hissed. "Do you want to hear the rest of the story or not?"

"When one married at the advanced age of twenty-six— at least when one was of my generation and the year was nineteen forty—one's only plans for the future consisted of having a child before one was thirty. I wanted to have Sam's baby as much as I wanted him to become a world-renowned sculptor—in short, as much as I wanted anything. What did I want for myself? That question is so easy to ask nowadays, when the important thing is to have a raised consciousness and to be out carving up the

world for oneself. Back then it didn't matter. I had found
what I wanted for that time. I saw making a baby as being
every bit as creative as sculpting or painting or anything
else. And Sam was my safe haven against the horrors that
had haunted me out of the convent. I didn't need anything
else for that moment. I finished my master's thesis and
kept on teaching until I was in my fifth month and
started to show. The nuns asked me to leave then. The
effect of my—ahem—condition upon impressionable young
girls . . . They thought babies grew under cabbage leaves,
I suppose.

"I used to sit and speculate about what might have
happened if that baby had lived, if I had had others. It's
possible I might have ended up exactly where I am today,
and it's equally possible I might have been just another
housewife, living her life through her children. But I
doubt that. Anyway, what purpose does it serve to think
about such things now? At this distance I can look back
and say there must have been a reason why it happened
that way, but at the time . . .

"I remember going to the doctor for checkups in the
early months. He used to tease me—most doctors have no
sense of humor, but this one was all right. He told me mine
was the most boring pregnancy he'd ever seen.

"The fact was, I felt marvelous. I never had morning
sickness. I did feel tired, found I needed ten hours' sleep
instead of my usual six, but other than that—my acne
cleared up, I gained weight for the first time in my life . . ."

. . . and watched her tiny breasts puff out into something resembling the genuine article—symbolizing fertility,
self-sufficiency: an organism capable, after its initial
awakening by the prodding sperm, of growing and nurtur-
ing an entirely perfect and separate person who was
swelling the hitherto flat, fish-white belly, with its misplaced freckle, until it looked as if it would burst, and the
freckle stretched and grew with it, and the whole apparatus

walked around ahead of her like an unwieldy parcel that kept bumping into things, a parcel moving and churning to its own private rhythm, slamming its feet against her spine and its head against her bladder until she had to pee sometimes twice in an hour and always in the middle of the night.

Until it got to be such a presence that she began holding long discourses with it, to which it responded with a coded pattern of thumps or else a thoughtful silence, especially when Sam put his big scarred hand on her belly to say hello And she began playing music for it and caressing it in rhythm until "it" became She without any doubt as to her sex and was given a name and imagined for dominant genes such as Sam's huge radiant eyes without his equally huge and only slightly less radiant ears Little She who would be perhaps a musical prodigy or a great actress or something incongruous like an anthropologist or a mathematician

And Europe rumbled Poland and France shrieking in disbelief and trickling rumors of atrocity washed across the ocean like the flotsam of a great shipwreck and a woman with waist-length auburn hair and unusually masculine hands and a swollen belly sat by the radio and prayed not the rote prayers Now I Lay Me Down to Sleep of her very orthodox childhood but the silent wordless plea of her newfound philosophical existential Christian If I Should Die Before I Wake freedom prayed for peace

And a mad swarm of Japanese planes long-anticipated because the Pentagon had cracked their code months before but the man in the whirlpool bath had decided that a war economy was just what the country needed to bring it its last big bootstrap step out of a too-long-for-his-political-health depression blasted several thousand men's souls into the warm oblivion of a Polynesian ocean

And Maidanek Dachau Bergen-Belsen kept spewing

their eye-stinging soot into the European sky until the sun drowned nightly in blood and the stench settled down onto the soil and the souls that in a thousand years or in such time as the chronicles of atrocity are no longer kept might by as many tears be finally washed clean

And the woman with the masculine hands and the swollen belly began to feel a tightening around her middle toward the end of the seventh month and the doctor said it didn't sound serious but she might as well come in during office hours that afternoon and they'd have a look

And six hours later what had seemed to be a normal if premature labor had become a problem of placental presentation the afterbirth breaking loose and putting its gory opacity between She and the open air throttling strangling struggling She *in utero* without a chance to catch the briefest glimpse of the world beyond And further complications threatened the now heavily drugged woman with the masculine hands limp against the just-as-white sterile sheeting her auburn hair cropped for the second time in her life insanely for supposedly hygienic reasons which didn't matter because it would fall out in clumps when the ordeal was over The attending surgeon zipping across the overblown freckle with the scalpel while a nurse with a scapular pinned to her bra readied to baptize the remains of She now tangled in her mother's intestines after the uterus exploded under the strain And they took what was left of the uterus and lopped it off cleanly at the top of the cervix leaving the ovaries bruised but intact sparing Sarah a few hormones to combat the rampant aging which is often a side effect of hysterectomy and began to restitch her.

The scar tissue would obliterate the freckle. The pain she felt when she finally hauled out from under the blanket of ether was so intermixed, physical with psychic, that it was months before she could recognize which was which, and then only because the physical had at last subsided. Months before she could stop staring at the stranger in her mirror and simply cry.

Cry in the arms of the newly assigned air-raid warden who had volunteered to do anything, *anything*, to keep his mind occupied while his wife was in the hospital. Cry in the arms of the man who could no longer bear to go to his studio, could no longer bear to work on his soul pieces, but who had given over to full-time teaching and, when the draft took most of his students, went to work sticking decals on gliders in a defense plant because pacifism could not pay the massive medical bills. . . .

"God, Sarah!" Joan said. "I mean, millions of women just have babies, with no medical attention or anything. Drop them like litters of kittens. One of my great-grand-mothers had twenty-two. It isn't right, that's all. Why do things like that have to happen to someone who—"

"Relax," Sarah told her, and released Joan's hands, as if realizing for the first time that the girl had slipped onto the couch beside her and was holding her hands as if her life depended on it. Some of the rigidity left Sarah's spine and she slumped back against the cushions.

"It was over thirty years ago," she said. "It doesn't bother me anymore."

She was lying. Joan's hands ached from the pressure Sarah had been exerting on them.

"I am no longer insulted by it," Sarah said grandly, try-ing to make Joan believe her.

"Really?" Joan was skeptical. "But it was as if part of your life was torn right out of your hands. It must have made you bitter."

Sarah looked at her sadly. "Blow your nose," she said, bossing a small child. "I told you, it was thirty years ago. More. And you have to understand what was going on around me. There was this thing called a war, you see. Other women were losing husbands, sons, in a situation that made even less sense than mine. My tragedy was a natural one, something that had happened to women for centuries. I was fortunate to have escaped with my life. It made a bizarre kind of sense, as opposed to this great idiotic man-made tragedy that was thundering all around us. I recovered quickly, believe me."

Joan wanted to have Eric with her, wanted to be able to squeeze him and hold his forty pounds of reassurance on her lap. She needed him to block out the phantom of Sarah's thirty-seven-year-old daughter. She kept seeing a second Sarah, younger but with the same intensity, the same vitality, perhaps bringing her own children—now approaching adolescence—to visit their grandmother for the weekend.

To be here in my place, Joan thought with a tremor. I am not your daughter! she wanted to remind the old woman; I'm nearly a decade too young, my coloring's wrong, and there is an unwritten law that dictates that daughters cannot coexist with their natural mothers. If I *were* your daughter, I would undoubtedly feel the same animosity toward you that I now feel for my real mother.

"This must be very depressing for you," Sarah apologized, trumpeting inelegantly into a handkerchief. "You're young, and you're sitting there thinking about your own child. You're much too close to it. I forget about things like that. I'm sorry."

"You're sorry!" Joan was unreasonably angry. "It happened to you, and you're apologizing to me? I should apologize to you for being so nosy."

Sarah raised her hands in mock-horror. "Spare me the pity, for God's sake!" she begged. "If there's anything I can't stand . . ."

She didn't finish, and neither of them spoke for a while. Sarah made supper, and Joan put the stereo on, and they listened in silence.

"You haven't asked me how your campaign is going,"

Joan said while they were eating, hoping to stay off the topic of children, past and present, dead and living.

"You keep using up my postage stamps," Sarah observed dryly, struggling with her knife. She was past the stage where she would allow anyone to help her cut her food, but the battle to control her weak right hand was unnerving to watch. "I assume you're putting them to good use."

"Let me show you what we've got so far." Joan put down her fork and got her tote bag. In it was a folder full of letters, possibly two dozen in all. "Okay," she said, riffling through them. "We've gotten nearly twenty letters back from alumnae, offering to help in any way they can."

She read off the names, and Sarah nodded. "Reliable types, every one of them," she said. "It's nice to know one's had some influence upon the people one sought to teach. But now that they've written to you, what do you propose to have them do?"

"There are two schools of thought," Joan said, an edge of irritation creeping into her voice.

"Meaning the Helen school and the Celia school," Sarah nodded, understanding. "Are those two still squabbling?"

"Yes," Joan sighed. "Anyway, Celia wants as many alumnae who are interested to show up at the college for a solidarity demonstration. Helen thinks they should just write individual letters of protest to Sister Francis."

"And what does the Joan school say?" Sarah raised her good eyebrow.

"I say try both," Joan said. "Letters first, to make our position clear. Then I'd like to hold some sort of rally on the day you have your hearing."

"The Great Compromiser." Sarah smiled her half-smile. "It's a joy to watch a legal mind at work."

"What do you think?" Joan asked, cutting short the lecture she knew was coming.

Sarah thought for a moment. "You're my campaign

manager," she said. "I'll take your advice. Who are the other letters from?"

Joan separated a handful of letters from the stack. These were printed on the best kinds of embossed letterhead stationery. Again she rattled off some names.

"I remember those girls particularly well," Sarah acknowledged. "Why did you separate them from the others?"

"Because the others are ordinary bourgeois citizens like you and me," Joan said, patting the special letters importantly, "but right here we have two doctors—an obstetrician/gynecologist and a shrink—one corporate executive, and one state assemblywoman. And they all have two things in common."

"Aside from a substantial income, you mean?"

"The income has something to do with it," Joan admitted. "All four of these women give huge amounts to the endowment fund every year."

"And?" Sarah asked.

"And all of them intend to withhold this year's contributions until you have your hearing," Joan said smugly. "And based on the outcome of the hearing . . ." She did not finish.

Sarah thought for a moment, digesting it. "It smacks of blackmail," she said finally, making sure it was the right word. "Definitely smacks of blackmail. I don't like it."

"It's not blackmail," Joan argued. "They're not demanding you be reinstated. They simply want a guarantee of a fair hearing. That's all you're asking for, isn't it?"

"Oh, but who's to say what's fair?" Sarah demanded suddenly, a plaintive note creeping into her voice. She passed a hand over her eyes, looking very tired and older than she should. "God, I don't know, Joan. Maybe we're getting in too deep with this thing. Maybe I'm not competent to teach after all, and getting all these people to put themselves on the line for me—I just don't know. Maybe we shouldn't be doing it this way."

Joan put the letters down on the kitchen table and said nothing. This was not like Sarah—at least it wasn't a side of Sarah she had ever seen before, or wanted to see. The Sarah she knew was confident, decisive.

"It's up to you," Joan said quietly, somewhat alarmed at what she had caused. She'd thought she was doing the right thing. "I thought you were a fighter, that's all."

"I *am* a fighter!" Sarah snapped, rallying a little. "When I know what I'm fighting for! But this—this smacks of pure egotism to me, and I'm not about to make a public spectacle of myself and embarrass a number of well-intentioned people in the process. I think this thing stinks."

"Or you think maybe you can't pull it off," Joan said impulsively.

"That too!" Sarah said, picking up her knife and fork again. She attacked the food on her plate, only to have the knife bounce out of her hand. "Shit!" she hissed as it clattered on the linoleum.

Joan reached under the table and retrieved the knife. She pulled Sarah's plate toward her and began to cut the food.

"There was a lady I knew once," she said evenly, without looking up from what she was doing. "A teacher of mine—marvelous person, really—who made a speech at an antiwar rally in—oh, I guess it must have been the late Sixties. And this lady said something that really impressed me. She said—"

"Don't remind me of that!" Sarah groaned, her hands clenching compulsively as if she would seize the plate from Joan.

"No, but really," Joan said, sliding the plate back toward Sarah and putting down the knife and fork, "I think I ought to tell you what this lady had to say. I think it has a lot to do with the situation at hand."

Sarah glowered. "I know. A lot of bullshit clichés about small individuals becoming powerful enough to stop the big guns . . . passive resistance . . . grains of sand in the machinery of war—I think that was a phrase I used. It got you kids all riled up, and got me a round of applause and a couple of hate letters from the YAF, but what the hell does that have to do with anything?"

"It's an analogous situation," Joan pointed out. Big words were starting to occur to her, a pleasant sensation after years of talking to babies and drunks and supermarket clerks. "I'm not saying your losing your job is exactly like the Vietnam War, but—"

"Jesus!" was all Sarah said.

"I'm not getting through to you at all, am I?" Joan exhaled. "Let's put it this way—have you noticed the one thing that Celia, Helen, and I agree on unanimously?"

"I can't say I have," Sarah remarked. "This is all such bullshit, really. Tomorrow I want you to draft a letter to each one of these lovely people and tell them to forget—"

"Sarah," Joan said patiently, her mind flickering back to find the first time she'd crossed the border from "Dr. Morrow" to "Sarah." She couldn't locate it; it was like the first time she'd referred to Mrs. O'Dell—Vicki's for Chrissake mother—as simply Helen. When did one become enough of an adult to call other adults by their first names?

"Sarah," Joan said again, "see if you can guess how come we never bothered to contact the students."

"I'll bite. Why?" Sarah demanded, playing along. "You ran out of stamps?"

"Not exactly," Joan said, in no mood for games. "We came to the conclusion that ninety percent of them don't give a shit."

She waited for a response, but none was forthcoming.

"So?" Sarah said after a long silence.

"Well, don't you agree?" was Joan's response. "Everybody you talk to says the same thing. These kids are completely self-interested. You mention something like Vietnam to them and they don't know what you're talking about."

"They were only children when that happened," Sarah explained. "You forget there's a decade between you."

"I mean anything like that," Joan argued. "Something contemporary—South Africa. They have no idea."

Sarah dismissed it. "You'll remember my field is medieval literature, not current events," she said. "I tend not to notice."

"Bullshit!" Joan sneered.

"All right, I notice!" Sarah shot back, out of patience. "But I don't judge. I teach. The Baby Boom ended in sixty-two, you know. Many of these kids are younger siblings of people your age who burned themselves out on drugs and hopeless causes. Many of these kids were unwanted—good Catholic parents and rhythm and all that jazz—and they see the world differently. Maybe they're not as creative and emotional as you people were, but they're decent human beings in their own way. And what the hell, I repeat, does it have to do with me?"

She was out of breath. She hauled herself up from the table and started clearing the dishes, slamming them into the sink, shoving leftovers into the refrigerator.

"You're in my way," she snapped at Joan the first time the younger woman attempted to help.

"Will you listen for a minute?" Joan sighed, feeling a headache creeping up the back of her neck. "All I wanted to say was that we feel—Celia and Helen and I—that the kids would not stand behind you, and the administration, knowing that, figured they could quietly usher you out the back door. That's why we wanted a show of support from important people who—"

"If the kids don't care about me, I've no business trying to teach them." Sarah slammed the refrigerator door a final time. "And if I cannot defend myself satisfactorily, the whole thing will be a bust. And I don't want to talk about it anymore!"

She stormed into the living room, and Joan followed her.

"You look exhausted," Joan observed. "Listen, I'm sorry if I'm harassing you. Let me leave early tonight so you can get some rest."

"Stay," Sarah said, but not as a command; it was an option: Stay if you want to, but don't feel obligated just because . . . "It is my intention to turn in a little early this evening, but I'd like you to stay. I like to have someone in the house."

To keep off the prowlers or the loneliness? Joan wondered, but didn't ask it. It was not a question a friend would ask, since a friend would already know the answer.

She picked up a magazine and began to read to herself, but her concentration didn't last long. The moment's argument was forgotten. She was thinking about Sarah's baby again.

How could anyone live with the loss of a child, with the knowledge that there could never be another one? Did you spend the rest of your life wondering what might have been?

"Yes and no," Sarah said suddenly, making Joan jump out of her skin.

"What?" Joan half-shouted, nearly dropping the magazine. She'd thought she was used to the old woman's psychic powers by now.

"Gradually there occur days when one doesn't think about it," Sarah said. "Then the days become weeks, and even months. When the time comes that you can no longer remember how old she would be without stopping and subtracting it in your head, then you know you have won some kind of victory."

Joan threw the magazine aside. "But you never accept something like that!" she challenged.

"There was a war going on," Sarah pointed out for the second time. "I managed to find other things to occupy my mind. I did volunteer work in a veterans' hospital for a while—that'll do it, let me tell you. I remember sitting up half the night with a woman whose husband had been shot up in Italy. He was a quadriplegic; half his face had been blown away; there were shell fragments in his spleen. He died that night, thank God, but she was sitting there for hours trying to figure out what to tell her children when she brought this horror home from the hospital. One of the chaplains finally took her home in a cab, and I went home to my own whole, beautiful husband and listened to him stomping around bitching about how keeping his hands in water all day sticking decals on 'those fucking death machines' was going to ruin him so he'd never sculpt again, and I realized—"

"That by helping others less fortunate than yourself you would become a stronger and better person," Joan said dryly, not wanting to hear it from Sarah. "God had given meaning to your life by depriving you of the one thing you wanted most."

"Don't be sarcastic; it's very unattractive," Sarah advised her strongly. "And whatever you do, don't anthropomorphize *my* God for me, will you?"

Her voice was brittle. Joan realized she had gone overboard. "I'm sorry," she said quickly. "I only meant—"

"You'd better be sorry," Sarah warned, her eyes glinting narrowly. "At your age, one would hope you had outgrown that adolescent tendency to sneer at someone's philosophy simply because it runs counter to your own.

"When you're my age," she continued, "you are allowed to indulge in the belief—however misplaced—that your life has had some meaning. To simpify it by saying that I was not permitted to have children in order that I might perform a greater service to mankind is immature. It's cheap. If I'd had any particular sense of mission, or whatever you'd like to call it, I would have taught in the slums or worked in the charity wards or volunteered for Europe when the slaughter was over; I'd have plunged in up to the elbows in the slime and disease and starvation that was there.

"Instead, I did my stint of charity work within a subway ride of my own warm, comfortable home. I couldn't teach for a while—technical things like my certification lapsing, and emotional things like not wanting to be near other people's children. I did a lot of miscellaneous things— secretarial work, real estate, one entire summer devoted to the writing of an epic poem that never got finished— and when I felt strong enough I went back to teaching. But as for a sense of mission—"

"All I meant was—" Joan began. What the hell *had* she meant anyway?

"What you meant was," Sarah interrupted, as if the words were written on Joan's forehead and she could read them there though she could not read them on a page, "what you meant was, did I accept what had happened in the sense that I felt there was a *reason* for it? I don't honestly know. One doesn't see things objectively at such times. You with your alcoholic husband ought to know that. One doesn't think at all, really. One reacts. One *does*. One survives. Later on there is time for philosophizing. Someday I will understand why my child had to die. Someday I will understand why I lost Sam the way I did. Someday I may even figure out the reason for this latest lunacy, this vanishing of the one thing that is essential to my way of life. Imagine, I am a Ph.D. who can't recognize the alphabet written on a set of flash cards. Was there ever anything more ludicrous? But right now all I have to do is survive. Outlive it. I'm not the type to curse God and die. I wouldn't give him the satisfaction."

She was trembling all over. Joan watched her cautiously, afraid to move, afraid to do anything that might increase her agitation. What would she do if the old woman had another stroke while she was standing there, or a heart attack, or . . . How could she get her to calm down?

"I'm sorry I said anything!" Joan said loudly, angrily. If Sarah didn't shut up soon, she was going to start throwing things. "Can we get off it for a while? Christ, you're a maniac!"

Sarah laughed suddenly, wildly, and stopped trembling. Joan relaxed.

"You're a pain in the ass, that's all," Sarah said lightly. "But you're right—enough is enough. I'm going to bed. Tomorrow I'll tell you about Sam. Sam requires at least a whole day's telling. Then we'll have the whole story done and we can concentrate on our reading and our— battle plan. Time is growing short."

"Agreed," Joan said, and helped the older woman up the stairs.

Joan didn't know why she should feel so exhausted; all she'd been doing was listening. It was not quite nine o'clock, but she was ready for bed. She would shower in Sarah's huge bathroom and then sack out. Sarah's guest room had become more comfortable almost than her own apartment.

She was heading down the hall on her way to the bathroom, pinning her hair up, her mouth full of clips, when she heard the phone ring in Sarah's room.

Joan was not an eavesdropper by nature, but Sarah's room was adjacent to the bathroom, and if one left the door open for a moment . . . Joan wondered who it could be. Sarah's brother had made his obligatory weekly call that afternoon. Who else . . . ?

In her room, Sarah sat down on the edge of the bed and lifted the receiver.

"Hello?"

"I'm back," the voice said gruffly, without introduction. "Plane got in suppertime."

"It's about time!" she said. "Weren't you supposed to get in by Labor Day?"

"Yeah, last weekend," he growled. "They just saved having to get a sub for my classes. I have exactly one day to unwind before I'm back at it again. Screws me up completely. Wanted to hit the beach for a few days at least, but tomorrow's rain, and I wanted to see you anyway, before I—oh, shit, how *are* you?"

There was a tenderness in the question that dissipated the bitterness of the first part of his monologue.

"I'm well," Sarah said strongly, refusing to let it be otherwise. "Extremely well."

"You sound clearer," he said, pleased. "Much better than when I left. The holes are gone."

"Joan has kept the rust from forming in your absence." Sarah half-smiled. "Lovely young lady. Poor self-concept, but we're working on it."

"Really?" he asked, not listening. "Jeez, it's good to hear your voice. I worried about you all summer. But you understand I couldn't write."

"Of course not!" Sarah giggled mischievously. "I should hate to have someone read one of your letters *to* me. All that florid prose. I couldn't stand it!"

"And I couldn't exactly make a whole lot of long-distance calls from where I was. I called my mother half a dozen times, that's about all. Cripes, the monastery where they put me up has a *pay phone* out in the hall—"

"Pietro," she interrupted him, "I under*stand*."

"I'm sorry," he said, exhaling wearily. "It's been such a long time. I can't wait to see you."

"Nor I you," Sarah replied.

"How about tomorrow?"

Sarah thought for a moment. "In the afternoon," she said. "Joan's spending the night, and—"

"Of course," Pietro said. She could see him nodding. "I have the twelve-thirty mass tomorrow anyway. Around two, then? . . . Fine. Sleep well."

"*Und du auch*," Sarah whispered. It was a small joke; they'd spoken in German for years until—

"Wonderful!" Pietro was surprised. "See? I told you it would come back. And the rest will, too, in time. You'll see. Tomorrow then. Goodnight."

(PRIEST: *Dominus vobiscum.*

FAITHFUL: *Et cum spiritu tuo.*)

"Goodnight," Sarah said.

When she had hung up the phone, Sarah could hear the water running in the shower.

XII

What is it we see in each other?
Absolutely nothing.
Oh, true, small things—
A look, the rococo of a character—
But most noticeable is the void,
The blank, the empty.
The silhouette etched into the landscape
Of that psyche,
Familiar because it is one's own. . . .

SARAH MORROW

There were three bedrooms in Sarah's house. There was the huge back bedroom that was Sarah's private lair; the odd little center room overlooking the courtyard, where Joan stayed most weekends; and the front room, once the master bedroom, now transformed into something of an archive.

They were sitting on an old steamer trunk since there were no chairs, and Joan's eyes were streaming from the dust. She sneezed several times, trying to be unobtrusive about it.

Sarah looked at the book in her lap a final time, then slammed it shut. Joan sneezed again.

"I'b sorry," she gasped. "Id's the dust."

"Gets to you after a while," Sarah nodded, her eyes watering for different reasons. She craned her thin neck to see to the top of the musty bookshelves, to take in at a single glance all the things she hadn't looked at since months before her stroke.

The room was a foreign country now. She could no longer read the titles on the books—Sam's books—that she'd kept in all their ragged finery for all these years. She'd made Joan read all the titles to her, pointing out with particular pride the one she'd given Sam one Christmas that had so entranced him he'd taken to bringing it to his studio to read. She showed Joan three chalky marks on the binding—fossilized prints from Sam's clay-covered fingers, preserved like the relics of some saint.

Sarah couldn't even read the titles of Sam's sculptures, their photos carefully preserved in the scrapbook she cradled in her lap. It didn't really matter, since she knew them all from memory, but it upset her especially. This scrapbook was the only extant record, a quarter of a century after his death, of the life and work of Samuel Morrow. The pictures had been taken by a friend, a professional photographer, who had put them in this album and presented them to Sarah only after Sam's death, afraid he would destroy the pictures as he'd almost succeeded in destroying the works themselves. Sarah held the book open on her lap, trying to make just one title spring forth recognizably from the page, but it was no use.

The only things, then, that Sarah could still feel comfortable with in this room were the photos of Sam—some blown up and retouched from miniatures, some only fuzzy snapshots taken with an old-fashioned Brownie Starmite. They were all black-and-white, and none of them did him justice, but they were all she had. There was Sam in his studio—a balding, hunched figure barely distinguishable from the stone he worked on except for the requisite flannel shirt. Sam in repose—asleep beneath a multicolored afghan by an empty fireplace, a large tiger cat dozing on his chest. Sam at a picnic with a crowd of someday-to-be-famous artists and actors and writers, a bottle of beer in one hand, the index finger of the other jabbing the air as he strove to make a point. And Sam in a formal portrait—a pipe weighing down his petulant lower lip, his great luminous eyes staring in melancholy disbelief over the photographer's shoulder.

Sarah's eyes were watering, but not from the dust.

"Let's get out of here," she said sharply, pulling herself up suddenly with her cane and thumping out of the room and down the stairs, shutting off the light and leaving Joan to scramble after her, barking her shin on the corner of the steamer trunk in the shades-down twilight.

"So," Sarah wheezed in the living room, breathless from the stairs, "now you've seen the professional Sam. What do you want now—the historical Sam, the private Sam, or the Sam that could have been if circumstances had been other than they were?"

"Whatever you want to tell me," Joan said quietly. "I'd be interested in all of them."

"Okay," Sarah said, making herself comfortable. "Settle in, because it's going to be a long story."

Why had the marriage worked? Why had the gnomish, taciturn artist in his forty-second year married the long-legged girl who in twenty-five years had never kissed a man? Why had the sculptor who could only speak through his work, who in adolescence had been kept by women older than his mother, who had no formal education beyond the tenth grade, seemed so well suited to the eloquent schoolmarm with her master's degree and her convent manners? Why had the combination clicked from the very beginning, and why did it get so much better with age?

Sarah's family clucked about it endlessly. Poor Sarah, they fretted. Just because everyone else she knew was long married and had at least three kids, and just because she'd flunked out of the convent, did she have to overcompensate by marrying such an old man? And the way they met! God only knew what had been going on in that studio. An old man, with a weak heart (rejected by the draft board, don't you know), who couldn't even hold a regular nine-to-five job, but had the gall to call himself an artist! Poor Sarah! She would end up supporting him someday, just you wait and see.

After she lost her baby, Sarah drifted further from the family, putting in her dutiful appearance at weddings and wakes, tolerating as much of the clucking as she could, and going her way. After a few years, when Sam neither deserted her nor dropped dead from a heart attack, some of the clucking stopped.

When the war was over, Sam got his teaching job back. Once in a great while there would be an exhibit of his work at the campus gallery, and he managed to sell a few existing sculptures or pick up a commission from time to time. These sales barely covered the rent on the studio and the cost of transporting the pieces from one place to another.

When Sarah turned thirty, she too went back to teaching. With two salaries, she and Sam were able to move from their cramped little apartment near the warehouses a block from his studio. They bought a fire-damaged brownstone for a pittance and redecorated it themselves, transforming it into an absolute showcase.

Creative people gravitated toward them, at least the sort of creative people who were chronically unemployed. There were actors who waited tables more often than they performed; poets who smoked hashish and left sam-

ples of their work on the bathroom wall; college kids with
the blueprint for world salvation but not enough carfare
to get downtown; painters who painted over unsold can-
vases because they couldn't afford to buy new ones; birth-
control activists; radicals; jazz musicians—the list was
endless.

They met at the Morrows' house once a month or so,
sat around drinking cheap wine and reordering the universe. At least one of them would be staying with Sarah
and Sam temporarily—"just until I get back on my feet"
—paying their room and board in weeded gardens, reup-
holstered couches, recipes for homemade wine. Some of
them left their paintings or manuscripts or portfolios
around for months at a time, "for safekeeping." The
house began to resemble a museum.

Sarah presided at the parties, gliding around in her
bare feet, feeding the hungry ones with spaghetti and
sausages, steering the heavy drinkers out to the yard
for some air, floating from one heady conversation to the
next. Sam stayed hunched in the corner by the mantel,
nursing a can of beer, holding forth on the Destiny of
Art in his plodding, monosyllabic manner, while everyone within earshot was polite enough to listen, if not to
agree.

"It don't make any difference who's doing what in
sculpture. My chief thing is stone. Epstein's spent years
trying to make bronze look like clay—don't ask me why.
Somebody else out in the boondocks may be fucking
around with wire coat hangers," he would say, jabbing
the index finger braced around the beer can at the nearest
of his listeners. "Who the hell says you got to belong to
some 'school' to be a legit artist? The first guy who
clawed his way into that cave and scratched that buffalo
on the wall at Lascaux—what the hell school'd he belong
to?"

They always laughed, ignoring the fact that he persisted in pronouncing it "lasscokes" no matter how often Sarah corrected him.

When they were all gone except the current boarder and those too drunk to stir, Sarah and Sam would clear away the debris, leave the dishes unwashed, and make love in the shower or in front of the fire or, once (in the middle of June and before there were tall buildings in the area or too many planes going over), up on the roof as the sun rose, after which they threw a blanket over themselves and went to sleep.

Some of the people at those parties did become famous eventually. One became a best-selling novelist, one a minor political figure, another an established actress. Several of the painters became proficient enough to earn a living. Of the rest, many went back to school for a degree in something useful, settling into respectable anonymity; several wasted their lives altogether—one died from an overdose of Nembutal, another from a botched abortion; and the others dropped out of sight completely.

Except for one aspiring art student. Sam once told him in a rage that he had absolutely no talent, that not only was he wasting his time and his parents' money, but he was using up valuable stone that would be better off paving somebody's driveway. Without a word, the young man dropped out of school and joined the marines; and just before his hitch was up, he found himself being recruited by the FBI.

And on February 9, 1950, Senator Joseph R. McCarthy of Wisconsin gave his infamous speech at Wheeling, West Virginia, in reference to "card-carrying Communists" in government and elsewhere, and the witch-hunt was on.

And the former aspiring art student, his FBI badge snug in his breast pocket and his crew cut freshly polished, paid a visit to the dean of his old college and casually mentioned the parties at Sam Morrow's house and some of the people he had seen, or thought he had seen, there.

And, yes, Sam and Sarah knew that several of their friends had flirted with the Party back in the Thirties, and at least one of them still kept his expired membership card tucked behind his Equity card for old times' sake, but neither of them had ever . . .

And within six months, Sam's contract had expired and was not renewed; and since he was a year shy of having tenure, he was faced with having to make a living solely through his sculptures. No other college was interested in his credentials.

He threw all his energies into a single massive exhibit, noising it about among his students that whatever didn't sell he was going to personally destroy with a sledgehammer. As the date of the exhibit approached, he and Sarah had endless roaring arguments. She tried to convince him to wait, to be patient, to survive on her salary until things got better. They had to get better, and in the meantime they could manage.

"I can't sit on my ass and let a woman support me," he would growl. "Can't you get that through your thick Kraut skull? When I was sixteen and I went days without eating, that was different. But I'm too old for that now. Jesus, Sarah, I love you. I'd do anything you ask, but I can't sit peacefully and watch you go off to work every day. If I can't work, they may as well throw me out with the garbage. I'm no good."

The exhibit was a debacle. Thirty-one of Sam's sculptures were shown. Four sold, and for less than he'd asked for them. On the last day, he holed up in the men's room with a quart of cheap whiskey and proceeded to drown in it. When he finally emerged with the prophesied sledgehammer clenched in his knotted fists, he was intercepted by two of his more muscular students; Sarah had called them and begged them to keep an eye on him. There was a scene. He managed a single abortive swing before they subdued him and all but carried him out of the hall, roaring obscenities and singing dirty songs while they stuffed him into the back seat of the car and took him home.

"I don't think he ever forgave me for that—for not letting him have the little scene he had orchestrated so grandly in his mind," Sarah said quietly, staring out the parlor window at the rain that had been spattering down for some time. The reflection of the rain on Sarah's face made her look as if she were crying, Joan thought, dismissing it as saccharine even as she thought it.

"Of course, I compounded my crime by taking it one step further." Sarah half-smiled, warmed by a particular thought. "Sam was too sick to move for nearly three days after that little episode. He never was much of a drinker. So while he was moaning and groaning upstairs with a big head and a queasy stomach, I quietly had all of his sculptures moved to a friend's studio for safekeeping. I wouldn't tell him what I'd done with them. I made him go to a notary with me and sign a statement swearing he wouldn't try to destroy them again. Oh, the names he called me that day! I think it was the closest he came to murder."

She was laughing now, an odd sound Joan hadn't heard since the classroom days, the cackle of a crazed witch. Joan wondered if she was pressing the old woman too much, pushing her too close to some sort of edge. What the hell was so funny?

"Sarah—" she began nervously, wanting to take hold of her and shake her until she stopped, "Sarah, for Chrissake—"

"Oh, God!" Sarah wheezed. "Hee-hee-hee! Oh, Jesus, the things we said to each other on the way home from the notary's office! Poor Sam! He was so damned pissed at what I was doing to him. He knew I had him this

time; knew I wasn't going to let him make his little gesture—going out with a bang and a crash. Poor Sam. If
he'd only known how it was going to turn out—if either
of us had only known—a bang and a crash . . ."

She was wiping the tears out of her eyes with her good
hand. Joan couldn't tell if they were tears of laughter or
tears from the sudden burst of sorrow that came with the
end of Sarah's monologue. The mood had changed so
drastically that neither of them had seen it coming.

"Oh, God, poor Sam!" Sarah said again. "He never
did find out how it was going to end."

She struggled for a long moment to control her voice,
while Joan scarcely breathed.

"After I made him sign the affidavit, we didn't speak
for the longest time," Sarah went on. "Oh, I don't mean
we were reduced to total silence or anything—we did
talk, but we weren't really saying anything. That went
on for a while, and he kept going out at all hours looking
for work. A commission—a birdbath—anything.

"He finally got something. There was a bank or something under construction in Manhattan—Upper East Side,
very posh—but they started running out of money at the
end. They'd already hired a big-name sculptor to do a
gigantic frieze for the front of the building, but he kept
raising his price until they refused to meet it, then he
walked out. They were stuck with all of these chunks of
precut marble sitting in the lobby of the building. They
couldn't install the vaults or the doors or anything until
they got the marble out of the way, and they decided
since they'd already bought and paid for it they might
just as well find a cut-rate sculptor to do something with
it. So they went around quietly looking for someone
who'd take a very small price for it. Sam heard about it,
showed up, and they couldn't refuse him. They insisted
he leave it unsigned—no point in raising eyebrows, after
all."

Joan was horrified. "I would have spit in their eyes!" she said with uncharacteristic vehemence.

"He had to do something," Sarah shrugged. "Besides, it was one of these neoclassical things—Apollo and the Muses or whatever, although what that has to do with banking is beyond me—and he'd never have wanted his name on something. like that, even if he had finished it.

"It was about two weeks from completion when it happened," Sarah continued, in a voice so sorrowful that Joan, even though she knew what was coming, felt a sudden chill. "He—overextended himself and—slipped—fell off the scaffold. He fell—over twenty feet to the marble floor below—brought the scaffold down with him—blood and dust and broken bits of wood and stone all over, they told me—later—I never saw—He—the coroner—said he broke his neck—but there was also—possibility of—heart attack. . . ."

The voice was mechanical, tapping the words out like a Teletype. Sarah had reverted to the speech pattern she'd had just after the stroke, her sentences fragmented and in a monotone. Joan was frightened. She went over to the couch to sit beside her, wanting to put her arm around Sarah's shoulder, but something in the old woman's posture told her she'd be rebuffed, all but thrown across the room, if she touched her now.

And then Sarah stopped, her head bowed, panting a little, bringing herself under control. Her eyes when she finally raised them were the saddest Joan had ever seen.

"When Sam was a child, they told his parents the rheumatic heart would kill him before he was fifty. He was fifty-five when he— I'd like to think it was a heart attack, and that it got to him before he hit the floor. I don't want to think of him having to fall twenty feet knowing he was going to die. And I should like to think that he was able to cheat the fates once before they broke him. No matter now. He was dead when he reached the floor. I didn't see

him then. I made them show me—the body—after I was
notified—after they'd cleaned him up and tried to recon-
struct—what was left of his face. It wasn't Sam. That
pulpy mess I forced them to show me was not Sam. I
don't know what it was. And I don't know whether it was
accident or his heart that killed him.

"I must have been in some kind of trance after they
took me home. They tried to sedate me, but I kept the
pills under my tongue and threw them out later. Even so,
how I got from that afternoon to the wake the following
day has always been fuzzy in my mind. I remember the
wake, though. I kept it simple—no flowers, no organ
music, certainly no religious service, though a lot of
people were upset by that. But Sam was a kind of pan-
theist, if such things can be in the twentieth century, and
a religious ceremony would have disgusted him. What
amazed me was the number of people who turned up.
The funeral director went berserk. All our friends, Sam's
only surviving sister, nearly every student he'd ever had
—except that FBI spook. I think he knew I'd kill him
with my bare hands. I'd even swear one of Sam's old
girl friends was there, but she was nearly eighty and
virtually deaf, so I never found out who she really was.
Oh, yes, it was quite a circus!"

"What happened to the—the thing he was working
on?" Joan ventured to ask, desperately wanting to get
away from the wake.

"One of life's little ironies there." Sarah's face was a
mask, impenetrable. "The building was completed the
week after the funeral, and the bank decided they didn't
need the frieze after all. Seems the falling scaffold broke
Apollo's nose, and nobody wanted to finish it. Sculptors
are a superstitious lot. I have no idea what they did with
the thing—cut it up into bathtubs for rich people, scrapped
it—I didn't care; it wasn't one of my priorities.

"And after the funeral, getting all his papers straightened out—he was a terrible slob about things like that, and the lawyers went through all manner of contortions settling the 'estate,' and ended up collecting most of it in fees. But it made me sit down and confront the fact that Sam was really dead. It was something I'd always considered in the abstract; there was his heart, and the heavy smoking, and the difference in our ages. You tell yourself that it's inevitable, but until it happens . . . Even then there's a kind of fuzzy denial that settles on you, and you're sometimes halfway through the day before you will acknowledge that you are alone.

"I think the only thing that kept me from going to pieces completely was the endless parade of pragmatic decisions that had to be made. What to do with his clothes, how to stop myself from setting his place at the table, how to learn to sleep alone again. And then there were the sculptures. God, the sculptures!

"They were still sitting in his friend's studio, and while the friend was good enough not to say anything, I knew he couldn't turn around without bumping into one of them. I had to make a decision quickly. Of course he'd gotten such touching obituaries in the papers, and people were getting tired of looking under their beds for communists. There was a great clamor to have a posthumous exhibit. But I couldn't bear to look at his works again, much less give the necrophiles the satisfaction of gloating over them in his absence, so I made an arrangement with the friend who was holding them. It's funny, he was the most promising of Sam's protégés, and later he became quite successful, but I can't even remember his name. I've blocked the whole thing from my mind. But I gave him instructions to keep whatever pieces he wanted, and to distribute the rest to certain others of Sam's students, and under no circumstances was anyone —least of all me—to know what became of them.

"Most of the ones who got them were starving, struggling along. I suppose they must have passed the stuff off as their own to pay the rent for a while. Maybe they even cut them down and reused the stone. But I think Sam would have been satisfied either way. His work was not completely destroyed, as he had wanted, but at least now nobody knew it was his."

"You mean you never kept any of them?" Joan was horrified, thinking of how meticulously she had written down and saved even the shittiest of Brian's songs and poems, even after he left. Even though she hated them, and him for writing them, knowing how much he had to drink to produce a single, disjointed bit of doggerel, she would never have considered parting with even a word of them.

"Only the pictures—the ones I showed you in the portfolio," Sarah said without apology. "Maybe someday they'll be of use to somebody."

There was a long silence. Joan fidgeted, wanting to say something, not knowing what. The old woman was watching the rain, lost in reverie, unconvinced of the need to speak ever again. Once she reached over and squeezed Joan's hand, absently, without looking away from the window. The silence dripped between them, broken by an occasional car pushing its way through the rivers in the street.

"The medieval concept of art was quite different from our own," Sarah said so suddenly that Joan nearly fell off the couch. It was the lecture voice; Joan hadn't heard it in ages. "The arts were an integral part of the chain of being, and as such were incorporated into everyday life. Patronage was given willingly, because the artist was viewed as someone who contributed directly to the community—just like the carpenter and the smith and the baker and everyone else. Artists didn't have to starve, or kiss people's asses to get grants and endowments. They didn't have to make excuses for their creativity. They created for the glory of God, and only incidentally for their patrons. One is not permitted to say such things these days. The chief prerequisite for creativity in the twentieth century is unquestioning atheism. After that comes either madness, or an angle that will make one rich. It's disgusting!"

The silence that followed this outburst seemed to go on forever. Joan got up and left the room. She went upstairs to pack her overnight bag and to run the vacuum cleaner around the bedrooms and the hall. She usually helped Sarah with the housework on the weekends, and thought it might help fill in the time now. When she finally returned to the living room, Sarah was still sitting by the window, watching the rain.

"Tell me," Sarah said, as if Joan had never left the room, "what, in your humble opinion, is the meaning of love? How is it possible in this world full of strangers for two people to find each other, and to love?"

Joan put down her overnight bag, sat on the arm of the couch, and thought about it.

"I'm not exactly the one to ask about that," she said finally. "I blew it the first time, remember?"

"All right then," Sarah nodded, accepting. "From your past experience at least you have discovered what love is *not*. But you do accept the premise that love exists, don't you?"

"Do I get credit for this course?" Joan joked feebly. "I mean, what department do I put down on my program card—English, Psychology, Philosophy? Or is it one of those interdepartmental things?"

"Don't be evasive," Sarah warned her. "Come, I need a definition."

"Why?" Joan demanded. "What brings this up all of a sudden?"

"I am trying to find a way to explain to someone who never met Sam, nor saw me in his presence, what it was that we meant to each other," Sarah said. "What I've told you are facts. Historical data. You know *what* Sam was, but not *who* he was, nor who *we* were—he and I— while we were together. We were married for only twelve years, you know, and I sometimes wonder if it would have been different if it had been twenty or thirty or forty. I don't think so. How can I explain what I mean?"

It was not a question that required an answer. Joan waited.

"What attracted you to Brian?" Sarah leaned forward, suddenly intense. "What made you think you were in love with him?"

"I—I don't know," Joan shrugged, caught off-guard. "He was very sexy. I was lonely. I found him easy to talk to. The rest just sort of happened."

"And what do you think attracted him to you?" Sarah wanted to know.

Joan opened her mouth, then closed it again. After six years of Brian, the only thing she could ever remember him saying to her was that she had sexy legs. And he had said that the night he met her. After that, there had been no compliments, no criticisms—nothing. Maybe he'd meant to say something else, but never got around to it.

"You haven't the vaguest idea, do you?" Sarah asked, a suggestion of pity in her voice. "Shall I tell you?"

"Um, since when are you a practicing shrink?" Joan was uneasy with this conversation, longed for the silences again. "And who authorized you to diagnose long-distance?"

"It's simple, really," Sarah said airily. "And obvious even long-distance. Brian needed a mother. The first time you laid eyes on him he was hanging onto a beer can the way a two-year-old clings to his bottle. Everything you ever did for him boils down to mothering. You kept

house for him, listened to his bragging, waited up for
him when he was out being a bad boy, blamed the world
for shortchanging him whenever he failed at anything.
And like a good mother, you kept waiting for him to
grow up, but he never did. And all you got out of the
bargain was sex, not love."

"Oh, come off it!" Joan blustered, beginning to cry.
"That's the biggest crock of bullshit I ever—"

"Come off it yourself!" Sarah challenged her. "You had
to show your girl friends you could get a man to fuck
you just like everybody else, and for that you adopted
this overgrown baby. Babying him didn't bother you at
first; women are taught to do for others all the time. It
was when you decided that you might occasionally like
to do something for yourself—after you discovered that
sex with a mama's boy isn't much fun—that your marriage fell apart."

"That's not the least bit accurate," Joan said grandly,
drying her eyes, knowing that it was.

Sarah ignored her. "The next time you meet a man
you think you might like to spend a considerable portion
of your life with, see if you can figure out what's missing.
I'm not talking about this 'opposites attract' crap. I mean,
see if you can look into his eyes and see that what's
missing is you. Then examine yourself and see if what's
missing in you is him."

"What are you talking about?" Joan demanded, although she thought she had a fair idea.

"It's a question of growth, my dear," Sarah said suc-
cinctly. "It's not as simple as making lists of things like
sexual compatibility, and the fact that you come from
similar backgrounds and have the same amount of education, and whether or not you can tolerate his cooking
or he yours. One and one don't always make two. If
you're too much alike, sometimes— God, what time is
it?"

"Two o'clock or so," Joan said, surprised at this sudden question. She squinted at the clock on the mantel. "Ten after."

Sarah became suddenly agitated, though Joan could see she was trying to hide it.

"Listen, we've talked enough for today," Sarah said abruptly, all but shoving the overnight bag into Joan's hands. "I just remembered there's something important I have to do this afternoon."

"Well, all right," Joan said, a little insulted and very suspicious. Then she remembered the phone call. She'd heard only one side of it, and only part of that, but she had a fair idea what was going on. The priest was back.

Joan went to get her raincoat from the front closet, taking her time, seeing how Sarah reacted. When she could stall no longer, she returned to the living room for her overnight bag, only to have it thrust into her hands by a distracted Sarah.

"Don't cross-examine me," Sarah said, leading her toward the door. "Just go, please, like a good girl? I'll explain some other time."

With that, she all but pushed Joan through the door. Joan was halfway down the stoop when she realized she hadn't even said goodbye. When she turned to wave, she saw that the door was already closed.

Joan smiled to herself, then looked up and down the street from under her umbrella. There was no one else out in the teeming rain. She had left the car—now more hers than Sarah's—almost at the corner. It was hard to find a parking spot in this neighborhood, especially on a Sunday, so she was not at all surprised to see another car creep up beside hers as she was getting in. The other driver honked. Are you leaving? he was asking. May I have your space?

Joan nodded to the other driver without looking at him, wrestling with her umbrella and sliding into the car. It wasn't until she had closed the door, started the motor and the wipers, and adjusted the rearview mirror that she really got a look at him.

It wasn't the sort of face one forgot easily. Few men in their fifties were as inordinately handsome as this man was. It was an objective observation; unlike many Catholic schoolgirls, Joan did not find priests a turn-on.

The plot thickens, she thought as she pulled away from the curb.

The other driver was not looking directly at Joan. Even if he could have seen her through the rain, he probably wouldn't have recognized her; she'd never been in his class.

It would take him a few minutes, she thought, to park the car, lock up, and walk up the block against the rain to Sarah's house. If, just out of idle curiosity, Joan happened to drive around the block . . .

When she rounded the corner at the top of Sarah's block, Joan could barely discern the large figure in the black raincoat hunched at the top of the stoop. As she drove past the house, she saw the door open and the figure slip inside. But she could not see, through the sudden downpour, the reaction of the woman who opened the door.

XIII

Severe and outspoken criticism of the ecclesiastical hierarchy or facetious treatment of the conventional rituals of Christian worship [in medieval times] did not . . . imply a lack of Christian belief.

D. W. ROBERTSON, JR.,
The Literature of Medieval England

"Celia? Is it really you?"

Herb had been squinting at her through a decade of elapsed time. He had been passing her in the hall as he had dozens of times ten years ago, and that had made the event familiar. But it was bizarre in that she had not changed in all of that time. She'd changed her hair, and her clothes were no longer Salvation Army specials, but she really hadn't changed. Why did she still look like an eighteen-year-old, when everybody else Herb knew, including himself, had aged ten years or more since the last time she'd sat in his ethics class and told him she was dropping out of school?

Celia, too, had been surprised by the unexpected *déjà vu*. She'd had to look at Herb twice before she could be sure.

"Herb!" she shrieked, trampling several students in

her delight, throwing her arms around him. They embraced for several moments, unaware that they were attracting attention in the crowded hall.

("Who the hell . . . ?" One of the men, a senior, had had his eye on Celia for some minutes before she'd jostled past him. "She go here, or what?"

("Search me!" His companion only noticed blondes. He shrugged. "Some chick. Sure not his wife.")

"Oh, wow!" Celia gasped finally, wiping the tears out of her eyes before they dislodged her contacts. "God, how *are* you?"

"Fine, fine," Herb nodded vaguely. "But listen, I'm free next period. Have you got some time? We could talk."

Herb had always had a special rapport with Celia and the other activists, one that frequently ignored the artificial barriers placed between student and professor.

"And you're still with—Mark, wasn't it?" he asked her after they'd talked for a while in the faculty lounge. "Maybe I shouldn't ask. It was so long ago."

"We're not living together anymore, no," Celia said, but with a secret smile. "We got married."

Herb was pleased. "Terrific!" he said. "Any kids?"

"No." Celia seemed to hesitate. "Mark's been out of work for a while, and I've been—"

"I understand." Herb held up his hand to stop the flow of information he didn't feel privileged enough to know. "I just don't know what to say to you after—Christ, ten years? It's like you just disappeared for a few weeks or months, not ten *years*. I can't believe it!"

"Yeah," Celia nodded, coping with unexpected emotions. She'd always felt like a misfit here, a hippie-weirdo, grass-smoking freak, and even now that she was a respectable citizen, married for several years, steadily employed, and hadn't smoked a joint in . . . she felt out of place here, and was not prepared for the rush of crazy nostalgia that came with seeing Herb again. He had been one of the few people here she could talk to—he and Sarah Morrow. "Yeah, I guess that's it."

"Hey!" Herb said suddenly, snapping his fingers. "And I bet I know why you're here! I don't know why it didn't come to me the minute I saw you. The strike!"

Celia frowned. "What strike?"

"Aren't you here because of the strike?" Herb seemed a little disappointed.

"I'm here for two reasons," Celia said, as if trying to remember why herself. "In the first place, I have to talk to Dr. Stern."

Herb's preconceptions were dashed to the ground. Stern taught modern languages and ran the little theater. As far as Herb knew, he was completely apolitical. Why on earth would Celia want to talk to him?

"Dr. Stern," Herb repeated slowly, feeling like an idiot.

"Yeah," Celia nodded. "He needs to rent some Leicos—stage lights—for the fall production. I can get him a discount by ordering them through my company."

"Your company?" Herb echoed, feeling more like an idiot. They'd been rapping about old times for nearly an hour, and he hadn't thought to ask her what she was doing now.

"Yeah. Didn't I tell you?" Celia was rather amazed at it herself. "I've been into theater for a while. There's a group called CRC—Classical Rep Company—we're about as far off-Broadway as you can get, I guess, but we get funding, and we do mostly revivals—Molière, Chekov, a little Neil Simon to keep the books balanced—"

"You're an actress?" Herb was incredulous.

"Me? No way!" Celia found it very amusing. "No, I'm strictly tech. Couple of months ago the lighting director left in a huff, so now I'm it. And I free-lance a little too. It helps if you want to eat. But I love it."

"That's amazing," Herb said quietly. "Somehow I've got this picture of a student radical in my head. I couldn't imagine what kind of work you'd be doing. Well, I'll have to come down and see one of your productions sometime."

"I'll send you a flyer," Celia promised. "And so you won't be disillusioned, I'm also here for political reasons. I wanted to check out the campus scene for Dr. Morrow."

Briefly she told Herb about the letter campaign, and the other plans in support of Sarah.

"And like, since Joan and the others work during the day and I'm free, they wanted me to come down and have a look around," she finished.

"But you just came in blind," Herb said. "You haven't heard about the strike?"

"What strike?" Celia repeated. Something told her she shouldn't ask, that she should put all of that sort of thing behind her as she'd almost succeeded in doing before Joan found her phone number and dragged her into the campaign. She was finished with half-assed causes, Celia thought; finished with marching around yelling for something that earned you sore feet, a hoarse voice, and maybe a dose of tear gas. She'd only agreed to do the Sarah Morrow thing because it seemed so tame, so provincial, so possible, and because she intended to crawl back into the woodwork as soon as she got the wheels turning. Strikes and demonstrations were not the way to do things, if such things could be done at all, and she really shouldn't ask Herb what he was talking about, but . . .

"Nobody told me about any strike," she said. "What's it all about?"

Vera Neil had made the phone call for Sister Francis. She'd known all along that she would have to do it; there were certain chores too demeaning for a college president to do herself. Vera Neil was accustomed to unpleasant tasks, could be counted upon to handle the most unsavory situation without a qualm, but this particular assignment made her apprehensive. She had been there, after all, the day last spring when Sarah Morrow came roaring out of the office, and she did not relish the possibility of having to cope with a similar scene over the telephone.

But Sister Francis had requested, in that unique manner that precluded all objections, that Vera make the call to inform Dr. Morrow of the date of the departmental hearing she had demanded.

Vera had no doubt that Dr. Morrow was extremely anxious to know the date of the hearing. She would not be pleased, however, to learn that it would be held on the last day before Christmas recess.

The reason for the choice of this date was simple: Very few classes were held on this day; nearly everyone left early, and those who lingered were in a festive mood, drifting from one Christmas party to another, and would not be perturbed by the passing events. Vera had not the slightest doubt that Sarah Morrow's hearing was a mere formality. She would have to retire after all, and there would be no student protests if she left quietly on the day before Christmas recess.

Sister Francis was being overcautious, of course. There would have been no student protest; this was not the Sixties. As for the faculty—well, everyone knew who the likely troublemakers were, and all of them were under careful scrutiny. They wouldn't go so far as to risk their own positions, after all. No, there would be no repercussions. This was not the Sixties.

Resignation to the inevitable made it no easier. Vera had tried to avoid making the call for over an hour, knowing she'd have to go through with it before lunch or she'd lose her nerve. But the strain of ignoring it made it impossible for her to do anything else, and so she kept trying. She actually dialed the number three times, but always panicked and hung up before the phone could ring.

On the fourth attempt, she finally followed through. She counted the number of times it rang, knowing she would have to wait awhile for Dr. Morrow to get to the phone. As she waited, Vera unconsciously picked at the leaves of the carefully nurtured plants on her desk. By the time her conversation with Dr. Morrow was completed, the Purple Passion in particular was nearly defoliated.

When she realized what she had done to the plant, she wanted to cry. This was odd for two reasons. In the first place, having survived the horrors of never-married menopause only last year, Vera Neil no longer cried about anything. Secondly, while she was inordinately fond of her plants, she found it disquieting that her destruction of one of them upset her more than her participation in the downfall of a human being.

She had not wanted to get involved in this nasty situation, but her job had forced her to do so. How could she square it with her conscience?

Later that morning, after Sister Francis had left to attend some vague intercollegiate conference, Vera Neil looked over her shoulder only once before she picked up the phone and dialed the cafeteria.

"They're *what?*" Sister Francis almost raised her voice when Vera told her the next morning. "Would you mind repeating that, Miss Neil? I'm not certain I understood you."

It was with great difficulty that Vera kept her face and voice from revealing her true emotions.

"There's a letter from the cafeteria and custodial staff," she said, repeating almost verbatim what had so startled her employer. "They wish to inform you that they are planning a work slowdown, beginning next Monday."

Vera held the note lightly in her hand, scanning Mario's agonized grade-school prose as if she had never seen it

before, when in actual fact she had typed it herself—
though on someone else's typewriter—before she went
home yesterday. Sister Francis did not react this time, so
Vera continued with her information.

"They haven't gone to the union about it," she went on
casually, "so I don't suppose it can exactly be considered
a strike, but—"

"Whatever they choose to call it, it amounts to the
same thing," Sister Francis interrupted. Her face had
acquired a strange mottled look, quite unlike its usual
alabaster, which made Vera a little nervous. "What on
earth is the matter with them?"

"From what I understand of the letter"—Vera looked
over the edge of it to see her employer's reaction—"it has
something to do with Dr. Morrow."

She held the letter out to Sister Francis, who would not
deign to touch it. From the expression on her face, it might
well have been a dagger pointed at her heart.

"Something *what* to do with Dr. Morrow?" Francis
demanded brittlely, throwing grammar to the four winds.
"What exactly does it mean?"

Vera hesitated. It would be difficult to make herself
clear without incriminating herself at the same time.

"They—they don't seem to think she's being treated
fairly," she stumbled. "They say something here about the
departmental hearing, and it seems they want it moved up
to an earlier date. Either that or they intend to stop working as of Mon—"

She stopped. Francis was leaning forward in her chair.
Her face had gone completely livid. Pieces were falling into
place in her head. "The only way they could know the date
of the hearing," Francis said, speaking very slowly, "is
if the information came directly from this office."

Vera Neil masked her terror with a look of wounded
pride. "Why, Sister, I certainly hope you don't think *I'd*
tell them anything?" she sniffed, ambiguous. "Dr. Mor-

row has known since yesterday, and she has lots of friends here. Word gets around fast, you know."

This evoked nothing from the nun but an icy stare. Vera let the letter flutter ever so gently onto the desk.

"And I'm sorry to say I won't be coming in on Monday," she rehearsed later, addressing her typewriter in a whisper. "I plan on having the flu."

That morning Bertie did not bring Sister Francis her coffee.

When the uproar began on Monday, the cafeteria became the hub of the disturbance. Boxes of frozen hamburger patties crammed the freezers while the grill sat cold and indifferent. Friday's coffee grounds silted the unwashed, inert urns. The soda machines were quickly depleted of their store, with cases of unchilled soda stacked solidly beside them; Mae had the keys to the machines, and she wasn't surrendering them to anybody. There were no sandwiches, and the opportunists who sought to buy up last week's pound cake and candy bars were told by Bertie in the most deferential manner that they must have exact change for all purchases since she was not going to open the cash register. There were no napkins, the garbage bins were brimming, and none of the tables had been wiped. Only the pinball machine—graduating gift of the Class of '77—operated intermittently throughout the morning, until one of the students, enraged at the lack of services, hit it too hard. The "tilt" sign now buzzed with maddening regularity.

Nearly everyone had noticed something odd when they'd arrived that morning. It was raining rather heavily, but no one had brought out the umbrella stands, or laid down the rubber-backed carpeting that always appeared in the main entrances on sloppy days. No one had emptied the ashtrays in the smokers, or the wastebaskets in the lounges.

Three toilets in the basement men's room had overflowed, and no one could find a mop, a plunger, or the key to the closet. The labs were running out of paper towels, and there was no soap in the ladies' rooms. All the thermostats had been shut off and locked, and those who usually grumbled about the overheating sat huddled in sweaters. And the unobtrusive, ever-present figures with the callused hands and rubber-soled shoes were nowhere to be seen.

Most of them had sequestered themselves in the back room, behind the cafeteria kitchen, where the now-silent dishwasher usually reigned in solitude. One coffee urn had been cleaned out and heated, and the somber figures served themselves periodically as they talked in half-whispers. None of them wanted to be caught roaming around out there alone; they had bunched together back here for moral support. Mae had locked the doors to the cafeteria when some of the students began growing hostile. Scuffling, pounding, and occasional curses could still be heard.

"What burns me," Mario said, wiping coffee off his tie (he'd decided to dress up for the occasion; even so, he spilled), "is that half of them little snotnoses don't even know what we're protesting about."

"Yeah," someone else chimed in. "One of 'em give me some lip about us getting paid damn good for what we do. I told her, I says, 'I got a daughter your age, and I'd whip her ass if she talked to me like that.' I says, 'We ain't in it for ourselves. It's for respect. An employee's got a right to respect from his boss, whether he's a college professor or a slob like me who just cleans toilets.' Little bitch didn't know what I was talking about."

"And sure, none of them's bothered to take this thing to the president," Mae grumbled, handing out the good china cups that were usually reserved for trustees and visiting dignitaries. "Even the ones that had the good lady for a teacher. None of them's bothered to stick their necks out."

"The thing is"—Mario interrupted the muttered assents that greeted this remark—"the thing is, what do we do now?"

Mae looked at him stupidly; the others were silent.

"What're you talking about?" Mae said finally.

"I mean, do we call this off after today, or do we keep it going until Sister Francis comes down off her high horse and talks to us?"

"Well, *I* surely don't know!" Mae exploded. "It was your idea, Mr. Hotshot. What do you think? Supposing she don't talk to us? Supposing she hears us out and tells us to go to hell?"

Mario was beginning to realize this would not be as easy as he'd thought.

"We have to take it to the local," Bertie chimed in, *sotto voce*. "If we want to keep it going, we got to take it to the union."

Mario hadn't thought of that. He'd expected some reaction from the president as soon as she'd gotten the letter. At worst, he'd expected a response this morning when the effects of their slowdown became apparent. But it was after noon, and the silence from the office was unnerving. He hadn't expected that. He'd expected—what? A reaction from the students, perhaps—a show of solidarity, some participation in this unofficial strike? There had been none, had been nothing but hostility because their stomachs were empty and they were cold. They were being inconvenienced, and that was all they cared about.

And where was the faculty? Mario wondered. The liberals had been conspicuously silent. They had all nodded sympathetically when told there would be no coffee, but none of them had offered to lend their support. Even that philosophy professor, the one who was always organizing protests against South Africa . . .

"Hey, Herb," Celia asked, surveying the turmoil from

the back of the cafeteria, "aren't you guys going to do anything?"

"How do you mean?" he asked vaguely, watching the behavior of the students with mild disgust. There was some satisfaction on his face as well; he'd never seen this particular batch of students so worked up about anything. He'd have liked to go back to the kitchen and personally shake the hand of every one of those hardworking individuals, to thank them for giving the kids something to think about. But wouldn't they interpret his action as condescending? He'd rather not chance it.

Celia was getting excited. She was literally hopping from one foot to the other in her anxiety to get into the action. "I mean, like, get together with all the people who signed your petition," she urged him. "Join in. Give the working people a little solidarity. Have everyone who signed your petition call in sick tomorrow."

"Oh," Herb said thoughtfully. "I'm not sure that would be wise."

Celia's eyes widened in astonishment. "Wise?" she echoed. "Well, shit, man! What do you mean 'wise'?"

"Well"—Herb avoided her eyes—"it's like this. We're having a faculty meeting Wednesday afternoon—the regular meeting, I mean, nothing special—and I'm going to bring up a proposal that we—"

"But that's two days from now," Celia objected. "By then they'll either call off the strike or Frannie'll put the screws to them. You have to do something now, while the issue's still hot."

"That's just the trouble," Herb said. "It's *too* hot."

"Come again?" Celia drew a blank. She was getting the uneasy feeling that Herb was trying to weasel out.

"Look, what is this—the last week of September?" Herb was being reasonable. "It's almost three months before this hearing comes up. If we fire our big guns now, what'll we have left by then?"

"Oh, my God!" Celia groaned, collapsing into herself. "I mean, that's really incredible! Isn't that what the strike is about? Because they realize if Sarah has to wait that long, nobody's going to take her seriously?"

Herb met her eyes for the first time. There was an uncharacteristic cynicism in his expression that gave Celia the shudders.

"Come off it, will you?" he said softly. "You really think the date makes a damn bit of difference? They're going to can the old girl and there's nothing any of us can do about it. We can make all the usual noises, sign all the petitions, but the same thing will happen that happened in sixty-eight. Wasn't that the year we tried to get that fat-cat from Dow off the board of trustees to protest his corporation's manufacture of napalm? What happened then? We lost, the administration won. And what happened when you petitioned for black-studies courses? They were introduced as electives for a few years, and taught by a nun with a degree in Napoleon; two years later they were phased out during budget cuts. And at least then you had some of the other students behind you."

"Oh, yeah, sure," Celia nodded, furious with him, furious with herself for not screaming at him. "Less than five percent of the population. Big deal!"

"But you were vocal!" Herb argued. "You were energetic and persistent and you tried to make a dent in things. Look at this crowd! You think you'd get a rise out of any of them?"

For a crazy moment, Celia wanted to prove him wrong. Ten years ago she would have plunged headlong into a group like this and made some kind of speech. She fidgeted, wanting to do it, knowing she wouldn't.

"Who's the Student Council president?" she asked Herb, trying to salvage the situation. "Maybe I can talk to her."

"You'd be wasting your time," Herb told her.

"I can try," she said, needing to get away from him and his shattering resignation.

"I'm sorry," he said, apologizing as much to the unseen group in the back kitchen as to Celia. "Please don't think I'm giving up on it. I just think it's too soon. If the minority of the faculty that's on Sarah's side is going to accomplish anything effective, I think we simply have to wait."

"Sure," Celia said, walking away without saying good-bye.

Aquinas had not seen Francis this angry since the day she'd found a half-empty box of condoms and three joints stashed behind the statue of Saint Joseph in the main foyer. She had come dangerously close to making a scene that time. Her first impulse had been to round up all male students and lecture them as a group before singling them out for individual interrogation. Aquinas had talked her out of it that time, and thought she bore watching this time as well.

"I want you to go over there this minute and tell them to stop!" Francis raged, pacing rapidly but methodically—three steps to the right, three steps back to her starting point, about-face and three steps to the right again—behind her desk. "This is an outrage!"

Aquinas blinked at her. Procrastination was her way of controlling the situation. "If we were going to do that," she said with painful deliberateness, seeking shelter behind the papal "we," "we ought to have done it first thing this morning. Or last week, before it even got started. They certainly gave us ample warning. But now that they've had their way with it for nearly four hours—"

"How *dare* they?" Francis stormed, her voice going up an octave and becoming quite strident. "They've always been so dependable, so—so docile. They've always been with *us*. Remember when that group of hippie types started handing out that subversive literature?"

"Of course," Aquinas nodded, grateful for the sidetrack. "It was a number of years ago. That Rinaldi girl— Cecelia, wasn't it?—and the rest of those unkempt individuals—"

"And the reek of cigarette smoke from their clothes!" Francis lamented, unaware she had been diverted. "At least, one prayed it was only from cigarettes. Oh, if only they'd combed their hair once in a while, one could almost have overlooked their aberrant behavior!"

She had stopped her pacing and was holding the back of her chair as if for support, though not gripping it tightly enough to spoil the alabaster symmetry of her lovely hands.

"Indeed," Aquinas mused, pleased that she had managed to buy some time.

"But what I meant was"—Francis resumed her anger and her pacing—"in regard to the cafeteria staff, when those students distributed all of that dreadful material about civilian casualties and napalm and profiteering, Mrs. Connaught and the others threw it all away, and tore the posters off the walls, and the very next day they all came to work with American-flag pins on their uniforms. I think that was commendable, don't you?"

"Of course," Aquinas agreed, wondering for the thousandth time why anyone as simplistic as Francis had been made president instead of her.

"And now this!" Francis said, sinking into her chair. "I simply cannot believe they would do this to m—to us. And for such an absurd reason!"

Aquinas said nothing. She would wait for Francis to complete the thought process that she herself had worked out days ago when she first heard about the impending strike.

"It's really none of their business!" Francis's voice was

rising again, and she had all but sprung out of her chair. "One might expect some objections from the faculty committee, but these people! How *dare* they?"

Aquinas waited until she was certain Francis was absolutely finished. "They are very union-conscious," she pointed out at last. "Perhaps they view Dr. Morrow as a fellow worker who, not having the benefit of union membership—"

"I want them stopped!" Francis seethed. "I want you to go over there and tell them to return to their jobs at once or—"

"That's not the way to do it," Aquinas said calmly.

The phone rang before Francis could respond. It rang several times, and the two nuns stared at it.

"Miss Neil has not come in today," Francis said, staring at the phone as if it were a viper. Aquinas looked at her mildly. Francis was beginning to rattle. "Well, I can't exactly answer it myself," she said.

"Do you expect me to—" Aquinas began, but in the middle of the fifth ring the sound suddenly ceased. "I wonder who that could have been."

Francis got up and roamed aimlessly around the office, shuffling and reshuffling the stacks of papers on her desk. The room, usually inordinately neat, was beginning to look messy. There was lint on the carpet, and things were becoming misplaced.

"She's in with them, you know," Francis said suddenly, conspiratorially.

"I beg your pardon?" Aquinas was startled.

"Vera Neil," Francis stated, a suggestion of paranoia creeping into her voice. "I'm positive she helped them draft that letter. And this morning she called in and said she had the flu. She's never had the flu! She's as healthy as a horse! And she took the keys to the file cabinets home over the weekend—I can't find a thing around here!"

There was genuine panic in her voice now. She had talked herself out at last. It was Aquinas's turn to speak.

"There's only one thing to do," she said, and she reached over to push the phone toward Francis. "And if it's going to be effective, you shall have to do it yourself."

"Uh-huh," the girl nodded yet again, snapping her gum in a way that made Celia want to stuff it up her nose. "Yeah. Uh-huh. I can see what you mean."

"And, like, I kind of thought somebody might he doing something already," Celia said, trying to be pleasant. *This* was the Student Council president?

"Well, you know," the girl said, fishing a compact out of her purse and putting the finishing touches on her eye makeup, "the kids in Morrow's classes, like, they've been sending her cards and stuff ever since she went in the hospital."

"But she can't—" Celia stopped. What was she doing, blowing Sarah's cover? "What I mean is, that's not the point. Moral support and all—that's cool—but there's something else that has to be done before they fire her."

The girl gave her hair a final flick with the comb and put her arsenal of brushes and colors away. "You mean that rumor that got all the cafeteria people so uptight? You don't really think that's true, do you?"

Celia wanted to grab her by the hair and shake her. Were they all this stupid? "You'd be amazed at what they'll try and get away with," she said, holding herself back. "If you let them."

The girl had to think about that. "But what could we do?"

It was as if the Eisenhower years had dovetailed strangely and without a wrinkle into the late Seventies. Where had this child been all her life?

"Get a group together," Celia explained slowly. "Sign some petitions. Have a protest march if you have to."

"Gosh," the girl sighed. "I don't think most of 'em would go for that. I mean, we all thought Morrow was a to-gether lady, but—"

"The majority don't have to get involved," Celia said, trying to persuade, "just a big enough minority to make some noise. If you got everybody on the Student Council, say—"

The girl's perfectly made-up eyes widened in horror. "Oh, no, we couldn't do that!" she gasped. "I mean, half of us are on Dean's List, and the rest—I mean, we're gonna be out there in the cold cruel world looking for jobs in a few months. We'll need recommendations from the faculty and the administration and—"

"Shit!" was all Celia could say.

The girl closed her purse, picked up her elementary-ed texts, and threw her Alberoy cardigan over her shoulders. "It was real interesting talking to someone from the Sixties," she said sweetly, "but I really have to split now or I'll be late for cheerleading practice."

Celia watched her go out the door, remembering after ten years that the clock on the wall of the downstairs john was always ten minutes slow. There was a performance tonight; she had to be at the theater before six to open up. After a day like this, she needed to get home and sack out for a couple of hours, and she'd promised to call Joan at work to let her know what she'd found. She couldn't possibly tell Joan that their worst fears had been con-firmed, that nothing at all was going on here except the cafeteria strike.

The cafeteria strike. That might actually turn out to be something, although without the support of anyone else . . . She would have to stick around and see how it turned out.

Exhausted, Celia went back to the cafeteria.

None of them spoke while Mae was on the phone. Most of them had barely breathed since it began ringing. They had all jumped when it rang the first time, and most had backed away from it, terrified lest the responsibility of answering it should fall upon them. Mario moved fastest and furthest. Everyone looked at Mae. Mae always said she wasn't afraid of anybody. Now was her chance to prove it.

They stood about silently, attaching deep significance to each of Mae's monosyllables and "Yes, Sister"'s. When she finally replaced the receiver on the wall extension, they crowded around her.

"She's giving us fifteen minutes to get back to work," Mae said dramatically, "or she'll contact the union and have us fined for wildcatting. As it stands now, she's docking us today's pay, and she said she wouldn't mind packing in the lot of us if she could."

There were murmurs, a few curses, and they began to drift away.

"Back to the salt mines!" Mario said cheerfully, the last but Bertie to leave. "Well, we had her going for a while, anyway!"

Mae glared at him with murderous intent as he disappeared through the door, keys jingling.

"You gutless little greaseball, you!" she hissed after him.

Joan left work right after Celia called. She told Mr. Werner she had a headache, and he let her leave at three. She hated like hell to lie to him, but she wasn't doing anything in the office that couldn't wait until tomorrow, and if she didn't get to Sarah's and talk to her this afternoon . . .

She was on the subway before it occurred to her that she ought to call Sarah first. But then, it wasn't as if the old woman wouldn't be home; it was only a question of whom she might be home with.

We are all adults, Joan thought, getting off the train. It's about time we started acting that way.

No one answered Sarah's bell when she rang. Ordinarily she would have used her key right away, but this being a surprise visit made Joan hesitate. She rang again, waited a decent interval, took the key out of her purse, and fumbled it into the lock.

There was no one on the first floor. Not daring to go upstairs, Joan called loudly a few times, only to be met by silence. Feeling like an intruder, and more than a little alarmed, she crept out to the kitchen a second time and noticed that the back door was slightly open.

She had never seen the backyard, had imagined it to be small and claustrophobic, typical of a brownstone. In others she'd seen, one was uncomfortably aware of other people's windows staring down—however serenely, always there. But something remarkable had been done to this garden, something that made it easy to forget Brooklyn and the sounds of clattering dishes and reggae and voices coming from open windows. Someone had constructed a miniature cloister—a colonnade, stone benches, a cruciform path between rosebushes and dwarf fig trees and weed-choked patches that might have been a medieval herb garden. Joan could visualize it, could smell each of the carefully named and symbol-laden herbs as they must have flourished when there was someone to care for them. It would be a lovely place when the weeds were pulled and the roses pruned and the untidy clogs of soggy dead leaves cleared away.

Sarah was here, in the midst of the great disarray, her back to Joan. She was wearing gardening gloves and a faded coverall, her cane propped against a column while she wrestled futilely with a pair of springblade rose clippers.

"Surprise, surprise!" Sarah said without turning when she heard the footsteps on the flagstones. "I thought you said you had confessions this afternoon—"

When she turned to see Joan instead of Pietro, her half-smile froze for an awkward moment, then became annoyance—not at Joan for sneaking up on her, but at her sixth sense for betraying her.

"What are you doing here?" Sarah demanded, trying not to sound hostile.

"Got out of work early," Joan said. "I had to talk to you."

There was an awkward silence. It was necessary to dismiss Pietro's presence.

"Do you like the cloister?" Sarah asked finally, waving at it, trying to be breezy. "Sam made it for me, although I know he must have hated it. He copied it from the Cuxa cloister at the Met, exactly to scale."

"It's beautiful," Joan said sincerely, lapsing into silence. What the hell right did she have barging in here and bothering the old woman with her news? It would only discourage her, maybe even dissuade her from going through with the departmental hearing. Just because Celia had succeeded in ruining her afternoon, did she have to do the same for Sarah?

"You're upset about something," Sarah observed casually, as if Joan had announced it on arrival. "And you took time off from work to come here. Personal problem?"

"No," Joan said, sitting on a stone bench and pulling a weed from a crack between the flagstones.

"What then?" Sarah demanded, attacking a rosebush with the clippers. Her bad hand could not manage the clippers. Joan tried to take them from her, but Sarah waved her away. "What then?" she repeated when Joan didn't answer. "And why come here with it? If it's not your problem, it must be one of mine. Out with it!"

Joan repeated everything Celia had told her. Sarah sat on the bench beside her during the narrative and swung the rose clippers in her left hand long after Joan had finished speaking.

"Those poor people!" Sarah said at last, and Joan could see that there were tears in her eyes, and that her voice was in danger of strangulation. "Those poor, brave, lovely people! I never thought they'd go out on a limb for me."

She was so overcome by the news of the strike, she'd completely disregarded the rest. Joan wanted to remind her, but Sarah was off and running now and had no intention of listening to anything negative.

"Well!" she breezed, pretending to have dust in her eyes, and spending some time elaborately removing her gardening gloves and wiping her eyes. "That's certainly encouraging, isn't it? Can't let the good people down now, can we?"

"But Sarah—" Joan began, knowing it was useless.

"And that bitch!" Sarah exploded with uncharacteristic fervor, flailing about with the rose clippers as if at an imaginary foe. "Why is it that type always floats to the top in small Catholic colleges?"

Joan was startled, and more than a little shocked. She knew Sarah hadn't been religious for eons, but since she worked in Catholic institutions she ought to have some degree of—

"It is because, my dear," Sarah went on, answering her own question, "the Church, after all, is just another human institution, and here as in all human institutions it is the cold-blooded, the unimaginative, the mediocre of intellect who climb over the other bodies to get to the top. That's why the creaky old mechanism is as fucked-up as it is today. I often try to imagine Christ—the same Christ who got high blood pressure over a handful of grubby little money-changers—coming back to have a look at this corporate conglomerate with its cutthroat political machinery, and running home to sharpen the old scourge. My, how the shit would fly then—"

She stopped when she saw the look on Joan's face. She had ranged quite far afield within the last five minutes; perhaps it had frightened the girl.

"Have I offended you?" Sarah asked suddenly. "I have no idea of your religious status right now—"

"No, it's all right," Joan said, shaking her head. "I've been out of it for a while. You just threw me for a minute. I—"

"You've given up your religion?" Sarah said in mock-horror, trying to inject a little humor into the situation. "Whatever for?"

"I don't know really," Joan frowned, taking it quite seriously. "Ever since I moved out on my parents, I've stopped going to church, just kind of avoided any kind of authority. We had Eric baptized, mostly to keep the families satisfied, but I don't think he needs any formal religious instruction until he's old enough to reason it out and decide for himself. As for me, I guess I'm still a Christian—in the sense that I believe in the message of Christ, not the crap they've tried to make out of it for the past two thousand years—but all of that churchgoing just doesn't move me one way or the other. I mean, I don't presume to understand God. I don't even understand elementary algebra, for Chrissake! You tell me the earth is round, I'll believe you. Six hundred years ago I would have gone with the consensus and said it was flat. None of it has anything to do with my everyday life, how I live, what kind of person I am. I think I'm leading an essentially moral life. Even though my background says divorce is a sin, I think I'm doing the right thing. Life should be growth and maturity, not stagnation. Living with Brian was stagnation, for both of us. I'm making a morally good decision by freeing both of us from that. And I don't think I have to sit in some badly decorated, drafty old barn every Sunday to be told what to do. Religion is a leveler. Maybe I'm a snob, but I think I've got a little more going for me than the old ladies with the rosary beads. I'm not a sheep, and I'm not a child, and I resent that stuff in the scriptures that says I have to be. And I resent some sterile old man sittng in an ivory tower half a planet away dictating to me about my sex life. And I resent the fact that women are kept down under a patriarchal structure that—"

"Whoa!" Sarah interrupted, though she looked immensely pleased. She had listened without interrupting while Joan got it out of her system. "I didn't ask for the whole lecture. I asked a simple question and got an entire philosophical discourse."

"I'm sorry," Joan said, embarrassed by her own eloquence.

"No, don't be," Sarah insisted, squeezing her hand. "It's good. Good that you can verbalize that kind of thing. Most often one gets so emotionally involved it's impossible to talk about religion. Cuts too close to the bone."

"It's probably the first time in my life I ever put it into words," Joan said wonderingly. "I used to get so mad, so incoherent. . . ."

"Well now that you can say it, don't ever apologize for your views," Sarah told her. "Essentially I agree with you. And I was older than you before I could express it quite so well. By the way, would you care to hear a little theory I've worked out? I have an awful lot of time to sit around and work things out in my head lately, you know, and, oh, Jesus, I have to admit this one's hysterical even if it is mine!"

Joan frowned. "What theory?" she asked, wanting to laugh but wondering if she was about to be witness to another of Sarah's mood swings.

"My theory—" Sarah said, "if that is the word I want —my theory on the future of the Catholic Church. Will you indulge me in this for a few minutes?"

"Why not?" Joan asked warily, watching the old woman's face for some sign of danger. All she saw was a twinkle in the back of her eyes, something she had seen often in the classroom, but never in this new phase of Sarah's life. What the hell, if it brightened Sarah's day just a little . . .

They sat together on the stone bench in the center of the cloister. A sneaky wind, promising rain, had begun trickling around their ankles. It was a perfectly Gothic setting.

"All right then," Sarah began, looking mischievous, "let us begin with a question. Reducing all organized religions to their most pragmatic form, what is the one thing they have in common?"

A profound answer was not required here. A strange sort of allegory was being written. Joan would have to tread carefully.

"It's your theory," she challenged Sarah. "You tell me."

"Come, come, the answer is obvious." Sarah nudged her in the ribs. "No religion, no organization of any kind, can exist without money. You know, that stuff they call the root of all evil? As long as it's still in the parishioners' pockets it is. Consequently, one subject that occupies much of the time of religious leaders—and let us for the sake of argument, since we are most familiar with it, stick with the One Holy and Apostolic Roman Church—is that of money, and how to acquire vast sums of same when the coffers start to ring hollow. Now, judging from the present course of Holy Mother Church, what with *Humanae Vita* making people gallop off in droves—and many of those who stay are using birth control all the same—what do you suppose will ultimately happen to the coffers?"

"They'll run out of money," Joan said, feeling like a child, waiting for the distant thunder.

"Precisely." Sarah smiled. "Now, before they go completely broke, they're going to have to do something drastic. What do you suppose would be a reasonable first step —in keeping with trends in other churches, let us say?"

"What?" Joan asked, deliberately playing it dumb.

"Come, come, you're supposed to be the liberated generation!" Sarah looked dismayed. "Ordination of women, obviously. We have to keep up with the Lutherans and Episcopalians, don't we? So as a last-ditch effort to acknowledge the existence of half the population of the churches—over half in actuality, since it's the women who drag the men and kids along—are you with me so far? It's going to get complicated, though. What the church fathers don't realize is that the addition of church mothers is going to open another can of worms altogether."

"I'm listening," Joan said, waiting for the old woman to smile and prove that she was joking. Her face was completely serious now, though there was still a suggestion of laughter in her voice.

"Things will start to get sticky," Sarah explained, "right after the first wave of ordinations—and I do mean a wave, because there are countless women in the convents and elsewhere who are dying for it to happen. Okay, even before they start ordaining all these new people, problems will arise. Problem number one: Where do we house all these women? There will be no funds from the still-depleted churches to build separate dorms. They can't put them in the convents, because the nuns will be horribly jealous. Nuns are very preoccupied with status, don't you know, but that's another matter. But what shall we do with all of these—ahem—female seminarians? Incidentally, we'll simply *have* to find another word, the idea of women being inseminated, even on an intellectual level, will have to be—oh, dear!"

Sarah was laughing, the same crazy laugh that had turned so rapidly to tears the day they'd talked about Sam. Joan watched her carefully, ready to head off another such scene, but Sarah went on laughing.

"Hee hee hee! Oh, God, where was I? Ah, yes, insemination—artificial or otherwise. The solution to this problem seems simple enough, though, at least at first glance. We must reopen the case for a married priesthood, stipulating that priests can only marry other priests. Think of all the money that can be saved by doubling up; think of all the furniture that won't be needed with two people to a bed. Good Lord, we might even be able to come to terms with that most touchy of subjects, homosexuality. Once we get that out in the open, we can cut the budgets for the religious orders as well."

"Sarah!" Joan gasped. "This is very cute, but really—"

"Wait," Sarah cautioned, raising an imperious hand. "I'm just getting started!"

"That's what worries me," Joan said sarcastically, hunching her shoulders in defeat.

She can't be serious, Joan thought. She's either kidding or she's cracked. Joan could see the corner of the Inquisitor's cowl peering past the side of the house by the garbage pails. If she wasn't careful, she might almost fall for the scenario; the cloister, the late-September wind, the austere-faced ex-nun by her side could easily transform a Brooklyn backyard into a real convent cloister, say somewhere near the Normandy coast, where the weather always— What was being spoken here was heresy. Joan looked at the Inquisitor again. His face was a black hole. There was a faggot of twigs balanced on his shoulder, ripe for burning. Cracked or sane, he would gladly haul the old heretic away as soon as she'd slipped the noose around her own talkative throat.

"Now then," Sarah continued, her good leg swinging slightly in time to the rapidity of her thoughts. "As soon as they've sold off those twin beds, and the convents and the monasteries are filling up, and the laity are flocking back in droves, fascinated by the new phenomenon of relaxed male and female people speaking to them from the altar, that's when we hit up against problem number two."

Joan waited, refusing even token participation in this madness. She hoped the Inquisitor took note.

"Pregnancy," Sarah said in pear-shaped tones. "Female priests, like female people in general, will tend to get pregnant with alarming frequency in a society that ignores the possibility of contraception. After the initial panic is over, and all those bulges start appearing under all those cassocks—assuming they're still wearing them, and I can't see any woman in her right mind . . . But *now* what do we do? We can't afford to feed all those extra mouths, and we mustn't have all those little munchkins scrambling around the rectories, wanting their diapers changed and their noses wiped. We can't spare the time from doing God's work—whatever that is. It's all right for lay people; has been for years. Keeps 'em in their place. If they can afford to get past eighth grade, they'll ask too many questions. It won't work for priests, though.

"Well, once the masses find out the clergy is on the Pill, there'll be an uproar. And finally, ass-backward, the Church will understand the need for birth control, and contraception will become part of the curriculum in Catholic grammar schools, which will lead to the eventual proliferation of the good word to all nations. Within a single generation, we will see the elimination of abortion, child abuse, crime, poverty, racism, militant nationalism—all the results of too many unwanted children growing up into monstrous, craving adults. For the first time in the history of the species, mankind will exist as a global entity, with enough space, enough food, enough opportunities for education and enlightenment—all because one major religion tried to economize on furniture and everyone else followed their example. Makes your heart throb, doesn't it?"

There was a long moment of silence.

"What about that first batch of pregnancies?" Joan asked doggedly, not about to buy the fairy tale outright.

Sarah shrugged. "Those children," she said, "will be absorbed into the life of the monastery, as they were in the medieval church, which was more sensitive to the human frailty of its members. They will grow up surrounded by the warmth and compassion of the new generation of priests, who will know from their own experience the agonies and joys of family life. The Church will become one glorious extended family, not the cranky, backbiting, hair-splitting conglomerate it is today. Not angels dancing on a pin but children dancing in the sacristy will be the image of the new Church. It brings tears to my eyes just to think of it!"

"You're crazy!" Joan said loudly. "Do you believe all that crap?" She was giving Sarah a chance to save herself, hoping the Inquisitor was listening.

Sarah shrugged again, her half-smile whimsical though her eyes were sad. "The medievalist deals in fable and allegory," she said. "Consider it a wistful fable for our time. What will really happen is that the present regime, who, though he may be Polish, is still under the thumb of the Roman Curia, will croak off eventually, and by some fluke—dare we call it the intervention of the Holy Spirit?—perhaps the dry old men will next time elect somebody with some compassion, not to mention sense. Over an agonizing period of years if we get lucky and there are no more Italian popes, the Latin disdain for women will be overcome by a little good sense, though

God knows I won't live to see it." She broke off suddenly. "It's cold. I'm going inside."

She rose with unusual spryness, gathering up her gardening tools and striding into the kitchen. Joan lingered a while, wondering which version of the story to believe, wondering which one Sarah really preferred. When she went to throw the rose clippings into the garbage can, the Inquisitor had vanished.

Pietro sat in the dank-smelling darkness, cramped into a confessional that had been designed for smaller men. The stuffing was coming out of the squashed-flat cushion on the bench that creaked ominously beneath his weight. Slumped down into the only position he could maintain for any appreciable length of time, he had to press his knees against the door with the little parquet crucifix that defined the limits of his prison. If he dozed during one of the nuns' endless recitations of trivia and the chapel caught fire, he'd be trapped, burned to a crisp along with the moldy maroon velvet draperies.

Damn Lipinsky, he thought. Last night they'd been playing chess as usual—Pietro had been on an unbroken losing streak since his return from Rome, preoccupied with the bitterness of a wasted summer and the worry over Sarah—and Father Lipinsky had suggested a way to spice up what for him was becoming a dull ritual. The wizened little cossack wasn't satisfied with merely winning, he thought it necessary to gamble just a little.

The ante in last night's game had been today's confessions in the college chapel, and Pietro had lost again. Lipinsky had in mind a soccer game or something that was on television this afternoon, and Pietro was stuck listening to the endless ticking-off of petty errata mumbled in dentured monotony by a dozen or so elderly nuns.

(Only the older nuns went to conventional confessions anymore; the younger set favored the less grueling general absolution that went with the new liturgy.) Pietro was trapped. How to die of boredom in a single afternoon . . . Damn Lipinsky! Pietro thought. Each time he heard the kneeler creak, he had to rouse himself from his self-induced stupor long enough to slide open the door that covered the nearly opaque grill through which the supposedly anonymous voices could seep. Discreet, Pietro kept his right hand over his eyes as he listened.

"Bless me, Father, for I have sinned. My last confession was one week ago. . . ."

The repetition of the formula was stupefying, but this time the voice sent a cold thrill down his spine. He was about to have the dubious honor of a glimpse into the very soul of Sister Francis Anne herself!

Pietro half-listened as she went on about some trivial thing—neglecting to say her morning prayers, he thought —while his mind groped about for another level of significance he felt certain was there. He thought he had a fix on it at last: Francis never went to Lipinsky's confessions; she managed to drop in at the bishop's office next door to the college at least once a week, and, while the bishop himself no longer heard confessions, he did have this marvelously discreet young aide. . . .

But what did it mean? Did Francis know who comprised her captive audience on the other side of the grill? Had she singled him out for a reason?

Pietro did not have to wait long for an answer. Francis was coming to the crux of her whispered narrative.

"Father—" She seemed to hesitate.

"Yes?" he rumbled evenly, resisting the urge to add "my child."

"There is a decision I have been wrestling with," she went on, the mellifluousness of her voice only partially muted by the fact that she was whispering. "A moral decision about which I need—counsel. Advice."

Pietro knew what was coming, and it threw him into a panic. His confessional experience had been sparse in recent years, limited to college kids with sexual hang-ups and seminarians with complex but manageable moral dilemmas. He'd spent his salad years in a slum parish and thought he'd heard everything, but academic life had spoiled him. And there was no precedent, in his experience, for this. He knew exactly what she was going to do, and simultaneously had not the vaguest idea what his own response would be.

"Yes?" he asked after the briefest pause, raising his voice a little above a whisper to make certain Francis knew who he was. "Go on, Sister, please."

"I do not wish to burden you with details—" she began.

Details with which I am already quite familiar, Pietro read between the lines.

—"but I am faced with a decision concerning the academic future of a colleague, and I am uncertain if my approach is completely objective in regard to this person."

"Has there been—conflict, perhaps a personality clash, between you in the past?" Pietro inquired, letting her lead him where she would.

"In a manner of speaking, yes," Francis acknowledged.

"Was it a personal matter, or one of a purely academic nature?" Pietro asked, wanting to laugh at this well-wrought charade, but sobered by the seriousness of its intent.

She had him by the short hairs, trussed up in the seal of the confessional, helpless. He couldn't repeat this conversation to Sarah, to anybody, without violating the sacred oath of his priesthood. John of the Cross had had his tongue cut out for less. Crafty bitch! he thought, and held himself back.

There was an inordinately long pause on Francis's side of the grill, as if she were struggling to frame a response. Perhaps she had not heard his question, or—

"This is the difficulty," she said at last, in a tone so plaintive that Pietro could almost believe her. "Who can say where objectivity ends and subjectivity begins? Because I take personal umbrage against a colleague whose personality is—unorthodox, can I be certain that it will affect my decision upon that person's competence to teach? And if, on the other hand, I had a close personal friend whose professional abilities were in question, could I be certain of objectivity in that case either?"

There was more, but Pietro wasn't listening. A stupider man would not have realized how neatly the package had been dropped into his lap. Loosely translated, she was telling him he was as prejudiced for Sarah as she was against Sarah. Let he who is without sin . . .

"As an objective viewer, Sister," he said after much thought, tongue in cheek, "I can only advise you to follow the dictates of your own conscience. In matters of an emotional nature, Holy Mother Church can merely provide guidelines, which the individual of clear conscience must weigh personally."

Plop. It was back in her lap, neatly packaged in platitudes. What would she do now?

There was a profound sigh from beyond the grill. If she hadn't taken the habit, Pietro thought grimly, Garbo wouldn't have stood a chance.

"Whatever course of action I take," Francis said weightily, "be advised that it will be a moral choice, and as such I intend to defend it."

In a kind of daze, Pietro assigned her some piddling conventional penance, and sat alone in the darkness for far longer than it would have taken her to rattle off the handful of Our Fathers and Hail Marys up at the communion rail. "Be advised," she had said. What the hell did that mean?

Whatever else happened between now and the week before Christmas, Pietro thought, getting up and stretching his aching bones, the next time he saw Lipinsky coming at him with that chessboard he was going to tell him where to put it.

XIV

For whatever we lost (like a you or a me)
it's always ourselves we find in the sea.
E.E. CUMMINGS,
maggie and milly and molly and may

"Oh, stop it, all of you!" Sarah bellowed above two voices
and the intermittent typewriter. "For God's sake, clear
out and let me alone!"

The three of them ground to a halt. Celia, who had
been typing letters to the important alumnae, spoke up
first.

"Hell," she snapped. "I've only got two more!"

Sarah merely glared at her. Celia sat indifferently at
the typewriter with her hands in her lap. She had
stopped what she was doing, but only temporarily. She
was not about to give up and put everything away.

"All right, then," Sarah said, as if she were doing
Celia a favor instead of the other way around. "Finish
them if you must. You're making the least amount of
noise, at any rate."

She turned her wrath on Joan and Helen, who sat
like chastened children while Celia's hunt-and-peck typing
resumed.

Sarah was growing more short-tempered as the date

of her hearing neared. At first, after initial misgivings, she had given Celia permission to write her polemical letters; later she'd decided they were indeed blackmail and ordered her to stop. Celia calmly put the letters aside for a few weeks until Sarah relented and let her continue. Celia worked daily with the vicissitudes of directors and stage managers. Sarah's moods disturbed her not at all.

This was the last weekend remaining before the hearing. Helen and Joan had been working alternate shifts—coaching Sarah, combing her vast collection of textbooks to prepare her for any question she could possibly be asked. They had made up cassettes for her to listen to in their absence. Until today she had been quite able to keep up with the two of them and the tape recorder. Now she had simply had enough. They had been babbling at her for what seemed like hours. For the next five days she intended to listen to nothing but silence and her own thoughts.

"Put them away!" she commanded, waving her good hand at the shambles of textbooks and notes that were strewn about the room. "Dante and Petrarch in the corner by the dining-room door, third shelf. Bede, Alcuin, and the Tancred chronicles by the mantel, left-hand side. And throw all the papers away!"

"But, Sarah—" Helen fluttered. She was the type who saved the string from bakery boxes; the idea of throwing away pages and pages of notes . . .

"*Leave* them then," Sarah roared, "but get them out of my sight or I'll use them for tinder the next time I start a fire. Do me a favor and go home and watch an old movie, or do your laundry, or clean out some closets, but please, please stop hovering! My blood pressure's gone up five points for each of you!"

Celia zipped the last envelope out of the typewriter and turned it off with a flourish.

"You're finished?" Sarah demanded, and Celia nodded silently. "Fine. Stick a stamp on it and clear out!"

"Fuck you!" Celia grinned affectionately. It was meant as an endearment, and Sarah took it as such. She smiled her half-smile in return.

Celia and Helen packed up and got their coats. Joan was about to join them when Sarah motioned her to stay where she was. Joan sat down and waited.

"I love you dearly," Sarah said, all but pushing Helen and Celia down the front steps, "but you're a collective pain in the ass!"

When she'd slammed the door, she pounced on Joan. "Get my winter coat from the hall closet," she ordered. "And the car keys. We're going to the beach."

Joan was stunned. "You want to run that by me again?" she asked. "Slowly?"

"I always go to the beach in December," Sarah explained simply, as if to an idiot. "Just as I always go to Stonehenge in the summer. Last year I missed both, and the next few weeks don't promise to lend themselves to leisure activities. You're here with the car today, so we go today."

"Hold it!" Joan exploded. Sarah's posturing all day had been getting on her nerves, and this latest order had tipped the scale. "I'm not going anywhere today. It was twenty-eight degrees when I left the house this morning, and it's not much warmer now."

"That's a valid point," Sarah said, considering it. "I guess you'd better let the car warm up a while before I put my coat on. Helluva day to have it stall on us."

"Helluva day to go to the beach!" Joan shot back, but Sarah had made up her mind, and there was no dissuading her.

Joan got her coat and the car keys, jingling them sarcastically as she went outside. She would warm up the car and drive it around to the front of the house so

Sarah wouldn't have to walk. She even intended to go inside and help the old woman down the steps, but Sarah was already waiting at the curb when she pulled up—cane clutched in one gloved hand, half her face shiny with eagerness.

"Okay, crazy lady," Joan said, after she'd gone around the car to let her in. "Where to?"

When she brought the car to a standstill in the empty, sand-swept parking lot and ran around it the second time to help Sarah out, it occurred to Joan that they were both crazy. What could be more idiotic than two unprotected women, one of whom had difficulty walking, alone on a seemingly deserted beach?

They stepped from the asphalt to the sand, cutting their limited speed in half. Sarah's weak leg kept buckling, and Joan had to grab her arm several times to keep her from toppling over.

"You're shivering," Sarah informed her over the wind. "Blanket's in the car."

Joan knew damn well there was a blanket in the car. Who had been driving the car for the past six months? She was not cold; she was terrified.

"I'm not cold," she snapped impatiently. "It's just so damn *weird* out here!"

They neared the water's edge, and it was easier to walk on the wet sand at the tide line. They stopped after only a few steps, arms linked, swaying slightly in the wind, the tips of their shoes and Sarah's cane teased gently by the spent waves.

"Over there," Sarah said after a moment, pointing with her cane toward a nearby breakwater.

The flailing cane dug deeply into the wet sand and seemed to propel her forward. Joan tramped dispiritedly beside her. Sarah sat finally on a damp flat rock on the breakwater, her feet just inches away from where the water surrendered to the insistent lunar tugging and retreated. Joan sat slightly behind her, careful to keep her feet dry, sheltering herself against the old woman's shoulder, downwind to catch every word of the lecture she knew was forthcoming.

"It's cold!" she whined like a spoiled child when Sarah seemed lost in thought and not about to begin her lecture at once. "If you're going to talk, can't we at least go back and sit in the car?"

"Coward," Sarah teased her. "No, we cannot. We are going to stay right here. I want to clear my head and prepare for what's coming. I don't want to do anything but just ramble for a while."

"Oh, swell," Joan growled.

"Think about something," Sarah said out of nowhere. "Have you ever been to the beach except to swim?"

"No," Joan replied. "I'm not crazy. Oh, maybe just to walk a little. But never this time of year."

"But why?" Sarah wanted to know. "People go to parks in the winter. Why don't they ever come to the beach? Is it just the cold, or are they afraid of being this much alone, looking out at this monstrous vacuum called the sea, without another human being in sight? What makes deserts so scary? Is it just the heat, the lack of water, or is it the total absence of structure, of that which is recognizably civilized? Why is it that NASA sent the straightest, sanest, passed-all-the-Rorschach-tests men they could find out into space? Not an imagination among them. No poets, no philosophers, no closet landscape painters, and—God forbid—no women. Carbon copies—with a little more intelligence, maybe—of Joe Mow-the-lawn-weekends America. And yet nearly every one of them came back with a strange glow in his eyes, and none of them fit into their little cubicles when they returned. They fell into drugs and booze and analysis, their marriages broke up, and so on. Why? Because they got too close to the undisguised face of God, that's why, and coming back to this old earth was too boring to be endured."

She's at it again, Joan thought, remembering the day in the backyard. There were traces of the old classroom rhetoric, but only traces. There was no logic to Sarah's ramblings, nothing to hold them together. The restraints of the classroom were gone, the syllogistic structure vanished. Lecture gave way to raving, ideas became more and more disjointed; there were leaps that defied comprehension. Was it a case of nerves over the upcoming events, the onset of senility, or simply a new form of mania? Why was it necessary to set a scene, to philosophize from a cold stone on a frozen beach? This was a further descent than the lecture in the garden. The miniature cloister with its lifeless shrubs and shuddering dead leaves had given way to this moonscape, where even the tide fled the sound of Sarah's voice. Joan kept an eye out for the Inquisitor, lurking perhaps in the damp lightlessness beneath the boardwalk, blocking their return to the warmth and safety of the car.

But there was no Inquisitor this time, and Joan was almost disappointed; he might have lent credibility to the landscape. Not that this was a religious monologue, at least not yet, but all the same . . . She burrowed down into her coat and decided that if she kept really quiet, Sarah would get tired of talking to herself and they could go home.

"Why do you suppose mankind has invented all of these essentially flimsy structures—governments, religions, secret organizations, fraternities, block associations, Cub Scouts? It's a herding instinct—a fear of standing alone like the one tree in the field that always gets struck by lightning. We are afraid to meet ourselves, or God, face-to-face. In previous centuries, we could hide in the churches, and the churches could hide behind the rules and formulas that obscure their real purpose. In the twentieth century, we are a little more free, hence a little more afraid. We can be atheists if we like—after all, denying the existence of God lets us do what we bloody well please without having to look over our shoulder, and, since it's all pointless, why must we obey rules? Or the frightened ones can still hide behind religion, whether it's one of the standard ones or something new like TM or spiritualism, as long as the herd is still there. The only place the herd can't follow us is to the special time and place when each one of us has to die. Oh, it's comforting to think that the priest will be in the same room with us, mumbling his incantations and keeping the beasties from snatching us down to hell at the last minute, but the sad fact is that he will still be in the room mumbling when each of us goes flying out the window. *Alone.*

"But how bad could it be? A baby cries at birth, if it has any sense, and if it had the slightest idea what it had to look forward to over the next three-score-and-ten it wouldn't be satisfied with a mouthful of warm milk and a warm place to sleep. In a sense, we spend the rest of our lives ducking the next phase, sucking our thumbs and squeezing our eyes shut against the light. We didn't want to leave the first womb, and, sure enough, look what happened when they did manage to drag us out of there. And none of us wants to leave the womb we inhabit now, however inhospitable it may be. We know what it's like, it's *familiar*, so we'll put up with it rather than try something new. Nobody really wants to be reborn. Not the priests and theologians. Not the old ladies with the rosary beads, either. Not even the atheists. Put a gun to any of their heads and they'd shit in their pants, just like you and me.

"You would like to ask me what there is out there, wouldn't you? As if I'm supposed to know solely because I'm closer to death than you are. 'What is the Answer?'

'What is the Meaning of Life?' As if there were only one. Jesus, child, I don't know what it's all about! There are people who have almost died and come back to tell us about it. They say it's beautiful beyond description. Most of them were reluctant to come back. I don't remember anything like that the two times it nearly got me, maybe because it wasn't the real thing. But I stopped shitting in my pants a while ago.

"The only answer I've come up with is this: The important thing is to be able to look back from the point of death and say an unqualified Yes. Yes, I have accomplished something. Yes, I have been true to myself. Yes, I have done something to jusify my birth, my taking up a given space in this universe. Does it sound arrogant? It isn't really. Talent is not self-generated, it's a gift—from God, if you believe in God, from Whatever-else if you believe in Whatever-else. What is truly arrogant is wasting the talents you have, spending your life bemoaning the ones you wanted and didn't get. Does that sound simplistic? Forgive me. Cynicism is a luxury of the immature. I'd like to see you come up with something better.

"It's very simple for me, if you must know. I have to see Sam again. We left a lot of things unfinished, he and I, and I can't believe they are to remain unfinished forever. And I cannot believe that a bad draw in the biological raffle means I will never come to know the little girl I wanted so much. And I have to meet a lot of people I've been reading about and teaching about for years—to see if I've done right by them, to see if my life *has* been meaningful. I would be content with this much; throw in the presence of God, too—whatever that means—and it's simply too much to contemplate. I have to believe there's a next step, regardless of how big a nose dive it may turn out to be. This life is not enough; I want more. Naïve? The old Leap-of-Faith syndrome?

Possibly. One doesn't escape that entirely, no matter how far one is removed from the Church. But you'll get no platitudes out of me. Make up your own answers, little jumping Joan. Before you start looking around for death, for God's sake do something intelligent with your life."

Joan waited, making sure it was over. "Are you quite through?" she asked finally.

"Quite." Sarah half-smiled, seeing how the tide had receded during her diatribe. "We can go now, if you like."

Joan led Sarah back to the car after the old woman had spent a long, silent moment looking out over the water, her white hair whipped about by the wind, her eyes feverish and more than a little mad.

In the car on the way back, Sarah invited Joan to stay for supper. This was not unusual in itself, except that she added, almost as an afterthought, "Pietro's coming."

Joan nearly drove right up on the sidewalk. "Are you sure it's all right for me to see the two of you together?" she asked lightly, trying to pass it off as a joke.

"How do you mean?" Sarah frowned. Why did her entire face register the frown, when only half of it could smile?

Joan was thinking of the time she'd watched Pietro climb the front steps of Sarah's house in the rain, of the number of times she'd arrived to find the seashell on the mantel full of burned-out Camels, and to all but see the wisps of smoke lingering in his recently accomplished absence.

"Up to now you've always managed to spirit one of us out the door just as the other was about to get there," she said. "Always made me wonder."

"I wasn't aware that it seemed that way to you,"

Sarah said, lying through her teeth. "There's really nothing to wonder about."

"Really?" Joan said, dripping with skepticism.

She pulled the car up in front of Sarah's house, waiting to see if there would be a response. There was none. Sarah sat placidly waiting to be helped from the car. Surrendering, Joan got out and ran around the car yet again.

"I've often wondered," Joan said later with lead-footed subtlety as she helped set the table, "why you never remarried."

Sarah considered it for a while. "I guess I never felt I had to," she said thoughtfully. "I felt that what Sam and I had was something too precious to try to duplicate —as if Sam had taken part of me with him when he died and I'd never be the same again. It never occurred to me to go traipsing around in pursuit of another man."

"Not even a temporary one?" Joan persisted, knowing she was being crass, but asking anyway.

Sarah shrugged. "I had a lot of male friends," she acknowledged. "Mutual friends from the parties Sam and I had, and a lot of academic types I met on those wacky lecture tours. But I never considered any of them to be anything more than friends, who incidentally happened to be male. There was never any kind of physical angle at all."

"No lovers at all then?" Joan seemed genuinely disappointed.

"Lovers? Me?" Sarah's laughter echoed through the house. "Good Lord, I'm much too much of an old prude for that!"

"But there must have been opportunities, even if you passed them up." Joan was getting in deeper and deeper, but until she got an answer to the particular question she wanted to ask . . . "I mean, you were still young."

Sarah considered this. "Mm. I suppose so," she said.

"Thirty-eight isn't exactly creaking. But remember, my hair started graying right after the hysterectomy. I looked older than I was."

"Still," Joan said naïvely, "it's hard to believe that you didn't have at least one little fling in all that—"

"You are such a child, aren't you?" Sarah asked evenly. "Why this question, and only today? What prompts it, truly? Why don't you ask the real question? Did I ever sleep with Pietro? No, baby, I didn't."

"I'm a nosy bastard, aren't I?" Joan said, chagrined now that she had the answer. What would she have done if Sarah had said yes?

"Yes, you are," Sarah said.

It had never really occurred to her until she had the doctorate safely hung over the desk where she typed her résumés two years after Sam died, but now it suddenly seemed apparent to Sarah that a woman's life was sharply delineated into pre- and postmenopause. Men's lives were a continuum; there was no noticeable line of demarcation between forty and forty-five. But a woman at forty was on the brink of something, standing on the divide between two quite separate portions of her life. Even she, whose artificial menopause had occurred suddenly when she was twenty-seven, could feel the difference. Her skin was drier, the fine lines crinkling at the corners of her eyes became more noticeable. Her chin seemed pointier, her prematurely graying hair became whiter almost daily. She still had her energy, thank God, and she had survived her period of mourning with no visible scars, but she had no delusions about her age.

She was looking for a quiet position in a small, noncompetitive college. For some reason, she was always drawn to Catholic institutions, despite her chronic disaffection with the Church. The job she finally got was precisely what she needed. Surrounded by priests and nuns, with a handful of lay people—some married, the rest hard-edged spinsters and chronic addled bachelors —she felt unthreatened, secure. No one tried matching her up. They accepted her widowhood and did not pity her.

As the newcomer in the English department, she was given the composition courses and the freshman lit courses, plus a Chaucer that the chairman was too overloaded to handle. Sarah shone. Within five years she was choosing the courses she wanted, rewriting the curriculum, creating a department of medieval literature that was unrivaled on the East Coast. She began to write— first isolated monographs published in low-profile scholarly annuals, then whole volumes of analysis and criticism. After a while she found it difficult to cover the full spectrum of her field without assigning her students at least one textbook or critical volume that she herself had written. She lectured, her scope limited only by an unreasonable terror of airplanes. During the summers, she traveled by boat, most frequently to England, where she bicycled from village to village, tramped around cathedrals and castles, researched, did brass rubbings, and danced at Stonehenge to her own private music under a full moon. She was happy.

After several years, she found she could learn to sleep alone again. She tried to keep in touch with Sam's friends, continuing to hold her famous parties, though not as often. She expanded the circle of invited guests by including certain colleagues and a select group of students from the college, becoming something of a cult figure on campus. Instead of a struggling artist living in the spare bedroom, there was often an indigent student or two camping out at her house. There was always someone around to wash the car, retar the roof, or help her move the piano. Most people liked her; only a few understood enough, and were permitted close enough, to love her. Of these few, one was a certain young priest.

He was barely thirty when she first met him. During his seminary training, he'd spent a lot of time working in the slums. Upon ordination he'd been sent to the Vatican as an assistant to a curial attaché. He was a Jesuit, a scholar. A Renaissance man, Sarah thought, getting to know him.

He had lasted a single year in Rome, sent back to New York at his own request. There had been a conflict of some sort with a superior; he was vague when questioned too closely about it. When Sarah first met him, he was cooling his heels while the order figured out what to do with him. Their decision was that a few years of teaching salvation history to sophomores might teach him the meaning of humility.

He behaved at first as if the assignment didn't particularly bother him, as if in fact he considered it something of a challenge, a new field of endeavor. He was trying a form of reverse psychology that he hoped would ultimately get him transferred somewhere—anywhere—else.

"I am surrounded by the largest collection of mediocrity ever assembled in one place!" he would sound off to anyone who cared to listen. "These kids are worse than mediocre; they're positively smug about it! They think morality is a neat little package you can wrap up and carry under your arm, not something you have to come to terms with every day of your life."

"They are only doing what your bishops and cardinals and popes and you scholarly types have taught them to do, Pete," Sarah would say, smiling at him over her cottage cheese. (It was in this phase of her life that she became a vegetarian.) "They're plugging in the right rules for the right situations, just as they've been taught from the Baltimore Catechism forward. Listen to some of your fellow professors—have you ever sat in on some-body else's course around here? They all teach essen-tially the same thing: Play by the rules and you get to go to heaven."

She loved to tease him; he took it so seriously. And she was getting to the age where she could afford to be amused at the passions of the younger generation.

"Bullshit!" he would say to her in private. "If only they'd send me someplace else! In the ghetto I felt like I was accomplishing something. I probably wasn't, but I felt like I was. All I managed to do in Rome was keep my fly zipped and my nose clean and my presence as un-obtrusive as possible. Even that doesn't work around here. God, I wish they'd send me someplace else!"

Sarah felt sorry for him. She invited him to one of her parties, hoping the conversation might cheer him up. He made the mistake of showing up in uniform, and was immediately set upon by every agnostic in the room. Watching him out of the corner of her eye, Sarah could see that he was eating it up.

She liked him, and though she was never so formal as to call him "Father," she never thought of him with-out automatically seeing the initials "S.J." after his name. She did not see their growing friendship as any-thing more than two intelligent people reaching out to each other across a morass of stupidity. She never con-sidered that he might be picking up vibrations, vibrations she was unaware she was emanating. Perhaps her still-unquiet longing for Sam made her unaware of how she appeared to others, particularly men, and especially men in Roman collars. And there was her age. She'd thought she was safe.

She was not completely dense, however. The first time she'd ever really looked at him, she'd held her breath for a long moment, letting it out in quiet admiration. Sam had taught her to see the body under the clothing that covered it, and all the cassocks in Christendom hid nothing from her practiced eye. And of course he was so different from Sam—tall, with masses of curly black hair and oddly gray eyes. And once, off campus, she'd seen him in his civvies—the dark hair spilled out of his open shirt collar attractively. Sam had been as hairless as a plucked chicken.

But she had filed her observations and gone about her business. She had been celibate until she met Sam, and she was well aware of the hazards from a woman's perspective. She did not know how any man could stand it, and she was not about to interfere, to upset the hair-trigger balance, however ephemerally.

At least that had been her conscious decision. She only became aware of her pulsating unconscious when it was nearly too late.

Sarah was surprised when Pietro began warming up to her, surprised and more than a little exhausted; she did not feel equipped to handle an infatuation at this point in her life. She watched Pietro with a mild amusement mixed with pity. It was sad how stunted that area of his development was, as if he were a fumble-footed adolescent instead of a mature man. He must have thought he was being so casual, going out of his way to talk to her when nobody else was around, aiming pointed phrases and meaningful glances, calf eyes, at her as if he were engaging in the subtlest of wordplay. She deflected these overtures untouched.

He began getting closer to her, touching her more than was necessary—a casual brush of the hand when passing her a book or a cafeteria tray, a friendly pat on the shoulder that lingered too long. Sarah might have let it go on longer rather than hurt his feelings, except that she saw that others were watching them. She didn't particularly care what they said about her, but she ought to spare him the humiliation, or worse, of being clucked about in this henhouse of an institution. Gossip could cost him his job. Not that he wouldn't *love* that.

She cornered him one afternoon in an empty classroom where he'd loitered, making conversation for an interminable amount of time. She was desperately hoping it *was* just a ruse to get himself transferred, something he felt safe in trying with her rather than getting mixed up with one of the students, many of whom were infatuated with *him*.

"Don't you think this has gone on long enough?" she asked.

"Absolutely!" he admitted, unabashed. "I think it's time we got it out into the open and came to terms with it."

Sarah's heart did a flip-flop. Good Lord, she thought. I am not equipped to handle this!

"What exactly do you mean by that?" she asked him carefully.

Pietro laughed and scratched his head, an irritating shaggy-dog habit he had. He was looking at the tips of his shoes under the long cassock, embarrassed. "I guess I'm not being fair when I say 'we.' It's not as if you've done anything to encourage me." He laughed again, desperately nervous. "But you must know—you must have seen that—that I'm attracted to you—violently attracted, I would say—and while I know you don't give a tinker's damn about me, I—"

"Wrong," Sarah said, keeping her voice in its lowest register to disprove her own nervousness.

"I don't understand." He was startled by her bluntness. He stopped scratching his head and looked up at her, perplexed.

"What I mean is," she tried to explain, "it isn't a question of your being attracted to me *per se*. Anyone female would do, I think, and I happen to be female. And you happen to be—horny, I guess I would call it. As for my own feelings—they are not exactly maternal."

She hadn't expected him to be pleased by this information, but she wasn't prepared for him to look quite that unhappy.

"You know," he sighed, defeated. "I've tried all the rational arguments. I've tried all the tricks they taught us in sem. Nothing works. It's not just a s-sexual thing, it's—"

"Are you sure?" Sarah demanded, cursing the blush that conquered her fair skin before she could even speak her thought. "Do you think about me all the time, or only when you masturbate?"

"All the time," he said, and his sincerity was pitiful.

She wished she hadn't said it. She wished she could hold his curly head in her arms and croon to him.

"I can't help you," she whispered, setting each word down like an unhatched egg. "I'm sorry. There's nothing I can do, really. I—"

"Just like that!" Pietro snapped, his voice cracking slightly. "It's so easy for you to say that, isn't it? How the fuck do you know when you haven't even tried?"

"That's not fair!" Sarah threw at him.

She was trapped in this room with him, and by her own design. Not that she thought he'd try anything, but still, it had been stupid to arrange for such a claustrophobic situation. Looking out the window, she could see the steady flow of pedestrians three floors below. They seemed so calm, purposeful, free of turmoil, while in this room . . .

"Do you think it's easy for me?" she asked him. "Easy to say 'I'm sorry' and try to leave it at that? You don't know how wrong you are!"

"Tell me about it," he rumbled, slouching against her desk, still unable to look her in the eye.

"Oh, don't be sardonic," she said over her shoulder, still looking out the window. "It's very unattractive. Shall I analyze it for you, this feeling, this drive of yours? Break it down into tidy little lists of possibilities?"

"Be my guest," Pietro said, half-defiantly.

"Fine," Sarah nodded, coming away from the window to confront him. She was in her element now, the archetypal teacher, delineating a plot, reducing the most torrid story line to a sanitary little outline.

"List number one," she began, counting them off on her fingers: "What you see in me. A woman of forty-four who perhaps does not look her age. Widowed, *ergo* lonely. Maternal, menopausal, *ergo* considerably safer than the dozens of nubile coeds who literally steam every time you pass them in the hall—"

"Oh, bullshit, Sarah!" Pietro protested. "They don't— you're not—will you give me a chance to—"

"No," she cut him off primly. "I'm not finished. List number two: What I see in you. A man, wearing a Roman collar. Please note that I include them both as a single entry. In my humble opinion, celibacy is one of the more perverse contributions of Judeo-Christian tradition to Western society, *and* I am quite aware of the body behind the collar. You're a very sexy man, Pietro. Never underestimate yourself in that respect. However, whatever my opinion of the priesthood, you at one time made a commitment to it, a commitment you were meant to keep.

"Which brings us," she continued, her voice rising to keep him from interrupting, "to list number three: What options we have at our disposal. One, we can ignore the whole thing and it will eventually go away. Not likely."

"Sarah—" he began, pleading.

"No! I have the floor," she said, shaking her head violently. If she let him stop her now . . . "Two, you can leave the priesthood as I left the convent many years ago, and we can get married and live happily ever after. We won't have to worry about children, because—"

"Sarah, please, for crying out loud!" His voice boomed across the room at her. "You don't understand anything—"

"But I do, darling. Believe me, I do."

She had dropped the mask entirely. Her voice was mellow with tenderness.

"I know you cannot leave," she said. "That collar is tattooed to your throat; you couldn't take it off if you wanted to. I know what you'd like us to do. You'd like to have an *affaire*, just to see. But an affair by its very nature is only temporary. What happens then? At what point do we decide to make a commitment? At what point do you decide to tear the collar from your neck and embark in a new direction? *What would you be if you weren't a priest?*"

"Maybe," he managed to say, "maybe a happy man."

"Because of me?" Sarah was incredulous. "No. You know what would happen? We would have our affair— for a month, a year, two years—and somewhere along the line you would convince yourself that you had committed a great sin. I would have to acknowledge that we were out of our minds, and we'd have to come to the parting of the ways, because I for one can't climb out of bed and spend the rest of my life nodding politely when I pass you in the halls. And I don't want to lose you, Pietro.

"You see, I need your friendship as desperately as you think you need sex, with me or with anybody. I think it is possible, in fact essential, that a woman and a man can have a close personal friendship without sex. I can't see fucking with you, honestly I can't. We both know any attempt would fail, and then we could no longer be friends. And I would lose one of the warmest, most intelligent, sparkling people I have ever known, all for a little sex. I can't call it love, because there's too much desperation in it, and I won't sacrifice a lifetime for a few nights of fireworks. It's totally selfish, but that's all I have to say."

She thought he was going to cry. His eyes were squeezed shut and he was biting his lower lip, his large body still hunched against her desk. She couldn't help it; she would have to touch him. She cradled his shaggy head against her shallow breasts and kissed his hair.

The contact electrified her. He threw his arms around her, clung to her. "I just need a little human contact!" he began to sob. "I'm an affectionate person. It's my background; I can't help it. But I'm a priest. I have to think before I even shake hands with someone. If it's a woman, she thinks I'm trying to make her. A man always wonders if I'm a fag. I'm supposed to spend my life reaching out to people, helping them. But I can't touch anyone. Is it me? Is it the collar? What is it?"

"Shhh!" Sarah soothed him, smiling foolishly, maternal. She clung to him, needing him as much as he needed her. She used to hug Sam a dozen times a day. Deprived of motherhood, she had added her maternal love to all the other loves she had for him, seeking every possible opportunity to fondle him, roughhouse with him, snuggle close to him while he growled in her ear. All of that love had been bottled up inside her since his death. Why should she waste it, let it spoil?

She clung to Pietro, though she knew his hands had left her waist and were finding their way up under her skirt. She did not try to stop him. Just this once, she thought. What harm? He'll find some kind of relief, and he'll discover that I'm not exotic, that I'm just a dried-up old woman whose mucous membranes aren't what they were. And I will have that feeling, just once more, and I will be satisfied. She relaxed, and did not try to stop him.

She had never worn a girdle. All he had to do was find his way past the garter belt and the practical cotton underpants. His hands were warm and dry; she could feel them through her stockings.

"Oh, God!" he groaned suddenly, pulling his hands away as if they'd been burned, crouching on his knees, covering his face.

Sarah came back to earth with a bump. "Pietro!" she whispered harshly, pushing at his shoulders.

He would not move. It had gone too far. She would have to help him. Shit! Sarah thought, hating herself. So busy thinking of what *you* wanted, you let him . . . She wondered wildly if he'd already come, if he was coming now, in this deathly silent, rigid immobility he'd no doubt practiced in the seminary.

"Move, damn you!" she ordered him, almost pulling him to his feet. He staggered against the blackboard ledge, his face contorted with the effort to stay in control. Not yet, Sarah thought. He's still up. If I can just . . .

She'd never unbuttoned a cassock before. She had no idea what they wore under them. Somehow, she had to . . . Blindly, she plunged her hands in, cupped them around him, and he let go.

He gave her his handkerchief later, and they did not look at each other for a long time, while she wiped both hands carefully, bunched up the handkerchief, and stuffed it into her purse. "I'll wash it for you," she managed to say. She was terrified of meeting his glance. Had they done what she'd been afraid they'd do—destroyed their friendship? And without even the pleasure of a few months'—

"No regrets," he rumbled suddenly. They had reversed roles. He was the stronger one now. "I started it. I'll take the rap." He was looking down at her averted face with great tenderness. "Besides, you didn't steal my virginity; I did a little fooling around the summer before I went into sem—had to make sure I could do without it."

"I should have—" she began.

"No," he said firmly, taking her by the shoulders. There was no electricity now. "I'm relieved. Washed clean. You've purged me of my evil humors. And you were right, I was horny. I'm sorry I had to burden you with it."

"No!" Sarah began to sob. She was shaking all over. "I shouldn't have—"

Pietro brought himself to his full height and placed both hands on her head. "*Te absolvo*—" he began. A feeble joke.

"No!" Sarah almost screamed, tearing loose from him. She calmed herself and stared right into his eyes. "Don't you understand? It isn't that easy for me. I have to forgive my own sins."

Sarah was being rather loud in her boredom. Joan was enjoying herself tremendously. She wondered that in four years at the same college she had not discovered what a charming individual this priest could be.

As for Pietro, any opportunity to tell one of his Vatican stories was not to be passed up. Sarah yawned again. He ignored her.

"Speaking of Roman summers," he was saying, "I have to share this little anecdote with you. You're a liberated young lady. You shouldn't mind a dirty story from an old priest."

"That's *not* a dirty story, Pete," Sarah interrupted crossly. "And you're not that old. Prematurely senile, perhaps, but not *old*. My God, you're not going to tell that one again!"

Pietro gave her a quizzical look. "Why not?" he demanded. "Joan hasn't heard this one yet."

"But *I* have," Sarah pointed out, playing the spoiled brat. "Along with every other story you've told tonight. Honestly, it's terrible to be such a bore you can only repeat the same tired old stories every time you get a new audience."

"A story is the same as a joke," Pietro argued. "If the audience hasn't heard it yet, it's still new."

"Never mind," Sarah sniffed. "Just get on with it."

Joan listened to them, trying not to giggle. What was it Vicki had said? "Like an old married couple." Vicki should only be here now, Joan thought, enjoying their happiness with each other, however disguised in crotchety arguments it might be.

"Well, apropos the heat of a Roman summer," Pietro addressed Joan, as if there had been no interruption. He glanced sideways at Sarah, who was deaf and blind. "You have no idea. It is simply incredible. Not as humid as New York, but *hot*. Deadly. So the first summer I was over there—newly ordained, green as the hills—I got into the habit of sleeping in the nude. I had a room of my own in the faculty dorm of a boys' school out in the suburbs. I said mass for them in the mornings before I trotted off to the archives, and they got to know me. Made fun of my accent, played all sorts of jokes on me —we got along well.

"Now, this school was a kind of preseminary prep school. Most of the boys who started there would eventually enter the priesthood. How they could arrive at a decision of that sort of the age of thirteen is beyond me, but you get the picture. Naturally the regimen was very strict, and the superiors were very concerned—almost paranoid—about homosexuality. I think if any of the boys had been found with a girl in his bed, they'd have been relieved. Better that than one of his classmates.

"They used to have bed checks every night—in the faculty quarters as well—to make sure everyone was in bed, alone, and not engaged in any covert activity. So here I am on this stifling night, windows thrown open and not even a suggestion of a breeze, and suddenly I hear this whispering. Am I losing my mind or what? I tiptoe to the door and look out into the hall. Nothing. I get back into bed, but I can still hear it. It's coming from outside the window! I am three stories above the ground in a sixteenth-century villa, with nothing between me and the ground but a little ledge about six inches wide that runs around the entire building. I look outside, and there, perched on the ledge in their skivvies, are two of the boys—both about fifteen—giggling their heads off and damn near killing themselves falling off the ledge.

"Now, I know if they're caught in my room I'm as good as dead, because the word has gotten around that I sleep in the nude, and nobody's going to believe that these two clowns are out for the night air. It's my conjecture they wanted to have a look for themselves, and they weren't counting on my being awake. I don't want to let them in, but I don't want them getting killed, either. So what am I going to do?"

"What *did* you do?" Joan asked, entranced.

"First I grabbed a pair of shorts—my pride will take precedence over their safety any day—then I grabbed them by the scruff of their necks and dragged them through the window. I was going to boot them out into the hall to fend for themselves when I heard the old lay brother waddling along with his flashlight, and being softhearted if not softheaded, I stashed the two of them under my bed and told them I'd personally kill them if they blew it.

"I swear to this day that he knew they were in there, but that he figured being a foreigner I had some sort of diplomatic immunity, so he'd have to be careful. All he did was grill me for about twenty minutes. Had I heard any strange noises, noticed anything peculiar? I kept yawning in his face and mumbling about the heavy work load I had in the morning, but I couldn't shake him. Finally he got tired of hearing his own voice, and I had to wait another ten minutes until I heard him walking around on the floor above. By this time the two idiots were practically suffocating, so I threw them out in the hall and that was that. They must have expected me to rat on them, but I never did. Crazy kids!"

It was a good story, and even Sarah laughed a little when he'd finished.

A silence ensued, and the three of them sat staring into the fire. Joan felt suddenly uneasy, as if for some reason she was not supposed to be there, not supposed to see the two of them like this. And it was late. She'd been so absorbed in the priest's stories, so amazed at the ease with which the two of them interacted, she'd had no idea how late it had gotten.

"If you'll excuse me . . ." She got up from her place on the floor at Sarah's feet. The domesticity of the scene was suddenly too much for her. She wished them both goodnight and had to stop herself from bolting up the stairs.

"It's this Friday," Sarah said without preamble when they heard the shower running upstairs.

"I know," Pietro said, getting up to take another pack of cigarettes out of his overcoat. He came back into the room to stand behind her chair and massage her shoulders. Her muscles were tense. "Scared?"

"You bet your ass I am," Sarah said, shrugging him off. "Sit down where I can see you without twisting!"

"Yes, ma'am," he said dryly. "Bitchy as hell."

"I'm entitled" was all she said.

"You can do this thing," he said earnestly, holding the

match for a moment before he lit the cigarette. "You know you can."

"It's not that," Sarah said vaguely. "Of course I know I can do it—academically. It's not that."

"Well?"

"It's whether or not it's *right*," she said.

Pietro leaned back on the couch, stretching his feet out toward the fire. "How 'right'?" he asked. "From your perspective, it isn't a question of right or wrong. They are the ones who are wrong in trying to push you out. You are perfectly justified in fighting for what is yours."

He was thinking of his dialogue with Francis in the confessional, wishing he could tell Sarah how ruthless an opponent she faced. But he could not.

"Oh, I don't mean that." Sarah waved it away with her good hand as being of no importance. "It's this business with the letters, and having all those people backing me. If I fail, or if I refuse to face the situation, I'm letting them down."

"But you won't," Pietro reasoned. "You won't fail. Or chicken out."

"And suppose I do come out on top of this thing." There was genuine anguish in her voice; she had obviously been weighing every facet of it with great soul-searching. "What happens to the kid who's got my job? He's back out on the street again. I hear he's got a five-month-old baby."

"He took it as a temporary assignment," Pietro said, trying to soothe her. "He probably started looking elsewhere the first week they hired him. Besides, you gave him a year's worth of employment he otherwise wouldn't have had."

"And he probably loves it," Sarah sighed. "And haven't you noticed that, with all the people plugging for me, the one group that doesn't care one way or the other is the students? This time last year I was in the classroom with these kids! Maybe I've lost my touch."

"Bullshit!" Pietro growled. "They don't deserve you. Pearls before swine, that's all."

"Then maybe it's high time I got out of the sty," Sarah said gloomily.

There was a long silence. Pietro got up to stir the fire, sat down and forced himself not to light another cigarette.

"There's an alternative," he said.

"I know that!" Sarah snapped, irritated that he had to point it out to her.

"Do you?" As a priest, he was obligated to disparage psychic phenomena. She would have to prove yet again that she could read his mind.

"Of course!" Sarah rattled it off as if he'd taught it to her by rote: "I go in on Friday and overwhelm them with my brilliance, answer all the questions right. Then when they come to kiss my ass and offer me the job back, I refuse it, knock them all on their faces, and limit myself to lecturing. That way I can still keep my hand in, but part-time, so I won't get exhausted. And then the bad guys will appreciate what they lost."

"Jesus!" Pietro exhaled, breaking his self-imposed restriction on misuse of the Deity's name. He recovered himself. "Is that what you want to do?"

Sarah looked into the fire for a long moment. "I don't know," she said at last.

XV

... he will be successful who directs his actions according to the spirit of the times, and ... he whose actions do not accord with the times will not be successful.

MACHIAVELLI, *The Prince*

Possibly it had been a mistake to choose the last day before Christmas vacation. Classes ended at noon. Sarah Morrow's departmental hearing was supposed to be at two. By twelve-thirty, an inordinately large number of people were buzzing around in front of the Little Theater.

The Little Theater was nothing more than a classroom with a handkerchief-size proscenium stage hugging one wall. It was never used for anything except advanced speech courses, oral interpretation and that sort of thing. Sister Aquinas, as chairman of the speech department as well as academic dean (somehow there was never enough work in either department to constitute a full-time job), had suggested it as an ideal forum for Dr. Morrow's hearing. It was thought at the time that the only persons present would be the English department, a few of Sarah's friends on the faculty, and of course Sister Francis.

But either Sarah had accumulated a substantial number

of friends, or else the people one would have expected to leave early were looking for some free entertainment. The entire faculty seemed to be gathered in the hall; there was an air of spectacle that made Aquinas nervous.

"There are too many to be accommodated in the Little Theater—" she began, but Francis silenced her.

"What are you suggesting?" she demanded irritably. Aquinas's recent air of superiority was getting to her, along with everything else. "None of them belongs there except English and the faculty grievance committee. Tell the rest to go home."

"And if they refuse to go?" Aquinas asked mildly. She could see the direction this thing was taking, and had begun to adopt a detachment that was enviable. "There is no way we can force them to leave without making it look like we're hiding something."

"Nonsense!" Francis hissed, then thought better of it. She'd been fueling her speeches at luncheons and alumni meetings with Watergate imagery long enough to realize what such an accusation could mean. "All right, then. Have Mario set up the chairs in the auditorium. If it's a show they want . . ."

Mario had been virtually invisible for most of the morning. He had been engaged in his own private work slowdown ever since the general strike had been squelched in September. He made himself as scarce as possible only long enough to warrant a reprimand from upstairs. He would then pick up production only long enough to make sure his job was safe, then systematically begin his slowdown again. Francis swore if she found the snow on the convent steps unshoveled one more time . . .

But as if by magic, Mario appeared within moments of the time Aquinas had been sent to look for him. He set up about two hundred folding chairs, brought out the lectern and the long table, checked the microphones and the heating system, with almost superhuman speed. Then he loitered in the back of the auditorium, smoking a contraband cigarette beneath the "No Smoking" sign and watching all the brainy types file in with the Styrofoam coffee cups he'd have to pick up when it was all over.

The cafeteria closed at one. At five after one, Mae and Bertie appeared in the auditorium, Christmas corsages pinned to their uniforms. They sat in the very last row. Mario stubbed the cigarette out on the sole of his shoe, put the butt in his pocket for later disposal, brushed the ashes off his pants, and joined them.

"Sure, I don't know if I can sit here an entire hour and then through the whole show," Mae complained. "What if I have to relieve myself?"

"You better take care of that now," Mario advised her, " 'cause I understand there's gonna be a mob here soon, and if you don't want to stand through it—"

"What mob?" Mae was surprised. "And how did you find out before I did?"

"I been hanging around by the front door all morning," Mario said mysteriously. "Not everything gets talked up over in the cafeteria. This is gonna be some blowup, let me tell you."

"Well, sure, God knows I'm used to standing," Mae sighed, getting to her feet. "But I don't want to miss this for nothing."

"We'll save your seat," Bertie offered, throwing her coat over it. "Pee fast."

The library was not supposed to close until four, but at one-fifteen it was empty, except for one ancient nun whose passion it was to sneak in and read *Cosmopolitan* from cover to cover, giggling softly to herself.

"Well, for crying out loud, she's not going to steal it!" Mildred insisted, putting her practical pumps into her tote bag and zipping up her fur-trimmed ankle boots. "I'll tell her to close the door after herself when she leaves. It'll lock itself. And the lights have to stay on for the cleaning women anyway."

"I don't know," Vicki frowned. The pinched white space between her eyebrows had become almost permanent lately, ever since her mother got mixed up in the Dr. Morrow affair. "It's not that I don't want to see what's going on as much as anybody else—"

"We have the option of closing the library early if no one is here," Mildred argued. "I'll tell Sister Chloe she can take the *Cosmo* home over the holidays and boot her out. She'll be delighted."

"It's not that." Vicki hesitated. "I just don't want anybody to think that because we're going to the hearing to observe we're somehow *involved* in it."

Mildred tied a plastic rain hat over her hair to protect her permanent from the fine sleet that had been falling for most of the day. "Well, *I'm* going," she announced. The little heels of her ankle boots made emphatic noises out in the foyer.

Vicki held out until one-thirty. When she peeked into the main reading room, she saw that Sister Chloe had fallen asleep. The copy of *Cosmopolitan* rode complacently up and down on her substantial stomach as she snored. Vicki was torn, indecisive. Going back to the desk, she tore a sheet off the memo pad and wrote a little note asking Sister Chloe to please lock up when she was ready to leave. She tiptoed into the reading room and stuck the note inside the cover of the magazine. She practically ran across the street to the main building.

In the English department office one floor above the auditorium, Sister Maryann had succeeded in biting her nails down until they bled. She was holding the door open as she listened to Herb, who was standing in the hall. She swung the door spasmodically from time to time, making no effort to let him in.

"I wish you'd get lost," she said plaintively. "Have you got your petition?"

"Signed and sealed," Herb said, waving it at her. "Just needs to be delivered."

"Then why don't you mosey down the hall and give it to Francis and leave me in peace?" Maryann begged. "I'm having a hard enough time as it is!"

She closed the door in his face and went back to the table where her papers lay scattered and unruly. She was going to have to ask most of the questions this afternoon. She wished she were someplace else, anyplace but here, doing this. As usual, she was trapped.

Most of the people who would be there this afternoon didn't know a whole lot about medieval literature. She could throw a half-dozen easy questions at Sarah and that would do the trick. But could she do that, really?

Maryann clumped the papers together in some semblance of order and cursed her waterlogged watch. There was no clock in the English office; she had to keep hopping out into the hall to see what time it was.

No, she couldn't do that, really. She would have to ask the toughest questions she could think of, in order to prove her objectivity. And her objectivity could determine Sarah's entire future. Would Sarah understand? Maryann cleaned the fog from her glasses on the hem of her skirt and peered out into the hall to see what time it was.

In the auditorium, necks were being craned. Nobody knew which direction Dr. Morrow would be coming from, whether she would be alone or in the company of the Jesuit. A surprising number of students had drifted in, curious. Most had really only gotten a grasp on the facts within the past week or so when they'd been sent a form letter, signed by an alumna nobody could find in the yearbooks.

"She didn't really graduate. My sister was in her class. She said she dropped out junior year."

Neither Sarah nor Joan nor even Helen O'Dell had been paying much attention to Celia in the past few weeks. True, her typing had served as background noise for most of their recent weekends, but nobody had bothered to check on how many letters she was sending out, or to whom. She had been putting out her own money for stamps rather than arouse their suspicions. She had not bothered to tell anyone she was spending many of her daylight hours roaming the campus, gleaning supporters for the cause wherever she could.

All of the students were here at her request—not to protest or declare themselves in any way, she'd assured them, only to observe. Celia herself was nowhere in sight.

"Jeez, looks like the whole school is here," another student said. "But who the hell are those big shots across the aisle?"

Celia's work had been thorough. Every one of the important alumnae she'd contacted was there, appointments and business lunches canceled for the day. Their entrance as a group had been greeted by a temporary lull in the cacophony, equaled only by that when—

"God help us, half the board's here!" Father Arpino gasped, groping for his nitro capsules.

"Oh, do be calm, Joseph." Sister Rosalie put a restraining hand on his arm. "They were due here for some sort of cocktail party this evening anyway."

Her serenity was only partly genuine. The trustees never involved themselves in the internal workings of the college unless it had something to do with student behavior giving the place a bad name. Rosalie was certain most of them hadn't the vaguest idea who Sarah Morrow was. What had brought them, and whose side were they on?

Every seat was filled. Onlookers lined the walls, and students had to be forcibly cleared from the aisles. A fire inspector could have a stroke. Except for Miss Turner, who had promised to take her mother Christmas shopping this afternoon, it was hard to say who *wasn't* there.

"Thank God Brigid's stuck out in Brentwood," Arpino rumbled, recovering from his shock at seeing the trustees. "All we need now is her loud mouth!"

"Joseph!" Rosalie hissed, suddenly excited.

Sarah Morrow's slight, lopsided form could be seen in the front foyer. Handing her coat to an unseen assistant, smoothing the white hair up off her forehead, and gripping her cane with her good hand, she made her entrance.

Sister Aquinas had already seated herself at the long table. Sister Maryann had just stumbled up the steps to the stage and was reshuffling her notes before sitting down.

Sister Francis's chair was conspicuously empty.

"Don't leave your desk" was Francis's terse command to her secretary. "I need you right here."

"Yes, Sister," Vera Neil whispered, suppressing a smug smile. She knew all about the petition from the faculty, and the letters from the alumnae.

"It doesn't matter, you know!" Francis hissed at her, trying to sound conspiratorial, but coming across as something of a hysteric. "They can sign all the letters and petitions they want, but if she opens her mouth up there at that lectern and comes out sounding like an idiot . . ."

Her thought trailed off. Vera looked up at her expectantly.

"We'll all know soon enough," Francis practically crowed, as if she could bring about Sarah's failure simply by craving it. "If she's had the courage to arrive at all, we should know very soon!"

She whirled into the inner office and slammed the door. Vera Neil started slightly at the sound, then looked about for some filing or something to take her mind off the simmering insanity in the next room. She pushed her chair away from the desk, intending to open the file cabinets. Before she was completely on her feet, she heard the intercom click.

"Where do you think you're going?" the voice demanded tremulously.

Vera Neil sat down again. "I was only going to—water my plants, Sister," she said weakly.

Sarah had been quite adamant about going in alone.

"I don't care where you go," she told her three guardian angels in the car as they pulled up in front of the main entrance. "Sit in the back of the room and watch. Go out for an ice-cream soda—or a drink, if you like. But don't trail after me like a flock of sheep!"

Joan and Helen left her at the front door and dashed down the hall, hoping to squeeze into the back of the auditorium.

"This stinks," Joan grumbled, pushing her way out the door again.

"Where are you going?" Helen asked, following her.

"To see if the stage entrance is unlocked," Joan explained, hurrying down the hall. "We can hang around behind the curtain. Even if we can't see what's going on, at least we can hear her!"

Pietro took Sarah's coat when they were inside.

"Bye-bye!" She waved him away as if he were an infant. "Go in and watch the circus."

"Good luck!" he whispered, at a loss for words, but she was already through the door, conscious of her audience and not of him.

One or two seats in the faculty section were not yet occupied. Pietro found his way into a chair next to Herb just as the silence accompanying Sarah's entrance engulfed the room. Only one additional figure managed to squeeze into the room.

"Hi!" Sister Brigid panted, trampling over Arpino's feet and throwing herself into the chair next to Rosalie. "God bless the Long Island Railroad! Thought I'd never make it!"

Sarah's grand entrance was slow, painstaking. She made no effort to disguise her physical handicap, but wanted to make certain that her audience recognized its exact dimensions. A very attractive pantsuit disguised the muscle degeneration of her right arm and leg, but the cane confirmed her limp, and the care with which she climbed the steps to the stage emphasized it. When Sister Maryann offered her a chair at the long table, she sat down slowly, but her sitting posture was erect and regal.

The procedure would be simple. Sister Aquinas, as proxy for Sister Francis, would ask Sarah a few preliminary questions of a general nature, to show those present whether or not she was oriented toward her surroundings and could express herself clearly. Sister Maryann would ask the technical questions, beginning with easy ones that any English major could answer and escalating to the more obscure and detailed ones that only a scholar could know.

There was a microphone at the lectern where Sister Maryann stood and two at the table, one each for Sarah and Sister Aquinas. Ideally, everyone in the room would be able to hear what was said.

Sister Aquinas cleared her throat, tapped the mike as was her wont before addressing any assemblage, and began.

"Good afternoon," she said. "Am I coming through all right?"

Assured by those in the front row that she was, she continued.

"I'm sure we would all like to welcome Dr. Morrow

back after her long absence, and to apologize to some degree for the circumstances under which her return takes place."

At heart, Aquinas was not a devious woman. It was only the tenuousness of her position that had made her fall into Francis's techniques. She had nothing whatsoever against Sarah Morrow, and if she herself had been president the whole matter would have been handled differently. Having laid her cards on the table, and receiving a nod of acknowledgment from Sarah, she went on.

"I'm sure, Dr. Morrow, that you are as surprised as we by the turnout today. We had no idea you had such a following!"

Sarah led the appreciative laughter that wafted lightly around the large room, but did not offer a reply.

"Bitch!" Joan hissed from behind the certain. Helen elbowed her in the ribs.

"You are looking well," Aquinas said slowly, weightily. "In fact, far better than we had expected, owing to the—severity—of your illness. How do you feel?"

Sarah leaned forward slightly to get within range of the microphone. "Quite well, thank you," she said softly, sitting back again.

A shock wave ran through the audience. Half had expected her to be unable to speak at all; the other half was surprised that she spoke so softly.

"Well, I'm sure we are all glad to hear that," Aquinas said. Even she had been slightly taken aback. "I think we can get down to the objective of our meeting as soon as Sister Maryann is prepared."

Maryann had been pointedly shuffling her papers for some moments. She flicked on the mike at the lectern and it began to screech. Nothing she could do would silence it, until it finally settled down of its own accord.

"I thought we were waiting for Sister Francis," Maryann said, too loudly. She had been told Francis wasn't coming, but she wanted to see what sort of excuse Aquinas would give the audience.

The mike began to screech again. Maryann flicked it off with uncharacteristic viciousness, and stood waiting for a response.

Aquinas, caught off-guard, did something she hounded her speech majors about. "Um—" she said, and again, "um—unfortunately, Sister Francis is unable to attend to-day's meeting. Certain urgent business must be concluded before the first of the year and—um—"

"I'll just bet!" Brigid stage-whispered to Rosalie. Rosalie ignored her.

There was some stirring and murmuring in the crowd.

"I think it would be best"—Aquinas raised her voice a little to command silence—"if we were to get on with our purpose here. I'm sure all of us would like to go home and enjoy our Christmas vacation. Sister Maryann?"

Maryann's glasses had fogged over as soon as she challenged Francis's absence. She knew she'd catch it later. She looked at the microphone as if it were booby-trapped, and gently flicked it on. It did not screech this time. Maryann adjusted her glasses and spoke.

"I'll start you off with the easy ones," she said to Sarah. "The toughies come later."

Everyone laughed.

"Fair enough," Sarah nodded, a little more audibly than before.

"I hope you won't be insulted if we start with *Piers Plowman*?" Maryann asked tentatively. There was in her voice a plea for understanding. "Just as a warm-up?"

Sarah leaned into the mike. I understand! she wanted to shout. I am not blaming you!

"Only if I hear one of my students prompting me from the back row," she said, breaking them up.

Even with the mikes, it was difficult to hear. The place was full of echoes, and there were too many people.

Sarah's voice was low, subdued, and whole portions of her answers were swallowed up or wafted away.

". . . the persona of Will being a structural device not intended to give us any absolute identification of the author, attributing the work definitively to William Langland is risky, particularly since discrepancies in the A, B, and C texts indicate the possibility . . ."

"What the hell is she talking about?" Mario growled, wondering if he dared a cigarette under Aquinas's watchful eye.

"Sure, I haven't the vaguest," Mae grinned happily. "But don't she sound grand?"

"What she's saying," Bertie said, as if to herself, "is the reason she's up there and we back here."

Mae and Mario stared at her. Mario had a new nickname for her lately—he called her "Mrs. Socrates." Bertie didn't seem to mind.

". . . Chaucer, as the premise of the prologue to *The Legend of Good Women*, has angered Eros with his unjust treatment of women, specifically in his composition of the *Troilus* and his translation of the *Roman de la Rose*. As punishment, Chaucer must write a legendary of Cupid's 'saints'—that is to say, those women whose religion is the religion of Love. . . ."

"Damn it, isn't she beautiful?" Brigid insisted, following every word. "It's all there—she hasn't lost any of it!"

"She has retained the scholarship, I'll give you that," Arpino mumbled grudgingly. "And her decorum is exemplary. I could almost welcome her back with open arms if I actually believed there was the slightest possibility they'd let her come back."

Brigid pounced on him. "So you'll admit this whole thing is a setup!" she said at nearly normal volume. She was greeted by a chorus of shushes which she complacently ignored. "Welcome to the side of justice!"

"Brigid—" Rosalie's lips barely formed the name, but

Brigid retreated. Rosalie did not so much as look at her; her attention was completely riveted on the stage.

". . . hence, although it is not at all historical, *Berta of Hungary*, which is neither a true epic nor a true romance but an amalgam of both, is most often classified with the Charlemagne cycle for purposes of clarity. Adenes li Rois is believed to have written it circa 1270, and since the historical personage Berta is known to have died in 783 . . ."

Herb leaned over toward Pietro, his curiosity overcoming him. "How come she doesn't have any notes?" he whispered. "You don't mean to tell me she's doing all that from memory?"

Nobody else had noticed. Pietro was alarmed. Could he trust Herb to be quiet if he knew the truth?

"Holy shit!" Herb said when Pietro told him. "Holy shit!"

There were murmurs in the audience. Sister Aquinas had risen slowly from her chair and was making her way as quietly as possible toward the parting in the curtain, intending to leave by the backstage exit. She nearly collided with Joan and Helen, who were still hidden behind the curtain, soaking up every word.

"Uh-oh," Helen whispered as Aquinas glided past her.

"It's really hit this time," Joan agreed. "Reverberations from upstairs any old time now."

Maryann had almost run out of questions. Sarah had not missed one, had barely seemed to hesitate before rolling out her responses. With Aquinas gone, they could very easily end it right here. Maryann looked over her glasses at Sarah. She had one more question. If Sarah could answer *this* one without having to look it up . . .

Sarah listened to the question intently, and there was a twinkle in her eye as she leaned into the mike.

"There are several origins for the story of Peredur, son of York. It appears in both the *Red Book of Hergest* and the *White Book of Rhydderch*, but an abridged version found in a manuscript referred to as Peniarth Four, which is part of the *White Book Mabinogion*, is the most frequently used. This last version appears to predate *Hergest*, which is believed from the character of the script to date circa 1375 to 1425."

Ninety percent of the audience knew nothing whatsoever about Welsh epic literature, but at Maryann's whispered "thank you" they began to applaud. Many rose to their feet, and the applause continued for some moments despite Sarah's attempts to still it.

Francis sat back in her swivel chair with an air of perverse enjoyment as she watched Aquinas scan the letters from the alumnae. Aquinas had not known about them until now, and the look on her face was pained.

"We're in rather deep, aren't we?" Aquinas asked finally, putting the letters back on the desk. "I don't suppose the faculty petition is terribly significant, but these—"

"What do you mean 'we'?" Francis demanded, her smugness replaced by the now-chronic paranoia. "Nobody's advising *you* to resign!"

Aquinas blinked at her, grasping for a way to make the ramifications clear. "Nobody has specifically told *you* to resign either," she pointed out. "As far as I can see, that's the solution you've worked out for yourself. And if you go, I go. We're part of the same structure."

Francis thought about it for a moment. It was becoming increasingly difficult for her to work out solutions to even the simplest problems. What had started out as a clear executive decision to rid the institution of a troublesome member had turned into a battle of wills in which the contestants were extremely ill-matched. Circumstances, Francis thought, had made it look as if she were picking on a defenseless old woman, when in actual fact . . .

"But I don't *want* to step down!" she whined suddenly, a petulant child forced into a take-it-or-leave-it decision. "I've done an efficient and orderly job for thirteen years, and I don't see why— Well, how can you sit there and be so blasé about it?" This last was almost a plea.

Aquinas shrugged. "As for me," she said, "you'll recall I never wanted to be dean at all."

She made no mention of her higher aim; that was out of the question now anyway. After thirteen years of running errands for someone else, it might be nice to be a speech teacher again, to catch up on her reading, see a few Broadway shows with her newfound free time. . . .

"You don't have to quit," she told Francis mildly. "You can tough it out."

"Can I?" Francis had grown surprisingly calm, as if the verge of hysteria had been worn so smooth by her psychological pacing that she no longer feared the precipice. "How?"

Again Aquinas blinked, trying to simplify it. "Give Sarah her job back and let the whole thing die down," she said. "There'll be some mumbling for a while, but when they get what they want, they'll settle down—and they'll view you as a fair and benevolent individual. If you make it look as if you're being generous—"

"No." Francis shook her head, and Aquinas was horrified to see tears in her eyes. Rages she expected. Hysteria was a commonplace. But *tears?* "Don't you see what's happened? What I've done? They don't respect me anymore."

Aquinas started to object. She could see that a gentle hand was required here. But Francis wouldn't let her speak.

"I'm not a fool, you know," she said, as if Aquinas would contradict her. "I've always known the students, the faculty—all of them—didn't *love* me. I am not a lovable person. Sarah Morrow, now, she is that kind of person. One either loves her or hates her. And most of them love her. I could never ask as much. I had to be satisfied with their respect. And now that that's gone . . ."

Aquinas stirred in her chair. "How will you go about it?" she asked. "Resigning?"

Francis sighed profoundly. "I should like you to go downstairs and take Dr. Morrow aside—into the alumni room, let us say—and let her know that she has—won. I shall have Miss Neil post a memorandum announcing my—our—resignation, after the crowd has dispersed. I expect by the time Christmas recess is over the word will have gotten around."

Aquinas considered it for a moment. It had a sense of diplomacy about it. No fingers were pointed, and yet the causal relationship between Sarah Morrow's rise and the administration's fall was clear. Let the crowd draw from it what conclusions they may.

"If you're sure this is the only way—" Aquinas began. Francis nodded, unable to speak. Aquinas rose from her seat. "I'd better be getting downstairs then."

When she'd gone, Francis covered her face with her hands for a moment, and then pressed the intercom button.

Vera Neil had been sitting on the very edge of her chair, feeling as if something momentous were about to happen. When the intercom buzzed, she actually leaped to her feet.

"Miss Neil—" Francis's voice stopped long enough to compose itself. "Would you kindly come in with your steno pad?"

No particular surprise was expressed by anyone in the alumni room when they were informed that Sarah would be invited back to teach in the fall. There were two other bombshells that would have far greater effect upon them. Sarah dropped the first one.

"Thank you, all of you!" she gasped, very flushed and a little hoarse. She was surrounded by well-wishers who had been wringing her hand and showering her with kisses, to the consternation of her three guardian angels, whose primary concern was that she not overexcite herself. "I love you all. Thank you for being here—taking the time—standing behind me when I needed you. . . ."

Joan slipped behind her chair and whispered in her ear. "Get rid of them," she hissed. "They're wearing you out."

Sarah looked up at her as if such a thing had never occurred to her. "You're my attorney," she said, only half-joking. "Tell them yourself."

Joan looked at the faces crowding the room, faces she had been partially responsible for bringing here in the first place. She didn't know how to get rid of them without hurting their feelings. Celia was so much better at crowd management. Where the hell was Celia?

"Um—people? Ladies and gentlemen?" Joan said loudly, trying to be heard. Gradually they became aware of her voice and settled down. "Listen, we're all tremendously grateful for your support today. . . ."

She went on and on. Most of them got the hint and started to drift away home, happy, feeling as if they'd accomplished something. Many of them didn't notice the sleet blowing into their faces until they were halfway down the block.

"Some of you—" Sarah began, and all eyes were upon her, "Maryann, Herb—would you stay? Mario, *please* don't leave yet. I want to talk to all of you."

She glanced at Pietro, who was frowning at her. "Yes, Machiavelli," she smiled at him, "you're going to have your way."

And when the chosen ones she'd asked to stay had settled themselves on the fat couches reserved for alumni teas and class reunions, Sarah told them she would no longer teach at the college.

There were gasps, murmurs, protests. Only Pietro was silent.

Joan howled the loudest. "How long have you been planning this—this grand little gesture?" she demanded. "And why couldn't you have saved us the trouble of—"

"The idea first came into my head," Sarah said in a low voice, but loudly enough to silence Joan, "some weeks ago. I didn't actually *decide* until I woke up this morning. And as for saving you the trouble, I'd say you for one have profited by all this."

Joan was furious. She'd had to lie about an imaginary doctor's appointment to get the day off from work. She'd spent every weekend and half her evenings for the past six months working for this arbitrary old—

"Profited? I'd like to know how!"

"Oh, you'll find out soon enough, baby," Sarah smiled gently. "I have plans for you."

"But what will you do now?" It was Maryann, her voice plaintive and weary as she imagined six months of sifting through hundreds of résumés, weighing, deciding on the one applicant equal to the task of replacing Sarah.

"Oh, I'm not ready for the rocking chair just yet," Sarah assured her. "You know that damned lecture tour I've been bitching about for all these years? They've asked me to do the New England circuit again, and it's suddenly beginning to look extremely attractive."

"You'll lecture, then?" Maryann repeated, not certain she'd heard it correctly. Assured that she had, she relaxed. "Now all I have to do is find somebody to replace you."

Sarah was surprised. "What about that young fellow who's been here all this time? I understand he's been doing a phenomenal job. Was he around at all today? Herb?"

Herb had suddenly grown very agitated. "He called in this morning," he said. "Said something about the baby— taking the baby to the doctor. Holy shit, I hope there's nothing wrong—"

He was on his way to find a phone.

"Poor Herb!" Sarah laughed, though she, too, was suddenly concerned about this baby she'd never met. "But seriously, Maryann, about hiring the young man—what's the obstacle there? He has his doctorate, doesn't he?"

"He's three credits shy—and the dissertation," Maryann replied. The simplicity of the solution entranced her. "If he gets those done before the fall—"

"Marvelous!" Sarah said. "Then you can hire him as a full professor, can't you?"

Maryann hedged. "Technically, no," she said, polishing her glasses on the hem of her skirt. "He's supposed to have a minimum of two years' experience postdoctoral, but—"

"Oh, for heaven's sake," Sarah said mildly, "I'm sure you can bend the thing a little."

They discussed it at some length, as if they had nothing better to do, and as if it were absolutely essential that John Spensieri's future be sealed that very afternoon. Joan fidgeted. She had to get home before six to meet Eric's school bus, and if they didn't leave soon . . .

Only Mario got up to leave. He'd been extremely uncomfortable ever since Sarah had invited him to stay. Any excuse would do to get him out of this room and back to the work he'd been avoiding so adroitly for months, but which now seemed necessary—nay, vital.

"Sleet's stopped," he said, grudgingly putting out a cigarette he'd gotten from Pietro. "Gotta go sweep the steps. Not that I think old Frannie's much interested in the weather report *this* afternoon, lemme tell you. But you were great, Dr. Morrow, and we around here are gonna miss you."

Sarah grasped his hand for so long that he became embarrassed. "Thank you, Mario," she said. "I couldn't have done it without you and Mae and Alberta and the others. That's not bullshit. I mean it. Thank them all for me, for having the guts to make the first move."

Mario grinned, shamed by her flow of emotion, and slipped away.

Joan took his exit as her cue. "It's getting late—" she began, when Herb suddenly reappeared, looking like the Ides of March.

"What happened?" Maryann jumped to her feet, thinking of all the terrible things that could happen to a six-month-old baby.

"Oh"—Herb shook his head as if it didn't matter, as if he'd forgotten why he'd left the room—"baby's fine. He just had to take her for a checkup—DPT shot, that kind of thing. And she cut her first tooth. But that's not it. Francis and Aquinas are resigning."

The second bombshell had fallen without a sound.

"What do you mean you have plans for me?" Joan demanded later in the car, after they'd said goodbye to Pietro and dropped Helen off at home.

"Oh, that," Sarah said airily, looking out the window at the winter evening. "I want you to go to law school."

Joan nearly drove right up onto the curb. "What the hell are you talking about?" she yelled, but Sarah waved it away.

"Another time," she said. "I'm too tired to think straight. Put the wipers on. It's starting to mist over again."

With that she settled back against the seat and closed her eyes. "Poor Francis!" she murmured before she dozed off. "I really didn't think she'd take it personally. . . ."

It was nearly six o'clock when the dinnertime rumble of her substantial stomach roused Sister Chloe from her *Cosmopolitan*-induced sleep. When she looked around and found that most of the lights in the library had been extinguished, and that the heat must have been shut down for hours, she became alarmed. She found Vicki's note, followed its instructions, and stuffed herself into her mackinaw, expecting nothing more when she crossed the courtyard to the convent than a hot dinner and a little commonplace gossip.

XVI

Enough! No more!
'Tis not so sweet now as it was before.
WILLIAM SHAKESPEARE, *Twelfth Night*

"Hand me that brown folder, will you, dear?" Sarah asked absently, rummaging through the clutter on her desk in search of the glasses she hadn't worn in over a year.

Joan was sitting cross-legged on the floor by the bed, taking inventory of the vast stack of books and papers on Sarah's night table. She opened the dime-store looseleaf binder and thumbed through it.

"*Twelfth Night*?" She passed it across the bed to Sarah. "Isn't Shakespeare kind of late for you?"

Sarah looked at her mildly. "Haven't you realized by now that I can do anything?" she joked. Joan giggled appreciatively. "Seriously though, I've done that lecture dozens of times. It's a good warm-up. Did I tell you where you're driving me tonight?"

Joan shook her head.

"Okay." Sarah sat on the edge of the bed, still holding the folder. She had cleaned the dust from her glasses and was wearing them now. She had not worn them in so long, they seemed to belong to someone else. "There's a little group in Manhattan—it's on some sort of private grant; I never ask about such things—known as the Mandrake Society. It consists mostly of rich ladies with time on their hands and perpetual students, people like that, and we sit around and discuss—or I lecture about—Renaissance and metaphysical poetry, for the most part, although they let me chime in with the older stuff now and again."

"Sounds interesting," Joan said, though without much enthusiasm. It wasn't really her field, after all. "The Mandrake Society. John Donne, wasn't it?"

" 'Get with child a mandrake root. . . .' Exactly," Sarah nodded. "And I've chosen *Twelfth Night* simply because it's the week after Christmas; it's appropriate to the season. And because I know it by heart, so I can concentrate on my act—on making it look as if I'm reading from my notes."

"Why the glasses?" Joan asked, getting up from the floor and stretching. "You didn't wear them for your 'trial.' Why now?"

Sarah took them off and studied her. "You're dense today," she said. "At the hearing, I *wanted* it to look as if I'd memorized the stuff. I'm wearing my reading glasses tonight to suggest the opposite."

"Excuse me for asking," Joan sniffed, pretending to be insulted. "I was just being conversational."

"Or changing the subject." Sarah put her glasses away and looked at Joan pointedly. "There's something we haven't finished."

"*I've* finished," Joan snapped, turning her back on Sarah and studying the Bayeux tapestry reproduction on the wall as if to terminate the conversation. "I don't want to talk about it."

"Why?" Sarah demanded, raising her good eyebrow. "Because you don't want to go to law school or because you do?"

"Because if I did want to, it would be impossible," Joan

said, turning on her. "And because I don't want to anyway."

Except for the few days either side of Chistmas when she and Eric had flown down to Houston to be with her parents, she had been in contact with Sarah almost daily since the hearing. When she couldn't be there, she phoned. Together they'd planned Sarah's future itinerary—a trial run at some private literary societies and local colleges, then the big East Coast tour in the fall. And they talked about Joan's future as well. She had made the mistake of telling Sarah she was not hiring an attorney for her divorce, which was coming up in the spring. She had been reading up on no-fault divorce, and decided she had enough background to handle it herself. That was when they'd started arguing in earnest about this law-school business that Sarah had been pestering her about for months.

"You have the brains and the temperament to make a good attorney. Go to law school! Deadlines are coming up soon. If you apply for the fall semester—"

"I'll have to rob a bank over the summer!" Joan shrieked, unable to keep silent. "For God's sake, Sarah, I'm earning a hundred and ninety-five dollars a week! By the time I pay for the baby-sitter, the nursery school, and the bus, I barely have enough for little incidentals like food and the rent. I'm not exactly fellowship material, and I couldn't afford the textbooks, the extra carfare, the—"

"You *do* want to go then," Sarah smiled, pleased that she'd read Joan's mind.

"Much good may it do me!" Joan said, disgusted, plopping down on the bed beside Sarah. "It's a dream deferred. I'd have to wait until Eric was old enough to stay home alone at night. It's too far in the future. If I think about it too much, I'll go crazy. So I don't think about it."

"A dream deferred . . ." Sarah repeated, stroking Joan's

hair absently. Joan did not start or pull away as she might have months ago, terrified of human affection after what it had cost her with Brian. Her back relaxed a little. "A dream to replace the dream of becoming a dancer, which was the last, the only, dream you've ever allowed yourself. Did it ever occur to you when you were in your teens and struggling through all those dance classes that what you wanted then was impossible? Of course not. Then why now? Far more people become lawyers than become dancers. Is it just the money? Because if you have the desire—"

"If I have the desire," Joan repeated cynically, in a turmoil about it. "Ever since I discovered that I could do what the three men I work for can do—as well, if not better; ever since I decided to handle my own divorce and started digging around in the library looking things up . . . When I was in school and I worked part-time in the law library, I used to snitch the reference books overnight, sit up all night reading them, get in before anyone else to return them the next morning. I've always been fascinated by the law—I just never considered it a possibility."

"Why not?" Sarah wanted to know. "Don't tell me you fell for that crap about it's being a man's profession? You're brighter than that."

"About the time Eric was born and I had a lot of time to sit around examining my life," Joan explained, "there was this great surge of opportunities for minorities and women, and I kept thinking that here was my chance, and I had blown it by tying myself down with a kid and a lousy marriage and no money. Nowadays the economy has the law schools tightening up again. It's hard for women to get in—we've got to be half again as good as the male applicants. I don't know if I'm that good."

"You think you're good enough to handle your own divorce," Sarah reasoned. "Aren't you afraid you'll fail?"

Joan shook her head. "Anybody with half a brain can

handle a no-fault. At least I can. Between the law library
and my present job I'm as knowledgeable as any lawyer,"
she said. "The legal profession is afraid of the competition,
so they try to scare people into thinking divorces are
tough."

"You're willing to take a chance of making an ass of
yourself in a divorce court, but you're afraid to apply to
law school because you might be rejected." Sarah raised
her hands in disbelief. "I don't understand you."

"It's all in the realm of conjecture anyway," Joan sighed,
getting up from the bed. "I can't afford it."

"You do have an option," Sarah pointed out. "I'm going
to suggest something, and before you bite my head off I
want you to hear me out."

"What? Borrow the money from you?" Joan snapped.
"Like a no-interest infinite student loan. Absolutely not!"

"I have something better," Sarah said, the Cheshire cat,
folding her hands in her lap and waiting for Joan to calm
down, "if you'll listen."

"I'll listen," Joan promised, "but I don't like the sound
of it already."

"This is my plan," Sarah began, ignoring the sarcasm.
"I want you and Eric to come live with me."

Joan's mouth opened. What new form of complication
was this?

"I don't understand" was all she said.

"It's not that difficult," Sarah said dryly. "You and your
son can move in here. Pack up everything you need, sell
your furniture or put it in storage, kiss your landlady
goodbye, and start applying to law schools. You can have
the front bedroom; Eric can have the little room. We'll
redecorate. Maybe we'll even put in a new bathroom. Eric
starts kindergarten in the fall, doesn't he? I can take care
of him after school, and whatever nights I'm not on tour.
There are lots of kids on the block. I'm sure he'll love it.

And I'll have all of that youth and energy running around my house."

Along with the grandchild you never had, Joan thought suddenly, her plans for sending Sarah on her lecture tour in the fall and gradually lessening the contact between them falling apart as she listened.

"That's very generous of you," she managed to say, "but I couldn't—"

"Why not?" Sarah asked gently.

"I can still read to you," Joan said, terrified of surrendering even one iota of the freedom she had found. "You don't have to offer me this."

"But I want to," Sarah said, as if it were the only humane thing to do. "What do you say?"

I can't do this, Joan thought, because I know damn well that within a month or even less we will both be disillusioned with this artificial extended family you are trying to construct, fed up with the phony symbiosis you are trying to create because neither of us has any real family, and by then we'll be trapped in it by economic circumstances and the fear of offending each other. We have done some exciting and interesting things over the past few months, but I am not a generous person, nor one who makes friends easily, and the fact that I've allowed you to monopolize this much of my life is frightening in itself, but I've done what I can, and it must stop here. Now. Don't try to get any closer! I will not be your surrogate daughter, and I will not let you play grandmother to my son, who has enough problems of his own. If I did move in with you, I would spend every hour in this house feeling that I should be doing more for you in exchange for what you were doing for me. I would feel indebted to you, and so far I can say that I've managed to pay back most of the debts I've accumulated in my life. I would worry constantly about your health, knowing that someday in the

future you would die on me and I would not be able to
cope with the loss of a person who knows me better than
I know myself. And I cannot do this most of all because I
think I love you, and I am not sure if that love is normal
or is the result of something lost or perverted in my life,
and because it is too soon for me to love again after what
happened with Brian, and because I am afraid, so very
afraid, of letting myself go again.

"I-I-I need t-to think about it," Joan said, stuttering
worse than she had in months. "I just don't know."

"It's a big step, I know. Don't answer now," Sarah
barely whispered. If she had touched Joan now, Joan
would have run right out of the room. "I only ask you to
think about it. I'm concerned about deadlines, that's all.
But if you feel you won't be ready in the fall, you can
put it off for six months—"

"It's not that!" Joan said wildly, though she couldn't
verbalize what it was.

"I *know*," Sarah emphasized.

I know *exactly* what it is, Sarah thought. I'm not trying
to pressure you!

Neither of them spoke for several moments. Finally
Sarah pulled herself up from the bed and groped for her
cane. "It's time to get ready," she said, not looking at
Joan as she headed for the door. "Won't do to be late
tonight. It's the start of my new career!"

The Mandrake Society was housed in what had once
been a plush private town house in the East Seventies.
It had been donated, along with most of the original
furnishings, as a tax write-off for a rich, unnamed dowager
whose greatest love had been the metaphysical poets.
Membership in the Society was open to anyone who had
the ten-dollar annual fee. Visiting international scholars

lectured regularly. It had been a home away from home for Sarah for nearly fifteen years.

Most of the people who greeted her when she came in with Joan that evening knew she had had a stroke a little over a year ago. None of them knew the extent of her infirmity, and the presence of the cane and her unbalanced walk made them uneasy. They would be studying her closely to see how fully she had recovered from her illness. If she could fool these people, who knew her so well, she could lecture anywhere.

All of this was on her mind as she passed the heavily carpeted staircase and under the cascading crystal chandelier on her way to the reception room. She was more frightened tonight than she had been the day of her hearing, but nobody knew that except Pietro, who followed her in after he had helped her up the front steps. Pietro knew her hands were always warm unless she was nervous. Tonight they felt like ice.

"Where are the other two?" Pietro asked Joan for the sake of conversation as they sat in the last row of folding chairs waiting for the jewel-dripping matrons and the debs in their Vanderbilt jeans to settle in among the white-haired professors and the threadbare graduate students.

"You mean Helen and Celia?" Joan whispered back. The priest nodded. "Helen decided her assignment was complete and went back to her remedial-reading kids. Celia just split—I think she may have a show opening this weekend. I haven't heard from her."

"Ah," Pietro nodded. "And Joan is ever faithful." He had adopted Sarah's irritating habit of addressing Joan in the third person.

"Bullshit," Joan hissed. "Joan just doesn't have anything else to do with her weekends."

They were hushed then by the president of the Society, who was introducing the guest speaker. Joan listened as if the person at the front of the room were a stranger, as if she herself were one of those graduate students in the first few rows who had seen a notice somewhere on a bulletin board and drifted in, curious. She listened to the seemingly endless list of credits and accomplishments, wondering that all of this was contained within the frame of the frail old lady whose hair she'd combed out only an hour ago, whose house she'd been keeping in order, whose conversation and companionship she'd enjoyed for so long. This same old lady, Joan thought, whom I've begun to treat as an equal. This same old lady who would take me in, practically adopt me, when six months ago we scarcely knew each other. Why?

A polite round of applause greeted the end of the introduction, and Sarah began to speak. Her tone was low at first, barely audible, as it had been at the hearing. But given a clear field, given an uninterrupted space in which to say what she had chosen to say, her voice began to swell, to expand, to roll over her audience like a great wave.

Joan closed her eyes and scrunched down in her seat, approximately familiar with the subject matter since Pietro had read Sarah's notes over to her in the car. She let the words and the texture of Sarah's voice wash over her as she wrestled with her decision.

". . . examining the moral context of Shakespeare's plays, to the extent where we find that, with the exception of certain passages in *A Midsummer Night's Dream*, there are not thirty uninterrupted lines that do not present us with some question of ethical behavior, of decisions between right and wrong. . . ."

What am I going to do? Joan wondered. For nearly a year she had been at peace, and now this. Once she had made the decision to break with Brian, it had simply been a matter of events falling into place. Once she had weathered the emotional imbalance of those succeeding months (with Sarah's desperately needed help; she wasn't denying that), the rest had been total tranquillity. Supporting herself and her son, alone, unaided, no longer terrified her. Getting through a sane divorce actually seemed possible. Living without a man around, without sex, for however long it might be necessary, seemed bearable. Everything seemed to have balanced. Why this? Why now?

". . . if we subscribe to Van Doren's theory that *Twelfth Night* is really a refined version of *The Merchant of Venice*, in which the threat to the tranquillity of a certain level of society is made by the intrusion of an alien voice—in the one case Malvolio, in the other Shylock—and that we are less offended by Malvolio's punishment because it seems so well deserved, whereas poor Shylock is victimized far more than is justifiable under the circumstances . . ."

What am I afraid of? Joan wondered. Is it only the idea of a big step like law school? How big a step can it be, when I think of what I've lived through in the past year? If I panic along the way, I can always drop out, can't I?

Is it rather the fear of being inextricably entangled in Sarah's life? And where does that come from? Is it because she is so much older than I am, and I can't face the thought that someday she will die? Is it because I'm afraid she will begin to treat me like a daughter, and I will be obligated to become her *de facto* daughter? If I can't get along with my own mother . . .

But what about all those other people who lived in her house along the way? All of them moved on eventually. Why couldn't I do the same? Suppose I met somebody and I wanted to remarry . . .

What am I afraid of?

". . . and a study of the majority of Shakespeare's women reveals that he almost never brings them to the extremities of character he visits upon the men. None of them are total fools or buffoons, yet none of them possess the sparkle and eloquence of his best male characters. *. .*"

If I don't take her up on her offer, Joan mused, what have I accomplished?

For one thing, as I told her this afternoon, I will have to put off any plans for the future until Eric is older. Unless I remarry, and what a helluva reason that would be for remarrying.

For another, I will have consigned Sarah to an awful lot of lonely hours, which after what she has done for me—and, let's be honest, what I have done for her as well—is hardly reasonable.

And where is it written that two unrelated women of different generations cannot live harmoniously in the same household?

What have I got to lose?

". . . it might almost be said that Shakespeare invented the 'and they all lived happily ever after' ending. It is found over and over in his happier plays, but perhaps best of all in *Much Ado* and in *Twelfth Night.* . . ."

I will give it a try, Joan thought, joining the polite applause that filled the cozy-shabby room. It is only possible to live happily ever after on a day-to-day basis.

XVII

Joan got her divorce in April. It was nearly June before she got around to moving in with Sarah.

Mostly what she did in that interim was cry. Every time she made any attempt to throw away the accumulated clutter of six years with Brian, she began to cry. It was as if moving out of this apartment, ridding herself of the fixtures that had witnessed so many domestic battles, was more final than the divorce. Leaving the arena meant that the war was really, finally, over.

She applied to four law schools. By early May she'd received two acceptances, one notification that her name was on a waiting list, and one rejection. What she had dreaded had not come to pass. She *could* get into law school.

She had also expected trouble from Eric about moving; expected recriminations and shouting matches about how she'd taken his father away and now she was taking him away from his friends, too. This did not come to pass either. Eric liked Sarah the first time he met her. He liked rattling up and down the long staircase and exploring in all the rooms and closets and secret places of her house. Sarah made him responsible for cleaning out the fireplace and stacking new logs when it was time to make a fire, and the boy was entranced. He was beginning to like his mother a little better, too.

Joan found it wasn't necessary to dump him on Brian every single weekend. Between sporadic efforts at packing, she would drag him to the park, and they spent hours kicking around a big neon-orange ball she'd picked up at the supermarket, and while it wasn't *exactly* a soccer ball . . .

She thought about it, as the ball whirled past her or bounced off her kneecap or, once, caught her smack in the chest ("Gotcha inna *breasts!*" Eric roared hilariously, delighted with the word; and Joan, instead of trying to kill him, had laughed as well), thought about the number of times she'd sat on a bench reading or doing a crossword puzzle while her son pedaled manically back and forth on his tricycle or sat in a bald patch in the grass covering his pants legs with dirt. This was so much fun!

They made up their own rules. They started at the far end of the field, and as long as Eric managed to keep the ball away from the benches, they kept on playing. When Joan's superior power eventually knocked the ball onto the concrete, they were both exhausted anyway, so it was easy to stop. But nobody ever lost.

Joan couldn't believe the recent transformation in her son. He was becoming less of a blob, or perhaps it was only that she treated him less like one; she couldn't tell which had happened first. Running after the ball, shrieking and windblown, he looked so goddamn normal, sane, healthy, she wanted to eat him.

And she watched his four-year-old's too-short legs scissoring so fast as he ran they actually blurred and she saw him growing, stretching out into something nearly as tall as his father with the dark wavy hair grown to his shoulders if they were still wearing it that way by then and the hint of the newly shaved stubble shadowed along his upper lip and the suddenly squared jaw, the big blue Brian eyes no longer opulent with innocence but rich with mock-cynicism that masked an often-wounded idealism. She heard the bizarre startling bass-note of a voice quite recently squeaky with adolescent nervousness now cracked into rumbling resonance better suited to the height and breadth of the new-shaped man-boy who liked to pick her up and stand her on a chair so he could still look up to her and call her "Ma." She could smell him, too—the six kinds of aftershave and the macho deodorant and the acne cream, not to mention the athlete's-foot powder, sweaty jockstrap, and last week's salami sandwich in the bottom of his schoolbag along with his economics text, gym socks, and the unopened box of Trojans he carried along just in case. She heard doors slamming and phones ringing at all hours, found handprints on the walls seven feet above the floor and black smudges on the ceiling in the hall near the cracked light fixture where the basketball just kind of, you know—

She watched the images whirl past, loving them, loving him, and determined not to stop him, not to hold him back from the future the way so many mothers did, particularly with sons. No, she thought, I will not do that! But treasure this moment now, she thought. Seize him now and hold him in your memory better than a photograph, and never forget the particular angle of the cowlick or the dimple in—which was it?—the left cheek when he smiled, and the space between his front teeth that would someday delight an orthodontist, and the way his face went white-red-purple when he threw a tantrum, and the way the tears hung on his eyelashes, defying gravity, when he cried or wanted sympathy. Hold him now in your mind and heart, Joan thought, because he is a boy, and boys so seldom let you hold them in your arms.

And he whooped when she kicked the ball a final ferocious shot onto the concrete and the game was over.

Joan flopped down under a tree, exhausted, as Eric scrambled to retrieve the ball, and she watched the naïve élan with which he pounced on it and galloped toward her, near-tripping on a tree root, recovering, and sliding down next to her on the damp grass. She lay belly-down, chin cupped in hands, feet dangling. Eric sat upright, solemn, sneaker soles together, hands clasping ankles, adult-looking. Joan's back began to ache from the odd position; she half-rolled onto her side and grabbed the boy around the middle, banging him into her rib cage and tickling him under the lightweight jacket until he squealed and chuckled and got the hiccups.

"Quit!" he yelled. "Quit! I wet my pants!"

Joan stopped, pushing him away a little. "Did you?" she demanded, pretending horror.

"Noo," he hedged. "But I will."

He hiccuped again, and Joan straightened his jacket, smoothed his hair, used every excuse to keep holding him.

"Okay," she said, "I'll quit. At least until your hiccups go away."

He sat up again, picking idly at the weeds around him. Joan plucked a single blade of grass and lay smoothing it between her thumb and forefinger.

"Tell me," she began, pretending to be serious, "if you could eat the biggest dessert in the world, what would it be?"

"Ice cream!" Eric crowed without a moment's hesitation. "Choclit!"

"Just chocolate?"

"An' bnilla fudge," he acknowledged, shrugging. "An' bananas."

"What else?" Joan asked, watching his eyes gleam at the imagining of it. His hiccups had stopped.

"Cool Whip. An' pickles."

"*Pickles?*" Joan asked. "Yuck!"

"Yeah. The funny ones daddy likes—little ones. Jerkins."

"Gherkins," Joan nodded. "Sweet ones. I like sour ones better. Let's see now—two kinds of ice cream, bananas, Cool Whip, and pickles. Nothing else?"

"Nope."

"No—asparagus?" Joan ventured, poking him in the ribs. It was a word that invariably sent him into convulsions.

"Nope," Eric said, eyes dancing, being mature, holding in the laugh. "Sumping else."

"What?"

"Nope." He shook his head, clamping his lips tight so that elephants couldn't drag it out of him.

Joan moved toward him, hands upraised like claws, as if to tickle it out of him. Eric shrieked and fell over giggling before she even touched him, helpless to defend himself.

"Noses!" he crowed. "Ice cream and noses!"

It was another private joke. For some reason the word "nose" had a double entendre that only Eric could appreciate.

Joan smiled softly, leaning down before he could stop her and kissing him on the forehead. He scowled and started to push her away, but didn't. He tolerated her, let her stare into his eyes for a long moment.

"I love you," Joan told him, pushing his hair back off his forehead. "You're a beautiful little boy, you know that? You're smart, and you're good, and you have beautiful eyes, and—"

"I *know* that!" Eric protested, bored with it. "You got gum?"

Joan sighed, released him, groped in her pockets. "Just cinnamon," she said, defeated by the sudden return to the mundane. "That too hot for you?"

"Nope," he said matter-of-factly. He shoved a piece into his cheek and pointed at the rest of the pack. "That says Trident," he said smugly.

"I *know* that!" Joan said, imitating him. She put the gum back in her pocket.

"An' I love you, mommy," Eric mumbled almost inaudibly, studying a ring-top he'd found in the grass.

And Joan stopped herself from telling him to put it down or he'd cut himself, and they picked up the neon-orange ball and went home.

Eventually Joan and Sarah got the closets emptied out, the extra furniture banished to the cellar, and shelves put up in the room that would be Eric's.

This is final, Joan told herself the first time she touched the paintbrush, almost ritually, to the wall. This means you'll have to see it through.

They moved in the first week of June, and Joan took a day off from work to drive Sarah to commencement exercises. Sarah had been invited by the new administration at the college to wear her academic robes and march up the rustic staircase to the stage with the rest of the faculty. She declined politely for fear of creating a scene, and was content to linger incognito on the fringes of the crowd of relatives and well-wishers trampling down the dandelions on the mall. A few of the graduates spotted her, however, and waved to her as they filed across the lawn in their identical caps and gowns. Sarah smiled, waved back, blew kisses at some of them.

"Ah, I love the ritual!" she exhaled as she and Joan

sat down. *"Pomp and Circumstance* always gives me goose bumps. D'you remember your own commencement?"

"Not especially," Joan said. "I remember sophomore year, though."

"Sixty-eight," Sarah nodded. "I remember that one, too. The year before they went coed. That old fart of a monsignor making a speech about how all a girl needs after she gets her B.A. is her M.R.S.! Unbelievable!"

"And Bobby Kennedy was dying," Joan reminded her.

"And about a dozen of you had the guts to raise the peace sign during the National Anthem. And Sister Francis later remarked that she thought it was in bad taste." Sarah sighed. "Poor old Frannie!"

Their voices were beginning to carry to the surrounding spectators. Joan poked Eric, who had crawled practically under the chair of the woman in front of him to retrieve a dandelion. He climbed back into his chair with much clattering and squirming.

"Why don't you remember your own graduation?" Sarah asked, trying to keep her voice to a whisper. "It wasn't that bad, was it?"

"I don't know," Joan whispered back. "It was about a month after I'd moved in with Brian. My period was three days late, and I was terrified that I might be pregnant."

"That could do it," Sarah nodded, seeming to listen to the speaker on the platform.

Eric was bored. He fidgeted, swung his legs back and forth beneath the chair, groped at his crotch until Joan poked him again. At this, he tapped her elbow to get her attention. "Ma," he half-whispered. "Ma, I'm thirsty."

"You have to wait," Joan hissed at him. "Sit still!"

"Ma! There's a *bee!"* he nearly shouted. Several heads turned in their direction. Joan wanted to strangle him.

"Leave it alone and it'll leave you alone," she stated. He slumped back in his seat and groped for his crotch

again. This time Joan ignored him. She leaned closer to
Sarah so that she could be heard without speaking too
loudly. "I understand the new administration's really been
ripping things up and starting fresh," she said, anxious to
hear Sarah's reaction.

"They're good girls, both of them," Sarah acknowledged. "I taught them both."

Both of the "girls" were nuns in their late forties. The
new president was a sociology professor, the new dean a
Shakespeare scholar. They had graduated from college
before they became nuns; their grasp on the twentieth
century was quite strong. Within the past six months,
fifty-odd years of infantile regulations had been abolished.
Efforts had been made to break down the walls, literal
and figurative, that separated the college from the community. Changes were being made, and they seemed all
for the good.

"It's all because of you, you know," Joan told Sarah as
they watched each graduate file up to kiss the bishop's
ring and receive a diploma.

"What is?" Sarah asked, absorbed in watching her last
class of graduates, only half-listening.

"The changes. The whole thing."

"Bullshit!" Sarah said, loud enough to be heard five
rows ahead. "It was an idea whose time had to come."

"Bullshit yourself!" Joan hissed, pulling Eric up out
of the grass again.

It was almost over. The figures in the long black robes
were beginning to stir on the stage. The organ played the
recessional, and the special guests strode down the rustic
staircase, followed by the faculty. Surprise, mingled with
varying degrees of pleasure, showed on their faces as they
recognized Sarah.

"Let's get out of here," she growled at Joan, "before we
get trampled!"

They pushed past a number of people, tripping over

feet, purses, and camera cases in their haste to escape. At the last minute, Sarah turned back toward the long black line, picking Pietro's towering figure out of the crowd. He waved tentatively in her direction, nodded at Joan. There was some question about whether or not he would have to go back to the Vatican this summer. He hadn't been able to be at Sarah's for over a week.

Sarah flapped her program at him to hold his attention. "Call me tonight, will you, dear?" she called, a little louder than necessary.

She did not wait to catch the embarrassment on his face, but grasped Joan's arm and pushed her toward the car. "I love to do that to him!" she giggled as they pulled away from the curb.

"That was mean," Joan said, locking Eric into his seat belt.

"Well, I have to keep the rumors going long-distance now." Sarah half-smiled disarmingly. She settled back against the seat, at peace.

On the Monday after Labor Day, Joan showed up for her first evening law class, appraised her professor—who, as it turned out, didn't think women ought to study law—and stopped at the bookstore to pick up the required texts.

There was something dazzling about the lights in the classroom and the bookstore, something magical in the smell of the fourth-hand textbooks as Joan skimmed through them wonderingly when she finally got home that night. Home. Sarah's home. Now Joan's home. Eric was asleep in the middle bedroom, where she used to spend her weekends. The baby-sitter, a neighborhood girl she'd befriended over the summer, had just left. Joan felt the weight of the books in her lap and stroked their ragged covers, awed and pleased.

She had driven Sarah to the Port Authority that morning, had sat next to her in the Connecticut-bound bus, making sure she'd packed everything, going over the details of the return trip and what time the bus would arrive tomorrow evening. She had embraced Sarah and scrambled out of the bus just as the driver started the engine, and she'd stood breathing in the exhaust fumes and waving like a fool long after the old woman could possibly have seen her.

And now she sat in the living room of Sarah's house—*her* house—breathing in the funny, stale smell of much-used textbooks. Anticipating . . .

While in a guest room at the dorm of a small New England college, an old woman sat on the edge of the single bed, her mouth dry from lecturing, her clear gray eyes tired from scanning a room full of faces. In her lap and beside her on the blanket were her books—the annotated Chaucer, and her own work contrasting the ideas of Thomas Aquinas and Duns Scotus. There had been no intelligent reason for lugging them along, but they were her good-luck charms and she never traveled without them.

She sat with the Chaucer open in her lap, staring at the page in the pool of light from the bedside lamp, waiting.

"Come on, damn you!" she whispered at the pages. "Give me back a word. One single, goddamn word! *Just —one—word!*"